I0762155

Kin
and
Clan

David Powers

Kin and Clan

First Edition - November 2022
Second Edition - December 2025

Library of Congress Cataloging-in-Publication Data
Powers, David.
Kin and Clan/David Powers.
293 p. 22 cm.

978-0-9985447-5-5 (hardcover)
978-0-9985447-6-2 (paperback)
978-0-9985447-7-9 (ebook)
979-8-9925863-2-9 (audiobook)

1. Murder--Fiction. 2. Murder--Investigation--Fiction. 3. Mystery Fiction. 4. Alabama--Fiction. 5. Mississippi--Fiction. 6. Louisiana--Fiction. I. Title.

Library of Congress Control Number: 2022920158
Printed in the United States of America

Eerie Forest
www.eerieforest.com

For My Mom and Dad

ALSO BY DAVID POWERS

UNBURIED MEMORIES

TIDINGS FROM THE ABYSS

THE MAN FROM BUZZARD ROOST

THE TANDOORI BOX

PROTECT THE FLOCK

THE ARMAGEDDON DIARIES – ALICE AND JULIE

Before

Winter 1988

BACK IN THE FIFTH GRADE, I sat in the Haworth Public School's auditorium, a spacious room that teachers utilized for lectures, plays, and band concerts when not serving as a gymnasium.

On the stage, the principal launched into a tirade about our school's string of recent bomb scares. Mr. Greenfield shook his fist each time he shouted, "Terrorism!" "Anarchism!" or when he really got into his isms, "Nazism!"

I knew who called in the phony threats using a nearby gas station's pay phone: Alan Bondy, the mohawked bully smirking in the front row.

Frank Benning, one of the cool kids, turned to me and said with pride, "*My* grandparents immigrated from Germany. Paul, what country is *your* family from?"

I had no ready answer for my classmate. For reasons unbeknownst to me, my mother and father never discussed my birth or the branches of our family tree. Embarrassed and, on a deeper level, troubled, I quickly made something up.

"They're from Scandinavia," I babbled, having no clue why I had named this block of Nordic countries. "That's where I came from, Frank. I'm Scandinavian."

Chapter One

Tuesday Early Morning—December 25, 2018

THE RINGING TELEPHONE AWAKENED ME. A dream—a repeating childhood nightmare—nebulized as I rolled onto my side to face the combination digital clock-weather station on the bedside table: *1:05 a.m.* The bedroom's temperature had plummeted to 63 degrees during the early hours.

Jennifer's eyes widened with concern. "Paul, it's your mother." My wife transferred the handset to me.

My heart, which languidly thumped at sixty beats per minute only a beat ago, revved up to an aorta-bursting one-twenty. "Mom?"

"Paul, your dad is," she sniffled, "gone."

My father fought a hateful form of malignant cancer for almost a year. This unpleasant news came as no surprise, yet the call's suddenness dragged my floundering psyche underwater in a spiraling death roll. I gulped for air, clicked on the speakerphone, and held the device between us. "When?"

"I couldn't sleep. At two-thirty, I went down to check on your father. That strange, labored panting—but otherwise, he seemed the same. Turning to go back upstairs, I heard a gasp. Right as I got to the hospital bed, Hale opened his eyes and asked, 'Am I still alive?' As I replied, 'Yes, honey, you are,' he stopped breathing. After I ran out of tears, I dialed the number for hospice. They'll send somebody to pronounce his death and arrange things with Volk in the morning. I'm with him now. Dad looks—like he's sleeping. Very peaceful."

The bleary scene my brain improvised wasn't peaceful at all. I wondered, *is my mother sugarcoating the truth?*

Jennifer slid closer to the phone. "How are you, Mom? What can we do to help?"

"Well, dear, there's nothing to be done at this moment." A long period of ragged respiration. "I'm just sitting here waiting for the knock on the door."

"Mom, we'll take the earliest flight to New Jersey." I now comprehended how it felt to lose a parent. "Try to get some rest."

My mother mumbled, "Merry Christmas, kids," and then hung up.

An empty, cold bed greeted me when I awakened the second time. This dream I remembered: My father showed me a small jewelry box containing the disease-ridden ear the surgeons had sliced from his skull. Downstairs, Jennifer sat at the kitchen table beneath a pendant lamp. Smokey rubbed his jaw on the corner of her MacBook, meowing when he saw me.

She shut the laptop's lid. "Our flight is at eleven-forty-five. Bereavement fare, nonstop to Newark. I still have to get ahold of the pet sitter." My wife stroked the cat's gray fur. "Hope Jean is available on such short notice."

I slumped onto a chair across from her. My head weighed a ton. I wanted to crawl back underneath the comforter and start the day over—*or never.* "What does bereavement get us?"

"Delta shoehorned us into the next flight and gave a discount on the airfare." Jennifer, the primary organizer in our eight-year marriage, checked the wall clock. "Shake a leg, sweetie. We only have thirty minutes to pack."

In the bedroom's walk-in closet, I ranked the condition of my three suits, which were so dated that I had no memory of when I had purchased them. I chose an off-the-rack jacket—*is this black or dark blue?*—and a white dress shirt. The yellow-ringed collar fit too snugly around my throat. My wife reminded me to bring a somber tie and to shine my shoes.

On the way to San Diego International Airport, the jolly, Santa-hatted Uber driver made small talk about his plans for the holidays. I glared out the dirty window, wishing he'd shut his trap and drive faster.

Delta hooked us up with complimentary first-class seats, my first flight not flying cattle class. As the plane taxied to the runway, I reclined in the roomy seat and closed my eyelids. An indeterminate time later, Jennifer elbowed me as the drink cart approached. "Paul, can you lower the blind? People are watching the movie." She passed me a Diet Pepsi and a bag of Snyder's of Hanover Mini Pretzels.

I tore the top off the foil sack. "How much longer?"

My wife touched the in-flight entertainment screen to load the destination map. "We're above Albuquerque. Four more hours." She shared her miniature pretzels with me. "What will we do with your mom?"

The knotted pastry tasted of coarse salt and processed flour. "Huh?"

"Paul, Edith cannot live in that big house on her own. All the family has moved or died. You're an only child. We need to find her a place closer to us."

We had discussed our parents' aging—vague prophecies over burritos at Armando's. With my father gone to meet his maker, my responsibility for my mother's well-being had become a stark reality. I said, "Let's deal with the funeral first. I can't think about that now."

My mom's brother recently died of a stroke. Uncle Charles' wife, Hilda, had relocated to Pennsylvania to be near their children and grandchildren. Jennifer was correct. Besides a few church friends, my mother faced the future alone.

I spent the remainder of the flight wide awake, finding no comfort in the extra-padded seat.

Tuesday Night—December 25, 2018

We took an uninspiring ride up the New Jersey Turnpike with an Uber driver who hadn't spoken to either of us since we got into her Prius. The sullen girl let us off in front of my parents' 1960s-era split-level house—*now my mother's house*—in the Manor section of suburban Haworth, New Jersey. Excluding snow in shady spots, my childhood home on Garfield Street appeared as it had a month ago when we came for Thanksgiving. Then it dawned on me—*no Christmas lights and no wreath on the front door.* On the first weekend of every December, my father decorated the trees and bushes with strings of old-fashioned multicolored bulbs.

Edith, alerted by my phone call informing her that we were just up the road, waited on the porch. She smiled with sadness as we rolled our luggage along the curved pathway. The woman who watched *The Wonder Years*, *Dallas*, and *Murder, She Wrote* with me while my dad toiled on mechanical projects in the basement had aged several years, if not a decade, in the past thirty days. Jennifer and I hugged her, expressing our sorrow for her and our loss.

Inside the foyer, I began to perspire. "Mom, what did you set the temp at?" I lowered the wall-mounted thermostat dial from 76 degrees to 72 degrees.

She perched on the edge of the neatly made hospital bed. "I've had a chill all day." She crossed her arms and rubbed them. "Can't shake it."

My wife increased the temperature to 74 degrees. "There we go. A compromise." She hung our parkas in the hall closet.

Mom peered at her wristwatch. "Oh my, it's so late. Do you kids want something to eat? Church members dropped off food this afternoon."

I was about to state that we had grabbed sandwiches on the way out of the airport, but I worried that she hadn't eaten supper. "I'm famished. Let's see what your friends brought."

Jennifer and I foraged among plastic containers and cling-wrapped bowls in the refrigerator. We singled out a casserole dish brimming with manicotti. As the ceramic tray slowly spun in the microwave oven, we got plates and filled glasses with water.

My mother listlessly picked at pasta overstuffed with ricotta cheese. I thought of my last day with my father. At Thanksgiving, he moaned continuously, his degenerating spinal disks a source of debilitating agony. For me, watching my mom spoon-feed her dying husband pureed turkey and mashed potatoes had been gut-wrenching. *He had difficulty swallowing, spasmodically choking so violently that he—*

Jennifer broke the silence. "Mom, do you feel like talking about this morning?" She extended her arm across the dining room table to clasp her mother-in-law's hand. "What time did they get here?"

Edith wiped her lips with a napkin, then sighed. "Megan from hospice rang the doorbell at eight. She notified the funeral home and prepared Hale for—well—she helped me get everything ready. The darling girl even brewed me a cup of tea. We have an appointment tomorrow afternoon at Volk with the director. I wrote the gentleman's name somewhere." Mom talked to herself as she sorted papers.

I dumped the offerings we had no hunger for in the garbage bin and stacked the dishes in the dishwasher. Outside the kitchen window, snowflakes fell softly onto the backyard. "When is the funeral? Isn't it ordinarily in three days?"

"Paul, that's one item we will talk over with," my mother read from a notepad, "James Whitmore. Mr. Whitmore said the ceremony usually takes place within three to seven days. The timing is entirely up to us."

Before I lugged our suitcases up the staircase to my boyhood bedroom, I lingered beside the deathbed, wishing to detect traces of my father's departed soul. Tears squirted from my closed eyes as I whispered, "Dad, can you hear me? Are you there? If you're here, please show me a sign." A black-and-white newsreel image of a feeble elderly man flickered on the interior of my eyelids. Throughout our Thanksgiving visit, my father became obsessed with confirming that his car still started. I helped him down the steps and into his gold Chevrolet Impala. My dad cranked the ignition key until the battery died for good. Dispirited by this remembrance, I shut off the lights and trudged upstairs.

Wednesday Morning—December 26, 2018

Jennifer gazed out the bedroom window. "Paul, come look. It's breathtaking."

Two or three inches of white powder coated the roadway. The solitary set of tire tracks carving the bend dissolved into whiteness.

I held her waist. "We used to sled down this street and at the hill by the high school. The snow was quite a bit deeper in my memories."

She poked me in my love handle. "Of course it was! You were just a wee whippersnapper." My wife, having grown up on the Big Island in Hawaii, found the sight and feel of crystalized water magical. "We'll monitor the weather. With luck, the drive to the funeral home this afternoon won't be too bad."

The forenoon hours crept by as we slouched in front of the television, watching the morning shows and cable news. In international news, over four hundred people died in Indonesia's tsunami. Domestically, our federal government would remain shut down unless Congress coughed up money for the Mexican border wall.

After I disassembled the hospital bed, Jennifer and I carted the unwieldy components to the garage. With the deathbed out of sight, the front room felt less like a death room and more like a living room.

Wednesday Afternoon—December 26, 2018

Following a lunch of ham-and-cheese sandwiches that my mother prepared, I backed her blue Ford Saturn out of the garage and onto the driveway, stopping parallel to my dad's dead Impala. Mom slipped on the icy surface, catching herself by snagging the Chevy's door handle.

Twenty minutes later, I parked in the lot adjacent to an imposing Colonial-style building in Teaneck. Pastor Seifert escorted us into Volk Funeral Home's tastefully furnished receiving area. The rotund man of the cloth had volunteered to help Edith plan the funeral. A woman at the reception desk welcomed us, made a call, and showed us where to sit.

The last time I had come to this stately home, owned and inhabited by generations of Volks, had been to attend my grandparents' funeral. Pastor Seifert had performed Grandpa Charles and Grandma Katherine's three-day-long service twelve years ago. I sat up front with my parents, staring with revulsion at the ventilation grills installed directly above the open caskets. My younger cousins fought boredom with giggling explorations to the stuffed and powdered stiffs in the home's many darkened chambers. I detested funerals, but today, I had to help organize my father's.

A gaunt beanstalk of a fellow attired in a black suit walked through a doorway. He put out his right hand to Edith. When she took his palm, he grasped the top of her fingers with his left. I questioned whether his semblance of a stereotypical undertaker got him the gig or if his career choice converted him into the caricature standing before me.

"Hello, Mrs. Crutcher. I'm James." Whitmore gazed into the grieving widow's eyes with what seemed to be genuine sympathy. "My condolences to you and your family." He pivoted to me. "And you must be Paul."

I gave his clammy hand a pump. "This is my wife, Jennifer, and do you know Pastor Seifert?"

"Elmer and I have known each other for years. I'm afraid it's the nature of our vocations. What a pleasure to make your acquaintances. Let's talk in the arrangement room."

There wasn't as much to work out as I had expected. Both of my parents had pre-planned their funerals. Aside from incidentals, including the number of death certificates and upgraded flower packages, they had prepaid all expenses in full. James presented a slideshow overview of the whole process, further demonstrating the "Eternal Peace" tribute website. We deliberated about music and obituaries, ultimately arriving at the topic I anticipated.

The funeral director faced the Lutheran minister. "Elmer, what is your schedule?"

Pastor Seifert checked his calendar. "Sunday afternoon is open for me."

James turned toward my mother. "Mrs. Crutcher, will that day be okay with you for the service?"

Her anguished expression sought counsel from me. I glanced at Jennifer, who dipped her chin.

"Sure," I said. "Sunday is fine."

No one uttered another word on the long journey home.

Thursday and Friday—December 27-28, 2018

Nothing memorable occurred on Thursday. On Friday, we drove to Hackensack to meet with the lawyer, a woman my parents met at church. Kay Rosewood's legal assistant, June, ushered us into her boss's office and shut the glass door. The straightforward language in my father's last will and testament quickened the reading. My mother inherited the entirety. Upon her death, the estate passed on to me in the form of a trust unless "something tragic" happened to me first. If that "unfortunate event ever presents itself," the funds will be transferred to my three older cousins.

After Kay answered our essential questions, the plump attorney tapped her pen on the ostentatious mahogany desk. "Edith, what are your intentions?"

My mother stammered, "Wha-what intentions?"

"That house is too much for one person to maintain. Have you considered downsizing?"

My parents had resided at that address since its construction five decades ago. I struggled to imagine Mom anywhere else.

June expressed the warmheartedness that her supervisor lacked. "Mrs. Crutcher, I know the future is hard to see right now. There are excellent retirement communities in Bergen County or, better yet, down by the shore. Manahawkin, Barnegat, Cape May? Such beautiful areas and a terrific way to introduce yourself to fascinating new people."

I read between the lines. *Is June coaxing my mom to conjugate with other men?*

"You mean move?" My mother's mouth sagged. "You want me to sell our home?"

Rosewood lifted her hand. "We're just tossing about options. Liquidating your assets will free up cash, giving you enough money to travel. It might be nice to get away for a change. Maybe stay with friends or relatives?"

My wife squeezed Edith's arm. "We want Mom to come to California."

"Jenn's right. Mom, sell the house. You should be near us."

My mother acted bewildered. I couldn't tell whether she hadn't contemplated this prospect or was amazed that we had.

The lawyer stood up to signal that the session had concluded. "That's a lot to mull over. Contact us if we can be of additional assistance."

Saturday Afternoon—December 29, 2018

The sky clouded over during Saturday's light lunch. At four o'clock, I stood at the bathroom mirror, tying my necktie. Frustrated, I restarted. With each attempt, the tail drooped lower than the blade.

"Need a hand with that, handsome?" Jennifer unknotted the botch job and smoothed the wrinkles. "Nervous?"

I scowled. "Don't want to see my father like that."

"Me neither." She finished putting me together and nodded with approval.

"What's the point of a viewing? Aside from morticians, what kind of person wants to hang around with corpses?"

"Visitation is a longstanding tradition. It allows everyone to pay their respects. Did you bring a tie clip?"

I flapped the decorative fabric against my chest. "People still wear them?"

My wife smiled. "Along with high-waisted jeans, necktie clips are back in style—keeps it neat. Your mother can lend us one of your dad's. Paul, it's heartbreaking to say goodbye to a loved one who's passed on. When my mom died, my stepfather had to drag me to the funeral parlor kicking and screaming. Even with

Roy holding my hand, I refused to walk up to the coffin. Such a little bitch."

"You were only eight." Jennifer's mother, Claire, a neonatal nurse, had perished in a tragic automobile accident. A drunk driver T-boned her Volvo as she drove home after a late shift. Severed fuel lines turned the station wagon into a funeral pyre.

"I should have—" My wife frowned as she brushed her long chestnut tresses. "Today, I will be with you every minute. We'll get through this." Jennifer gave me the hairbrush. "Put a dab of Dippity-do on those strays. I'll ask your mom if she'd like help with her outfit."

My mother gripped my arm as we entered the reposing room. At a distance and below a diffused light fixture, my father appeared to be sleeping. *Dad's taking another one of his famous "Saturday Afternoon Siestas" on the living room couch.* As I stepped closer, this serene illusion crumbled. *My dad's lying in that wooden box, and he's never, ever, getting out of it.*

The lyrics to a macabre nursery rhyme that my boyhood buddies chanted came to mind. *"On looking up, on looking down, she saw a dead man on the ground. And from his nose unto his chin, the worms crawled out, the worms crawled in."* I pictured worms, ants, and centipedes wriggling in and out of my father's nostrils and mouth. *"Then, she unto the parson said, 'Shall I be so when I am dead?' 'O yes! O yes!' the parson said, 'You will be so when you are dead.'"* My peripheral vision grayed, and my legs weakened.

Jennifer clenched my arm. "Paul?"

"Think I'll—sit down for a sec." I collapsed in the first row, focusing on the intricate floral patterns woven into the Persian rug. *Am I having a panic attack? Heart failure?* I rubbed my dad's gold tie clasp, a hand cradling a steam turbine generator. *Didn't he receive this clip when he retired as a mechanical engineer from General Electric?*

The first hands patted my shoulder. I stood to accept embraces as a stream of mourners filed into the space. Close relatives, distant relatives, neighbors, friends, and past coworkers came up to offer condolences. Plentiful stories, some hilarious, of their relationships with my dad boosted my courage to stand alongside the casket. I dared fleeting glances at my father's waxen face framed by sprays of mums, carnations, and lilies between handshakes and hugs.

As the minutes ticked by on the grandfather clock, Hale Crutcher resembled every inanimate object in the room—nothing scarier than wall art or a piece of furniture. The man who had raised me was no more.

Sunday Morning—December 30, 2018

I stirred to the muffled rumble of a passing truck. The weather had degraded overnight into a nasty storm. I couldn't make out the house across the street.

To allow Jennifer well-deserved shuteye, I dressed quietly and descended to the mudroom. I donned my parka and tugged on my dad's heavy boots. In the garage, I unhooked a fifty-year-old red shovel from the rack, rolled up the sectional door, and clomped into a foot and a half of fluff. Brisk and clean air energized my lungs with a healthy sting. With the snowplow excavating remote parts of town, I marveled at the quiescence that only trees draped in white and mountainous snowdrifts bestowed. This tranquility ended when I heard the scrape of other homeowners shoveling their driveways. I felt a modicum of shame as I destroyed the pristine beauty surrounding me, but I had to clear a path for my mother's car. This afternoon, we would lower Hale Crutcher into the ground. By the time I sprinkled rock salt on the walkway, my rubber soles had left waffle imprints in the fresh powder.

The scent of sizzling bacon and percolating coffee wafted into the mudroom. My stomach growled as I climbed the stairs to the kitchen.

Mom swiveled from the stove. "Paul, how deep was it? Did you work up an appetite?"

"It snowed an inch since I finished. Why didn't Dad buy a snowblower?"

"Your father shopped for them at Sears. Couldn't settle on the model or didn't want to spend the money." She put plates of scrambled eggs and bacon on the same Formica tabletop where I'd wolfed down countless meals growing up. "Said he needed the exercise."

I harkened back to my youth: every spring trimming hedges, every summer cutting grass, every fall raking leaves, and every winter shoveling the driveway. All that exertion only to have the hedges and grass swiftly regrow, more falling leaves to blanket the lawn, and, in the worst insult, watching the snowplow push mounds of shoveled slush back onto the cleared driveway. *Such fun.* I grumbled, "From the looks of it, I'll be outside after breakfast." I sat and scooped hearty helpings onto my dish. "What time should we leave for the funeral home?"

Jennifer shuffled into the kitchen in a robe. A terrycloth towel coiled her wet hair. "Wow, it's really coming down."

I poured a round of orange juices. "Yup. I just asked Mom when she intended to head over to Volk." Again and again, my mother referred to her list. *She sure writes lots of notes.*

"The service begins at two. Afterward, a limo will chauffeur us to George Washington Memorial Park for the burial. Pastor Seifert can ride with us." Edith dashed to the stove, cognizant that she hadn't switched off the burner.

My wife guided her to the table. "Relax, Mom. Paul and I shall take care of everything. If we leave at one, we'll have plenty of time."

I battled the raging snow gods every hour to stay ahead of the game, tense about the drive to Teaneck. In the old days, my dad wrapped chains around the car's rear tires. Nowadays, vehicles come equipped with all-season treads—practically useless on anything slick. Having lived in California for so long, I wasn't used to driving in the snow. I stressed over the eulogy I had composed for my father. Throughout the morning, I rehearsed the brief speech, with the words exiting my mouth and entering my ears always sounding cliché. *Or false.*

Jennifer shouted from the garage. "Paul, Volk just called! The director postponed the funeral service and burial due to the inclement weather."

I propped myself up with the red shovel. Now, my stomach ached in tandem with my back. "Until when? Tomorrow?"

"There aren't any openings on the calendar. Plus, James Whitmore said the ground froze last night—too hard for a backhoe to dig a grave. Interment may have to wait for the spring thaw."

"That's crazy." A large crow landed on a tree branch. The black bird regarded me with one black eye. *An omen?* I threw a snowball at the harbinger of ill tidings. The raven cawed in rancor and flew off. "What will they do with him in the meantime?"

"I overheard James saying the cemetery has a special vault for these occasions." My wife crossed her arms and shivered. "Your mom is pretty upset."

I jammed the scoop into a snowbank. "Shit, no ceremony for my dad."

"Yeah, sucks big time."

Edith stood in the kitchen holding a lengthy list and the landline receiver. "I started phoning people. The majority saw the forecast and decided not to risk the trip, but what if someone shows up at the funeral home and nobody's there?"

Jennifer took the names. "We'll call them on our cell phones." She ripped the paper and gave me half.

Dejected, I flung my hat and coat onto the countertop. "Mom, are you all right? I can't believe this is happening."

"Paul, it's winter." She pulled a chair from underneath the table and plopped down with a grunt. "Only God controls the weather."

"We're unable even to bury him." My egotistical id, Selfish, experienced relief. *This is good news, Paul. Now you don't have to speak before that crowd and prove you're a total idiot.* I wanted the whole horrible affair to be over with—*done.* A battered briefcase sat beside the sink. Manila folders strapped together with rubber bands covered the counter. *Where did I see that aluminum case?* "Mom, what's all this?"

"They're Hale's papers. So I'd know how to pay the bills after his death."

Now it occurred to me. Several years ago, when we visited my folks in the midst of summer, my father led me down the rickety steps to the cooler cellar to show me what he called the "Emergency Kit." He opened a briefcase crammed with papers and gestured for me to peek inside. "Paul, I organized our monetary and legal documents." He selected a folder labeled BANK OF NEW YORK and handed it to me. "The banking and financial accounts are stored with the life insurance policies and my pension. I keep the notarized wills and healthcare directives in this upper pocket. Our attorney, Kay Rosewood, has copies. When the time comes, please help your mom figure this all out."

Overwhelmed by the notion of his (and my own) mortality, I forced the folder back into his hands. "Dad, let's talk about this later. You'll live forever!" My father hadn't lived forevermore, only eighty-five years—the final six months in unendurable torment.

Sunday Afternoon—December 30, 2018

That afternoon, clearing the driveway a bygone priority, I set the briefcase on the dining room table. I put the dozen folders in order with more of a sense of obligation than curiosity.

"Whatcha doing?" Jennifer had been napping on the sofa. "Ah." She kneaded a crick in her neck.

"I'm looking at my dad's financial records."

She frowned. "Should you be doing that?"

"He asked me to."

"When was that?"

"Two, three years back? Didn't think my mom could handle it."

"I noticed she's forgetful. Can I lend a hand?"

"Sure." I indicated a bundle of envelopes. "Check those out."

I was reviewing my dad's will—its legalese duplicating the paperwork we had gone over in the lawyer's office—when my wife voiced discomfort.

"Is your neck bothering you?" I dropped the documents and stood behind her. "Shall I massage your shoulders?"

She clutched a standard-sized envelope with my mother's longhand inscribed on the front. Jennifer's honey-brown eyes turned up to me, her eyelids squinching shut in contrition. "Sorry, I opened her personal papers."

"What's in there?" Subconscious, the horned hellion always in charge of my physical being, commanded my stomach to execute a full gainer off the high board—a perfect 10 belly flop. I prayed that this day would not come. Nonetheless, I hoped my conjecture was wrong. I popped the question I'd been fearful of broaching. "Am I adopted?"

Jennifer's head rocked backward in shock. "You knew?"

"I always had a suspicion."

"Why didn't you tell me?"

"I wasn't positive. Mom and Dad didn't divulge details about my birth. Most mothers love to boast about when and where their water broke or the speedy trip to the hospital, followed by endless hours of labor. Fathers pass out cigars, bragging about their baby's length and weight."

"Not a thing?"

"I have a fuzzy recollection of sitting on a man's or woman's lap while they read a picture book aloud. An alarming title like, *Why Was I Adopted?* I can't recall exactly. My grandparents or godparents?"

"And you never grilled your parents?"

"Nah. Might have been too terrified to hear the truth. As a pre-teen, I discovered a confusing birth certificate or a similar document at the bottom of a dresser drawer. Even so, I wasn't certain. I always felt different, often wondering why I was an only child." An infant's chubby face floated in front of me. "And there was Patty."

"Your sister?"

Patricia died in 1974, four years before my birth. She had lived to be one or two years old. My mom and dad didn't openly discuss my older sister, and if they told me about her, I was too young or too absorbed in my daily existence to memorize (or desire to memorize) the disturbing details. From what I understood, Patty had been born with a severe birth defect: medical and mental issues caused by Down's syndrome or spina bifida. Framed baby pictures of Patty and me hung above the upright piano in the living room. In sixth grade, my mother signed me up for music lessons. As I sat on the hard bench in front of our shiny Baldwin, taking a break from practicing "Chopsticks" or, as I progressed, "Poor Lonesome Cowboy", I'd compare my set of five photographs (each shot at various angles by the same photographer) to Patty's. We were both lying on our tummies, grinning the same sweet toothless grins. In these carefully posed portraits, she always seemed normal to me. I frequently fretted over why God allowed Patty to die, cheated of a chance to gurgle "Mama" or "Dada." Reminiscing about my youth, a tsunami of guilt pounded me. *I should have asked my mother and father more about their lives and shown more sensitivity.*

I replied to Jennifer. "Patty is the reason my parents adopted me. When old Fido kicks the bucket, you get puppy Fido to ease the pain. I now realize I was a replacement child."

My wife shook her head. "That's not right. Edith and Hale loved you as much as they loved Patty. You can't blame them for still wanting to start a family."

"I get that, but although Patty was my sibling, I didn't have strong feelings toward her." My facial skin tightened. "I had a rough time explaining a dead sister to my friends." I visualized Patty in her baby photo staring down at me. "She was just a faded picture hanging on the wall."

"How could you develop any type of kinship?" Jennifer shrugged. "You never even knew her." She reluctantly held out an envelope. "This contains your birth certificate. It has the date, the hospital, and the name of your biological mother." My true origins were within reach. "Do you want to see who she is?"

I reared back as if my wife spewed virulent Ebola. "Put the papers away. I have zero interest in knowing."

Chapter Two

June-August 2019

AS IT CAME TO PASS, I CRAVED TO KNOW WHO BORE ME and *why the fuck they let me go.*

The two seasons following my father's death sped by in a busy blur. We flew to New Jersey in June to help my mother clean out the house. Dad enjoyed numerous hobbies, all of which filled the basement, attic, and garage with specialty tools, parts, and materials. I quickly learned that going through my parents' belongings could reveal items of interest, as well as those of a perplexing nature. Hale's formative years during the Great Depression had molded him into a man incapable of letting go—a hoarder. We opened six-foot-tall file cabinets stacked with hundreds of *Popular Science* and *Popular Mechanics* magazines from the 1950s to the present and smaller card cabinets crammed with every leather wallet and belt he had ever owned. My father seemed rational to me in my youth, but as an adult, seeing his odd habits, nothing convinced me that he had all his marbles.

Mom gave much of the excess to my cousins. She also donated scrap metal and metalworking implements to the machine shop at the local technical school. Nevertheless, it required two large dumpsters and a weekend garage sale to dispose of all goods not designated for shipment to a storage unit near our house in California.

A real estate agent sold my parents' property to a podiatrist. Jennifer and I once again crossed to the East Coast during the Fourth of July weekend to oversee the loading of an enormous Atlas moving van. My mother and I waved a woeful farewell to our mutual history, then the three of us took the red-eye to San Diego.

In Carlsbad, my wife and I moved my mom into our upstairs guest bedroom. With a Realtor's assistance, we searched for nearby homes for her to inhabit. Every house or condominium Judy walked us through, Edith had a gripe. "This is too big," "This is too small," or "I don't like the color."

Weeks of being chauffeured about in the backseat of a plush Lexus wore on me. Jennifer and I, who were used to doing our own things, spent all our spare time evaluating floor plans, peeking in closets, and flipping light switches.

Back home, after an interminable day listening to Judy extol the virtues of each abode, I pried the cap off a Corona Extra and plopped on the couch next to Jennifer. "Why can't my mother make up her damn mind?"

"Have patience." She drank a third of my beer. "We'll find her someplace soon."

"It's as if Mom hasn't any ambition to purchase her own place."

"Why would she?" My wife snapped her fingers, and Smokey jumped onto the hassock. "Edith doesn't know anyone in San Diego except for us. She's lonely."

"I'm going bonkers!"

"Calm down! She's your mother. It's not so bad with her here."

"Jenn, just yesterday, you complained you had no privacy!"

"Well, I *was* in the bath!"

We stared at one another, convulsing with laughter until our cheeks turned red. As long as this wonderful woman walked beside me through life, I could overcome any problems that came my way. "You're right, as usual, babe. Mom living with us isn't that bad."

One day, I arrived home to the odor of burned metal. I found a blackened cooking pot in the kitchen sink alongside an empty can of Campbell's Chicken Noodle Soup.

My mother hurried into the room, wringing her hands. "Paul, I forgot to switch off the stove."

"Mom, you almost burned the house down!" Exasperated, I showed her the saucepan's melted bottom before making a big production of dropping the ruined cookware in the trash.

"Sorry, I'll buy you a new pot." Heartache contorted my mother's face into an emotion I hated myself for provoking. "I was watching TV and lost track of time. It won't happen again."

"Come here." I wrapped my arms around her. "Everything's fine and dandy. It's only a stupid pot."

But things weren't dandy or fine. Next came the night my mom accidentally let the cat out the front door. The hand of God led me to the neighbor's bushes where Smokey hid. Of even greater concern, we couldn't rouse Mom for breakfast one morning. Jennifer inspected Edith's pill packs, discovering she had swallowed three days' worth of blood pressure pills.

The doctor tested my mother for dementia. The results, mild to moderate mental decline, startled us. Now that we knew the cause of Edith's absentmindedness, her extensive notes and lists made perfect sense. Jennifer and I both agreed my mom shouldn't be left alone. We alternated our work schedules so that one of us was always home. The babysitting ended the afternoon my mother slipped on a cat toy and fell down the stairs. As her back hurt too severely for her to stand, I set up a cot convenient to the ground-floor bathroom. After a single, long, hectic day, my wife and I felt the full weight of a one-hundred-and-seventy-pound woman as we lifted her on and off a toilet seat. We couldn't properly care for her.

Jennifer located a nice assisted living facility with an immediate opening. We transferred Edith and her few possessions into a room at the Meadows the next afternoon. Our house felt empty without Mom puttering about, but it took a load off my mind knowing she now had 24/7 nursing supervision.

On the last Sunday of July, I rummaged through cardboard cartons for my mother's Social Security number. My duties had expanded to filling out and submitting her healthcare documents. I held an envelope labeled EDITH CRUTCHER'S PRIVATE PAPERS. The sunlight slanting into the kitchen window generated a low-resolution X-ray of the rectangle's interior. Words were printed across folded pages. The thicker scalloped squares had to be photographs. I exhaled and tossed the vexation into the box. "Not even curious."

Thursday Early Morning—August 1, 2019

I never thought of myself as a liar, but I suppose we all constantly tell ourselves untruths. As the calendar page flipped from July to August, dropping into dreamland came easily, but staying there became more taxing. Ever since my father died seven months ago at 2:30 a.m. Eastern time, for reasons that struck me as supernatural, I regularly woke up at 2:30 a.m. Pacific time.

This morning, instead of returning to bed after draining my bladder, I plodded into the living room to check on Smokey. The miniature mountain lion wasn't curled up in his favorite spot on the couch. I found the cat on the kitchen table sitting on a carton packed with my mom's papers.

"Smokey, what are you doing here?" His amber eyes blinked once before he hopped down and wandered off to his food bowl.

I flipped on the ceiling light and dragged out a chair. As my pupils adjusted to the brightness, I slid the moving box toward me and spread the flaps. *Am I really up to doing this?* My hand burrowed into the depths to free the envelope containing my birth parents' names. My mother's identification markings, EDITH CRUTCHER'S PRIVATE PAPERS, gave no argument for misinterpretation. The capitalized letters screamed, "STAY OUT!"

I peeled off the piece of transparent tape sealing the envelope. *Paul, there's no turning back now.* I shook the contents onto the square table, gazed at the tiny pile, then positioned the objects into a semicircle.

I picked up the first black-and-white photograph—a grassy field, horses under trees, and a barn in the distance. *Why would my mother keep a rural landscape? She grew up in Hoboken!* A KODAK PAPER watermarked the rear.

In the second photo, also black-and-white, a youthful man in a Navy uniform stood in front of a Huey helicopter. *Not my dad or Uncle Charles. They served in the Air Force.* Nothing on the backside.

I scrutinized the third picture. In this color image, an adolescent female was lying in a hospital bed holding a baby swaddled in a blue receiving blanket. Her whole demeanor, like a deer caught in the headlights acutely aware Father Time was not her ally, deeply distressed me. *Is that my mother—my real mother?* I used a magnifying glass to enlarge the room's details—red roses in a half-filled vase on a wooden side table, chiffon curtains blowing inward from the open window, gray-speckled tile floor, and a barely visible porcelain hand-wash basin in the corner. A steel chair leg and a man's shoe tip extended into the frame.

None of these minutiae held any importance to me, but the girl on the white sheets cradling the infant intrigued me—*a lot.* She appeared to be in her mid-teens. Brown curly hair fringed a roundish face. Despondency circled her hazel eyes. The defiant chin spoke more than the clinched lips. Beyond these elemental characteristics? If I had to describe her lineaments to a police sketch artist, I might only add, "Officer, she looks strikingly familiar."

Topped with a blue knit cap, the newborn's face resembled all male babies—squinty-eyed, wrinkly old men—yet I recognized this boy. *That little butterball is me.*

I read the handwritten date on the back of the print, 5/15/78, and the name, PAUL. When I stood abruptly, the chair tipped rearward, hitting the floor with a bang—a 7.0 earthquake shaking the mental mansion that I had tediously built off its foundation. A framed photograph of Edith and Hale hung in the hallway. I brought the portraits into the kitchen to study the well-known visages underneath the harsh fluorescent bulbs. *Oh, no, no, no!* I always believed that my physique and facial features mirrored those of my parents, especially my mom's. People often commented on how I looked like my mother. But now, *who the hell am I?*

I set the fallen chair upright and sat down, ready to examine the remaining items—a newspaper clipping, a pamphlet, two official-looking documents, and something encased in foil. The unfolded aluminum leaf exposed a lock of blond hair tied with a red thread. A yellowed *Bergen Record* article announced Patty's death, summarized her short life in a single rosy paragraph, and posted a location and time for her funeral service. I rewrapped my sister's hair in the foil. The vibrant *Do's and Don'ts for Adoptive Parents* brochure—chock-full of cartoon families holding hands and playing games—listed the ten steps of the adoption process. Several phone numbers and agencies were underlined.

The final sheets, including adoption papers and a birth certificate, provided the enlightenment I longed for and simultaneously abhorred. PART I - INFORMATION ABOUT CHILD of the Mississippi Report of Adoption included the FULL NAME OF CHILD AT BIRTH: PAUL GIBBS; the PLACE OF BIRTH: GULFPORT, MISSISSIPPI; the DATE OF BIRTH: 5/15/1978; and the SEX: M. The blank fields, FULL MAIDEN NAME OF NATURAL MOTHER and FULL NAME OF LEGAL FATHER, made me quizzical until I noticed this note: IF THE OFFICIAL BIRTH CERTIFICATE NUMBER IS ENTERED, THE NAMES OF THE FATHER AND MOTHER MAY BE OMITTED. PART II - INFORMATION AFTER ADOPTION listed the FULL NAME OF CHILD AFTER ADOPTION: PAUL CHARLES CRUTCHER. *Charles is my grandfather's and my uncle's first name.* The bottom section of the form recorded my adoptive parents' data—*nothing unexpected here.*

The CERTIFICATE OF BIRTH issued by the State of Mississippi Bureau of Vital Statistics told a more complete story. Paul Gibbs—*me*—breathed my initial breath on Monday, 5/15/1978, at 7:02 a.m. in Gulfport, Mississippi, at Memorial Hospital. Sixteen-year-old unmarried Jane Gibbs, date of birth 8/14/1962, a Caucasian high school student, was, *and is*, my birth mother. No doctor or father listed.

Paul Charles Crutcher, formerly known as Paul Gibbs, entered the world illegitimate. *What could have been so wrong that my mother decided to get rid of me?*

Chapter Three

Monday Morning—August 12, 2019—Day 1

THE DICTIONARY DEFINES "CLARITY" AS "clearness or lucidity as to perception or understanding." Clarity can be exceptionally good or extremely bad. Sometimes we yearn for the true awareness of whatever lies ahead, but in affairs of the heart, keeping our heads stuck in the sand often seems safer. In my case, for years, I had buried the concept of Edith and Hale not being my actual parents under layers upon layers of mental safeguards.

Today, Monday, on board a flight headed east from southern California to southern Alabama, my dear friend Clarity felt like an eight-hundred-pound gorilla squashing my heart into tomato paste. My wife and I had relaxed in extra-wide first-class seats when we jetted to my father's funeral. This time, the cramped coach seat I now crammed my six-foot frame into approximated a 21st-century torture device. Jennifer was not here on this trip to rest her pretty head on my shoulder or dole out her salty snacks. I already missed her desperately. Although my wife had wanted to accompany me on my "Origin Journey," I dissuaded her with ambiguous reasons why I had to meet my birth parents solo. Alone at thirty-eight thousand feet above Glamis' drifting dunes, all my justifications sounded self-centered and just plain dumb.

During a three-hour layover at Dallas-Fort Worth International Airport, I kicked my sneakers onto an unoccupied chair and opened the Notes application on my iPhone. I reviewed my outline for the steps I would take after landing at Mobile Regional Airport: 1. PICK UP RENTAL CAR FROM BUDGET. 2. CHECK-IN QUALITY INN. 3. EAT SOMETHING. 4. had no instructions written beside the numeral, so I shifted the first line downward and typed GET SUITCASE on top of it. I renumbered the paltry list and dropped the phone on my lap. *What am I doing here?*

Prior to leaving home, I did a fair amount of online research. A *Google* search turned up several Jane Gibbses and one Jane Gibbs Baker in the Southern states. Only Jane Gibbs Baker of Hurricane, Alabama, came close to the correct age of fifty-seven. I spent many minutes on *Zillow* staring at a two-hundred-and-thirty-two-thousand-dollar gray, single-level house surrounded by swampland. The front yard needed a mowing or a heavy dose of Roundup. A 1950s-era Dodge truck rusting on flat tires sat in the side yard. In *Google Maps Street View*, as I roamed up and down Bayou Road, I happened upon a slim female walking an unleashed German shepherd. Her featureless face (blurred for privacy) appeared and disappeared amid my minute mouse movements as if lost for all time in the seams of multiple stitched-together panoramic images.

I analyzed the saved screenshot of this enigmatic woman—the blue blouse, the red shorts, and the brown sandals. The dog-walker beckoned or waved to someone. *Or is she reining in the straying animal?* I rubbed my thumb over her face in an ineffectual effort to wipe away *Google's* programmed obscurity. *Is she my mother or just a neighbor taking her pet outdoors to pee on a fire hydrant?*

I returned to my tiny text file and typed 5. DRIVE TO HURRICANE TOMORROW MORNING.

My flight arrived in Mobile at 8:48 p.m.

Chapter Four

Tuesday Morning—August 13, 2019—Day 2

I ENTERED JANE GIBBS BAKER'S ADDRESS INTO THE RENTAL CAR'S GPS, then drove the green Subaru Forester out of the Quality Inn parking lot in downtown Mobile, Alabama. The two-star hotel in the touristy "Historic District" by no means rivaled New York City's Waldorf Astoria. Still, at $69 a night, the sheets and towels were clean enough for my liking, and the TV was big enough to see from the bed. After dark, the 18th-century brick buildings outside my window were invisible. However, in daybreak's blush, as I passed Colonial Fort Condé to get on US 98, I admired Mobile as an appealing region for Jennifer and me to explore in the future. I followed Old Spanish Trail across the cable-stayed Cochrane-Africatown USA Bridge and into the "Historic Spot of the Deep South," officially known as Spanish Fort. While I motored through the congested town, the splendid antiquity wowed me, yet I couldn't help but count the number of indistinguishable strip malls.

At a United Methodist church (here in the Bible Belt, there had to be as many houses of worship as gun shops), I turned north onto AL-225. The land spread out and grew more beautiful as I drove past a succession of McMansion developments, each larger than the last. The two-lane street progressed through backwater locales where 1800s settlers had assigned quaint place names, such as Buzbee Fish Camp and Muddy Branch. This inscrutable landscape, with homesteads overrun by clinging vines and encroaching woodland, replicated the charming South that I had seen on TV dramas and on the silver screen. I found the bucolic scenery eerie yet alluring overall. *I was born here.* The lyrics of a rock song by Wet Willie—"smilin' through the rain and laughin' at the pain"—blared from the radio. I cranked up the volume, glancing at myself in the rearview mirror. "You're a Southern man, Mr. Crutcher!" I did my best hoot and holler, honking the horn twice.

I swung left onto Hurricane Road at the Crossroads, a four-way intersection with a fire station, a marine service business, a gas station, and a church occupying the corners. The GPS displayed 2.5 miles to my destination.

I had probed *Wikipedia* for information on Hurricane, an unincorporated community in Baldwin County. Dubbed "Tensaw Station" during the Civil War, the former Confederate supply depot was renamed Hurricane Bayou in the aftermath of the gory conflict. In 1895, the town council abbreviated the designation to Hurricane. Excluding the citation of a post office closing in 1962, no other events appeared worth documenting.

In four minutes, I'd be standing in front of the house where I believed my birth mother resided. As my determination evaporated in the heat of the day, I contemplated making a quick U-turn at the Assembly of God Church and retreating home.

Five hundred feet farther, a neighboring Baptist church, Saint Mary's, whispered my name. Unusually tired, I pulled into the lot, parked under a shade tree, and rolled down the side glass. Without the purr of the four pistons and the whishing of the August winds, the profound quietude sounded unnatural. The fragrance of blooming magnolias wafted into the car. A fly buzzed in one window, alighted on my nose, and flew outside to freedom. My eyes tracked dark clouds coiling to the east, and my ears detected the steady scrapings of a rake. The 90-degree, 90 percent humidity air pressed my cranium into the headrest. I reclined the seat and closed my eyes.

> Two men walked arm in arm. One wore a green and white golfing outfit, the man who nurtured me. The other, cloaked in folds black as pitch, remained unrecognizable. The figures' shadows gradually elongated, fading to nothing as an exhausted sun sank below a snowcapped peak. When my lips parted to hail my father and his curious companion, hesitancy clamped my tongue into submission. My dad accompanied the shapeless stranger down a pathway lit by fireflies toward a forest of tall evergreens. I scurried underneath a canopy of blighted vegetation, my flannel pajamas ensnaring here and there on prickly thorns. Only bits and pieces of their conversation reached my attentive eardrums.
>
> My father's staccato utterances—*"Paul's my son," "You abandoned him,"* and *"Leave Paul alone"*—curled the short hairs on my neck.
>
> Arid whirlwinds, dervishes trapped in a ritualistic moonlight dance, stank of smoke and ancient decay. Although I longed to overhear the arcane man's responses, his prolonged silence exemplified his opinion of me. Yonder dying trees, the rugged footpath terminated at a small lake nestled in a tapering canyon. Water, a sheet of obsidian glass, reflected the vastness of the Milky Way. The

> interloper clasped my father's hand and led him like a child to the end of a lengthy wooden dock.
>
> As the freshwater surface turned an unhealthy stain of orange, I began to worry.
>
> *In this world, the sun rises too early.*
>
> Snow fell from the sky. I shortly realized the gray flakes sticking to my sweaty cheeks were actually ashes. Horned goats stampeded through the flaming timber, their cloven hooves trampling plants and slower animals. Noxious vapors suffocated gasping lungs as the towering inferno suctioned the last ounces of oxygen out of the atmosphere. My eyes darted along the rocky shoreline. I cupped my quivering fingers to my mouth. "Dad! Where are you?" Yards from the dock, circular ripples and a buoyant golf cap hinted at my father's cruel fate. I raced to the boggy edge, tearing off my jammies.
>
> While I waded into the roiling whirlpool, a thunderous voice commanded, "Come unto me, my son." I splashed to a halt, swiveling to gaze into the fiery eyes of the being I knew to be my birth father. His veined arms extended to me. "Paul, I've waited for ages to meet you."

My own strangled shriek awakened me. I held the Forester's steering wheel in a death grip. Behind the church, a worker in overalls burned leaves in a fifty-gallon drum. He spotted me and ambled toward my car. I started the engine and peeled out of the parking area.

I headed west on Hurricane Road. The dream had spooked me—every horrible moment so lifelike. My dad had feared the man in black. Did my adoptive father know my biological father? I snickered to myself. *Just a nightmare.*

I slowed at a bend and steered right onto Bayou Road. Tense, I turned off the radio to concentrate. A BNSF freight train loaded with coal chugged past on shining railroad tracks. As I rounded a curve, the diesel locomotive rolled onto a steel truss bridge crossing the wide Tensaw River. A string of grandiose houses faced the water, each having a private landing pier. The scene evoked the wooden dock from my latest bad dream. Speedboats, water scooters, and kayaks sped or paddled over the brackish expanse.

I lucklessly scanned for number 296. These four-thousand-square-foot luxury homes didn't resemble the matchbox dwellings in *Google Maps Street View.* At a dead end, I turned around in a driveway. *Where the heck is it?* Near where Bayou Road first branched, an offshoot sheltered by trees came into my line of sight. A bent BAYOU ROAD sign perforated with bullet holes sat atop a heap of bald tires. *How many Bayou Roads are there?* On both sides of the washboard lane, small cabins, cottages, double-wide trailers, and less elegantly hammered-together shanties wedged themselves between cypress trees. Spanish moss tendrils swayed in the limp breeze.

I saw the rusted Dodge truck first, its hollow headlight sockets glaring at the approaching intruder. With no place to park on the narrow tract, I drove by the unmarked house, striving not to gawk.

I stopped at Perkins Hurricane Landing. Apart from a handful of permanent lodgings and mobile homes, not much else was here. At a concrete ramp in want of patching, two men garbed in fishing apparel winched an aluminum boat onto a trailer. Powerboats bobbed under canvas awnings beyond a screened structure named the Hurricane Bream Club. Perkins

Landing, a boarded-up building adjacent to my parking spot, may have been a bar or restaurant in more prosperous times.

A Budweiser truck jounced into the clearing and, gears grinding, backed up to a ramshackle store. The potbellied driver offloaded cases of Bud Light onto a hand truck. A red COCA-COLA sign bleached in the subtropical sun. I strolled over to buy a drink, keen to lubricate my parched throat.

On The Tavern's wooden deck, soda and newspaper vending machines flanked an iron bench. A herd of deer antlers adorned the gable roof. The stuffed alligator fastened beneath a LIVE BAIT SOLD HERE poster flaunted rows of razor-sharp teeth. Fascinated and a bit out of my depth, I turned the doorknob and went inside. Once my pupils dilated in the dim lighting, my retinas registered fishing equipment (rods and tackle) and sundry items (sunscreen, bug repellent, toothpaste, first aid kits, and ammunition) crowding the walls and shelves.

A thick-set woman heard the shopkeeper bell and paused from stocking the beverage refrigerator with fresh beer. She closed the glass door. "So, what can I get ya, hun?" Above her head, a blackboard advertised canoe rentals for twenty dollars a day.

Maybe the Bayou Road backyards are visible from the river. I snagged a ham-and-cheese sandwich wrapped in plastic and a cold Diet Coke, placing my lunch on the counter. "Can I rent a canoe?"

"Sure thing." The storekeeper grabbed an orange life vest and a single-bladed paddle out of a rack. She sized up my meet-my-biological-mother-for-the-first-time clothes. "Will you be fishing or only paddling today?"

Never having cast a hook in the water or stepped into a small boat, I peered at my leather shoes. "I left my pole at home. Just out for a little exercise."

"That'll be twenty-nine thirty-seven." The clerk noticed my thinning scalp and nodded at the toiletries shelf. "Might be wise to bring some sunblock and bug spray."

I chose bottles of Deep Woods OFF! and Banana Boat Ultra Sport Sunscreen Lotion, returning to the counter to fork over another Jackson.

She dropped the change in my palm. "The canoes are in back. Check the hull for cracks. Remain in the tributary. The Tensaw'll suck you clear down to the Gulf of Mexico if you ain't mindful."

"Thanks for the warning." I turned to depart.

"And no matter how hot you get, don't be dippin' your fingers in the river. A twelve-footer took ol' Mrs. Bailey's Tony last Friday."

"Twelve-footer?"

"Gator. Folks feed chickens and suchlike to the reptiles for entertainment." The shopkeeper stretched below the countertop and lifted a scoped rifle. "The end of August is hunting season. Requires a permit to bag one."

"An alligator ate her husband?"

The storekeeper's retracted lips unveiled several gaps. "Don't I wish! Travis is a boozehound and enjoys usin' his fists. Tony is Mrs. Bailey's bird dog. Damn shame. He was such a good boy. I'm Marge, the owner. Let me know if you need anything else."

I tossed the plastic sack filled with fifty bucks of provisions, along with the life jacket and maple paddle, into a red canoe. My loafers' smooth soles provided insufficient traction as I dragged the fiberglass hull across the silt to the tributary's edge.

"Mister, you got it in backwards." A girl of thirteen or so in a MORE BACON PLEASE!!! T-shirt pointed at the rear webbed seat. "You sit there—the stern—facing thataway."

"Can you tell," I confided, taking off my shoes and socks, "that I've never done this?"

"Canoeing isn't difficult, but on your own, you'll struggle if the wind picks up. Spins you round like a top. If that happens, kneel in the middle."

I rolled up the bottom of my pants. "Any additional seafaring tips?"

"Don't put your hands in the water. Mrs. Bailey lost her dog last week."

"Tony?"

"Yup. I used to walk Tony on days when her arthritis flared up. If the canoe flips, stay calm. Try not to splash too much."

"I'll keep that in mind." I towed the slender boat after me as I waded into the murk. The canoe rocked precariously when I stepped over the side. Seated securely, I twisted my body to wave. "Hey, what's your name?"

"Sarah."

"I'm Paul. See ya, Sarah."

Tuesday Afternoon—August 13, 2019—Day 2

The canoe meandered north with moderate paddling on either side of the hull to glide forward, and more vigorous paddle strokes on the opposite side to steer in the direction I wanted to go. Every log or twig poking out of the water simulated the horny scutes on an alligator's back or the ridges above their protruding eyes. Landings on the tributary, shorter than the sheltered ones fronting the big houses on the main trunk of the Tensaw River, jutted into the constricted waterway. Residents moored watercraft of various sizes and seaworthiness to do-it-yourself docks in varying stages of disrepair. At a landing newly constructed from pressure-treated pine, the *Lickety-Split* glimmered beneath the mid-afternoon sun. The powerboat's dual outboard motors were tipped up from the corrosive brine.

This house's gray siding matched the house that I had espied from Bayou Road. *And there's the rusty truck!* I drifted with the sluggish current, paddling to hold in place. A giant Goodyear tire knotted by a long rope to a live oak hung over the riverbank. *Swimming? What about the gators?* Four plastic chairs and piles of scrap lumber circled a stone firepit. As I studied the home that my real mother might own or rent, particular objects stood out. On the recently shingled roof, a disconnected wire flapped from a television antenna bolted alongside a gleaming DirecTV dish. An unopened carton for a built-in Summerset stainless-steel barbecue grill sat on a freshly poured cement pad. Stacks of bricks leaned against a partially plumbed outdoor kitchen island. The sliding patio doors and all the windows still had manufacturer's stickers on the glass. *It looks like the Bakers hit the lottery.*

A black and tan German shepherd trotted down the embankment to bark at me—the trespasser. The huge dog plunged into the water and swam toward me. I clumsily reversed the canoe and hastily paddled to Perkins Hurricane Landing.

Marge accepted the life vest and paddle. She appraised my mud-caked shoes and saturated slacks. "Didja see anything interesting?"

"Not really." I selected an 18-pack of Budweiser from the cooler. "Just birds." I itched my bug-bitten arm and gingerly patted the top of my sunburned scalp.

Marge shook her head in bemusement. "You shoulda put on the redneck cologne and worn a hat."

I hesitated. "Does Jane Gibbs Baker live around here?"

Marge shook a smoke out of a flip-top box of Marlboros as I got out my wallet. "Why you askin'?"

I compelled my mind to concoct a simple cover story. "I was told Jane may be in the area. Just wanted to drop by and say hi."

The Tavern's proprietor lit the cigarette. "Sorry, don't know her." She blew a cloud of nicotine in my face. "Have a nice day."

Tuckered out from jet lag, I caught a few Z's in the Subaru's backseat before returning to Mobile.

I hunched over the hotel room's undersized table, gnawing on beef ribs and scarfing spoonfuls of "Southern Style" macaroni salad. The pale lager rinsed the greasy nutrients down my esophagus. My digestive system swiftly mainlined the ethyl alcohol to my muddled frontal cortex. Marge's questioning of my motives gave away that she knew Jane Gibbs Baker. *In a small town, everybody has to know everybody. What is The Tavern's owner concealing and why? Did Marge's reticence have something to do with all the Bakers' new purchases?*

I guzzled a substantial amount of liquefied rice, hops, and barley malt, then called Jennifer.

"Hey, sweetie! How are you? Were you able to meet her, your mother?"

"Nope." I shuffled to the bed and put her on speakerphone while lying on my back. "Not yet."

"Why not?" I heard the television shut off. "Did you have a rough day?"

"More of a weird day. I rented a canoe."

"What?" My wife chuckled. "You can't even dog paddle."

"Ha, ha. I dog-paddle as good as any one-legged Labrador Retriever. I located Jane Gibbs Baker's house. That's the reason I canoed on the Tensaw River. Thought I'd check out where she lives from a distance." *Should I tell Jenn about the canine-eating alligators?*

"Are the people friendly? Hold on. Here's Smokey."

Loud purring permeated the empty space.

"Besides the guy at Budget Rent a Car and the gal staffing the Quality Inn's front desk, I only spoke to two others. First, the lady in Perkins Hurricane Landing who rents the canoes and, second, a local kid who taught me the proper way to sit in the tipsy thing."

"Going back to Hurricane tomorrow?"

"That's the plan."

"Well, take care. I miss you so much. Smokey sends you kisses."

"I love both of you, too. Talk to you soon."

I hung up, conscious that I hadn't inquired about my mom. I muttered, "Aren't you a shitty son," as I exited the room to find the ice machine. At the time, filling the bathroom sink with ice cubes to chill the surviving Buds seemed like a bright idea to me.

Chapter Five

Tuesday Night—August 13, 2019—Day 2

Out in the corridor, I groped my pants for the Quality Inn key card before clicking the door shut. The ice maker hummed while I filled the plastic bucket in an alcove near the elevators. Two male guests barreled around the corner as I turned to dodder back to my room. Upon returning from my expedition to Hurricane, I noticed the bearded pair parking their black pickup truck. I reckoned the coarse-looking duo were out-of-town construction workers bunking at the hotel.

My toothy grin and my hand shaking the container of ice cubes in their faces jolted them. "Hey, guys! I left you a couple!" Too late, I failed to notice that the identical men neither carried an ice bucket nor were in the mood for light comedy.

The man wearing a BASS PRO SHOPS sweatshirt grunted.

His accomplice, muscles flexing under his skintight GOLD'S GYM T-shirt, slammed my spine against the Ice-O-Matic. "Who the fuck are you?" Moist breath reeking of overcooked hot dogs and fermented sauerkraut made me gag.

The frozen water rained to the floor, crushing underfoot as Bass Pro Shops slugged me in the stomach. "Why were you on the river spying on us? Tell me, or I'll knock out all your teeth, beginning with your back molars."

Clearly, my airless gulp wasn't the justification either thug wanted to hear. Gold's Gym kneed me in the groin. The world tinged bile-green as my exploding balls ordered my legs to throw in the towel. On the wet tiles, I searched my pockets for the three hundred dollars I had grabbed from the ATM. *My wallet is on the nightstand.*

Bass Pro Shops nodded. "Punch him. This time harder."

"The money's in my room." I held out the yellow Quality Inn key card. "Take it." A fist blurred forth. The nothingness of unconsciousness eased the anxiety and pain until. . . .

. . . .somebody dumped a pail of ice water on my head. *The hotel room.* Electrical cords strapped my wrists and ankles to a chair. A washcloth stuffed my mouth. My chest and stomach hurt. *Broken rib? Busted spleen?* A warmish substance dripped down my sore jawbone. My tongue, tasting copper, counted my teeth. *All accounted for?*

"He's awake, Ernie!"

Bass Pro Shops rushed from the desk, waving a folder. "What is this crap? Marvin, get the rag outta his yap."

I drooled a gob of blood onto the beige carpet. "Are you twins?"

Ernie held the adoption papers in one hand, the birth certificate and my California driver's license in the other. "You think *my* mother is *your* mother?"

"*Our* mother," Marvin corrected. "Utter bullshit. The son of a bitch is lyin'."

"Am I a son of a bitch?"

Marvin smacked my contusions. He unfolded a tactical knife. "Say that filth again, and I'll cut your fuckin' tongue out through your fuckin' ass."

Ernie waggled his hand. "Marv, he's not a cop." He snagged my drenched collar, drawing me close. Hazel irises inventoried my facial features. "It's true, isn't it?" The man let go of me. "We're related."

"That's why I came here. To find out."

Marvin cracked a Budweiser, quaffed the room-temperature suds, belched in the key of E, and lobbed the empty can into the trash basket. He cut the electrical cord binding me to the chair with his blade and outstretched a meaty palm. "Welcome to the family, bro!"

On the way to Hurricane in the black Ford F150, Ernie and his younger sibling (by two minutes), Marvin, revealed small slices of themselves. Initially, I surmised Ernie inherited the brains and Marvin the brawn. After conversing with both, I concluded that the boys were of equal intelligence. And why not? *They're identical twins.* What also became immediately apparent—*these brothers are not to be messed with.*

When I queried them about their father, Marvin grumbled, "Jonas? We haven't laid eyes on that cum stain since—"

"May 18th, 2008." Ernie rolled down the window to spit out a wad of chaw.

I had hoped to be introduced to the man whose seed created me. Marvin poked me in the arm as we swung into the rutted space in front of the home on Bayou Road. "Don't tell Maw we roughed you up! I texted her. She's awful eager to meet you."

Up the cinder block steps, I stood at the screen door, gazing at the woman I believed to be my biological mother vacuuming the rug. *She's tidying up the place for me.* My legs wanted to go any which way but forward. *Are her nerves as frayed as mine?*

Marvin gave me a gentle shove. "Open the door, Paul. Just 'cause your belly's full doesn't mean we ain't starving."

She saw us from the corner of her eye or heard us speaking. My mother (I instantly knew our relation to be factual) shut off the Hoover upright and straightened her back. In my dreamlike state, her shoes hovered above the floor as she drifted toward me. The walls of the room bedimmed. A never-ending freight train of emotions chugged over my heart, each boxcar laden with good and bad sensations—anticipation, fear, excitement, surprise, joy, trust, distrust, contempt, disgust, anger, shame, guilt, sorrow. *Have I journeyed these many miles only to feel like dying?*

Tinier than I expected, Jane Gibbs Baker appeared tougher than I had imagined. The woman could hold court in any room. She took me into a mother's warm embrace, her sobs penetrating my shirt. The domineering human yearning enveloped me—unconditional love. *Was Edith and Hale's bond to me this strong?* My arms encircled her trembling shoulders.

She cupped my cheeks in her hands. "Lordy be, who did this to you?" When my swollen lips remained together, she frowned. "What, are you mute?"

"Maw," Marvin aimed a finger at his brother, "Ernie did it!"

Ernie's clenched fists matched the hue of his face. "Snitch!"

Jane stepped between her sons to referee. "Simmer down, boys. Why did you hit him?"

Marvin held a tube of ChapStick. "I went to The Tavern to buy some odds and ends. Marge mentioned she rented a canoe to a man asking about you. Said he was parked outside, sleeping in his car. I called Ernie, and we followed him to his hotel."

Her eyes focused on me. "And this gash on his cheek?" She dabbed at the coagulated wound with a damp tissue.

Marvin stooped to her ear. One word sounded like "Narc."

I backed away. "Hey, I'm not the police. After my father died, my wife found my birth certificate and adoption papers in my mother's belongings—with your name on them. My aim isn't to stir up trouble. I only want to get to know you."

"We had to be sure. Turned his whole hotel room upside down. Nothing except the stuff Paul's tellin' ya about. Oh, and this here." Ernie produced a rectangular box, the wrapping paper torn open on one end.

Jane hefted the package. "What is it?"

"Jennifer thought I should give you a gift."

"For?"

"Your birthday."

"You know it's tomorrow?" Jane palmed her forehead. "The date is on the birth certificate. Jennifer. Is that your wife?"

"Yes. Married eight years now."

"Kids? Do I have grandkiddies?"

"Just a cat, Smokey."

"Hmm." Jane ripped off the particolored balloon gift wrap—an assortment of dark chocolates. "Thank your wife for me. You had supper?"

Marvin chimed in. "He ate already. Had Moe's barbecue sauce smeared all over his face."

I stared him down. "Still hungry because I never got to eat my dessert, a nice fat slice of sweet potato pie."

I snooped about while Ernie and Marvin set the dining room table. The living room and dining room were typical of any house, with tables, chairs, lamps, and couches. Hummels lined a shelf, along with baseball and bowling trophies. Family photos hung on the walls. I can't say what I wished to find. *Baby pictures of me?*

Jane (calling her Mother, Mom, or especially *"Maw"* was inconceivable to me) brought steaming dishes of meat, potatoes, and green beans from the kitchen. Satisfied with her effort, she hollered, "Sarah!"

I'll admit, I wasn't overly astounded to see the canoeing expert who had warned me to keep my appendages out of the alligator-infested waters race into the dining area. Sarah, recognizing the dinner guest, put on the brakes. "Oh! It's you!"

The tallish brunette stroked her cheekbone. "Paul, did you fall overboard?"

"No." I scratched at one of my bruises. "Southern mosquitoes love my sweet Northern blood. I neglected to use the bug repellent." I assumed Marvin or Ernie was her father, yet the youth didn't gravitate toward either man.

Sarah sat between Jane and me.

Jane handed Sarah a platter of carved marinated flank steak. "How did you two meet?"

"I've never been in a boat." I forked a slab of meat onto my plate. "Sarah gave me a few good pointers this afternoon. Very helpful."

Jane passed the roasted potatoes garnished with fresh rosemary. "Our girl's a smart cookie. Straight A's. Sarah is in the Mathletes Club and the Environmental Awareness Club. She wants to be a doctor or lawyer when she's all grown up."

Sarah wagged her hand. "I intend to be an environmental scientist. Or an activist like Greta Thunberg."

Sammy, the German shepherd who had chased me away on my canoe outing, waited for table scraps by the teenager's feet. Her lineage interested me. "What's your dad think of that?" No reaction from Marvin or Ernie.

Sarah pierced a strip of beef. "What dad? He killed my mom and ran off when I was still a fetus."

In disbelief, I swallowed hard. The half-masticated steak lodged in my esophagus. I couldn't inhale or exhale.

Marvin, first to detect my life-or-death predicament (my fingers clutching my throat), shouted, "Hey, the new guy ain't breathin'!"

Earnie hotfooted up behind me, jerking me out of my seat. He pounded my back with the heel of his palm before wrapping his arms around my waist. My personal emergency medical technician grasped his fist with his other hand and began abdominal thrusts. The uncorked chunk of cow ejected from my mouth, landing in the dish of potatoes. I coughed and wheezed for air.

Marvin's snigger echoed in the small room. "Jesus H. Christ. What did I just see?"

Ernie struck me on the shoulder. "You're welcome, bro. Next time, chew your food." He returned to his chair to shovel more vittles into his maw.

Sarah patted my arm. "Are you all right?"

"Yeah. Being that *I nearly died.*" Relieved to live to see another day, I joined in the laughter until tears spilled down my cheeks.

"Paul," Marvin rubbed his thumb on two fingers, "now you owe Ernie your life."

"He beat me up, so I'd say we're even." I pivoted to Sarah. "Is it true about your parents?"

Ernie reached across the tablecloth to pass me an icy Pabst Blue Ribbon. "Me and Marvin's paw, Jonas Baker, took a liking to a young barmaid in Spanish Fort. Thought he loved her."

"Obsessed." Marvin rapped the side of his skull. "Paw lost his mind."

Ernie agreed with his brother. "The tramp drained him dry—ahem—his bank accounts, I mean. Well, anyway, Paw—"

Jane stood. "My husband was a jealous man." Marvin dutifully got up to clear the table. "Jonas stabbed Sally Davenport in the neck with a Phillips screwdriver the night he learned she'd played him and just 'bout everyone else at that damn roadhouse for fools. The dirty whore didn't bleed out soon enough. Pardon me for being blunt, Sarah. The ambulance carted her to the emergency room. Right off, the surgeons discovered she had a bun in the oven. Put Sally into a medically induced coma. Six months later, out popped our tiny bundle of joy. Sarah's a blessing born out of an unholy coupling."

I wondered how the family verified Jonas as the father. *DNA test? Or are they confident his sperm were superior swimmers?* "Did the mother awaken from the coma? What happened to Jonas?"

"Sally's EEG showed zero brain activity, so Doc Khan pulled the plug. My husband? After three years on the run, Jonas got himself shot in the head by the Denver police. Once again, over a woman! Sometimes," she tipped the spoiled potatoes into the garbage, "I miss the big galoot. Jonas had a sugary way with words and, on his sober days, he made a gal feel special."

My words to Sarah held infinitesimal weight. "Sorry. That had to be dreadful for you."

"No biggie." The girl lifted her chin with gratitude and affection. "I never knew my parents—can't miss them. A mom and two dads? Well, Ernie and Marvin are really half-brothers, but I call them 'uncles' because they're so much older. Confusing, right?" She beamed. "I'm lucky Jane adopted me! This poor orphan coulda wound up locked in a foster home till I turned eighteen."

When I leaned forward to ask Jane if Jonas was also my biological father, she changed the subject. "What are you doing to get by, Paul?"

"I'm an author."

She acted intrigued. "For a magazine or newspaper? *The New York Times*?"

"No, nothing so prestigious. I write books. Novels and short stories."

"You must do well for yourself. That Stephen King fella is drowning in cash money."

"The Master of Horror is a prolific wordsmith. I'm nowhere near his intellect. My current ambition is to find a literary agent to represent me. How about you?"

Marvin answered for her. "Maw worked as a caregiver at the old folks home in Daphne. She retired two years ago. Now she's living the good life. Right, Maw?" Jane's eyes rotated to the eighty-two-inch wide-screen TV and high-fidelity sound system. Marvin polished his skinned knuckles on his Gold's Gym tee. "Me and Ern, we started our own business."

"Oh, nice." I pictured the hopped-up pleasure craft outside. "What are you into?"

Ernie reined in his talkative brother. "A li'l bit of this, and a li'l bit of that."

"That's cool." I covered my yawn with my hand, then checked my wristwatch. "It's almost eleven. I'd better get back."

Marvin pointed at the couch. "Paul, you're family." He shook his hand horizontally. "Why waste money staying in that swank hotel?"

The previous twenty-four hours had been emotionally eventful, and the six or more beers had taken their toll in dead brain cells. *I need to go to bed.*

"It's a two-star Quality Inn," I replied. "I also have to phone my wife. She'll want to hear about my day."

"Yeah, I'll bet!" Marvin seized my shoulders. "Meeting your real clan is a huge deal." He eyed the wall clock. "We can drop you off at the hotel on our way to our job. Ern?"

The older brother corkscrewed the strands of his brown beard. "We're already late." His one arched eyebrow formed a question. "Paul, are you up for a boat ride? A little midnight cruise?"

Even though the wise man in charge of my higher-tier cognitive functions advised, "Say no!" the inebriate pulling the strings to my jaw muscles had a game plan of his own. "Sure. Where we off to?"

"Fishing." Ernie unrolled a topographical map on the dining room table and touched a dot. "This is us, Hurricane." He dragged his forefinger south down a tributary to the Tensaw River's mainstem. "We go here." Ernie tapped the paper. "Big Lizard Creek."

I bent to read the fine print. In the W. L. Holland Wildlife Management Area, below Negro Lake—*what year is this, 1940?*—a thin stream wound its way to the much larger Mobile River. "We're going up that? It's nighttime."

Marvin unlocked a vertical metal cabinet in the hallway. He handed his twin an assault rifle plus two ammunition magazines, then selected a pump-action shotgun for himself.

I didn't appreciate what my eyeballs were showing me. "Why all the firepower?"

"Alligators." Marvin loaded the Remington 870 with red shells. "You've seen 'em. Long as Cadillac Eldorados and twice as mean."

Ernie checked the optic on his SIG Sauer M400 AR-15. "And venomous snakes. In the marshes, there're the copperheads, the cottonmouths, and those pretty things, the, the—"

"Coral snakes." Marvin packed extra ammunition into a pouch. "Those puny ankle biters have the red, yellow, and black rings round their bellies. But, Paul, the one you gotta look for is the—"

"Eastern diamondback." Ernie reveled in the banter. "A single drop of their rattlesnake venom will turn your insides to chocolate puddin'. After two hours shitting out your bloody guts, the turkey vultures will peck your eyes out. And don't forget all the black bears and wild boars running around raising havoc."

Jane's cheeks flushed red. "Paul's tired, and you're upsetting him. Can you please bring him to the hotel?"

Ernie judged my manliness. His lowered eyebrows, wrinkled nose, and inverted upper lip pronounced his verdict.

Like Marvin said, we're clan, and clan takes care of one another. I muttered, "I'll be fine."

Marvin slapped a massive pistol into my right hand. "And for you, Paul, Jonas' Desert Eagle. He was so fond of this gun, he named her Big Bertha." He pressed two pre-loaded clips into my left palm. "Nine rounds, full metal jacket. You know how to operate one of these babies?"

The howitzer-sized Magnum Research .357 Magnum weighed a metric ton. I'd watched enough Sylvester Stallone films to fake my way through firing every type of weapon. "Of course I do. You stick this whatchamacallit that holds the ammo—" It took me several attempts to insert the magazine into the bottom of the grip. "Then you pull the top part to load a bullet." Yanking the slide back with my fingers demanded more force than I predicted. "And, ladies and gentlemen, we're ready for any critter that comes a crawling."

Ernie nudged my elbow to aim the semi-automatic away from delicate human flesh. "You got the hang of it, Sundance. Remember to flick off the safety before you squeeze the trigger." He rubbed his hands together. "Okay, let's roll."

Chapter Six

Wednesday Early Morning—August 14, 2019—Day 3

AT THE TWENTY-FIVE-FOOT, GRAY BOSTON WHALER'S CENTER CONSOLE, Ernie guided the Guardian onto the Tensaw River and steered south. The padded leaning post that Marvin and I were perched upon canted backward as our captain pushed the throttle control. Twin Honda 225-horsepower engines quit rumbling and began to roar. The agile speedboat, stripped of anything deemed unessential, abruptly sped up, practically knocking me off my seat. Two long duffel bags slid from side to side on the forward deck. Clumps of swamp tupelo flitted past in the illumination provided by red and green running lights. While the relaxing beer buzz had decomposed into a dull headache, the pounding hull amplified the throbbing in my temples. Ernie had stowed the assault rifle, shotgun, and handgun in the metal locker behind our cushioned bench. *Why do we need heavy weaponry to fish? What's in those sacks? Cocaine? Heroin?* I searched for nearby lights, ogling at the distant stars and galaxies spinning above my open mouth. *Infinitely beautiful. Can't see these in California. I can almost reach out and touch—*

A submerged branch or log smacking the boat's aluminum skin brought me to my senses. *Nobody knows I'm out here. Will these guys kill me and dump my body in the river?* Antsy as an ant peering up at a boot heel, my lips neared my seatmate's ear. "Marvin! Where are you taking me?"

Even in the darkness that only comes after midnight, my half-brother must have seen my jittery eyes. "Don't get your balls in a knot, big brother! We're just dropping off something to one of our clients." He crowed wildly as the powerboat gathered momentum around a bend in the creek. "Like *Grubhub* or *Uber Eats*, we deliver right to your doorstep!"

I pointed at a reinforced steel bracket bolted to the front platform. "Is that a tripod for a camera?"

"50-caliber machine gun mount. Those 30-caliber posts on either gunwale cover the port and starboard. US Navy SEALS owned the *Lickety-Split* before we won her last spring at a public auction."

Ernie, consulting the onboard GPS, pulled the throttle lever. The arrowlike bow dived into a spray of water.

Marvin extracted our firearms from the weapons locker as we drifted up to a brown Manitou XT, the *Avid Angler*. He pumped a shell into the Remington's chamber. "Cock and lock, boys."

Ernie flung a rope to a pair of armed males. Marvin hurried to the prow to unload our cargo onto the pontoon boat. When he hoisted the second duffel over the *Avid Angler's* railing, a strap caught on a cleat, and it crashed to the deck.

The bearded man had a strawberry birthmark extending from his forehead across his eye and to his cheek. He growled, "Watch it, moron!" and knelt to unzip the canvas bag.

Marvin's shotgun elevated until Ernie blocked his forearm. "Get ahold of yourself, bro. Chill."

The Desert Eagle's heft in my hand frightened me, but I also perceived an increasing inclination to defend my new sibling's honor. I disengaged the safety, my finger tight against the trigger guard.

The one with the mother's mark inspected a dozen assault rifles.

A python tattoo snaked out of the older guy's Hawaiian shirt and coiled around his neck. He twirled an impatient forefinger at his younger companion. "Well?"

"They're packed in bubble wrap." The unshaven man zipped the zipper and set both cylindrical bags side by side. "Not a single scratch."

The *Avid Angler's* inked commander threw a container to his one-person crew. "Pay these stooges, and let's scram."

Marvin snatched the Tupperware and opened the lid. He counted a stack of bills and nodded to Ernie. The skipper of our little ship shifted into reverse, spun the hull 180 degrees, and rammed the lever forward.

I thought we traveled at the speed of light on the way out here. Evidently, the Boston Whaler's dual engines had horses to spare. The front of the deck rose higher and higher until I couldn't see obstacles lying in wait.

Ernie whooped. His twin shook a fist at the Sturgeon Moon. I held on, worried they might fire bullets into the sky like the Taliban. *Am I now a gunrunner?* Before long, we glided up to the dock behind Jane's—*my mother's*—house. I helped my half-brothers tie up the boat and tilt the outboard motors away from the brine.

When they dropped me off at the Quality Inn, Marvin offered me a roll of twenties.

"I can't take that."

"Sure you can, Paul. You earned your share."

"No, I didn't."

"Yeah, you did. Augustus Dawson and his doofus son, Jasper, are shady as fuck. Those dirtbags will slit your throat if you glance at them sideways. Paul, you were our muscle. Three against two always makes for better odds. Take the two grand. Everybody can use financial help."

I crammed the money into my front pants pocket. Now it's official: *I'm a gunrunner.*

As my cheekbone sank into the down pillow on the hotel room's queen-sized bed, I visualized the two thousand dollars in the closet safe. *It's dirty money, it's dirty money, it's dirty. . . .*

> My father, the man who reared me, passed me a photo album. "Care to peek inside, Pauly?"
>
> We sat in the basement of my childhood home, with a solitary bulb flickering overhead. Playthings from my boyhood—stuffed animals, car and airplane models, sports equipment—spilled out of dusty toy boxes in the gloom. I laid the thick tome on my lap, innocently enunciating the two words embossed in gold on the leather front cover. *"Our Family."* Below a stamped chrysanthemum, baroque script spelled out a surname. I squinted, inept at deciphering the characters. "Dad, what language is this?"
>
> He slapped his knee and cackled. "Sanskrit, Egyptian, Hebrew, Greek? Modern French or German? Emoji? Son, I'm not a linguist. Go on, open the book."
>
> An ornate tree illustrated the inner panel. *My family tree.* The hand-drawn rectangles atop each leafless branch contained no first and last names, only manners of death: Stoning, Poisoning, Burning at the Stake, Lynching, Human Sacrifice, Suicide, and a word I didn't know—*Parricide.* My forefinger smudged the still-wet ink on the lower levels. On the first page, clear acetate, pressed flat, color

portraits of Jane, Marvin, Ernie, and Sarah. A sepia print at the bottom of the sheet showed the same foursome happily traipsing through a field of swaying sunflowers. The words under the picture revived a memory of a satirical motivational poster a coworker had hung in his cubicle, depicting sooty, sweaty stokers in the Titanic's fire room, chanting, "Just another day in paradise!" as they shoveled coal into flooding, red-hot boilers. Upon closer scrutiny, I realized that my family's gleaming teeth weren't Colgate smiles, but mouths gasping for air—*or screaming? What are they running from?* The next leaf held a white-bordered 8x10-inch photograph of a man and woman locked in lusty copulation. *Jonas and Sally? Are the lovers in Pain, or is it Ecstasy?* Disturbed, I turned the page to view a flipbook image of Jonas thrusting a screwdriver into Sally's windpipe and her body collapsing to the ground in a bloody heap. The hideous motion picture repeated ad nauseam. *Where is the stop icon?* I shut the photo album to cry. "Paw, these pictures are awful. Where is Maw?" *When did I start calling Mom and Dad Maw and Paw?* "Why must I see this?"

Someone else had replaced my dad. The cowl of a flowing black cloak shrouded his facial characteristics, excluding an aquiline nose ruined by rhinophyma. "Paul, *I* am your father." His gaping jaws exposed infected gums and decaying fangs. "Come nigh. We have much to palaver." I ran up the cellar stairs, shouting, "Wake up, wake up! Dear God, please let me wake up!"

Thankfully, when my eyes flew open, the hooded man in the black cloak was no longer there.

Chapter Seven

Wednesday Morning—August 14, 2019—Day 3

"SO, WHAT'S JANE LIKE?"

Excellent question, I thought. *What is my mother like?* "Jenn, I don't really know. I just met the woman yesterday."

"Do you resemble her? Was there any chemistry? Do you call her 'Mom'? Your half-brothers are twins? Tell me more!"

My urge to disclose the particulars of last evening's motorboat ride totaled less than zero. I had ridden on an adrenaline high ever since my fellow gunrunners let me off at the hotel. The first thing I did in my room? I snapped the rubber band holding the bundle of money together and spread one hundred Andrew Jackson faces across the bedcover. I repressed my impulse to roll around naked in the bills, but sleep? What sleep? "Ernie and Marvin seem okay. Jane, my mother," the maternal words tasted alien, "cooked me dinner."

"That's so nice of her. What did she make?"

"Steak and potatoes." I also withheld from my wife the humiliating choking event when Ernie saved my life. *Why alarm her?* "Believe it or not, I have a teenage half-sister. Wait, I take that back. Sarah might not be related to me at all."

"Who's Sarah?"

"My mother, Jane Gibbs, married Jonas Baker." I paused to recall the sordid details. "Jonas had an affair with a bartender,

Sally Davenport. He found out his mistress was the town pump and plunged a screwdriver through her neck. She fell into a coma—braindead. Jonas ran north to evade arrest. The second Sally gave birth to Sarah, the doctor shut off the ventilator, and three years later, the Colorado police shot Jonas in the melon. With both parents gone, Jane took it upon herself to adopt Sarah."

"That's nuts!"

"For real," I agreed, shaking my head.

"But," Jennifer cleared her throat, "this Jonas, he's your real father?"

"I didn't ask."

"Paul, why not? Because you're concerned you may be related to him?"

"Wouldn't you be?"

"Well, you wanted to know, right? Isn't that the reason you flew all the way down there?"

I had witnessed the sketchy deeds Ernie and Marvin were capable of. Did I long to learn whether Jonas' murderous genetic code lurked inside of me? I replied, "They invited me to Jane's birthday party this afternoon."

"That's gracious of them. I never meant to press you about locating your biological father. Sweetie, I get that you're under lots of stress. I haven't the faintest clue what I'd do."

After several minutes of idle chitchat, I hung up the phone, depressed and very much alone. *Once more, I neglected to inquire about my mom's health.*

Wednesday Afternoon—August 14, 2019—Day 3

"Keep working on your follow-through, Uncle Paul." Sarah tossed the horseshoe in a high arc. She danced a jubilant jig when the steel shoe clanged against the iron stake. "Nailed it! Nine to two."

My next throw wasn't any better. The talisman of good luck somersaulted into a pricker bush. At the beginning of the match, I deliberately played poorly so the kid could win. I soon comprehended that losing to my "niece" would not be an issue. "What grade are you in?"

"I start eighth grade in September." Her aura clouded. "God, I'm so looking forward to high school—one step closer to getting out of this stinking backwater."

"Is Hurricane that bad?"

"Too small. Everybody's meddling. I can't wait to blow this popsicle stand."

I mourned all that Sarah had endured. *Jesus, her father killed her mother in cold blood, and now he's dead.* "Is college in your future?"

"That's the goal. I'm shooting for a Master of Science in environmental policy and management." Glumness twisted Sarah's lip downward. "*If* we can afford it."

I glanced at the Boston Whaler bobbing in the ebb and flow. "Ernie and Marvin are doing all right. You have years to save up, or you can get a student loan."

"I guess so. Uncle Marvin says they're raking in the dough. 'Like taking candy from a baby.'"

I handed her a horseshoe. "What *is* their business?"

Sarah wavered in the middle of her windup. "You're asking me? Uncle Paul, *you* went out with them." Her pitched ring missed the post by a foot.

I retrieved the four horseshoes. "Wasn't paying attention. Just enjoying my first ride on a speedboat." I threw a ringer. The reverberation of steel striking iron spun Ernie's head. He smiled, then resumed attaching a paper bull's-eye to a wooden frame. "Three points?"

"See? You're improving. Nine to five." She won the game with a leaner. All the same, her earlier glee had diminished—no happy dance. "I should check if Mom needs my help in the kitchen."

"Paul!" Ernie summoned me to the river. He gave me Jonas' Desert Eagle. Marvin came from the house carrying the shotgun and the assault rifle. "Let's get in some target practice before supper. You handled yourself last night. Even so, I'd like to see if you can hit anything."

I chambered a round, switched off the safety, and aimed.

"Hold on, Paul." Ernie took the gun. "There are two main shooting stances. Isosceles and Weaver. Let's begin with the Isosceles." He faced the target squarely, his feet parallel and shoulder-width apart. Ernie cocked out his butt and inclined his torso forward with his arms extended. "Here. Big Bertha's a cannon. Use both hands, locking your right elbow." My half-brother folded my fingers properly around the grip, instructing, "When you're ready to fire, exhale and hold your breath." He slid a pair of earmuffs over my ears.

I placed my finger on the cold trigger. The instant the front and rear sights lined up on the bull's-eye's inner circle, I put pressure on the metal tongue. Hot flames roared out of the long muzzle. My arms flew upward, the powerful recoil almost making me drop the weighty semi-automatic. Water spouted from the Tensaw. Shaken, I peered at the target. *No hole.* I turned to the twins. "Sorry," I joked, "I didn't wear my glasses."

Marvin chuckled. "No need to apologize. She's a handful. At least you didn't plug one of us. The Weaver stance might be more your style. Move your right shoe back 45 degrees. A smidge forward. There you go."

I braced for the kickback. The bull's-eye displayed a round perforation in the upper left corner, along with a white plume in the river.

A nod from Ernie encouraged me to continue.

I shot the paper target seven more times. Marvin equipped me with a fresh magazine. I swapped the clips and blasted away until the gun had emptied. He demonstrated checking the chamber to be certain no bullets remained.

We tramped down the riverbank. "Not too shabby, bro." Ernie circled the tightest pattern on the bull's-eye with his finger. "Once you got the sights dialed in, you were fairly accurate. Damn good start for a novice. Marv, let him try the shotgun." He ripped off the sheet to hang a new black-and-white graphic: a scruffy cowboy drawing two six-shooters.

The Remington 870 felt deadly in my hands. "Don't your neighbors complain about the noise?"

Marvin sneered. "Nah. Here in 'Merica—we do what we please. Grasp firmly and aim for his chest."

I trained the lengthy barrel at the cartoon character pointing pistols at me. The lead pellets pulverized the outlaw's head.

"Paul, I suppose you're prepped for your final class." Ernie handed me the SIG Sauer AR-15. I saw myself as Rambo mowing down corrupt law enforcement in *First Blood*. "It's loaded. Pull the charging handle. Yeah, grab there. Flip this selector from Safe to Fire. Now, we're ready to rock."

I squeezed off one round. *Boom!* Another two. *Boom! Boom!* "This gun is loud! Amazing—hardly any recoil."

Marvin opened an American Eagle 5.56x45mm military-grade ammunition box and removed a cartridge. "The projectile is about the size of a .22, but this 55-grain shell packs a punch. Do not underestimate the power of this tiny bullet!"

A bell rang at the house. Ernie reached for the AR-15. "Come on, boys. I could eat a whole buffalo. Let's fire up the barbecue!"

On the cement patio, beside the unopened built-in gas stainless-steel grill carton, Marvin dumped a sack of Kingsford Original into the Weber Red Kettle portable barbecue. He doused the charcoal briquettes with Kingsford lighter fluid, then lit the pyramid with a Diamond kitchen match. The flames soared.

Ernie nudged me with a tray. “Dude, whatever you do, don’t cremate Chicken Little.”

While I sipped a beer, leisurely rotating the browning thighs, legs, breasts, and wings with the steel tongs, I completely forgot about my kin in San Diego. Here in the Alabama delta, I felt on top of the world. Free. Alive. *This is my clan.*

I monitored the four family members’ interactions at the rustic picnic table on the back lawn.

Ernie acted as the dominant force, serious yet with a biting sense of humor. The older twin primarily led the conversations (unless Sarah spoke). This alpha male was always on the alert and quite protective. I test-swallowed, relieved that no chunks of chicken obstructed my upper airway.

The junior twin? Marvin’s true personality eluded me. On one hand, he took on, and even relished, the subservient role of the underachieving bumbler. On the other hand, rare moments surfaced when he allowed his intellect to shine. I still had a long way to figure this brother out.

Jonas and Sally’s offspring, Sarah, struck me as a missing piece in the family puzzle. She plainly adored them all, but the youngster always appeared to be on guard. *Aloof?* “Apart” may be a more descriptive word. Perhaps the brainy girl feared turning into one of them. *Sarah mentioned she couldn’t wait to see Hurricane in the rearview mirror.* I wished her the best of luck.

Jane. *My mother is a riddle.* So far, I had gleaned little information about her. Come to think of it, I hadn’t talked beyond trivialities to the person I desired to learn the most about. *Why is that? Are you scared? No. Probably. Yes, I’m scared.* In any case, I connected to her on a primal level.

On multiple occurrences over the afternoon, I caught Jane studying me. In turn, I itemized her physical characteristics, contrasting shapes and sizes to my own. The woman stood at an average height with a slender build, as was I. Her flawless, heart-shaped face didn't match my rectangular, chickenpox-scarred mug. *Is her nose Roman like mine? No, pointed. More refined. Noble. Prominent chin below thin lips? Her lips are fuller.* Hooded eyes—hazel irises with flecks of blue and green—didn't duplicate my steel-blue irises. *Jennifer always says she loves the color of my eyes.* For some inexplicable reason, I hated them. Jane's hair? Golden-brown, lighter, and wavier than my own. *Would a stranger on the street ask whether I was her son?* A windowpane reflected my inquisitive expression. *Possibly?*

I suspected Jane Gibbs Baker experienced psychological trauma. *Of course she did!* Her husband, the father of her two sons, brutally murdered his mistress. *Is there something more?* I thought so. The woman, carefully shielded by a guise of optimism, seemed damaged—a pretty bird with a broken wing.

As we sang the simple lyrics to "Happy Birthday to You", I knew one thing for sure: Before leaving for home, I had to find out why my mother abandoned me.

Chapter Eight

Thursday Early Morning—August 15, 2019—Day 4

THE BOSTON WHALER'S DUAL OUTBOARDS REVVED TO AN INSANE LEVEL as we skimmed across the Tensaw River's placid surface. The GPS screen displayed a watercourse five hundred feet ahead. Ernie decelerated, cranking the steering wheel to the right. Beneath a cloud-obscured moon, the Guardian entered the opening to Big Briar Creek. We continued along the Mobile-Tensaw Cut-Off Channel until we reached the Mobile River. Our captain turned the boat north. Onward, atop a railway crossing, a light flashed once, twice, thrice. He guided the hull under the steel truss bridge, holding the craft steady in the stiff current.

Overhead, an indistinct figure lowered an orange bag over a railing and onto the front deck. Marvin unknotted the rope and covered the buoyant waterproof container with a tarpaulin. Ernie floored the speedboat, advancing northward.

I yelled at Marvin, "What's in there?"

"Don't know." The wind fanned his brown hair backward. "And don't need to know."

We sped through the darkness for a way, angling onto Big Bayou Canot and, at a small island, into Dead Lake. I worried the engines would run out of fuel, leaving us stranded. To my left, the city glittered. Further on, vehicle headlights zipped by on a highway.

Marvin inserted a thick clip into the Desert Eagle when brighter lights became visible. He held Big Bertha out to me. I threw my hands up in rejection. "Nuh, no. Uh-uh. Don't want it."

Although Marvin restrained himself, I realized the man was close to blowing his lid. "Paul, you just have to deliver that orange bag to campsite number fifty-eight. You'll see a brown and tan Fleetwood Frontier. The middle storage compartment will be unlocked. Swap the sack with the one in there, close 'er up, and mosey on back here. Nobody's awake at this hour. Piece o' cake."

"Marvin, if delivering that thing is so easy, why don't *you* do it?" My heart skipped a beat. "And why do *I* need a gun?"

Ernie eased the Boston Whaler into a vacant slip at the Mobile County River Delta Marina and Campground. He kept the motor idling. "Paul, no one knows you in these parts. Just another camper carrying his soap and shampoo to the bathroom to shit, shower, and shave."

"At midnight?"

"Could be, your bunkmate ain't givin' you none, and you gotta spank your monkey. I'm not saying your mission will be hazard-free," the older brother grinned, "but if you drop off this sack and bring us the other one, a third of our cut is yours." He wiggled two fingers and winked. "Twenty large in your pocket is nothing to sneeze at. And, Mr. Shakespeare, as a bonus, after tonight, you might write the story of a lifetime!"

My mind saw a slot machine spitting out gold coins. *Crime is certainly more lucrative than creative writing.* "What's in that dry bag?"

Ernie shrugged. "The roll-top is sealed, and I guaranteed our customer it's gonna stay sealed. What'll it be, big brother? Are you in, or are you out?"

I disliked how the twins called me "big brother," as if I had a birthright superior to theirs. *Really, Paul? Or do you truly like being part of their family?* I snapped my fingers at Marvin. "Give me the goddamn gun." Again, referring to the method all action movie heroes use to conceal a weapon, I inserted the bulky firearm in the back of my pants and pulled my shirt over the butt. The metal slide stop pressed against my spine, and the long, fat barrel dug into my crack. I hopped onto the wooden dock with the bag's strap slung across my shoulder. Afraid I would falter, I refused to look back.

A pebble pathway on the marina's grassy shore led to a pavilion abutting the concrete boat ramp. Except for an occasional nightbird winging skyward and the electrical hum of an outdoor Pepsi machine, the campground remained as still as the City of the Dead. A map on a signpost pointed me toward campsites past the pool. I walked on a sandy track, jumping at every rustle. At the terminus of a dirt road, a bus-sized motorhome awaited me. I crouched beneath the branches of a longleaf pine to listen and observe, only hearing a forlorn pond frog croaking and seeing a cloud of oversexed lightning bugs.

My senses on high alert, I hurried among the shadows. *Nearly there. You can do this.*

A door banged open. I scurried behind an SUV. A man wearing polka dot pajamas stepped out of a pop-up camper and shambled to the restroom. When the coast had cleared, I hastened down the lane.

I passed the post marked 58 and crept up the campsite's driveway to the front of the recreational vehicle. The enormous glass windshield glared downward at me—a Cyclops' single eyeball. My gut warned me that something besides the speckled trout carcass on the cutting board smelled fishy.

The forty-foot rolling house had six recessed handles on the lowermost section of the chassis: four large hatches in the center and two smaller hatches on the ends. *Marvin said the middle compartment isn't secured. Which one? Fifty-fifty probability.* I tried the right door. *Locked.* Anxious to retreat to the refuge of my hotel room, I set the dry bag below a flowering rhododendron. I placed my fingers on the left door's chrome latch. As it happened, my stomach had developed a sensitive olfactory system.

A tubular object drilled into my skull. A feminine voice rasped, "Caught me a Peepin' Tom. Turn to me, Peeper. Slowly now."

I raised my palms high, pivoting as directed to face an Amazonian woman in a pink velour Juicy Couture tracksuit. The giant antiquated revolver in her elevated fist made seeing her face difficult and impossible for me not to stutter, "Da-don't shoot. Just making a delivery."

"Stand up, so I can look at you." On my feet, she shined a tactical flashlight in my eyes. "Why are you slinking about in the dead of night?"

If this lady doesn't like my response, she will put a bullet in my head. I felt cold metal pressing against my lower back. *I have a gun, but she'll shoot me before I touch it.* "Ma'am, is this your Fleetwood?" The woman did not reply, nor did she execute me. "I brought you a—" I indicated the rhododendron. "Over by that bush."

The penlight beam shifted to the spiky shrub, then to me. "What's in it?"

"Got me. They sent me to exchange this bag for another—that's all."

"Describe your boss." Her finger extended to the Colt's trigger. "Tall, short, bald, hairy, skinny, fat as fuck?"

How did Ernie and Marvin become my masters? "The bearded men I work for are identical twins. Six-foot-two? One is more muscular, but either could kick my ass all the way to New Jersey with both hands tied behind their back."

The woman's chortle, oddly musical in the hushed hours before dawn, took the edge off the tense situation. She lowered the American Civil War-era relic and stooped to examine the orange sack's contents. Lighted by strings of multicolored Christmas bulbs, I estimated her age to be approximately the same as Jane's. Satisfied, she aimed the handgun's lengthy barrel at the hatchway I had been about to open. "In that one." I slid a blue rucksack from the storage locker. "What's your name, kid?"

I slung the sixty thousand dollars onto my back. *Six or seven pounds? Not heavy for a small fortune.* "If it's okay with you, ma'am, I'd rather keep that information private."

The woman shut the compartment and climbed into the Frontier. Her hand resting on the door, she swiveled. "Want to come inside for a drink?"

I shook the rucksack. "Perhaps some other time." I hightailed it out of there.

Marvin reached up to help me into the rocking Boston Whaler. He stowed the moneybag and the Desert Eagle in the locker. "Any problems?"

I had kept my act together on my stealthy return trip through the campground. Now, clinching the leaning post as Ernie gave the engines full throttle, my consuming trepidation transformed to pure anger. "That psycho almost blew my brains out!"

Marvin, laughing uproariously, socked my bicep. "Who do you mean, Ruby?"

Ernie swung his eyes off the horizon. "Humph. No holes in you. Ruby knew you were coming. There were no bullets in either of your guns. The ol' gal was just playing with you. Having a little sport."

"'Sport'? You shoulda told me!"

Ernie hurtled around a blind bend in the creek. "Didn't wanna put you in a tailspin." His lazy smile pissed me off. "Plus, we bet on how you'd perform under pressure. I lost ten bucks."

I wedged my back into a corner on the slippery deck, sulking for the remainder of the ride to Hurricane. *Tomorrow, I'm on a plane. If I can't get a reservation, I'll drive the rental the whole way to California. Outta here.*

At my car, Marvin counted out wrinkled bills. "Your third of the take."

I fanned the Jacksons. "Five thousand? Is this a joke? You swore I'd bring home twenty."

He smirked. "That much to transport a bag? Give me a break, Paul. We ain't the US Postal Service. Sweetenin' the pot was Ernie's idea. Figured you wouldn't do the job unless the stakes were high." Marvin raised his shoulders. "Still a fantastic payout."

I slammed the Subaru's door. Muck flying from the spinning tires splattered my half-brothers. *Screw them. I don't care.*

Thursday Morning—August 15, 2019—Day 4

The *Star Wars* R2-D2 ringtone dragged me up from the depths of a perplexing nightmare. My father, not Hale, led me through a maze of jumbo-sized corn stalks with a firm grip. He wanted me to see a bottomless pit in the cultivated rows of fertile earth. *Sinkhole? A mass grave?* Although my wife was the caller, I wasn't in the mood to answer. I considered myself a scrupulous person, not the lying criminal I had evolved into in a mere three days. "Hey, Jenn."

"What's wrong? You sound—"

"I'm fine. Just tired."

"From the birthday party?"

"Uh-huh. The barbecue went late." Fabulist, the imp operating the controls in my prefrontal cortex, scrolled through a list of lame excuses. "Can't pound 'em down like I used to. I woke up with a wicked hangover."

"Did you ask your mom about your dad?"

"Never got around to that ticklish conversation. In fact, I'm thinking of flying back to San Diego today."

"Why so soon?"

"People are different here. Not exactly my cup of tea."

"Trouble getting along with your family? Or not diggin' the Southern hospitality?"

I tumbled from the bed, approached the window, and watched a man edging the sidewalk with a string trimmer. "It must be weird for them, too. Me showing up out of the blue, expecting everyone to welcome me with open arms."

"Well, Jane obviously knew about you. While you're there, you might as well talk to her. You may not get a second chance."

The landscaper stopped the machine to drain a bottle of orange Gatorade. "I want to be with you and Smokey."

"We miss you too, sweetheart. If you found what you needed, get on the next plane."

Mom! "Hey, how's my mother?"

"I dropped by the Meadows this morning. We sat in the courtyard underneath her favorite tree. She loved listening to the birds singing."

"I'm glad Mom had fun! Maybe I'll drive to Hurricane this afternoon and have it out with Jane. One final time."

"Paul, don't be aggressive. She'll clam up. Tolerance is key. Remember, your mother was just a child when she gave birth to you."

"I promise to be nice!" A physical memory—*pleasurable?*—of the Desert Eagle shoved in my belt made me ponder. *Am I nice? Am I one of the good guys?*

Chapter Nine

Thursday Afternoon—August 15, 2019—Day 4

I GRIPPED THE SUBARU'S STEERING WHEEL ON THE ROAD TO HURRICANE, fretting over the best way to bring up the worriment that kept me restless at night. Jane was behind her house, mortaring bricks for the new outdoor kitchen. She didn't express astonishment as I strode into the backyard.

"Paul, I've been waitin' on ya." She passed me a hand tool and pointed at a green hose connected to a spigot. "Can you please bring me that pail, then rinse the mud off this trowel?" While I cleaned the triangular blade, Jane submerged the mortar in an inch of water and tamped down the plastic lid. "Now, the cement will keep till tomorrow." She frowned at the sun. "Good golly!" My mother shucked her work gloves to swab perspiration from her forehead. "Even Satan's sweatin' bullets today. Paul, would you like to get some ice cream with me?"

I have yet to meet a red-blooded male or female who doesn't love frozen desserts (and I wouldn't trust them if I did), so I agreed to her proposal. "Sure, sounds good."

Jane's eyes lit up. "Cammie's isn't around the bend, but she and her husband, Larry, make the best darn rocky road in southern Alabama."

"Where's Ernie and Marvin?"

She rolled her eyes. "Dollars to doughnuts at home asleep."

"They don't live here?"

"In my house? Lord, no! The twins got their own places over in Whitehouse Forks. Most days, my boys stop by to see if I need anything or to take the boat for a spin. Sarah's lived with me since—well, you know." Jane glanced at her wristwatch. "She won't be back till suppertime. Went to hang out with her friend in one of the riverfront houses. I'll leave her a note in case she comes home early."

The ice cream parlor, located nearby my downtown hotel, was indeed a journey. As we began the forty-minute trip up around the delta and down the 65 through Mobile's suburban outskirts, we talked about topics unrelated to the REALLY BIG ISSUE.

My mother, belted in the white Buick Enclave's driver's seat, muted the radio. "After high school, you went directly to college?"

"My parents were pretty strict. They didn't offer me the opportunity to take a few years off to tour the world." She nodded wholeheartedly as if this subject concerned her. "When my guidance counselor determined I had strong math skills, he advised me to major in economics—specializing in quantitative analysis."

"What's that?"

"We use mathematical and statistical modeling to comprehend human behavior to a greater degree. Governments rely on quantitative analysts to make recommendations on important economic policies. Upon graduation from the University of San Diego, I worked at two financial institutions and for the State of California until all the bean counting burned me out. Quants earn big bucks, but I have always longed to be an author. So, I discussed my career change with Jennifer. We put aside enough moolah to get by for a while. Felt liberating to punch the time clock, salute my boss, and walk out the door. I've written four novels and one book of short stories over the last seven years."

Jane shifted her eyes off the highway. "And are you pleased with that decision?"

"Some days go well; you've typed a couple of pages. Other days, I'm tempted to chuck the damn laptop out the window, then jump out after it." I squirmed in the leather seat. "Writing is the hardest thing I've ever done. A year or two cultivating the plot, followed by months of weeding out all the crap you thought was so extraordinary when you put the words to paper. You're overjoyed the day you self-publish the hardcover and ebook, downcast the next morning as you realize nobody on Planet Earth will read a single word."

"Paul, you could always return to being a," Jane tapped her fingers on the Buick's steering wheel, "whatta you call it? Quant? Why write if you feel unsuccessful?"

I daydreamed about the seven thousand dollars I had scored in two evenings with Ernie and Marvin. *Easy money.* A valid response to her valid query stumped me.

My mother changed lanes to pass a logging truck with MAKE AMERICA GREAT AGAIN and INSURED BY THE SECOND AMENDMENT stickers on the rear bumper. "What does Jennifer do?"

"She's a senior software engineer at Cardinal Health. Without her steady paycheck, we'd be camping on the street. Do you miss the nursing facility?"

"I cherished our residents and my coworkers. Ernie begged and begged for me to retire. Coulda worn the scrubs for ten more years. Still not comfortable sitting on my bum twiddling my thumbs."

"I bet Sarah appreciates you being around."

Jane beamed. "True! Being home when she gets out of school is a perk. Sarah's such a doll, much easier than the twins ever were. Those boys have been a handful. Always digging themselves out of a hole, only to throw themselves into a deeper pit."

Ernie and Marvin's father stabbed Sarah's mother to death. Why wouldn't the children be basket cases? "What was your husband like? How did you meet?"

"Hmm. Where young people of my generation partied—a discotheque."

I recalled a PBS documentary about a rock-and-roll disk jockey blowing up crates of vinyl disco records at a baseball game. Jane had entered her twenties in the early '80s. "Wasn't disco dead by then?"

"The doors on a scattering of clubs remained open for the loyal. Jonas loved to dance. Have you watched *Saturday Night Fever*?"

"Mighta caught a scene or two while channel surfing."

"As God is my witness, John Travolta had all the moves. Jonas musta seen that flick a million and one times. The man practiced his routine in front of a full-length mirror for hours straight. He thought he was Michael Jackson. Me? More of a punk rock girl—always first in line at Atomic Music to buy the latest Ramones and Dead Kennedys. In those days, I dressed in black to imitate Patti Smith and Joan Jett."

Confounded by that image, I swung to her. "You met Jonas in a discotheque?"

"Paul, the Creator works in mysterious ways. Or perhaps it's the Devil's doin'. Either way, my two girlfriends took me out on the town for my birthday. I'd have preferred the Mudd Club, but Naomi and Loretta had crushes on a barman at the Flamingo. My friends were paying, so why put up a fuss? The Flamingo's dance floor had strobe lights in the bottom and a revolving mirror ball hung from the ceiling. I remember that Saturday like it was yesterday. There he was, Jonas Baker, dancing the bump with some wannabe Chaka Khan. He wore the whole Tony Manero getup—black shirt, white vest, white suit, and white slacks. Nowhere as smooth as Travolta, but after three Moscow Mules, Jonas looked perfect to this country gal. I strutted right over, shoved ol' Chaka's bony ass out of my way, and paired with him in the Brooklyn shuffle."

"Then you two got hitched?"

"No choice. Shotgun wedding. Jonas didn't believe in birth control because of his strict Catholic upbringing. At any rate, he had no qualms with premarital sex, nor, down the road, lyin' and cheatin'. Wasn't all bad. Had a few giggles here and there. Jonas and I were married twenty-six years, the final three with him on the lam after he shanked Miss Sally Davenport."

"You said the Denver police shot him?"

"The news stated Jonas held a female against her will inside her apartment. A SWAT officer judged the armed man intended to harm the hostage. A sniper received the green light to squeeze the trigger. End of story."

But the story never ends when you want it to, does it? "That's terrible! I cannot imagine how Ernie, Marvin, and Sarah felt."

"I had a hunch where Jonas holed himself up. Ratted him out to the cops—'twas me who got my husband killed."

Now—or— "Was Jonas my father?"

My mother pulled the Enclave into the parking lot of Cammie's Old Dutch Ice Cream Shoppe. She shut off the engine. "Paul, I'm aware uncertainty is searing a hole through your heart and into your soul. Before I answer that critical question, and you decide you never want to set eyes on me again, let's sit a spell. We can savor God's greatest gift—a nice big bowl of Heaven on Earth."

The white-and-yellow building with garage-door-type windows might have formerly been a gas station. We passed beneath the gambrel-roofed entrance and into the store. I requested an Old Timer banana split from the teenage confectioner at the dipping cabinet. Jane ordered a Dutch Chocolate Tulip Sundae and paid with cash.

She slid over a napkin at an oval table near the front window. "It's not very often a fifty-seven-year-old mother gets to take her forty-one-year-old son out for ice cream for the very first time." Tears welled up in her eyes as she jammed the spoon into the double scoops of chocolate. The woman who bore me buried her face in her hands. "You must despise me."

On the ride to Hurricane, I had rehearsed a plethora of pithy retorts, endless variations of, "Go fuck yourself!" After listening to Jane's wretched saga, I had no stomach to shun her. *Do I love her?* I grasped her palm in mine. "It's all right, Mom. Better late than never." *Did I just call her Mom?*

We ate in companionable silence until the frozen desserts were purely sweet memories. Cars and trucks whooshed by on the street. On the sidewalk, an elderly woman in a filthy black house dress pushed a wobbly shopping cart overflowing with stuffed animals. *What's her tale of woe? Does anyone know her name or care if she exists?* I glimpsed her soiled panties when she bent over to rescue a fallen teddy bear. *That could be me if Jennifer leaves me for someone earning a living.* I turned from the extraneous distraction. "Jonas Baker isn't my father?"

Jane Gibbs had numerous anxiety-filled years to prepare for a reunion she prayed would or wouldn't occur. She stacked the paper bowls, dropped the plastic spoons inside, wiped chocolate off the tabletop, and crammed the brown napkin into the sticky mess. My mother stared me right in the eye. "Paul, there's no good way of saying this. Your biological father—raped me."

In the months after I learned of my adoption, my powers of invention hammered out multiple relationship scenarios, forcible intercourse not being anywhere in the current lineup. I had hoped the man my mother lost her virginity to had been a high school sweetheart, an older college student, or even the boy next door. My tormented brain didn't allow me to consider incest or— *Jesus, I am a child of rape.* Heartburn scorched my esophagus. My tongue squeegeed the curdled cream back down my gullet. I rushed to fill a cup at the water dispenser. The cold liquid flushed the gastric acid coating my throat. "Tell me."

Jane blinked twice before her mouth opened. "I grew up in Gulfport, Mississippi. My dad served in the Seabees at the naval base. Between my junior and senior high school years, I left a classmate's house at eight-thirty on a Wednesday evening. Mr. Radcliff, our summer school science teacher, paired Gail and me to work on a science fair project. We had to submit our assignment the next day. They drum it into you from infancy not to walk alone, especially after nightfall, and specifically if you're female. And whoever 'they' might be, they weren't kidding."

I pictured the faces of all the missing milk carton kids and shivered.

Jane straightened her shoulders. "So, I'm cutting down an alley behind Ace Hardware when a white van pulls alongside me. In every slasher film, the maniac drives a creepy, rusted van, the rear windows covered with cardboard or painted black. This Chevrolet appeared fairly new. A commercial vehicle, but no PETER'S PLUMBING printed over Donald Duck waving a pipe wrench. The passenger glass cranks down, and a dark-haired man asks me where 28th Street is. Claims he's visiting a friend. I thought this peculiar, as the original Gulfport City Council sequentially numbered the streets and avenues. Any dummy can figure out how to navigate anywhere blindfolded. Now I'm freaking out 'cause I knew August 24th, 1977, wouldn't end well for little Janey Gibbs.

"I've booted myself in the rump a thousand times for being so stupid. The guy opens the driver's door and sprints around the front. You want me to describe his face, but I can't. No streetlights were installed behind the hardware store, and my eyeglasses were in my schoolbag." Jane patted her temple. "I wear contacts now." Her head swiveled left and right. "I peered up and down the alleyway. There are just two ways to escape. The way I came, or toward my house on 30th Street—three blocks farther. I'm five-foot-nothing, and this four-hundred-pound sack of testosterone could play professional basketball. Whichever direction I pick, Shaq is gonna catch me.

"As I backed away, ready for the marathon of my life, he yells, 'Jane! Mike sent me to get you.' What a crock! My dad—God rest his soul—threw a tantrum anytime somebody didn't call him by his full name. Michael.

"I did the only thing I could. Turned tail and ran for it. As a freshman, I joined the cross-country team, building stamina and decent speed for my size. I'm almost to where the alley meets the street when he tackles me. We fall, and he lands on my back. The man drags me inside his van by my hair." My mother deliberated. "For both of our sakes, I'll skip over the worst part." She used my cup of water to wet her lips.

"The guy slapped me and whammed my forehead against the metal floor. I pleaded with him to let me go. He said I was a liar, a thief, and a name I couldn't make out. Tanya or Tabitha? By the time the fiend finished his business, one look in his eyes told me all I had to know. Prayers alone weren't enough to stop this schizo from strangling me."

Still listening to her, I flexed my knuckles, rotating my right palm upward. A small blemish crossed the crease arcing from above my thumb to my wrist. *When did this scar surface on my life line?* My fingers clenched into a fist. *Are these my father's hands?*

"Paul, as you can see, I'm still alive and kicking and, knock on wood, have the majority of my faculties. NASA scheduled the launch of the Voyager I space probe for the fall of 1977. For our astronomy science fair project, Gail and I charted the spacecraft's flight path past the planets Jupiter and Saturn on poster board. In such a hurry to leave Gail's house, I hadn't stored the pair of compasses I used for plotting the Voyager's orbit in my book bag. I tucked the drawing tool into my jacket instead.

"The beast straddled my stomach, holding down my arms. Not sure if he was wallowing in the evil he had done or just recharging his batteries for round two. I had a single roll of the dice, so I screamed at the top of my lungs. While he raised his hand to cover my mouth, I slipped the compasses out of my pocket. I aimed to stick him in the eye, but the demon read my mind and blocked my arm. Yet, I got him plenty good—gripped the metal handle in my fist and raked the needle point across his left cheekbone. Stabbed and jabbed till the ogre rolled off. Bled like a stuck pig, the whites of his teeth gleaming through a gash in the side of his ugly face.

"I leaped from the van and ran home. His blood, mixed with my blood, stained my arms. My parents were in the TV room laughing up a storm. Funny how, even now, I can remember what program was on—*All in the Family*. I called out, 'Tired, going to bed,' and scooted by. My knees and elbows had scrapes, and my eye turned black and blue by morning. Long sleeves and pants, plus a gallon of makeup, fixed these temporary matters. After twelve weeks, a more serious dilemma emerged. When I started to show, my schoolmates gave me grief about my baby bump. I waved it away. 'Ha, I better lay off the jelly doughnuts!'

"Four weeks later, wisecracks failed to divert attention from my pregnancy. My mom put the screws to me. 'Who's this boy you been with?' Ashamed, I kept my mouth shut. She informed my dad. He went ballistic, hollering he'd send me to an out-of-state abortion clinic. My mother, who was brought up a devout evangelical Christian, preached on and on about the sanctity of life. 'There will be no murdering of innocents in this family!' Me? I had no say whatsoever. Mom shipped me off to the town of Wiggins to stay with her sister, Aunt Vivian."

Although it was rude for me to interrupt her, I lifted my palm. Jane gestured for me to speak. "Weren't you stressed your, um, assailant would come for you? He had your dad's name and must have known your address."

"Oh, I spent many a sleepless night worrying about him slithering in the bedroom window to slit my throat. I hid a kitchen knife under the pillow and placed glass bottles on the windowsills as primitive alarms. As time passed, I got the notion that the ghoul of my dreams could just ring the doorbell, stroll in, and butcher us all. Once I moved in with Aunt Vivian, and several months droned by, I became complacent. I had a being growing in my belly to dwell on, in addition to the homeschooling. Sure, I peeked over my shoulder. Still do." She unsnapped the flaps of her alligator skin handbag to reveal a pearl-handled pocket pistol. "I pray the man who raped me is dead. My only power over him is appealing to the Almighty for his untimely demise."

"My father?"

"Yes, Paul. Your actual father." Jane's cheeks turned scarlet. "That animal nearly killed me."

"Why did you give me away?" My eyes burned. "You could have raised me."

She dropped the Colt Model 1908 into her bag. "My parents were so embarrassed, and even if they permitted me to keep you, look at me! I'm not worthy. You've seen where I live. Ernie and Marvin? Sweet Jesus, if those boys don't stop trafficking death, they'll wind up in Talladega." Jane clutched my hand. "Paul, aren't you grateful Edith and Hale adopted you?"

"By all means! My mom and dad did everything for me. They changed my dirty diapers and hugged me when I woke up, wailing from nightmares. My mother drove me to the doctor if I had a fever. My father taught me how to ride a bicycle. Both assisted me with my homework and paid for my college education." I sighed. "They loved me, and I loved them back, but—"

"No buts about it. Putting you up for adoption was my only option. God knows what would have happened to either of us if you had stayed with me. Paul, you turned out finer than I ever dreamed."

I saw my reflection in a mirror mounted behind the dipping cabinet. "If you look at my face, do you see his? That man in the van?"

When Jane's feedback took excessive seconds to form, I understood why she handed me over to those carrying far less emotional baggage. "As I said, without my glasses—" She closed her eyes. "In Psalm 30, David sang about his enemies, 'O Lord my God, I cried to you for help, and you healed me.'"

My mother conveyed the impression of being ultra-religious. Edith and Hale attended the early service at the local Lutheran church each Sunday and sent me to Bible school. Years had passed since I stepped inside a house of worship. *Was the last time a wedding? Or could it have been Uncle Charles' funeral?* "Mom, does praying help?"

Crow's feet, I hadn't noticed until now, tracked the outer corners of her eyes. "No, Paul. Not yet." She tossed the empty ice cream bowls in the trash and went outside.

The Buick hit every dip in the road leading to Hurricane. Neither of us spoke much. My mind repeated the phrase: *My father is a rapist.* Near Red Hill Creek, my mother let up on the gas to point out a pandemonium of soaring wild parrots.

Otherwise, Jane Gibbs Baker kept the pedal to the metal and her lips sealed. *Is she angry with me? Am I angry with her?*

Chapter Ten

Thursday Afternoon—August 15, 2019—Day 4

STICKS, BRANCHES, LOGS, AND DEBRIS OF A LESS ORGANIC ORIGIN floated by me on the swiftly moving Tensaw River. A few days ago, I feared the creatures lurking beneath the turbid surface. Now, sitting next to the moored Boston Whaler, my shriveled toes resembled white worms wiggling in the tepid water. I gave the daddy of all gators permission to take the juicy bait and drag me under. My conversation with Jane at Cammie's had devastated my entire being. *Isn't it a God-given rule that eating ice cream is always supposed to be fun?* My junket to southern Alabama, a naïve attempt to get back to my roots, had quickly turned unpleasant—a real train wreck.

"Sorry, it's not 190 proof." My mother handed me a Pabst Blue Ribbon. She sat beside me on the wooden dock.

"This is fine," I said. The descending sun's amber rays highlighted her waves of golden-brown hair and formed a triangle of light across her cheekbone. I visualized the photograph of sixteen-year-old Jane Gibbs lying in a hospital bed, cradling me in a blue blanket. *This woman retained her beauty through hell and high water.*

"Quite a day! Paul, you're the first person I've spoken to about that horrid night." She downed half the bottle of beer. "I'm still figuring out if I feel better or worse. How 'bout you? Worser than worse?"

I felt dreadful. My world had tilted on its axis, casting shadows on footpaths I once trod securely upon. Weaker me cried: *Why did this have to happen to me?* My introspective self whispered: *At least now I know the reason I'm so fucked up.* I asked her, "What if I'm like my father or will turn into him?"

She scratched her cheek. "We all inherit personality traits from our biological parents. My dad, a military man, was extremely strict, but fair. My mother? The complete opposite. Spiritual, but free-spirited. Mom let me do whatever I wanted as long as I kept my grades up and stayed out of juvenile court. I raised the twins as she raised me. In hindsight, I shoulda been like my father, much tougher. They—well, you've seen how those boys act. My sons love me. Even so, I cannot say I'm proud of the men they've become." Jane finished her drink and set the glass bottle on the dock.

"Ernie and Marvin aren't that bad. Never too late to change."

"Would you talk to them? Maybe you can steer your brothers in the right direction?" She wrung her hands, desperate for me to agree.

I soaked up the last drops of lukewarm lager and placed the brown bottle alongside her empty one. The sight of the two dead soldiers somehow saddened me. "Jane, I'm going home tomorrow. I miss Jennifer. There's my writing, and I—"

"Paul, I accept you want to get as far from this part of the country as possible. Will you come to visit?"

"To be honest, I intended to leave today. I couldn't take off without saying goodbye."

"And asking me about your father."

"That too." *Shall I return to Alabama? Eh? Not likely.* "My wife can't wait to meet you. It might be a while until we, uh—"

"You need time to sort this all out, but please don't forget about us." Jane tipped her head backward to prevent tears from rolling down her cheeks—a futile effort. "At this stage of my life, I'm so emotional. A sappy beer commercial can set me off, or anything with a cute animal."

I put my arm around my mother's shoulders, awkward at first, then natural. "Have you established the identity of the man who abused you? You told me he may have used his van for business purposes. Did you ever see the same white Chevy on the streets?"

Jane conversed internally with her id, ego, and superego. Hazel eyes drifted from the nearby water, to the far riverbank, to the distant horizon, and finally fixated on me. Libido—the driving force of all behavior—apparently won the psychological confrontation. "I've something to show you." My mother went up to the house and reappeared a few minutes later with the German shepherd. She laid a yellowed, unaddressed envelope on my lap.

I opened the flap to remove a three-by-six-inch remnant of heavy-duty paper. The word CAUTION centered a blue diamond. I flattened the creases to piece together the torn sentences: READ THE LABL and KEEP OUT OF REACH OF CHIL. DICHLORO DIPHENYL TRICHLOROETHANE (DDT) . . . 50%, INERT ADDITIVES . . . 50%, DDT MIN. SETTING POINT . . . 89°C. were listed as ingredients. The unfolded bottom edge stated: MONTROSE CHEMICAL CORPORATION, TORRANCE, CALIFORNIA. *DDT. Where did I hear of this chemical?* "What is this from?"

Jane grimaced. "DDT has been used worldwide since the late 1800s. Farmers applied tons of this powerful insecticide to their crops. Governmental agencies sprayed mosquitoes and fleas spreading malaria and bubonic plague. Diligent housewives sprinkled the granules everywhere to rid their homes of cockroaches and ants. School nurses dusted the heads of children to kill lice. The chemical leached into the streams, rivers, and eventually the oceans. In the 1970s, the EPA banned the use of DDT in the United States. Too hazardous to wildlife, primarily birds."

I remembered how I learned about DDT. "Our high school biology teacher assigned the class to read *Silent Spring*, a book detailing the harmful environmental effects of synthetic pesticides. Even after the ban, the US sold DDT to foreign countries. Doctors claim trace elements are still in our bloodstreams."

She crinkled her nose. "Toxic stuff. When I became convinced I'd never get out of that van alive, I searched for a clue to leave behind. Things were heaped between the front seats. While the man struggled to zip down his fly, I jammed this strip of a bag in my pocket. I hoped that if detectives found my body, they'd tie this evidence to him."

The ancient scrap of wood pulp contaminated my fingers. "What were the other items?"

"They mystified me, so I did some research. The library collected publications on DDT, its uses, and proper application methods in various circumstances. In one illustration, a technician had a pump sprayer strapped to his back. Clothing partially covered a cylindrical object with 'REGA' stamped in the metal. Rega is an Australian manufacturer of pump sprayers. And that's not all. The beige clothes on the tank were full-body coveralls. I believe my attacker was an exterminator."

Chilled, I clenched her arm. "He could have worked in your neighborhood or been inside your home."

"A man came every month to spray outside our house. Bugs? Weeds? As a youth, I paid him no mind and didn't see him up close. So, I can't really say."

"That's scary!" Sammy, dozing on the dock, lifted his muzzle. "You should have gone to the cops."

"Of course! How many more girls did he yank inside his van? Was I the only survivor able to report him? I've lived with that sin on my conscience."

"You were young. Very few sexually assaulted women go to the police."

"I needed to move on and forget the past." She scowled. "Pure fantasy."

I clasped my hands. "Then along comes Jonas."

She nodded. "The murderer. For years, my self-esteem lay in the gutter. Jonas showered me with attention, an act my gullible brain mistook as love." Jane gripped both of my hands. "Paul, I apologize for letting you down. Can you ever forgive me?"

"What's going on here?" Ernie called. "A little mommy-sonny time?" The twins ambled down the hill with a 24-pack of stoopid juice.

Chapter Eleven

Friday Early Morning—August 16, 2019—Day 5

AGAIN, WITH ERNIE MANNING THE HELM, the Boston Whaler skipped across small waves. Six beers and two double shots of golden alcohol that poured without the slightest resistance from a "Jesus Jug" made recalling how I got talked into another night of nefarious activity very difficult. The twins acted more amped up than they had been on our previous two excursions. After dinner, I asked Ernie where we were going. His pinched lips signified what lay ahead. The Desert Eagle tucked in my belt felt like a fatal accident waiting to happen.

For the first leg of this trip, I kept track of our boat on the glowing GPS. We progressed north up the Middle River, a stretch of water clearly in the middle of noplace and nowhere. Ernie slowed the Guardian while his brother shined a flashlight along the shoreline. When Marvin twirled his hand, Ernie stopped by a giant can of Hunt's Tomato Sauce bobbing in the reeds.

Marvin bent over the side to snag the steel can attached to a nylon rope. "Paul, help me reel 'er in."

Ernie clapped twice. "Hurry! They're only waterproof for so long."

We hauled a chain of brick-sized plastic boxes, each anchored to a lead weight, onto the deck. White granular powder filled the eight clear containers.

Marvin used the flashlight to inspect the parcels for leakage. "Dry as a bone." He hefted one block and smiled at me. "Eight kilograms equals four million doses of pure fentanyl. That's twelve-mil street value. Nice booty for a couple hours of labor, don't you agree?"

I focused on Ernie. "You're getting paid to deliver this poison to some drug dealer, correct? Don't tell me you're planning to sell it."

The twin bared his teeth for the first time this evening. "Paul, we're taking the Dragon's Breath for ourselves." If I hadn't been gripping the leaning post when he slammed the throttle control forward, the sudden spurring would have jettisoned me into the backwash.

I lurched to the center console and shouted above the thundering motors, "Ernie, you can't just steal it! Your mother wants you to stop breaking the law!" I reached for the throttle handle.

Ernie thrust me aside. "I don't hear Maw complaining about all the new stuff we bought her. We've been takin' care of her since our father ran for the hills." He sneered. "But what do you know of family values, bastard boy?"

I withstood the impulse to clobber the man piloting our boat through dark, uncharted waters. "What happens now?"

"We're paying a friendly little visit to Augustus and Jasper."

"The Neanderthals you sold the firearms to? Are they part of the mob?"

"Augustus Dawson and his son work for the Silverio drug cartel. Auggie recruited us. The Mexicans shall believe the Dawsons ripped them off."

I rocked Ernie's shoulder. "What are you going to do—kill them?"

Marvin jabbed me in the kidney and laughed. "We ain't sicarios, big brother. Bakers are born devious, but not murderous. We'll bamboozle those nitwits."

I considered Jonas, the twins' murderous father. "How?"

Ernie helmed our vessel into a natural cove. The two huge outboard engines of a thirty-one-foot SeaHunter speedboat emerged from the duskiness.

I squinted to determine whether the forms in the cockpit were human. "Is that the Dawsons?"

Ernie guided the Boston Whaler side by side with the unoccupied *Chum Runner*. "No. We borrowed this."

Marvin leaped into the stolen boat and held the hulls together. "Hop aboard, Paul."

I threw up my hands. "Why?"

"Just do it!"

I climbed over the gunwales onto the *Chum Runner's* non-skid platform.

Marvin hot-wired the Mercury motors. He stowed the anchor and jumped back into the *Lickety-Split*.

The current captured my floating craft. "Hey, how about me?"

The senior twin beckoned with his fingers. "Follow us!"

"Ernie, I know zilch about boats!"

He separated his palms. "Easy as driving a Tesla on autopilot. You've watched me enough. When Marvin flashes his light three times, stop and lower the anchor. Don't even think of taking off!" Seconds later, men and motorboat raced far ahead.

I stood at the center console, my left hand gripping the SeaHunter's steering wheel, my right hand pushing the throttle. Nothing. *The lever's stuck.* I fumbled with the handle, at last locating a button. Unlocked and in gear, the dual 250-

horsepower outboards surged onward. As the controls became familiar, I accelerated faster and faster until I rode in their wake. Marvin gave me the thumbs-up.

We backtracked south down the Middle River. On a Sunday afternoon, freewheeling throughout Mobile Bay would have exhilarated me. Tonight, the incredible power beneath my fingertips only produced anxiety. *We're not on a pleasure cruise, are we? Jane's sons are up to no good, and I'm neck-deep in their horseshit.*

A light blinked thrice. I decelerated and jerked the shift to neutral. The *Chum Runner's* nose dipped into the river, gliding to a standstill. The *Lickety-Split* faded beyond a bend, leaving me alone to wrestle with my demons. Internal voices screamed at me. *Should I wait until Ernie and Marvin finish robbing or murdering Augustus and Jasper? Paul, run while you still can! What about the money? Stay, Paul, stay. Stop being a coward!* I cast the anchor into the black ink. After all, as a long-dead German once recited at an Alsace poetry slam: *Blood is thicker than water.*

I scanned the ghostly riverbanks and monitored the gauges. The purpose of half the instrumentation baffled me, but the plummeting fuel needle gave me agita. My cupped ears perceived the bass notes of cavitation reverberating from where I had last seen the Boston Whaler.

The *Lickety-Split* careened around the oxbow, splashing to a dramatic halt. I clung to the SeaHunter's console to keep from tipping over.

Ernie tied the bouncing boats together as his brother dropped the Guardian's anchor in the waterway.

The eight plastic containers filled with whitish powder were gone. "Did you get paid?" I shut off the engines. "Can we please go home now?"

I never foresaw the twins vaulting into the *Chum Runner.*

"Help Marvin. Then we bolt on the T-top." Ernie uncovered a pile of aluminum and began assembling the curved tubes.

Marvin unfurled a wide roll of contact paper. When I read the three capitalized words, I considered swimming the entire way back to San Diego.

A beach towel flew through the buggy air. Marvin ordered, "Wipe off the sides so the glue sticks." After the sections above the waterline were moistureless, he passed me one end of the long vinyl strip. "Peel carefully. *Don't* let the bottoms touch." We adhered decals to both sides of the SeaHunter's hull and the stern, adding two official emblems to the diagonal black stripes on the front of the boat.

As a team, we fastened the T-top to the center console's frame. Ernie grinned with satisfaction at the navy-blue canvas roof. "Well done." He flung stuffed plastic bags at his brother and me. "Put on these uniforms, pronto!"

My sack contained dark blue trousers and a light blue shirt, a personal floatation device, and a duty belt. Patches on the sleeve matched the identifications Marvin and I had affixed to the sides of the SeaHunter: *ALABAMA MARINE POLICE.* "No way!" I shouted. "No fucking way!" As I lunged toward the Boston Whaler, Marvin hooked my wrist.

"We are well past the point of no return, Paul." Ernie unbuckled his jeans. "That train already left Grand Central Station. Be a good boy and get changed. Put your street clothes in the garbage bags." He checked a timer on his cell phone. "We're on a tight schedule."

Fully outfitted with the cumbersome life jacket positioned over my shoulders, after feeling the bulletproof vest on my chest, I realized I'd sink to Davy Jones' Locker if I fell overboard. I glanced up to find myself under review by a pair of identical police officers.

"Oh, I almost forgot." Ernie handed out self-adhesive "Freddie Mercury" mustaches.

I had set the Desert Eagle on the floor to undress. Marvin gave me the .357 Magnum. "Paul, the handgun is just for show. We're taking Augustus and Jasper by surprise. No gunplay unless those jackoffs are stupid enough to shoot first." I inserted Big Bertha into my holster.

Ernie fired up the *Chum Runner's* dual outboards, swinging the phony police boat to face certain danger. And with two hurrahs and one murmured objection, we were off to rob the Dawsons of twelve million dollars in illegal drugs.

Robert Burns once scribed this verse in a famous poem, *To A Mouse*: "The best-laid schemes o' mice an' men Gang aft agley." If I hadn't enrolled in an advanced placement literature class in high school, I wouldn't have known the translation of his last few words. Burns' eloquent line, written in Scots, basically means: *You're always bound to screw everything up royally, regardless of how detailed your plan may be.*

When the stern lights of the Dawsons' brown pontoon motorboat came into sight, the GPS showed them heading south to Mobile Bay. Ernie killed our running lights, decreasing our velocity to remain unnoticed.

Marvin plugged an electric cord into an outlet on the center console. He retracted a short antenna from a box the size of a pack of cigarettes and held out the gadget. "Paul, will you perform the honors?"

"Is this a detonator? Are we blowing up the Dawsons' boat?" I backpedaled from the red button protected by a transparent guard.

Marvin scoffed at me. "While you were in bed dreaming of whistles and wagons, Ernie and I installed remote shut-off valves on their fuel pumps. This wireless doodad stalls the engines. Then—hippity hip hooray!—the sea cavalry comes to the rescue."

Ernie whirled to glower. "What's the holdup? We gotta hit those asswipes before they get to the river fork at Blakeley. Paul? Snap out of it!"

I thumbed up the hinged switch guard as if Lucifer himself puppeteered my muscular reflexes. The ethanol that had permeated my judgmental lobes had long since dissipated in my bloodstream. God help me, I knew exactly what I was doing when I mashed the trigger.

The Manitou XT didn't explode. The outboard motors, burning a quart of fuel every minute, simply fell silent.

Unable to restrain his excitement, Ernie rubbed his palms. "Perfect!" He eyed his stopwatch. "Let them fiddle-diddle with the engines for five minutes." Ernie pulled a banged-up flask from his pocket and took a healthy swig.

Once Marvin had his fill, I drained the dregs of the foul-tasting liquid courage. I accosted our pirate captain with my throat on fire and the contents in my stomach fermenting. "If we take the fentanyl, won't the cartel come for us?"

Misgivings rippled Ernie's broad face. "The Mexicans will blame Augustus and Jasper. They're responsible for losing the shipment to the police."

"Who left the drugs for the underwater pickup?"

"Ruby Dawson."

My jaw sagged. "The lady at the campground is a Dawson?"

"Yep." Ernie took the assault rifle from his brother. "Auggie's sister. And, just to be clear, Ruby's no lady."

"She also works for the cartel?"

"Not directly." He examined the AR-15's detachable magazine, nodded in approval, then hammered the metal receptacle home. "Ruby's freelance, same as us."

I squeezed my sore head, a gigantic pimple ripe for popping. After binge-watching seasons one and two of *Narcos* on Netflix, men like Pablo Escobar gave me the willies. I stated the obvious. "We will be trapped in the middle."

A tremor ran through Marvin's hands as he sighted along the shotgun's barrel. "When we complete our business here, we're leaving town. You're flying home to San Diego."

"What about Sarah and your mother? Alabama will not be safe for them."

"Paul, Jane's your mother as well. The women are coming with us."

"You told them about what you're doing?"

"Hell, no!" Marvin adjusted the Velcro side straps on his ballistic vest. "I'm not cuckoo!" The twins wore handguns on their hips.

"Where can you go? The cartel will hunt you down wherever you hide."

"They may try. Safer for us all if you don't know our whereabouts. Once things settle, we'll invite you and your wife to a family reunion. They say the island of Fiji is paradise on Earth." Marvin's hazel eyes pursued the Dawsons' directionless motorboat. "Check your weapon, big brother. Get ready to rumble."

I finally got to meet my real mother, and now she's abandoning me again. Adrift in maudlin reveries, I drew the Desert Eagle from the waistband holster and stared into the muzzle.

"Check the clip, Paul!" Ernie clicked the gearshift. "Keep extra ammo close at hand!" With my loaded handgun returned to its Kydex sheath, the Mercury Verados' dual screws propelled the SeaHunter forward at a moderate speed.

Our skipper activated a spotlight as soon as we were near enough to read the name painted on the stern of the twenty-six-foot pontoon boat. He spoke into a white and red bullhorn, enunciating the words in an exaggerated Northern accent. "*Avid Angler*, are you in need of assistance?"

Augustus blocked the blinding light with his palm. "We're fine, officer. Our engines quit. There's fuel in the tank, and the battery has voltage, so my son reckons the problem is just a disconnected hose or wire."

We were only seventy-five feet from trouble and rapidly closing in. The closest EVINRUDE cowl lay beside the outboard motor. Jasper used a screwdriver and a pair of pliers to tinker with a cylindrical device, his strawberry birthmark vivid under the bright beam.

Marvin confided. "That rig is quicker than she looks. See the size of those suckers? They might get away if the kid figures out what's wrong."

Ernie raised the bullhorn. "We'll tow you to Sunset Marina. Their repair shop opens in four hours. Get breakfast at Mave's Café. You can be back on the water reeling in king mackerel before you know it."

Augustus called out, "My boy tells me he found an electrical issue. He's a genius when it comes to fixin' anything mechanical." The man waved us off. "Thanks for your service, officers!"

Jasper stood up to give his father the okay sign. When Augustus stabbed the Manitou's ignition button, three spins of the two starters primed the fuel injectors with gasoline. The instant the combustible kissed the sparking plugs, the sixteen pistons were off to the races.

Something inside me (or someone inside of me I hadn't been formally introduced to) goaded me to seize command. I sidled up to Ernie. "Cut the motherfuckers off."

"What?"

"You heard me."

Although my half-brother's lower lip plunged in unbelief, he angled the *Chum Runner* on a collision course with the *Avid Angler*.

You've sat breathlessly through Hollywood shoot 'em ups, perhaps Bruce Willis annihilating a dozen terrorists to save his wife in *Die Hard*, or Clint Eastwood raining fire and brimstone on Logo's sinful townsfolk in *High Plains Drifter*. However, if you've never been in an authentic shootout, you have no concept of what live fire is actually like. Not even close. You aren't munching buckets of buttery popcorn in a darkened theater. Flesh-and-blood people are doing their damnedest to bore holes in you.

The glitzy advertisements for the Manitou XT portray bevies of sexy women lounging on plush seats. Look beyond the itty-bitty red bikinis to the mechanical specifications, and you'd learn that Manitou engineers expressly designed this pontoon motorboat for men lusting for the fastest way to get from Point A to Point B.

Ernie understood that our 500-horsepower boat was no match for the Dawsons' 600 horses. "Cutting the motherfuckers off," as I had suggested, would slice our fiberglass hull in two, squashing us like a family of jellyfish crossing an interstate. So, rather than jockeying the *Chum Runner* to blockade their getaway, he rammed our bow into the *Avid Angler's* revving engines.

The bracket that hitched the right outboard to the Manitou's transom broke free. For an instant, the screaming motor hung from cables, wires, and hoses before submerging below the water. The left outboard, smoking and slanted sideways, steered the *Avid Angler* in concentric circles. Augustus and Jasper weren't going anywhere.

Marvin, his fake mustache dangling off his upper lip, bellowed, "This is the police! Drop your weapons." Stripped of his Remington (the shotgun had fallen overboard during the collision), he cocked his Glock Model 22.

I prayed for the father and son to surrender. As Jasper put his weight into straightening the six-hundred-pound power plant, Augustus opened fire with an AK-47. I had fallen on impact, my face smacking against the cold deck as he riddled our boat with gilding metal. Fiberglass filaments snowed horizontally as hardened projectiles penetrated the hull's port side to fly through the starboard. Ernie snapped the SeaHunter into reverse to maneuver us out of range.

Marvin crouched. "Paul, why aren't you shooting?" He discharged his handgun above the gunwale while Augustus reloaded the Kalashnikov. "Let 'em have it!"

Ernie, no longer in favor of retreat, fired his AR-15 at Augustus. With our speedboat undulating in the waves and the Dawsons' pontoon boat still moving in expanding rings, I doubted any bullets came close to their objectives. I yanked the Desert Eagle from the holster, jacked a round into the chamber, and peeked over the port side. As Augustus hoisted the fully automatic weapon again, I peered along my ten-inch barrel. Granted, aiming at a paper bull's-eye does not equate to zeroing in on a human being, but if your adrenaline is boiling, a target is merely a target. My hands steady and my breath held, I compressed Big Bertha's curvy trigger. *Ka-boom!* When I lowered the cannon from twelve inches of recoil to take more shots, the man had vanished.

"Paul, you plugged him!" Marvin cheered. "He's down!"

A red rose blooming on his left shoulder, Augustus climbed into view. My next shot missed. He propped himself on the prow to let loose another barrage.

Marvin crumpled to the deck in agony. "I'm hit!" He clutched the bottom of his right leg. "Shit, shit, oh shit."

I crawled across the spreading blood as bullets whizzed over my head. Not trained as a combat medic, I did the first thing that came to mind. I pressed my palm on the spouting wound. "Ernie, get us out of here! Marvin needs a doctor!"

Ernie had sheltered behind the tallest object on our boat, the center console. "They're escaping!" He let off two bursts from his assault rifle before grasping the steering wheel. "Don't let my brother bleed to death. Use a rope for a tourniquet."

Jasper miraculously had aligned the still-running engine. While Augustus pumped the throttle, his son steered the skeg rudder by brute force.

As the *Chum Runner* reared up on its haunches, Marvin and I slipped down the slick platform, smashing into the stern. I tore off the bulletproof vest, doffing my uniform shirt to access my T-shirt. With the makeshift bandage wrapped around Marvin's calf, I tightened a length of cord about his lower thigh. These emergency procedures stemmed the gusher to a trickle.

Ernie slid the SIG Sauer downhill to me. "Sharpshooter, see what you can do while I give chase!"

I clambered to the machine gun mount to brace the AR-15. My forefinger switched the safety selector to Fire. Hot brass ejected from the semi-automatic's chamber as I peppered the *Avid Angler's* posterior with full metal jacket. If I survived today, the future might hold quiet moments for me to contemplate my homicidal tendencies. At present, I had no time for: *Am I doing this to help my family, or am I really doing this for the money?* And the most disturbing thought of all: *Do I enjoy shooting people?*

Smoke billowed from the guts of the Manitou's destroyed outboard motor. Jasper sprayed the Evinrude with an extinguisher until the flames guttered out. On the listing deck, Augustus calculated the success of his limited avenues for flight. He leveled his AK-47 at us.

Ernie, dropping the elaborate pretense, brought the bullhorn to his lips. "Auggie! Lay down your weapons." He set his Glock on the deck. "Give us the drugs, and we'll let you off on shore. You have my word!"

Young Dawson flipped his middle finger. "Baker, your word is worthless! You tried to rob us. Juan Carlos Delgado will flay you all alive when he finds out."

Marvin threatened with his handgun. "If that's the way you feel, how 'bout we finish the both of you off right now!"

I obstructed my half-brother. "Mr. Dawson!" I laid the AR-15 on the platform. "I'm Paul. Five days ago, I flew to Alabama to track down my birth mother. Now that I've met her, I just want to go home to California and be with my wife. The *Avid Angler* is in bad shape. It's sinking. These currents are strong! Good luck if you think you can pick off the three of us, then swim to our boat with your injured arm dragging twenty pounds of dope. I shot you, and you shot Marvin. In my book, we're square. If you chuck your guns overboard, I swear we'll split the fentanyl fifty-fifty. You guys need to disappear, as do we. Tomorrow, when the *Avid Angler* washes up on some beach, the Mexicans will presume you drowned."

Augustus trembled with rage. "Delgado won't believe me and my boy didn't steal his goods."

I stood high on the prow, my bare chest an easy target. "What if we stash a kilo of his drugs in your boat to throw them off? That leaves us three bricks and four for you and Jasper. Is that fair?"

Ernie's hand clamped my forearm. "Who put you in charge? You're giving it all away!"

"Look at your brother." Gore coated the entire deck. Marvin's lips cracked open in pain. "If you don't want to bring him to an emergency room, we can stitch him up at your house. From what I can tell, the bullet passed right through his calf, missing the bone." I took ahold of Ernie's shoulders and glared into his hazel irises, carbon copies of Marvin's. "If we stick around much longer, your twin will die."

Ernie lifted his mouth to the stars and howled. The tall man shook his head in wonder, his furor dissipating to the heavens. "Paul, you're right. I got caught up in the—no excuse." He scrambled over the deck to tend to his brother.

While I locked horns with Ernie, the Dawsons also had been arguing.

"What's it gonna be, Augustus?" I extended a long-distance handshake. "Do we have an agreement?"

"I don't like it, but yeah." He hocked into his fist and raised his palm for me to see the dripping loogie.

I spit onto my life line to seal the deal before wiping the bloody saliva on my pants.

The father and son reluctantly ditched their hardware in the water. Augustus held his glowing phone. "I called Ruby. Take *my* word. You don't want my big sis showin' up on your mother's doorstep if we ain't home by sunrise."

Chapter Twelve

Friday Morning—August 16, 2019—Day 5

AFTER WE DROPPED THE DAWSONS OFF ON A REMOTE PIER NEAR BLAKELEY, we transferred the gear to the Boston Whaler. As we hurried to Hurricane, the torched SeaHunter's flames warmed my back but not my soul. When the repercussions of what we had just done walloped me, I emptied my stomach over the stern. *I just shot a man. Tried to kill him.*

Jane gave Ernie the third degree as he and I snuck in through the back door at 4:30 a.m. "Where were you? What are you up to? Who's in that car parked outside my house?" Her cheeks blanched when she became aware that the twins weren't conjoined at the hip. "Marvin?"

Ernie hustled to the front window. "Phew, Ruby's gone." He stripped the kitchen table down to the faux marble Formica. "Marv's okay. Let's make room. Maw, do you have a needle and thread? Is Dad's wheelchair still in the garage from the time he blew out his Achilles tendon dancing?"

"Why do you need that old thing?"

"Marv's shot. We're going to sew him up."

Jane helped us lift Marvin out of the *Lickety-Split* and roll the top-heavy wheelchair up the backyard hill into the kitchen. She sheared off his pants at the knee with poultry scissors.

"Easy, Maw. Hurts worse than it looks."

Her hands stilled, reassured that her youngest son possessed the strength to kick up a fuss. "Paul, bring me that floor lamp in the living room."

Sarah shuffled into the kitchen as I placed the standing light close to the wound. She noticed the bloody shirt encircling Marvin's leg and rushed forward. "What happened? Is he all right?"

Ernie pointed to her bedroom. "Pack a bag. We're leaving in an hour."

"Why? Where to? What's going on?"

He lost his temper. "Do as I say!"

Sarah reappeared with her iPad. "Any of you even know how to treat a gunshot?" She scrolled through a list of medical websites. "Move aside." Her gloved finger probed the hole in the front of Marvin's calf and the wider cavity in the back. "First, we clean the area. There's a possibility of bone or bullet fragments, but I'm not seeing any. Luckily, it's not deep. Uncle Paul, we need to reduce the bleeding. Please get a pillow from the sofa to elevate his leg. Mom, gather paper towels, a bowl of water, and that bottle of hydrogen peroxide you keep in the medicine cabinet. Also, find your blood pressure cuff." Now came Sarah's turn to be indignant. "Uncle Ernie, while Mom and I care for Uncle Marvin, why don't *you* go pack our bags? Whatever you jackasses did this time must be bad enough for us to have to run off. Pretty crappy of you to force me to miss my last year of middle school and leave all my friends. I'll never forgive you if you've messed up my college plans." She shooed her half-brother away like a buzzing fly.

By the time Ernie dropped four suitcases at the front door, Marvin's trauma had been flushed, sterilized, sutured, and dressed with a fresh bandage. Jane and I assisted in small ways as Sarah proficiently completed the intricate work amid Marvin's screams of pain.

After the budding surgeon recorded her patient's vital signs, she helped Marvin sit upright. "You lost a lot of blood. Are you dizzy or lightheaded?"

"Tired is all." He sipped water from a glass. "Ern, it's almost seven o'clock."

"Give it to me straight." Sarah shook her bloodstained hands. "Who's coming for you? The police?"

Ernie boosted his brother off the table and onto the wheelchair. "Sarah, it's better if you're left in the dark. Put Sammy on a leash and fetch his dog food. We're dropping him off to stay at Mrs. Bailey's house."

"Tell me now, or I'm not going anywhere."

The words flowed out of my mouth, unbidden and too late to take back. "These two half-wits stole eight kilos of fentanyl from the Silverio drug cartel. Enough to kill everyone in Mobile twenty times over."

Ernie—face fire alarm red—raised his fist to strike me. "Fuckin' little tattletale. Marv wouldn't be sitting in that goddamn crip chair if you hadn't shot Augustus in the wing!"

"Shut up, Ernie." Marvin used both hands to roll the wheelchair toward the front door. A yard into the shag carpet, he gave up. "Ever since the moment I was born, I've done everything you asked of me. The magazine scams when we were teenagers? Your brilliant scheme. The counterfeit bank checks? You, again. Trafficking guns and drugs? What were you thinking? *Me?* Why did I go along with it? Am I that dumb, so meek, so obedient? Then, you got greedy—had to grab it all. Paul came to Alabama to find his birth mother, not to rot in prison or stare skyward at six feet of packed dirt. Ernie, you forced our new brother to join our crew as an accessory to our crimes. The sorry son of a bitch had no clue the trouble he was gettin' into." Marvin's ashen face tilted upward. "Maw, I didn't mean that as an insult. You've always been good to us."

Jane patted her injured child's head. "Honey, I gave it my best shot, and Lord as my witness, bringing you two up was no bowl of cherries."

Marvin continued. "Paul talked us out of that shitshow by using his brains to negotiate with the Dawsons. Instead of busting his balls, Ernie oughta kiss Paul's toes for getting us home alive." His bearded chin drooped. "Christ on a cracker, all I ever wanted to be was an accountant."

Ernie flopped onto a kitchen chair. "Marv, I had no idea you felt this way. What an asshole I've been." The stoic mask the man hid behind for years fractured, shattered, and fell. He gaped at each of us. "You all must hate me."

Jane clasped Ernie's hand. "You were a playful boy, happy as a lark. When your father left us and then died, you gradually changed into somebody I hardly recognized. My fault. I should have brought you and your brother to family counseling." A solitary tear ran down her cheekbone, chased by a deluge. "I got too caught up in my own sense of loss."

The senior twin rose to wrap his mother in his arms. The junior twin wheeled over to them. Sarah and I enfolded ourselves in the family huddle—good and bad emotions flooding over me in concert.

Our vehicles zoomed away—me to my "kin" in San Diego and my "clan" off to parts unknown.

Chapter Thirteen

Friday Morning—August 16, 2019—Day 5

BACK AT THE HOTEL IN BED, AS I EVENTUALLY FELL ASLEEP, I had never experienced such a feeling of loneliness.

> I clung to the dashboard pad as the white van careened around another hairpin curve. The transmission automatically downshifted when the winding roadway steepened. Tree trunks, their circumferences surpassing the redwoods I had seen on a family vacation to the Santa Cruz Mountains, streaked past the rolled-down windows. I stuck my nose outside, queasy from motion sickness. Frigid gusts whipped my hair and watered my eyes. The forest smelled of rotting vegetation, acidic earth, and— *Is that smoke?* In the distance, three tall smokestacks belched blackness into the heavens. Snowflakes sticking to my tongue tasted of sadness—with an aftertaste of sorrow. *That's not snow. Those are crematory ashes.* A dense canopy of arm-shaped branches sprouting yellow leaves blocked illumination from all celestial bodies. The tachometer's needle redlined as the speedometer's needle passed 100 and pinned at 120 miles per hour.

"Dad, slow down!" Neither of us wore a seatbelt. The '60s Chevy had been stripped of safety features. "Why the big rush?"

The man leaned into the windshield, the headlights' gleam bathing his cheeks in a radioactive glow. He ignored the oncoming orange switchback sign to lock his eyes on mine. Strips of raw flesh parted to speak. "My meat is to do the will of Him that sent Me, and to finish His work."

I shouted above the exhaust's roar, "What, Dad?" *Did he just say "meat"?*

The driver no longer resembled Hale Crutcher in any aspect. "Pauly, my blood runs hot in your arteries. Your heart beats in sync with mine. We are both cast from the same mold." The steering wheel and brake pedal vanished as I watched black oil gush from the red-hot engine through cracks in the firewall. "Although," my real father floored the gas pedal, "I believe God broke the damn mold the day he created us."

The speeding van hurdled through the metal guardrail, over the icy edge, and into the void.

I shut my eyelids, bracing for an impact that surely will hurt.

The crepuscular cerebral image merged with an unfamiliar view. *I'm in a hotel room—my phone is ringing.* I threw back the sheets and stretched for the iPhone next to the digital clock. *10:43 a.m. Late. Ugh—Jennifer. Can't talk to her right now.* The R2-D2 ringtone ended as waves of guilt began.

Face up on the lumpy mattress, I counted the seconds between each blink of the smoke detector's red LED. *One second.*

I'd better return her call. Two seconds. The Mexican cartel wants to get its hands on Ernie and Marvin. Three seconds. And me! Four seconds. Four million lethal doses of fentanyl. Five seconds. Time to leave Alabama and go home. Six seconds. My father is a very. . . . As I drifted off into the same bad dream, R2-D2 again chirped with urgency.

"Hey, Jenn." I glanced at the clock. *Already 11:55.* I set the cell phone on the bathroom basin. "Sorry, I was, ah, asleep." I splashed cold tap water on my cheeks, attempting to mop away the cobwebs clinging to my mind. The reflection in the dripping mirror startled me. *Vampire? Not a vampire—a zombie.*

"Paul, you sound awful. Are you hungover? It's almost two here. Did you speak with your mother? Why didn't you call me?"

My wife's harsh interrogation sapped my spirit and gnawed a hole in my heart. Until my trip to Hurricane, we had based our marriage on complete honesty. I kept my wrongful activities from the most important person in my life—*my best friend.* Now, I lacked the fortitude to come clean. *I'll start with the simple answers, the truthful ones.* "Last night, I mighta overdone it on the alcohol."

"Because of something she told you?"

"Yeah. It's terrible." The screamed chorus of a vulgar nursery rhyme earwormed through my brain. *I'm a child of rape, how about you? I'm a child of rape, did your mom abandon you, too?*

"Jonas is your father?"

"No, Jenn." At the window, I observed an older couple bickering in the parking lot. When the stony-faced woman strutted off in a huff into the hotel lobby, the potbellied man stubbed out a cigarette and trotted after her. "The identity of my biological father is unknown. Someone attacked my mother as she walked home from a friend's house."

"Are you saying she was—"

"Raped." I collapsed onto the room's only chair, an armless thing with skimpy cushioning. "I wish I had never come to Alabama. What a huge mistake." I waited for my wife to offer words of solace.

"That's—uh—Jesus. You okay?"

"Once I'm home with you and Smokey, everything will be right as rain. I love you!"

The words I spoke to Jennifer were true. Still and all, that Friday, I didn't board any planes destined for San Diego.

Friday Afternoon—August 16, 2019—Day 5

After I checked out of the Quality Inn, I walked for ten minutes to the Ben May Main Library, a boxy Classical Revival building hemmed in by a Burger King and a sizeable bone orchard. Patrons of all generations roamed the cavernous interior, working at tables or leafing through books and magazines while seated in lounge chairs. I found an unused computer and *Googled* the names of local newspapers. Of the dailies in publication throughout the seventies, only two continued to publish regularly, and neither provided online archives, so I climbed the limestone stairs to the reference desk.

A young woman with a NANCY nametag pinned to her plum sweater grinned up from a screen. "How can I help you?"

"Hi, I'm doing the groundwork for a book. I'd like to see past editions of *The Mobile Beacon & Alabama Citizen* and the *Press-Register*. Very little on the web."

"What year?"

"1977."

Nancy tapped a few keys before jotting numbers on a notepad. "Anything before 2010 is on microfiche or microfilm." She pushed over a form. "Please fill this out."

I wrote my name, email address, the names of the newspapers, and the year.

Nancy went to the file cabinets in the back room, doubling back with two rectangular sheets of photographic film. "The microfiche readers are in the corner. Come to me with your questions."

The desktop machine I powered on had features comparable to those of the units at my neighborhood library. I loaded the *Press-Register* film under the glass lid, spun the focus knob, then slid the carrier to August 24, 1977. Most of us don't know their precise moment of conception. Unfortunately, I did.

On a Wednesday, the front page appeared no different than any other day in history. Clear skies and a high of 90 degrees. Wealthy politicians violated campaign finance laws. Countries were in constant global conflict. People still mourned Elvis Presley's early demise. In the back sections, black-and-white comics were followed by tons of automobile and furniture advertisements. The expensive-to-produce newspapers typeset during journalism's glory days contrasted dramatically with today's free online media. I had researched many articles for my novels, but digging up write-ups about real-life events soon became an onerous chore. An hour later, I hit December. *Nothing of interest. The Mobile Beacon & Alabama Citizen* dished out more of the same humdrum.

What did I expect to gain? My mother resided in Mississippi at the time of the assault. She refused to report the incident to the authorities. *Why am I reading Alabama papers?* I unloaded the microfiche carrier. *So stupid.*

The library closed in fifteen minutes. I returned the film to Nancy. "Do you have Gulfport-area newspapers?"

The librarian shook her blond braids. "Sorry. Did you check online?"

"You're required to pay a subscription fee to enable keyword searches. I want to read the complete edition from front to back."

"Perhaps I can be of assistance. What do you need?"

I spread my hands. "It's kind of complicated."

"How about going to Gulfport? Regional libraries usually archive local publications."

I swore to Jennifer I'd come home. "Is that far?"

"Gulfport's only an hour away. My friends and I drive to the Mississippi beaches every weekend." She chuckled. "We mostly go for the happy hour pub crawls. Can't beat two for the price of one margaritas."

"I guess not. Well, have a nice evening."

Outside the library, I sat on a bench overlooking a breadth of grass. The shadows were elongated, yet the orange ball smoldering through the purple haze wouldn't sink below the glimmering bay for two more hours. I gauged the distance from Mobile to Gulfport on *Google Maps.* Seventy-four miles, all interstate. Nancy was correct. I could be in the town my mother grew up in by sunset.

I oriented my head toward Hurricane. *Jane, Ernie, Marvin, and Sarah—gone. Where can they hide? North, south, east, west? Aren't the Mexican cartels everywhere?*

I got out my phone and typed SILVERIO CARTEL in *Wikipedia.* "Established in the late 1980s and based in Culiacan, Sinaloa state, Mexico, the Silverio Cartel (also known as the Association and the Blood Confederation) is a global drug trafficking, money laundering, and organized crime syndicate. Videos of atrocities, including beheadings, hanging police officers from highway overpasses, and dissolving informers in vats of alkali, are posted daily on the internet as overt warnings to the authorities and rival gangs."

I selected the biography hyperlink for the Silverio crime boss. "Juan Carlos Delgado (born May 27th, 1958, in Navolato, Mexico), a former federal judge, holds the highest position in the Silverio drug cartel organization. As a Drug Lord, Delgado manages the lieutenants (Spanish: *tenientes*), the hitmen (Spanish: *sicarios*), and low-ranking falcons (Spanish: *halcones*) within their controlled territories. Delgado oversees the trafficking of heroin, cocaine, and crystal meth into the southern United States, utilizing aircraft, container ships, fishing vessels, go-fast boats, narco-submarines, rail cars, tractor-trailers, buses, and automobiles. *El Gato Montés* (English: The Wildcat) is considered armed and extremely dangerous."

I paced the front lawn, unaware of my surroundings. Perspiration stung my eyes. *What if the Wildcat knows about me?* The world oscillated and grayed. I hunched over, clenching my knees. *Gonna puke.*

"Hey, are you sick?" With her car keys in one hand, Nancy waved tentatively with a free arm.

I waggled my palm. "I'm fine. Stood up too fast." Distrust distorted her worried expression into disgust. *She doesn't recall who I am. They think I'm homeless or a tweaker.*

The reference librarian hurried to the parking lot.

Inside my rental car, after I entered Gulfport, Mississippi as the destination on the dashboard GPS, I realized I had made the decision instinctively. *I'm going to find my father*—my fist hammered the Forester's steering wheel—*and confront him.*

With Mobile and, subsequently, Alabama, distant memories in my rearview mirror, I recapped each life-changing event from my stay. Meeting my biological mother for the initial session had been exceedingly intense. Jane, no longer the adolescent girl in the faded photograph cradling an infant, had suffered much. For all that, now in middle age, the woman remained confident of her abilities to survive any trauma. I admired her grit, and I loved her as only a son can love his mother. Ernie hadn't dealt so well with his inner demons. The man, his ethics worn as thin as a sheet of rice paper, had eroded into a common crook. Hopefully, his twin brother's fervent plea to change his ways will have a lasting effect. I visualized Marvin sprawled on the *Chum Runner's* pitching deck, blood spreading from his leg wound like an infection. *Can he get gangrene?* Sarah's there to help—smarter and stronger than any of them. *Augustus Dawson.* I shot *him* in the shoulder. *If Augustus dies from complications—I will be a murderer.*

I booked a room at the sixty-five-bucks-a-night Shangri-La Inn, a fleabag on the edge of the railroad tracks but conveniently located two blocks from Gulfport Beach. After I shaved away the stubborn stubble of a bad day, I squeegeed the water droplets from my reflection with my palm. "Paul Charles Crutcher. What sort of person are you becoming?"

Chapter Fourteen

Saturday Morning—August 17, 2019—Day 6

I AWOKE FOR A FEW MINUTES AT 2:30 A.M., then, totally exhausted, splashed into this dream.

> Alone in a yellow rowboat, I hovered above a black sea. Far away, on a granite ridge, a beacon of hope blinked thrice, then stopped. *The lighthouse keeper must have forgotten to pay the fuel bill this month.* I asked myself, *What month is it, Paul? And the year?* I sat on a wooden plank worn concave by generations of fishermen's buttocks. The single oar popped free of the oarlock, slipped overboard, and sank into the abyss. Saltwater leaked through the skiff's paper-thin skin. A fishing bobber floated in the oily bilge. Never one for caution, I yanked the string linking the red and white sphere to the cork plugging a hole in the hull—*a trap.* The fountain of seawater shot the bobber and stopper into the air. A jumping swordfish swallowed them hook, line, and sinker. The rowboat flooded with glacial water as distant tongues joined in song.
>
> A masculine voice resonated from a bank of mist. "Ahoy, there!"

> I stood on the tipsy seat to get a better view. "Help me!" I shouted. "I'm stranded!"
>
> The prow of a 16th-century sloop parted the reddening miasma, the Jolly Rodger flying atop its tallest mast.
>
> "Here I come, Son! Hold tight!"
>
> With a thousand women shackled below decks, the blazing pirate ship bore down upon me.

I rolled out from beneath the sweat-soaked bedsheets and strolled to a mom-and-pop coffee shop. The sidewalk bench presented an outstanding perspective of the Gulf of Mexico and T-shaped Cat Island. I called Jennifer.

"Hey, sweetie! When is your flight arriving? I've scheduled meetings for this afternoon, but—"

"Jenn."

"Huh? Checking my calendar. Guess I can skip the daily scrum if—"

"Jenn, I'm not sure which day I am coming back."

"You weren't able to arrange a flight?"

"I'm here in Gulfport."

A garbage truck rattled by.

"Paul, I couldn't hear you. What did you—?"

"Gulfport. I'm in Gulfport."

"Where's that?"

"Mississippi."

"Mississippi? What's in Mississippi?"

"I'm looking for my father."

"You exposed who he is?"

"No, I'm still on a fishing expedition. Yesterday, I visited the library in Mobile. Nothing there, but the librarian said—"

"You're hunting for the man who attacked your mother? Are you out of your freakin' mind?"

"Jenn, it sounds crazy, but I can't sleep at night thinking about him."

She whispered, "I pray he's dead."

I spilled the cold coffee grinds into a potted plant. The almond bear claw, tasting of old sawdust, went to the birds. "I need to know one way or the other."

"Well, if that sociopath isn't planted in the ground, he's still walking the earth sexually assaulting women. What are you proposing to do if you identify where your father lives? Ring his doorbell, and say, 'Hi! You've never met me, but I'm your son, Paul. You raped my mom back in 1977. May I come inside for milk and cookies? We'll catch up on the last forty-one years. I'll read my books aloud, and you'll show me your panty collection.' Paul, the man is a predator!"

"I can handle myself."

"You're not Jackie Chan. Remember that taekwondo class we enrolled in? You dropped out when you fractured your toe. Get your ass home!"

"Not till—"

The phone connection ended. My wife had hung up. *She's pissed.*

I accessed the Harrison County Library System website. The Biloxi Public Library housed the local periodicals. US-90, aptly named Beach Boulevard, took me on a thirty-minute drive down the spectacular coast. Today, the tranquil ocean and smooth sand did little to improve my mood. The recent dialogue with my spouse left me overwhelmed with self-reproach.

Once more, I challenged my purpose. Jennifer, as always, was right. *My real father is most likely pushing up daisies.* On the thoroughfare's bushy median strip, armed sheriff's deputies supervised green-and-white-banded inmates stuffing plastic sacks with litter. *Or he's in lockup.*

I swung into the Biloxi Civic Center, shutting off the engine at the Public Library. *If I can't gain anything of worth here—which I doubt I will—I'll pack my suitcase and go home. Even if I determine my father's identity, how can I locate him? If the man is a serial rapist, why would he be dumb enough to stay in the vicinity?* I slammed the car door. *Let's get this over with. The second I finish my research, I will call Jennifer and beg for her forgiveness.*

I entered a building newer than the Mobile library, its architecture much more strip-mallish. In the voluminous lobby, a volunteer at the information desk directed me to a separate wing. I filled out a form at the Local History and Genealogy Department. Debbie handed me a stack of microfiche from 1977 and 1978 for *The Daily Herald, The Biloxi Press,* and *South Mississippi Sun*. The librarian warned me that there was a 60-minute limit on the reader if patrons were waiting.

I plugged AirPods into my ears and cued up the Screaming Trees' sixth album, *Sweet Oblivion*. Mark Lanegan's gravelly vocalizations kept me awake skimming through hundreds of *The Daily Herald* editions. I created photocopies of articles regarding molestations, murders, or missing persons for August 1977 and the twelve subsequent months. Furthermore, I noted the advertisements for pest eradication services. The *South Mississippi Sun*, its printing presses grinding to a halt in 1985, reported slightly conflicting versions of, or updates to, the same stories printed in *The Daily Herald.* At this point in my investigation, I could not correlate any of the events. My eyes were tired from scanning thousands of black-and-white pages. My neck ached from checking whether anyone was standing in line to use the microfiche reader.

The last newspaper I reviewed, *The Biloxi Press,* operated from May 1977 to December 1986. While I flipped through the skeletal weekly of chiefly automotive ads, I overheard a male voice placing a request for the *Sun Herald*.

"Right away, Professor Evans." Debbie hustled to the file cabinets.

The Biloxi Press' classifieds for Thursday, September 8, 1977, were five sheets long. Among the public notices for MAKE $5 AN HOUR STUFFING ENVELOPES IN THE COMFORT OF YOUR OWN HOME, LOST PERSIAN CAT, and SWF SEEKING SWM WITH VIKING GOOD LOOKS, an eighth-of-a-page color ad for RUGGER PEST CONTROL caught my attention. A cartoon cockroach labeled BLATTO ran for dear life, his segmented arms, legs, and twin antennae covered with prickly hairs. The brown insect's bulging eyeballs twisted rearward in terror. As Blatto's red tongue drooped out of his open mouth, magnified perspiration droplets showered from his furrowed brow.

"Ahem."

I spun to encounter a goateed man in a tweed suit clutching a leather briefcase. "Sir, I'm almost done. Please allow me one more minute?"

He aimed his forefinger at the MICROFICHE READERS – ONE-HOUR LIMIT IF OTHERS ARE WAITING sign tacked to the wall. "Can't you read?"

My amygdala fired neurons into my hypothalamus, and I couldn't restrain my adrenal glands from injecting adrenaline and cortisol into my bloodstream. "Yeah, professor, I can read." I stood and whispered in his ear, "Get going, egghead, or I'll rip your fucking balls off and shove them up your fucking ass."

The academic scurried out the door.

I jabbed the print button and gathered my photocopies, feeling like a bit of a douchebag myself. Debbie, suppressing a smile, watched me exit the library.

In the Subaru, I examined the image for Rugger Pest Control. Underneath FREE ESTIMATES and LICENSED & BONDED came the pronouncement WE PROUDLY USE MONTROSE CHEMICAL PRODUCTS. *Montrose? That slip of paper Jane snagged from the Chevy van—the pesticide bag. Montrose manufactured DDT.*

I breathed the deepest breath of my life, then dialed the listed phone number. A woman intoned, "When placing a call, it is necessary to enter an area code plus the seven-digit line number." I preceded the exchange code with 228 and punched in the remaining numerals. The same lady robot relayed the bad news, "We're sorry, you have reached a number that has been disconnected or is no longer in service." *Figures. But did I really want him to answer?*

Again, I studied the four-decade-old Rugger Pest Control advertisement. *Rugger. Could that be my father's last name? Nah. Is Rugger my actual last name?* I *Googled* RUGGER, discovering its Italian origin and that it is one of the rarest surnames in America. *Do I look Italian? What does an Italian look like?* More *Googling*. "Italians generally exhibit brown eyes and hair with skin nearly as fair as northern Europeans. Italians frequently feature Roman-shaped noses." I color-graded the amount of melanin in my arm and massaged the prominent bridge above my nostrils. "Perhaps? Hmm, except for my blue eyes."

In the hotel room, I booted my laptop. As Jane and I parted ways, we agreed to stay in touch through back channels. I started the *Chrome* browser and opened an Incognito window. On *Craigslist* for Mobile, Alabama, I searched for BEAUTYREST KING-SIZED MATTRESS in the free items category. *Nada. She's okay.*

I laid out the newspaper photocopies of articles referencing sexual offenses, homicides, and missing persons on the bed. From August 1977 through August 1978, forty-eight sex violations and fifteen slayings occurred in the Gulfport-Biloxi region. Fifty-four people had been declared missing, predominantly female. *Are these felonies high, low, or normal?*

The spotty criminal data online only went back to 1999. In most years, Gulfport recorded the highest murder rate in Mississippi, significantly higher than the rest of the country. Conversely, local rape statistics were lower than average. I couldn't find adequate information on people who were nowhere to be seen.

I phoned Jennifer and was miffed to hear her voicemail message. "Hi, Jenn. It's me. I'm sorry about how our conversation ended this morning. Hey, please call me when you get a chance. Love you."

The frightened bug in the Rugger Pest Control newspaper ad gave me the heebie-jeebies. *What was his name? Blatto. Wikipedia* stated: "Blattodea is the order of insects encompassing termites and cockroaches." *A clever moniker for an extermination business's mascot. Aren't cuddly animals supposed to entice you to throw down money for the service?* Blatto's panic-stricken expression brought to mind the countenance of death row prisoners walking their final mile.

The Biloxi Press called it quits in 1986. There'd be no silverfish-eaten classified advertisement invoices in a dank cellar for me to paw through. *Can it be that easy?* I typed RUGGER in the online *Whitepages.* One hundred and fifty-three Ruggers populate the United States, mostly in Iowa. Mississippi listed three. I selected the hyperlink, both hoping and afraid I'd hit pay dirt.

Lois P. Rugger, age 89, resided three hundred miles away in Oxford. Four relatives, all women. *Too old, too female, and too far north.*

Gary Anthony Rugger, age 69, dwelled in Cuevas, a mere ten miles west of Gulfport. Leslie C. Rugger, age 37, the only family member mentioned, had relocated to Bakersfield, California. *Gary's age is about right. In 1977, he would be in his late twenties.* No photos of Gary Anthony Rugger, Gary A. Rugger, or just plain Gary Rugger were found on *Google Images.*

Hunter Rugger, age 67, hung his hat in nearby Pass Christian. No middle name and no connections. My face drifted to the screen as if to lay eyes on him. "Hunter. Such a fitting handle for an exterminator." *If Hunter's the guy, he'd be twenty-five the year of Jane's attack.* Combing the internet for pictures of Hunter Rugger proved unfruitful as well.

I had to drop coin to unlock the current and past street addresses and phone numbers. I opened a Premium All-Access account for twelve bucks a month.

On *Zillow*, I input Gary Anthony Rugger's address. I clicked through a dozen photographs of his three-hundred-thousand-dollar, three-bedroom, two-bath, single-story property. The suburban development showcased weedless lawns, healthy trees, and manicured shrubs. *What did you imagine you'd see? A medieval castle complete with a moat?* No S&M dungeon in the interior shots.

I cannot tell you why the looks of Hunter Rugger's five-hundred-and-forty-thousand-dollar domicile caused me angst. Certainly not the design, a rectangular box mounted high on stilts to avoid seasonal flooding from nearby tidewaters, nor the choice of pigment, cheerful blue with yellow trim. By all appearances, it was an ordinary house on an ordinary street owned by an ordinary man. I enlarged the pixels of a red and amber taillight poking out from behind a support column. *Is that a white van?*

Saturday Afternoon—August 17, 2019—Day 6

I stopped at Kajun Kick to grab a poboy and a soda, then drove to Gary Rugger's address in Cuevas. Pecan Drive happened to be on the route to Hunter Rugger's residence in Pass Christian. After I parked the Subaru two houses away, I tore into the crispy French bread sandwich, washing the fried catfish down my throat with Diet Pepsi. Passenger cars and commercial vehicles zoomed back and forth. Dog-walkers waited patiently for their fur babies to evacuate. A postal carrier delivered bills and junk mail to each curbside mailbox.

Insistent knocking and "Sir, lower your window" shocked me out of a pleasant slumber. A Pass Christian policewoman pantomimed cranking a door handle.

I fumbled with the Forester's ignition button to activate the electric window switch. "Hey there."

"We received a call concerning a suspicious male loitering in the neighborhood." Officer Warner put forth her hand not resting on the holster. "Can I see your ID?"

"Yes, ma'am." I passed her my driver's license. "Felt sleepy after lunch, so I took a nap." Across the lane, a witch-like woman glared from an upper window.

As Officer Warner hurried to her vehicle to verify my identity, visions of my mug plastered on a wanted poster doubled my pulse.

The policewoman returned my card with an air I took to be disdain. "California. Are you traveling on business or for pleasure?"

I'm absolutely not in Mississippi for pleasure. "Just visiting with family." I kept my palms on the steering wheel. "Thought I'd check out the area before heading home to San Diego."

"Next time you're tired, pull over in a public park. Good day, Mr. Crutcher."

"Thank you, officer."

Warner swaggered to her SUV and sped off.

After I shot the nosy neighbor the evil eye, I cruised by Gary Rugger's house. A twentyish couple tossed a ball to a giggling toddler in the front yard. The friendly man upraised a hand as I rolled past. I waved back. *He can't be Gary—musta moved.*

My mental state vacillated between the bitter disappointment of not tracking down my biological father and the sweet relief that he wasn't physically within reach. *Yet.* I recollected the *Zillow* image of Hunter Rugger's taillight. *That damned van.*

Horseshoe-shaped Pall Mall Road overlooked a section of the Mallini Bayou and the two dozen homes bordering the greenish inland waterway. I spotted the house Hunter Rugger might still inhabit. A gravel drive transitioned to a concrete pad. Under the building, a backup light suddenly turned white. I stomped the gas. When the medium-sized van reversed into the street and departed in the opposite direction, I braked onto the earthen shoulder. *Should I follow him?* Brownish graphic art and a trade name covered the vehicle's back doors—now too far to read in my side mirror. While I frantically analyzed my options, the Chevrolet merged with the afternoon traffic.

A flattened piece of cardboard was lying by the curb. I locked the rental car, folded the carton's flaps, and carried the fabricated delivery up the blue house's driveway. *Don't see any security cameras. Vigilant neighbors?* I tilted the brim of my Padres baseball cap over my sunglasses. At the place next door, a dog strained against a chain secured to a doghouse stenciled BRUNO. The excited Doberman pinscher wagged his docked tail in friendship instead of barking.

I approached the slab underneath the structure. An enclosed storage space filled the area bounded by stout supports. Out back, beyond an expanse of sunbaked grass, a boat, *THE TERMINATOR,* bobbed in a protected slip. A twelve-foot-tall stairway ascended to the main level. As I climbed the twenty-one steps to the yellow front door, the wooden treads creaked under my weight.

Holding the empty package, I rang the doorbell. Westminster chimes resounded within the seventeen-hundred-square-foot home. About to retreat to the safety of my car, I elected to walk the deck encircling the upper story. Shades drawn to the windowsills, with reflections on the plate glass, made viewing the interior impossible.

A week ago, I wouldn't have had the mettle to try all the windows and doors. The lower frame was freed from the bottom track when I lifted the sliding door's handle. I unlocked the slider and set the door back in the groove.

No audible alarms shrieked as my sneakers trod the modern kitchen's sandstone tiles. A stainless-steel refrigerator hummed from a recess in the cherry wood cabinets. Curious, I opened the freezer to see stacks of DiGiorno frozen pepperoni pizzas and Stouffer's frozen dinners, all Salisbury steak. Bottled water and condiments stocked the lower compartment. From a wall clock above the double bowl sink, the masked Lone Ranger and his faithful horse, Silver, marked my every movement. A bag of sliced white bread and jars of peanut butter and jelly lined the soapstone countertop. I perused a Mississippi Power gas and electric bill for Hunter Rugger, 1086 Pall Mall Road, Pass Christian, MS 39571. *He definitely lives at this address.* I glanced again at the watchful ex-Texas Ranger, allowing myself ten minutes to explore the entire house and get out.

A lengthy hallway divided the three-bedroom, two-bath home. In the living room's midpoint, a threadbare La-Z-Boy recliner faced a large flat-screen television. Lone Ranger and Tonto salt-and-pepper shakers sat atop a secondhand end table stained with circular spots. *He eats his TV dinners in here. A single chair, no couch. Hunter does not appear to have many guests over to play tiddlywinks or beer pong.* Next, I set foot in a small bedroom, peeking underneath the bed and pulling out dresser drawers. *Zippo.* The adjacent room comprised a toilet, a washbasin, and a bare medicine cabinet. *No mirror. Strange.*

The master bedroom featured a full-sized mattress, overlaid with a Wild West cowboys-and-Indians bedspread. I slid a long case from under the bed. *Locked.* I shoved the dusty cedar box back. Identical table lamps rested upon two mahogany nightstands—black-masked Lone Rangers riding rearing white Silvers below 100-watt suns. Underwear and socks crammed the top drawers of a vertical chest. The bottom drawers held T-shirts, jeans, and sweatpants. I opened the door to a walk-in closet and flipped the switch. The seven-by-ten-foot space had been converted into a photographic darkroom. On a workbench bathed by orange safelights, three plastic 8x10-inch chemical trays were positioned between an Omega enlarger and a fully plumbed sink. No prints hung from the string of clothespins stretched wall to wall.

In the attached bathroom, a medicine cabinet (also missing a mirror) stored a tube of Crest, an Oral-B toothbrush, disposable Gillette razors, a bottle of Ambien sleeping pills, and a nail clipper. A sliver of white projected from the chrome trimmer's curved blades. I tucked the vestigial claw into my wallet.

At the dark end of the carpeted corridor, the third bedroom served as an office. A laptop and an inkjet printer sat atop a desk. My hand swept the trash bin. *If Hunter packs up to move, all his possessions will fit in a single suitcase.* I checked my wristwatch. *Time to go.*

On my way through the kitchen, I noticed a bi-fold door. The laundry room reeked of chemicals. A mound of beige coveralls filled a blue basket. I shook the wrinkles out of a one-piece work garment. RUGGER PEST CONTROL was embroidered on the left pocket. Blatto, the cockroach, scared shitless as ever, embellished the right pocket.

"Jenn, there weren't any paintings on the walls or knickknacks on the shelves. Just the Wild West memorabilia in his bedroom. No mirrors anywhere! The entire house seemed staged by someone clueless about how conventional people live."

She laughed. "Like we're professional interior decorators? Paul, what about your collection of meerkats?"

"Aren't the furry little critters adorable?" I pressed the cell phone to my ear. *At least she's talking to me.* "Babe, you love meerkats."

"The first stuffed animal we bought at the zoo's gift shop was fine. Now, the 'Rat Patrol' is infesting our house."

"This could be him." I marched around the hotel room. "He may be my—"

"Father? You're saying the only evidence tying Hunter Rugger to Jane Gibbs is that he runs a pest eradication company?"

"Rugger is the correct age."

"Have you checked the Better Business Bureau? I did. There are over thirty pest management companies within twenty miles of Pass Christian. You're not even positive the deviant who abused your mother sprayed ants for profit."

"It's hard to explain. I sent you a photo of Blatto, that tortured cockroach in his advertisement. I'm telling you, Jenn, I got a creepy-crawly sensation inside his house."

"Paul, you broke into somebody's home. What if you set off an alarm? The police might have shot you."

"There were no security pads or video cameras."

"Doesn't that strike you as being odd?"

"Why?"

"Paul, if Hunter Rugger *is* a multiple offender, don't you reckon he'd be more—how do you say, *'on the alert'?*"

Her sarcasm struck a nerve. "The crime took place over forty years ago. Enough time for a man to change his ways." I hated to acknowledge the person who spawned me was a monster. "Maybe he got drunk and only did it once?"

"And you believe that? The statistics for sexual perpetrators not repeating are negligible." Jennifer paused. "Were you careful?"

I retraced my steps from the moment I carried the bogus shipment up the crushed stone driveway to the swish of the fake delivery box dropping into the Shangri-La Inn's recycling dumpster. I looked at my hands, remembering that I had handled his belongings. My fingers verified that my wallet, keys, and iPhone remained in my pockets. "Of course. I double-checked the sliding door when I left. He'll never suspect I stepped into his lair." *Did I leave fingerprints in the dust?*

"'Lair'? Paul, this isn't a joke."

She's not wrong. I should be content, even thrilled! My dream of locating my real mother came true. As a bonus, I learned that I had two half-brothers—two gangster half-brothers. And young Sarah, the brains in that family.

"You're acting on impulse. Reckless. Sweetie, please come home!"

I thought it over. *Playing detective clearly isn't my thing. If Hunter Rugger is my father, there's not a thing I can do about it other than get my ass in hotter water. And he sure as shit has no desire to meet me, his bastard son.*

"Jenn, just give me a few more days."

For the second time today, my wife hung up on me.

Chapter Fifteen

Sunday Early Morning—August 18, 2019—Day 7

THE SANDMAN'S POUCH MUST HAVE RUN OUT OF MAGICAL DUST while lulling the more worthy to sleep. At 1 a.m., I drove the Subaru down to Pass Christian and parked in a vacant lot on Pall Mall Road. The pulverized stone crunched underfoot as I crept along Hunter Rugger's drive. Luckily for me, the next-door neighbor's big Doberman pinscher didn't pounce to give me a lick bath. *Bruno is in his doghouse, dreaming of chasing cats or safe indoors, snuggling with his family.* My mission? Check the storage area below the stilt house.

After my midnight perils under the tutelage of Ernie and Marvin, I felt more comfortable prowling around beneath the mantle of darkness. I crouched by a concrete support pillar, only hearing metallic ticking. Behind a wooden divider, the engine block in a white late-model Chevrolet Express cooled in the gentle breeze. I touched the hood. *Still hot. Where was he at this hour?*

I stroked the vinyl cockroach burnished to the back doors of the RUGGER PEST CONTROL van. Blatto's bulgy bug eyes pleaded for me to end his misery. Inside the Chevy's cabin, the Lone Ranger stared sternly from the side of a plastic cup in the center console. A bundle of invoices lay on the passenger seat. As were the rooms above me, the vehicle's interior appeared deliberately orchestrated. The windowless rear doors kept the cargo area unviewable. I shot Blatto an empathetic glance before crossing to the garage-sized storage space.

A hefty padlock and a sturdy hasp secured the solid door. The walls rose straight to the rafters. *No way to get in. Moronic of me to snoop.* Infuriated at my failings, I joggled the keyed lock. The steel shackle popped up. I removed the brass case, flipped the hinge plate, and hung the shank on the loop. The plywood door opened and closed on oiled hinges. I scrabbled about for a light switch. The LED tubes mounted high on the ceiling hurt my eyes. Pungent chemicals irritated my nostrils.

Pest deterrents and accessories packed the ten-by-fifteen-foot room. The racks on the left wall held safety gear and personal protective equipment: first-aid kits, latex gloves, N95 masks, full-face respirators, paper booties, earmuffs, and hooded bee suits. I also counted flashlights, headlamps, lanterns, and endoscopes. Hooks attached to the back wall suspended different-length stepladders, sectioned spider web brushes, bed bug steamers, and pump sprayers. Chemicals and traps were stocked on shelves on the right wall. The caution labels on the gallon jugs of TAURUS SC and PERMETHRIN SFR classified the liquids as TERMITICIDE/INSECTICIDE. Then came the pesticide foamers, aerosol foggers, bulb and electric dusters, bait guns, and bait stations.

Hunter Rugger had amassed an impressive array of sticky traps, snap traps, box traps, and live animal cage traps reserved for more humane customers. T. REX—a plastic rat trap endowed with long, sharp teeth—fell out of my sweaty fingers, clattering onto the cement. I angled my ear upward—no roused feet traversing the upper floor.

On my hands and knees, I reached underneath the bottom shelf for the errant dinosaur. T. was lying among dust bunnies and a ball of fur which, on closer inspection, had a tail. My whiskers sensed a draft as I backed away in repulsion from the mummified mouse. I crawled between the cobweb dusters to see a slot at the wall's base. My eyes followed a crevice up the sheet of plywood, spotting the glimmer of metal. *Hinges. From the outside, this room did seem larger.*

Once you knew the trick, locating the catch merely demanded perseverance—a recessed thumbturn deadbolt hidden behind a 1982 Montrose Chemical Company wall calendar. The concealed entryway sprang open.

The LED dot on my iPhone only extended an arm's length into the five-by-ten-foot space—so quiet inside, I felt, rather than heard, a motorcycle rumble past. *These walls must be soundproofed with thick insulation.* I grabbed a big flashlight from the main room. The violet beam also failed to illuminate the narrow area. I read the sticker on the device's oversized head: BLACK LIGHT ULTRAVIOLET TORCH. Stains—some glowing fiercely in the long-wavelength radiation—ran down the matte black surfaces.

I shut the door, turned the deadbolt, hung the calendar, and flipped the month to August. With T. Rex perched on the shelf precisely where I found him, I broke all traffic rules racing back to the hotel.

Tonight's lucid dream: a nightmare coiled within a rattlesnake den of nightmares.

> I came to on a cold floor, the windowless chamber's dimensions long and narrow. The highest point? Too murky to see if a ceiling—or heaven itself—even existed. Undecipherable passages brushed by a madman with a pail of sanguine paint oozed down the walls. Something fast and furry scampered across my bare ribs before vanishing into a nest woven from tiny bones.

The room shrank as the light eclipsed. I attempted to sit up, my forehead thumping a puffy, yet ungiving, substance. My hands groped the yards of silky fabric. Small, rounded disks filled rows of indentations. *Upholstery buttons.* No space to expand my elbows or lift my knees. "Hey!"

My fists pummeled the padding. The barrier raised enough to let a slice of warm sunshine caress my face. *Thank you, God.* Fetid soil shoveled by chain-smoking workers in unwashed overalls sprinkled my cheeks and salted my eyes. Worms voracious for an easy meal wriggled in the cracks until a muddy boot stamped the lid shut. Clay rained upon the top of the wooden box—*pitter-patter-pitter-patter*—then ceased. *I'm buried alive under six feet of earth.* My soul beseeched my ancestors for mercy. More silence. *Don't lose it, Paul. There's always a way out of any jam. Think.* Restive creatures hissed by my toes and squeaked by my head. Continuously growing incisors honed by eons of gnawing through gristle tore off my earlobe. I crushed the life from the squirming rodent, hot fluid flowing down my neck to drench the satin pillow. "Help! Mom, I'm trapped in here! Where are you, Dad? Can anybody hear me?"

Hollow segments of keratin rattled—a beehive bursting with insanity. The serpent—*only fools say its name aloud*—squeezed past the cellulite in my thigh on a perpetual crusade for human blood. I hammered the coffin's lid, screaming, "Help me! Help! Help! Help!"

Sunday Morning—August 18, 2019—Day 7

My fingers knocked the cell phone off the nightstand. As my arm stretched between the mattress and the headboard, the incessant buzzing quit. I read Jennifer's message. *What room are you in?*

I typed *Why?* and shuffled to the toilet.

A banner notification said: *In the lobby.*

I scrubbed my hands and face, having no comprehension of what "lobby" she referred to. Confused, I answered, *102.*

While I awaited her response, I switched on the Samsung. CNN televised horrendous scenes of bloody bodies strewn throughout a bombed-out banquet hall. Ana Cabrera read from a teleprompter, "Saturday evening, sixty-three people died at a wedding ceremony in Kabul." An image of a weeping father holding a gray baby filled the screen. "Another one-hundred-and-eighty-two injured, including women and children. ISIS claims responsibility for. . . ."

Soft rapping on the door. *Housekeeping. I thought I hung the DO NOT DISTURB sign on the doorknob.* "Hi," I said loudly, "it's okay if you skip today."

"Paul, open up!"

I squinted through the peephole, then yanked the door wide. "What in the world are you doing here?"

Jennifer elbowed her way into the hotel room. She eyeballed my not-so-sexy boxers. "You're not dressed. Did you just wake up?"

"Yeah, I—"

My wife prodded me in the chest. "Tell me what you're up to!"

"Up to?" My smile felt false, even to me. "I'm not up to anything."

"We've been together a long time." She splayed ten fingers. "You're in some kind of trouble. Spill it!"

I married a gorgeous, intelligent, witty woman. Most days, I wondered what she saw in me. "It's—"

Jennifer stabbed her forefinger into my sternum, this time forcibly enough to send me stumbling backward. "Come on now, what are you keeping from me?"

"Na-nothing."

"Whatever's bothering you must be serious." My wife toppled me onto the bed. "Very serious indeed." She stripped off her blouse and straddled my hips. "Don't worry, Paul. I'll get you to talk."

"We always do everything as partners." Jennifer put down the menu. "You hurt my feelings when you came to Alabama on your own." Late for lunch and early for dinner, we had the restaurant's outdoor patio to ourselves.

"I'm sorry, babe. The day I learned my mom and dad weren't my actual parents, I dismissed that major news item as unimportant. I figured, if my real folks didn't want me—fuck 'em." I gave the entrée list a once-over, my eyes not absorbing any of the mouth-watering offerings. "Burying my past only worked for so long. The emotional dam burst after I opened the envelope containing the adoption papers and the photograph of my mother. I became obsessed with finding my actual family."

"Welcome to Shaggy's. My name is Jim." Our server held an iPad. "Can I get you drinks?"

My wife grinned at the ruddy-complexioned teenager. "I need the Relaxer."

Jim swiveled to me. "And for you, sir?"

"A Modelo, please."

In a jiffy, Jim set two frosty beverages on coasters. "Need another minute to decide?"

"No," Jennifer replied. "I'd like the Captain's Seafood Platter."

"Shrimp, oyster, or catfish? Or all three?"

"What the hell. Get me all three."

My index finger glided across the laminated menu, apparently guided by phantom hands on a Ouija board. The headstrong digit landed on a bowl of noodles. "Shaggy's Alfredo for me. Shrimp."

"Excellent choices." Jim left a pile of napkins and hurried to the kitchen.

Jennifer sipped the coconut rum served over strawberry purée. I sucked down the ice-cold lager as if I possessed the last cerveza on Earth.

She seized my hand. "Why did you come alone? Didn't you suppose I'd be interested in meeting your family?"

"Sure, but in retrospect, I can't recall the thoughts going through my mind. I *can* confirm your husband is a selfish dolt."

My wife twinkled a perfect set of pearly whites. "Paul, you're not selfish."

I laughed until I cried. "Thanks, babe." I used the hair on my wrist to dry my eyes. "Perhaps, I didn't want you to see where I came from. My humble roots."

Jennifer gazed beyond the railing at the white beach and aquamarine water. She smiled. "Don't get what you mean. From all that I've seen, the South is beautiful."

I scowled. "Right here in Gulfport, my biological father sexually assaulted my biological mother. A sixteen-year-old schoolgirl! If she hadn't escaped, he might have killed her. Walking around this seaside town, that's the only thing I see."

I braced to divulge the honest-to-God truth, the whole enchilada. "My half-brothers, Ernie and Marvin, are into some nasty shit. Illegal shit. They brought me along on their 'Midnight Cruises'. I may have gotten myself—or us—into deeper shit." I spilled my guts, beginning with the powerboat ride that transported a load of firearms to Augustus and Jasper Dawson, and with how I delivered a bag filled with the unknown to

Augustus' sister, Ruby. Finally, the cherry on top: our shootout with father and son, thereby ripping off the Silverio drug cartel for a fortune in fentanyl. I waited breathlessly for my wife to respond.

Her eyebrows nearly met her hairline. "Wow. That's—"

I heartily agreed. "Wow, is right."

"You shot a man."

I tapped my arm. "In the shoulder."

My wife tented her fingers. "How do you know Augustus is still alive?"

"I don't."

"Oh boy." She used a ball of napkins to polish a grease spot on the tabletop.

I captured her fidgety hand. "Jenn, I apologize for keeping this horror show to myself. I didn't want you mixed up in this."

Her honey-brown irises drilled into me. "I appreciate your concern, but tell me the real reason you hid what you were doing from me?"

My first finger felt the curve of Big Bertha's metal trigger. My ears heard the percussive blast. My nose smelled burned gunpowder. My brain experienced extreme satisfaction seeing blood jet out of Augustus' back. I replied, "I can distinguish right from wrong. Good from bad. I confess I got high living dangerously. Such a rush! I talked the Dawsons into giving up their drugs while getting shot at! Influence over others felt powerful."

"Paul, you're a principled person. I have no concerns regarding your moral character."

"And there was the money." My face burned with guilt. "Lots of it."

Jim slid dishes of steaming food in front of us. "Shall I bring you anything else?"

I waved the server off. "Something is the matter with me. Fundamentally."

"You flew here to connect with your family." Jennifer skewered a flame-grilled shrimp. "It's not your fault your brothers railroaded you into doing their dirty work. What you did was done in self-defense. Sweetie, it's okay. Don't beat yourself up."

"That pervert's DNA is running through my veins."

My wife's averted eyes, and her torso's slight recoil let slip a new aversion festered within her: my heredity. "That's a lot to unpack."

"There's more."

Jennifer finished her daiquiri in a single gulp, choking on a chip of ice. She signaled Jim with her empty glass. "Go on."

"Last night, I broke into the storage unit under Hunter Rugger's house."

Her hands clamped the table. "You did what?"

"He forgot to clasp the padlock, so technically I wasn't breaking and—"

"'Thou shalt not steal' is one of the six Ten Commandments not pertaining to God himself."

"I took nothing of his." *Or did I?* "Just poked about."

"And?"

"The shelves were filled with pesticides, traps, and, you know, all the supplies required to run a pest management business." I softened my voice. "When I accidentally knocked T. Rex onto the floor, I—"

"T. Rex?" Jennifer elevated her forearms, wiggling her fingers. "Like the big dinosaur waving the dinky arms?"

"Uh-huh. A rat trap with gigantic teeth. I stooped to pick him up and discovered a door in the back wall."

My wife leaned in, her eyes glinting with curiosity. "And what did you find?"

"A hidden space. Black as King Tut's tomb. Technicians use ultraviolet bulbs to track rodent urine droppings. I clicked on one of his special flashlights. Stains covered the walls. Some splashes were dark. Other splotches radiated below the UV light. The cause of the discolorations? I can't rightly say."

"Could it be his man cave? He carts in stacks of porno magazines to tickle his pickle."

She doesn't believe anything I'm telling her. Or doesn't want to. Christ, neither do I. "Babe, an empty room. Not a stick of furniture. Not even a chair." Bone-weary, I closed my eyes, opening both after seeing gruesome patterns spraying the insides of my eyelids. "Unless the guy has a garden hose for a dick, that's not how the male anatomy works."

Her eyes bulged out of her head. "So, you—?"

"I suspect," the uneaten noodles drowning in pinkish sauce resembled eviscerated cadavers, "my father uses that secret room to murder people."

"Oh, God." Jennifer pushed her refreshed Relaxer away as though she, too, had lost her appetite for reddish liquids. On the street, a pair of police officers clad in blue shorts rode by on electric bicycles. "Should we tip off the cops? Get the heck out of Mississippi? Going home gets my vote. Forget Hunter Rugger."

"He's my father, Jenn."

"Paul, you have no evidence that you are related to that man."

"I—know—he—is."

Her forefinger darted across her iPhone's screen. "Let's see. The DNA Center's website states that paternity tests take only 24 hours. The map shows their building is just three blocks south." She read further. "I doubt our subject will submit to a cheek swabbing. Consent to blood or semen samples? Likewise, problematic. For hair, they need the entire root bulb, whatever that is. Oh, the root bulb is the base of the hair follicle. Might be a few roots stuck in his hairbrush. Or saliva on his toothbrush.

Here's a list of unusual specimens. Does he smoke? Did you notice any cigarette butts on the ground?"

"No."

"Umbilical cords?"

"Jenn, that's not remotely funny."

"We can dig through his trash for chewing gum, tissues, straws, and, yuck, used Q-Tips."

I sighed. "Not necessary."

"Hmm?"

I slipped the wallet from my pants and dumped its contents onto the tabletop.

My wife focused on the little shaving resting atop the smushed aspirin packet. "Whoa! Paul, is that a—?"

"I found his nail clipper."

"You swiped a fingernail for a souvenir?" She nudged the semicircle of keratin with a knife. "Let's go."

"Where to?" My hunger had reappeared unheralded. "We haven't finished lunch."

Jennifer flagged down our server. "Jim, two to-go boxes!"

Chapter Sixteen

Sunday Afternoon—August 18, 2019—Day 7

JENNIFER AND I SAT ON A BENCH IN JONES PARK, observing pleasure boats slip in and out of the harbor. At the Port of Gulfport, a cruise ship preparing to get underway tooted a horn four times. A woman at the DNA Center informed us that the paternity results would be available late tomorrow afternoon, barring complications. The entire process of bringing my ancestry into daylight made me uptight. Even so, the prospect of a conclusive resolution motivated me to proceed.

Hungry seagulls sailed in descending orbits as my wife crammed our takeout containers into an overstuffed garbage receptacle. One of the bigger fellows, his breast as white as Siberian snow, knocked a Styrofoam carton onto the ground. A throng of squawking birds fought over the leftovers.

"Jenn, who's feeding the cat?"

"Jean."

I chuckled. "Smokey will gain ten pounds the way she spoils him with all those treats."

"He needs some meat on his bones. Tell me more about Jane and the rest. I wish I could have met them."

"Again, I regret not bringing you with me." I endeavored to summon images of my new family, their faces already evaporating from my memory. "Jane, ah, my mother—still sounds strange saying that word—wasn't the person I envisioned. At first, she acted standoffish. Like, 'Why are you standing on my doorstep? I abandoned you for a good reason.' When Jane took me to an ice cream parlor and explained her plight, I understood that, at her young age, she had no choice."

"I cannot fathom how you didn't go to pieces after hearing of your mother's assault." Jennifer draped her arm across my shoulders. "If something that awful happened to me, I doubt I'd be able to live with the shame. Jane is definitely a brave woman."

"She spent her whole life helping others in need. Ernie is the son who urged her to quit her job at an assisted living facility. All he cares about is making easy money."

"Paul, you said Marvin gave Ernie a real come-to-Jesus moment the day you guys split up. Did Marvin being upfront with his brother have an impact?"

"Hard to say. The twins grew up aware that their father had killed his lover. They're a couple of screwed-up dudes. Glad I had a dad who cared for me, but now," my throat muscles tensed, "what do I do if that DNA test comes back positive?"

"Sweetie, let's not get ahead of ourselves. What's Sarah like?"

"Although she had the same destructive father as Ernie and Marvin, she somehow turned out very well-adjusted."

Jennifer stood before me. "People bottle up all kinds of pain. I worked with a gal at Cardinal Health. Melissa O'Keeffe, or was it O'Kafferty?" Jennifer shrugged. "To me, Melissa seemed to be the happiest person on the planet. Always upbeat. She never complained—almost to the point of being obnoxious. Nobody in their right mind deserves to be so content. The company threw a big shindig for the employees during the year-end holidays. After three or four Long Island iced teas, my coworker opens up about her childhood—shit I didn't want to know. One afternoon, she and her younger brother came home from grade school to hear water running in the kitchen. The kids discover an overflowing sink *and* their mom and dad. Their mother was washing dishes when their father blasted the back of her head off—a textbook murder-suicide. Two weeks into January, Melissa doesn't show up at our office or phone in. She experienced a complete mental breakdown and needed to be institutionalized. Paul, you can't comprehend the tonnage others carry on their shoulders. Or how friends and family are holding on to sanity by a single thread."

I slowly shook my head. "Such a sad story."

"Indeed, and the detail that always haunts me? Melissa kept her dad's shotgun. She mounted the accursed thing on her kitchen wall above the sink. *Fully loaded.*"

"Sarah has her noggin screwed on tight. Wants to be the next Greta Thunberg."

"An exemplary goal." Jennifer's eyes darkened. "What of the Mexican cartel? Will Juan Carlos Delgado be a problem?"

A blood vessel inside my skull throbbed. "Oh, I nearly forgot about the Wildcat."

"You're dealing with some heavy stuff." My wife paced along the crushed-rock pathway, agitated. "Can he connect you to Ernie or Marvin?"

"I-I don't think so."

Her skidding shoes sent up a small cloud of dust. "Where *is* your family? Are they out of harm's way?"

I unlocked my iPhone. "Twice a day, I search for a free king-sized Beautyrest mattress in the Mobile, Alabama *Craigslist*. If there's trouble, Jane will—"

"What is it?" Jennifer plucked the rectangular screen from my quivering fingers. "Do we use this phone number?"

I extended my palm. "Give it to me. I'll call."

"This notice is four hours old. We need a burner phone."

"Burner what?"

"Untraceable cell phones. We just finished watching *The Wire* on HBO. All the pushers employed by Stringer Bell used prepaid phones."

I sprang to my feet. "Where can we get one?"

"Walmart or Target. 7-Elevens are on every street corner."

I performed a series of *Google* inquiries. "Can't get a damn Slurpee in this town! Walmart is eight miles away. And Target is twenty."

My wife aimed her index finger over my shoulder. "That store will stock them."

Dollar General had a prodigious display of prepaid phones. Out on the sidewalk, I ripped open one of the three plastic TracFone packages. *DG must be where all the local dope peddlers purchase their burner phones.* I powered up the $4.99 reconditioned MyFlip and dialed the number listed in the *Craigslist* ad.

A female bawled from the speakerphone. "They kidnapped Sarah!"

"Jane?"

"She's gone!"

"What do you mean she's gone?"

"Sarah got bored being stuck inside the hotel room. I gave her money for the candy machine. When she didn't return, we went looking."

"Maybe Sarah is exploring the town. You know the way teens treasure their independence."

"Paul! Ernie and Marvin left hours ago. They're not answering their phones."

"Who took her?"

"You tell me!"

"Where are you?"

"The French Quarter. L'Hôtel Corbeau."

"How many miles is New Orleans from Gulfport?"

"Eighty. Ninety minutes in the fast lane."

Jennifer spoke into the MyFlip's microphone. "Mrs. Baker, stay in your hotel room. Don't open the door for anybody. We'll be there soon."

"Paul, who's that speaking?"

"My wife, Jennifer. We'll contact you when we're close."

We sprinted the whole distance to the Shangri-La Inn's parking lot. I depressed the unlock button on the Subaru's remote.

Jennifer cupped her hands. "Toss me the keys."

"You don't want me to drive?"

She clicked her fingers. "We're in a hurry." On US Route 90, my wife flipped on the right directional indicator in the town of Pass Christian.

"Why are you turning?" I pointed forward. "The Bay Saint Louis Bridge is just ahead."

"I need to see Hunter Rugger's place with my own eyes."

"Jenn, somebody abducted Sarah. We don't have time for sightseeing." The determined set of her jawbone persuaded me to give in. "Left on Poindexter. Pall Mall is that short loop street." I indicated the house supported by stilts. "That blue one with the big deck."

My wife slowed on Poindexter Drive, not steering onto Pall Mall Road. "That's a good-sized lot with a decent view of the water." Her eyelids constricted with repugnance. "Oh, I see what you were saying about the storage room. The shape itself oozes bad vibes." Jennifer spun gravel, making a U-turn.

I pivoted to the rear to check the driveway. "Rugger's van isn't under the house."

My wife frowned. "Doctor Death's probably out and about crucifying cockroaches."

I pictured Blatto on a miniature Mount Calvary with his six legs nailed to crossed popsicle sticks. "My God, my God," his mouthparts opened to shriek, "why hast thou forsaken me?"

We burned rubber across rural Mississippi's marshy flatlands, got on Interstate 10 to bridge the Pearl River, and headed southwest into rural Louisiana's marshy flatlands. *The trees are all identical—even the houses.* On Lake Pontchartrain, at the midpoint of the Twin Span Bridge, the rising anxiety engulfed me. I wondered if I could swim three miles to shore. *Conceivably, if I do the backstroke?* My lips blurted the thoughts whirling between my ears. "What happens when we get to New Orleans?"

Jennifer's opinion took longer than usual to formulate. "We ferret out whoever snatched Sarah and bring her home." My wife ignored the zigzagging traffic to stare into my eyes. "Then, before we board the next nonstop jet to sunny San Diego, you'll take me out for chicory coffee and beignets at Café du Monde." From the faith she exuded, I believed every word she said.

Despite the fear paralyzing my heart muscles, I smiled. "That's a date, but really, how do we deal with Sarah's kidnappers?"

We rolled down an exit ramp, waiting at the bottom while a drunk man weaved along the crosswalk to a corner liquor store. A heavily inked woman beaming from an enormous billboard advertised LOOK BETTER NAKED ART ACCENT TATTOOS.

My wife guided the Forester onto Saint Bernard Avenue, stomping on the brakes to avoid pancaking a stray dog. "You suspect Juan Carlos Delgado nabbed Sarah?"

Construction vehicles were parked in front of water-damaged structures. *Hurricane Katrina wrecked the Seventh Ward.* "Yeah, I do. The Wildcat lost a ton of money."

"Ernie and Marvin must give back the stolen goods to the cartel. The Dawsons kept the bulk of the fentanyl?"

"Yes. The twins took three bricks. Augustus and Jasper held onto four, plus the decoy they left in their boat." I directed Jennifer to North Rampart, and six blocks later, we turned at Saint Ann. "L'Hôtel Corbeau is two streets up." I texted Jane about our arrival.

My mother stood on the steps of a Greek Revival building. A large wooden black bird, a limp snake dangling out of its beak, hung over her head. When we pulled the car into a space, she dashed to us. "Praise God you're here!"

I hugged her. "Heard from Marvin or Ernie?"

Jane clenched her elbows. "Not yet."

My wife got to the point. "Where did your sons hide the drugs, Mrs. Baker?"

My mother, reluctant to disclose incriminating information to an outsider, bit her lip.

The band of tension winding within me sprung. "Tell Jenn everything she wants to know! How can you expect us to help you?"

Jane stepped backward as though my words physically hurt. "Sorry, today has been exceptionally nerve-racking." She embraced my wife. "Thank you for coming, Jennifer." They continued holding hands. "And you don't have to call me Mrs. Baker. Jane is fine. It may be awkward at first, but I wouldn't mind if you—"

My wife took the hint and ran with it. "Mom, where did you stash the fentanyl?"

Jane scanned for passersby. "Ernie and Marvin buried the containers in a safe place. We stopped in the Pearl River Wildlife Management Area on the way to New Orleans. I saved the exact GPS coordinates on my cell phone." Her chest rose and fell. "What do we do?"

From its lofty perch above L'Hôtel Corbeau's battered doorway, the raven's carved eyes watched our huddle. My brain shifted into overdrive, each of my solutions more harebrained than the last. I remembered the bike patrol on the beach outside of Shaggy's. "Should we go to the police?"

Jennifer rubbed her chin. "It's your decision, Mom." She rotated to me. "Still, I might have an idea."

My blood pressure dropped a few millimeters. "Whew, I couldn't come up with anything productive."

"Augustus has a sister?"

I groaned. "Yeah. Ruby's the scary lady at the campground I gave the dry bag to. What's she gotta do with Sarah's disappearance? And now, Marvin and Ernie?"

"Her brother and nephew are in the wind, so they're outta the picture. And we can't just pick up the nearest telephone to call Delgado. 'Hey, Juan Carlos, how's it hanging? Great to hear you bought a brand-new Learjet. By the way, Juan, did you kidnap a schoolgirl named Sarah Baker?'"

I asked, "You're hoping Ruby will act as a go-between to negotiate?"

"Let's find out." Jennifer shook a new burner phone at me. "How do we contact her?"

I flung up my hands in desperation. "How should I—?"

"I'll reach out to Ruby." My wife and I faced Jane. "Ruby Dawson and I graduated from high school together. She's the main reason Ernie and Marvin gravitated to the dark side."

Jennifer acted surprised. "You know her?"

"We didn't travel in the same circles, and we weren't tight, but—" Jane toed a cigarette butt.

I wanted to pull my hair out at the roots. "Mom!"

"Before Jonas Baker, I dated Augustus Dawson for a few months. Ruby sometimes hung with us—movies, barbecues, whatever. Hurricane is a tight-knit community. You can't itch your ass without some busybody sending up smoke signals. I knew Auggie didn't buy the speedboats and luxury cars with money earned from operating the moonshine still in his shed. After Jonas died, Ruby dropped by every other day to ask how I was holding up. She'd bring my kids gifts—a baseball bat and glove for Ernie or a skateboard and helmet for Marvin—pricey things to make the twins like her more than me. When the boys stayed out later and later, I got to the bottom of Ruby's shenanigans. She was grooming my sons to do Auggie's funny business."

I needed my mother to apologize for my half-brothers' poor behavior. "Didn't you attempt to stop them?"

Jane bowed her head in self-condemnation. "Sure, I did." Her eyes, glistening with remorse, leveled with mine. "You've been around long enough to see how bullheaded those two can be once their backs are up. Short of having my boys arrested, what else could I do?"

I peered at Jennifer, mulling over why we had never discussed raising children. *I'm flawed. She knows I'd be a lousy father.* "Ernie and Marvin went to look for Sarah. Did they say which way they were going?"

"No. When Sarah wasn't at the snack machine, Marvin decided to walk the block." My mother's throat convulsed as if she had swallowed a sharp stone. "Neither of them came back. Both of their cell phones go straight to voicemail."

My wife opened the burner phone's plastic clamshell. "Call Ruby."

"Her number is unlisted." Jane typed into the messaging application. "There's someone who can get it for me." The TracFone beeped. "Got it." She dialed and squished the MyFlip to her ear.

Jennifer moved forward. "Put Ruby on speakerphone."

"Hello?"

"Ruby, this is Jane Ba—"

The minuscule speaker squealed, "You bitch!"

"Ruby!"

"One of your crotchlings shot my little brother!"

"I had no—"

"The hell you didn't. Robbin' Auggie wasn't enough for you. You had to shoot him!"

"Ruby, they were trying to—"

"You wouldn't be livin' like royalty in that fancy house if it weren't for my brother."

"You know my house is far from fancy."

Jennifer shouted into the microphone, "Ruby, shut the fuck up!" She gritted her teeth before adding, "Please, will you just listen?"

"Jane, who's askin' to get their potty mouth washed out with laundry soap?"

"Jennifer. My son's wife."

"Wife? Ernie or Marvin? Ha! What ding-dong is dumb enough to tie the knot to either of those oxen?"

"She's married to Paul."

"And Paul is?"

"He's my eldest." My mother glanced at me. "I gave him up at birth. He recently tracked me down."

The three of us scowled at the luminous screen.

"Paul's the kid who delivered the orange bag to the campground?"

"Yes, Ruby," I said loudly, "you aimed a gun at me!"

"It wasn't loaded."

"Are you communicating with Augustus and Jasper?"

"They took off."

"Can you get a hold of them?"

"Why should I do that?"

"We think the—uh—people you do business with—uh—may have—"

"Spit it out, boy. My Metamucil is kicking in!"

"They grabbed Sarah. Ernie and Marvin are also missing."

"Oh, I'm crying in my soup. My brother told me a guy new to your gang shot him. Was that you, Paul?"

I jabbed my finger at the phone. "Your family shot first."

Ruby sighed. "How did the Mexicans locate you?"

Jane spoke up. "Dunno. We paid for everything in cash, except for the hotel rooms, which I paid for with my credit card. Are you still at home?"

"This chick wasn't hatched yesterday. I cleared out the second Auggie and Jasper flew the coop. Only the Father, Son, or the Holy Rollin' Ghost can find where I parked my RV."

Jennifer bent closer to the TracFone. "Juan Carlos Delgado kidnapped Sarah because he wants something in exchange. Ruby, we're returning his merchandise."

"Girl, I'm no imbecile. After graduating from high school, I took cosmetology classes at Remington College. What do you need me to do?"

Jennifer scowled in frustration. "Drug lords aren't listed in the white pages. Is there anyone who works for Delgado who will relay a message?"

"There is," Ruby moaned, "but you can bet your britches, this ain't gonna end well."

Jane gave the MyFlip to Jennifer. "Now what?"

My wife stuck the device in her purse. "We wait for Ruby to get back to us."

I gazed upward with mistrust at L'Hôtel Corbeau's feathered mascot. The eavesdropping bird emanated waves of bad juju. I pointed at the horizon. "Sunset is in half an hour. A different hotel will be safer for us."

My mother's eyes swept Saint Ann Street. "If Sarah or the boys show up," she stepped off the curb, "how shall they know where we are?"

Jennifer yanked Jane from the path of a swerving yellow cab. "Did you notify your family members about the *Craigslist* mattress ad?"

"Yes. And we went over creating a post. I'll update my message with one of your phone numbers."

Jane checked out of L'Hôtel Corbeau. We booked a room in the Hotel St. Marie. The balcony overlooking the hubbub on Toulouse Street cost a pretty penny, but the security personnel patrolling the premises were worth the added expense.

We turned in after the late news without hearing the burner cell phone ring or seeing any current *Craigslist* posts for free mattresses.

Chapter Seventeen

Monday Morning—August 19, 2019—Day 8

IT AMAZES ME HOW A PERSON CAN MAINTAIN AN APPETITE under incredible pressure. I guess no matter how close the gallows' rope is to stretching your neck, your stomach still sweet-talks you into tying on to the old feed bag for one last meal. Seated beside Jane and Jennifer at a corner table in the Hotel St. Marie's breakfast area, I drowned buttered Belgian waffles in Dickinson's Pure Maple Syrup. To initiate conversation, or more likely, to release tension, I mentioned the nightmare I had before waking up. "Such a weird dream! So realistic!"

My wife was well aware that she had married a heavy dreamer. My constant tossing, turning, moans, and groans prevented her from ever getting a night of restful sleep. "Oh, yeah?" She broke off a piece of blueberry muffin. "What about?"

"We were up in the clouds on an airplane, the only passengers on board."

Jane yawned. "Me too?"

I noticed the dark circles beneath her hazel eyes. "Not right away. You arrived on the scene sometime later."

She covered her mouth and yawned again. "Where were we going?"

I scratched my cheek. "It might have been an intercontinental flight—to Europe? An old plane, the interior painted olive drab like a B-17."

"Paul, that's your favorite aircraft." Jennifer sliced a turkey sausage into a dozen penny-sized disks. "We toured the restored B-17 at Palomar Airport last summer. You were against shelling out a thousand bucks for a ride. 'Money doesn't grow on trees,' you told me."

I nodded emphatically. "It doesn't! As a child, I glued together a Revell Flying Fortress model. A birthday present given to me by my parents. Thought those World War II bombers were cool, so many guns sticking out at every angle." I sipped orange juice from a Dixie cup. "I love crawling inside the belly of a warplane. Soaring around in a four-engine B-17 would be quite an adventure. Still, I'm not sure I'd spend—"

"Are those rusted relics reliable?" My mother dumped two packets of sugar into her steaming coffee. "Didn't one of those bombers crash recently?"

"A motor caught fire, and they made an emergency landing. Illinois? I don't recall anybody dying. Back to my dream. We fell asleep on the long flight. A noise wakes me. I leave my seat and walk to the cockpit. No pilot, no copilot. The plane is flying itself."

My wife scrunched her eyebrows in skepticism. "B-17s had autopilots? Isn't that modern technology?"

"Jenn, I didn't say the airplane was a B-17. I said it looked old, similar to a B-17. Anyhow, I believe some aeronautical genius invented the automatic pilot during the First World War."

"My apologies for interrupting." She sopped up runny eggs with a triangle of toasted bread. "Please continue."

"I call out. Nobody comes. The dozens of round gauges on the instrument panel have needles pointing to different numbers. I don't understand the functions of most of them, but no alarms, no red bulbs blinking, so I hope we're safe until I see the—"

The TracFone rang. Unnerved, I dropped my fork on the floor.

Jennifer jammed the burner phone to her ear. "Hello?" She mouthed, "Ruby" to Jane and me. "No, it's not with us. Uh-huh. I need to speak with Sarah first. How about Ernie and Marvin?" Seconds elongated. "Nonnegotiable. Roger, text me the information." When my wife disconnected, I had a hard time decoding her expression. Happy? Sad? Shaken? *Is she losing her confidence?*

"What did Ruby say?" Perspiration stood out on Jane's forehead. "How is Sarah?"

Jennifer's worried eyes evaded my mother's frightened eyes. "Ruby doesn't know. There's positive news, if you can call it that. Marvin and Ernie are with her."

"Oh, Jesus!" Jane's arm tipped over her cup of java. "The Mexicans took my boys!" Nearby diners, who had been picking at their complimentary breakfasts, stopped to tune in.

My mother's hand trembled under my tight grasp. "Relax, Mom. They won't hurt your family. Sarah and the twins are worth millions to them."

"Delgado could make examples of my kids. Drug lords have no code of ethics. They are," she rooted through her vocabulary for a suitable word, "barbarians!"

"Juan Carlos is a reasonable man." My lies flowed as effortlessly as the syrup smothering my half-eaten waffles. "He won't touch a hair on their heads. Jenn, what is Augustus' sister texting you?"

"Ruby thinks she can get someone to let us talk to Sarah and your brothers. If so, she'll send me a number to call."

"Proof of life?"

My wife nodded.

I felt like an actor in a movie I hadn't auditioned to be cast in. "That's good, right?"

My mother looked lost. "What is this 'proof of life'?"

Jennifer frowned. "The hostage-takers submit evidence authenticating that their hostages are still alive and unharmed. If you can't talk directly to the victim, the abductors provide a picture of the person holding something current, like today's newspaper. Kidnapping is big business in Mexico." My wife and I had watched a segment on Vice News about how prevalent abducting people for ransom has become south of the border. Her finger tapped the tabletop. "I informed Ruby we'll only commit to moving further if we can speak to Sarah."

Decaf blotched Jane's white shirt sleeve. "You mean, dig up the drugs and bring them to the dealers?"

I shushed her.

Jennifer grabbed her vibrating burner phone. "A message from Ruby." She held the device in front of her face for what seemed like an eon.

My mother wrenched the inexpensive TracFone out of my wife's fingers. A guttural sound rattled in the back of her throat.

I bent over to see. The image, hard to discern on the teeny screen, showed Sarah tied to a leather office armchair with rope. An electric camping lantern hung close by; the recesses of the room were veiled in darkness. The defiant glint in her eyes struck a sympathetic chord in my heart. "Is that the only photo? Where are the twins? And how do we know when this was taken?"

Jennifer shook her chestnut tresses in irritation. "That's all there is. At least Sarah—" Ringtone. "Ruby's calling." She selected speakerphone. "Give me a sec." We followed her past the lookie-loos, through the hotel lobby, and to the street. "Where's Ernie and Marvin's picture?" An automotive horn honked from the tiny speaker. "Hello?"

A disgruntled voice exclaimed, "Cocksucker!"

My wife pressed the MyFlip to her lips. "Ruby, is that you? Are you mad at me?"

"Not you. A gasoline truck cut me off. Prick won't be smilin' if I smash fifteen tons of RV into his sorry ass. He'll burn in everlasting fire." A laugh. "So will I, I reckon."

"Are you driving?"

"Yep. Figured it might be wise for ol' Rubes to go on an extended holiday. Head west. Or east, if the Lamb of God leads me in that direction. Christ for Christmas, even up north where Pelosi and all the other libtards mope around wasting space. Cabo San Lucas is obviously out of the question. Could be I'll join Auggie and Jasper and never come back to this hellhole."

Jennifer arched her eyebrows at Jane and me. "Why, what's the word?"

"You should—" Honking.

"Are you there?"

"The Silverio will—" Louder honking. "The morning commute traffic boils my blood. Stop and go. Go, then stop. Motorcycle jockeys ride up the middle like they own the road. I get so worked up I want to—"

"Ruby," I hollered into the MyFlip, "unlike you, we can't run away. Ernie and Marvin dug their own graves," my mother shot me a perturbed stare, "but Sarah had nothing to do with their conniving. We're going to save her and, *goddamnit it all to hell, we'll save her even if I have to kill every last one of those fucking parasites!*"

My companions must have detected a tone they had not previously heard in my voice. When our eyes met above the cell phone, they saw a new expression there, too. *Am I reading their emotions correctly? Are they afraid of me?*

"Good luck with that," Ruby said. "If it all goes tits up, don't call the cops. They're not to be trusted."

I steadied my nerves by focusing on a piece of green gum stuck to the sidewalk. "So *can* you or *can't* you hook us up with Juan Carlos Delgado or one of his men?"

"I'm texting you. Be at that address at ten tonight."

"Ruby, who are we meeting?" I visualized Sarah strapped to the armchair, the belligerent upturn of her chin. "Will we see Sarah? And Marvin and Ernie?"

"I'm just a messenger, not privy to the nitty-gritty. Don't be late. These cutthroats will not wait. Oh, and bring the Dragon's Breath. All three kilos."

I asked, "What's the deal with Augustus and Jasper's four kilos?"

"My brother says it's taken care of."

"What is 'taken care of' supposed to imply? Augustus already returned the drugs?"

Ruby hung up.

Monday Noon—August 19, 2019—Day 8

As we crossed the lengthy bridge spanning Lake Pontchartrain on the way to pick up the drugs, I didn't measure my capability to swim safely to shore. I fretted about Sarah, Ernie, and Marvin, dreading this evening's showdown with the bloodthirsty Mexican cartel.

We drove the single-lane Ronald Reagan Memorial Highway to an industrial town named after the Confederate ambassador to France: Slidell. Jane was hunched over in the passenger seat, her forefinger scrolling every which way on *Google Maps.* Jennifer adhered to my mother's directions, shifting the Subaru into reverse or turning around if we missed a turnoff. In the role of a backseat driver, I had serious concerns about whether we'd be able to reacquire the drugs and beat the traffic to New Orleans in time for the important meeting. I pestered our navigator until she ordered me to be quiet.

Camp Road, a tarred byway slightly wider and smoother than a cow path, meandered through dense undergrowth. Jane peered out of the side window. "It should be," she rolled down the glass, letting in the oppressive air, "there!"

Jennifer eased the Forester past an open pipe gate. A quarter of a mile along the unpaved roadway, a trio of pit bulls ran out of the woods to chase our trail of dust. The bumpy lane ended at a decrepit house trailer squatting on a waterway's eroding banks. A Confederate flag flapped listlessly from a pole stuck in a tire filled with concrete.

A bearded Colonel Sanders look-alike wearing a red TRUMP 2020 KEEP AMERICA GREAT cap opened the mobile home's screen door. The fleshy septuagenarian descended the cinder block steps to stand on a rectangle of green artificial turf. He extracted a corncob pipe from the bib of his patched overalls.

My wife murmured, "What country are we in?"

I whispered, "The Confederate States of America. That there's Robert E. Lee's great-great-grandson."

"Ace, Spencer, *Jolene*, get over here! Now!" The two black pit bulls sat by the man's feet, long tongues lolling out of their drooling mouths. The white dog with a black spot around its blue eye bared its menacing teeth. "Jolene!" When the animal kept growling at us, he snagged her spiked collar, chained her to a post, and rubbed her square head affectionately. "Good girl!" His spine cracked as he stood erect. "Morning, folks!" He checked the LCD display on his vintage Casio wristwatch. "Heh. Guess the afternoon began twenty minutes ago. Where does all the time go? Name's Merle. My friends call me 'Merle the Pearl.' You can too." Merle the Pearl tamped a clump of Backwoods Natural inside his pipe, irked after a curly string of tobacco fell to the ground.

Jane held her pinkie and thumb to her ear. "We phoned about renting a boat?"

Merle struck a strike-anywhere match on his boot, dipping the flame into the corncob bowl. Bluish smog repelled the crown of gnats swarming above his sweat-stained red hat. "Knew your voice sounded familiar on the tele. You're the gal who rented the boat with the two younger fellas last Friday. Didn't recognize you in the daylight." After he looked Jennifer and me over—his bulbous schnoz crinkling as if getting a whiff of something feculent—he reverted his attention to Jane. "How was the night fishing? Catch any perch or even a couple of crappies? I heard the bass are bitin'. Somebody in White Kitchen reeled in a largemouth the size of a Volkswagen bus."

I stepped forward. "Merle, we don't have all day. We have to drive back to New Orleans."

"Well, I oughta quit jawin' and get my ass in gear." Ace and Spencer followed us down a grassy slope to the riverbank, where three aluminum rowboats bobbed at a wooden dock. *Dixie* had a 3-horsepower outboard engine clamped to the transom, not exactly a speedboat. An electric trolling motor propelled *Trillie* to neighboring fishing grounds. Oars (and a pair of muscular biceps) powered *Viola*. All the watercraft leaked. Merle indicated the rowboat rigged with the Yamaha. "*Dixie's* the one you took last time. Still want 'er?"

"She'll do." I sloshed into an inch of brown bilge, stretching to receive the empty duffel bag and help my wife sit next to me on the front bench. At home on the water, my mother jumped into Dixie and settled onto the rear seat. She choked the carburetor, made certain the gearshift was in neutral, and yanked the rope start. The two-stroke sputtered to life after three pulls.

"Folks, I require a two-hundred-and-fifty-dollar deposit in addition to a rental payment. Forty bucks an hour or three hundred for the day." Merle the Pearl extended his palm. "Cash on the barrel."

We got out our wallets and purses and pooled $290.

Jane handed him the money. "We'll be back in an hour."

I unknotted the rope and shoved us away from the dock. My mother twisted the throttle on the tiller, and we putt-putted north up the Old Pearl River. Merle's *Dixie* possessed none of the gumption of Ernie and Marvin's *Lickety-Split*. Still, physically, she had the narrow width to squeeze through reedy sections and the low depth to skim over submerged blowdowns and mud bars typical of the Wildlife Management Area.

The floating Salvinia and flowering duckweed-obstructed marsh transitioned into stands of moss-draped cypress trees. Dabbling ducks tipped their hind ends in the air, grubbing for subaquatic plants and insects. Long-legged herons and egrets waded in the shallows, occasionally spearing small fish with their dagger-like bills.

A tour boat, *Cajun Eco-Encounters*, passed by. Chattering vacationers gawked at flora and fauna. We concentrated on the task ahead. Fifteen minutes after we slipped (I had to duck) under a Chef Menteur Highway drawbridge, Jane checked the map on her phone and clucked her tongue. She pushed the tiller to the right. The motorboat swung left to a tributary. As we neared a ramshackle structure, I realized the object lying on the disintegrating dock wasn't a detached length of lumber but rather an alligator as long as my mother's Buick Enclave basking in the noonday sun.

Jennifer caught her breath. "Is that an—?"

"Shoo!" Jane slapped the river water with an oar. "Shoo! Scat!" The reptile remained still as death. *Is that thing alive?* She smacked the surface again. "Off with you!"

The alligator eyed us with annoyance (if cold-blooded vertebrates are capable of emotions aside from pure hunger) before slithering over the edge of the dock. Its horny tail slid into the water without making a splash.

I shifted toward the middle of the seat. "That monster will capsize our boat!"

My mother harrumphed. "That might occur," she gestured with her chin at the approaching thunderclouds, "but there are greater odds God shall smite you with a bolt of lightning." *Dixie* glided up to the landing. "Paul, the drugs are inside the shack. Ernie hid them underneath the floor."

I hoisted myself above the gunwale and climbed onto the dock, my contracted abdomen anticipating sudden disembowelment by the leaping beast. My hands steered clear of the rows of rusty nails protruding from the weathered planks. However, a pine splinter penetrated my knee and snapped off. "Ouch."

Jennifer yelled, "You okay, Paul?"

"Sure." My fingernail forced the sliver in deeper. "Only a scratch." *Until my leg swells up with bacterial sepsis.*

The swamp shanty's porch hovered above a carpet of spider lilies so close-knit I couldn't identify what supported the foundation—pontoons, pilings, or earth. Abundant overgrowth cloaked the rear of the dwelling. *One way in, one way out.* Layers of blue, green, and red paint peeled from the warped clapboard siding. Once upon a time, someone lazed on a rustic bench smoking (evidenced by plastic Tiparillo stubs overtopping a Dinty Moore tin can) while casting a fishing line in the river (a White Owl cigar box was filled with assorted tackle). The former owner had hand-chiseled KEZAR'S KASTLE into a board, which was nailed above the entrance. A LIVE, LOVE, LAUGH sign poked from a Bed Bath & Beyond shopping bag. I turned the doorknob, unoiled hinges creaking as I shouldered my way inside the one-room hunting lodge. The corrugated steel roof had collapsed in multiple areas, allowing beams of misty light to spotlight the table, three chairs, and wood-burning stove. A broom and shovel leaned against a wall. Beer cans and bottles were scattered on the floor. The place stank of mildewed *Field & Stream* magazines—and utter loneliness.

Two sets of shoe prints in the dust (overlapped by two return sets) led me to a single set of handprints on a pair of floorboards. I used my house key to pry up the planking. Beneath the building, three kilograms of uncut fentanyl rested on a bed of dirt. For a heartbeat, I forgot about Sarah, Ernie, and Marvin. I considered taking the dope for myself. *Four and a half million dollars would be a nice little nest egg for me and the wife.* The image of Sarah bound to an armchair shimmered before me. *Hurry.* I reached into the cache.

As my fingers touched the top plastic container, the rattle of a maraca made my lungs lock up. *Snake?* An object coiled in the shadows, thicker than my forearm and—*oh, God*—covered with hourglass-patterned scales. I weighed the pros and cons of yelping for help as its triangular, copper-colored head—

A flash of metal whooshed past my cheek, severing the serpent's neck. The reptile's body twitched for an instant or two, then lay there motionless. I hadn't perceived Jane sneaking up behind me.

"Copperhead," she said. "Be thankful it wasn't a diamondback." The spade clanged when she pitched the bloody tool in the corner. "Let's go, Son."

I hauled the three kilos out of the hole, brushed a huge daddy-longlegs off my wrist, and rushed after her to the boat.

She called me Son!

Jennifer stuffed the drugs into the duffel bag. "Paul, you're white as a ghost. What happened in there?"

I bent my two fingers into fangs. "Only a baby copperhead." I regarded my mother with new respect. *She saved my life.* "Jennifer, Mom sent the snake straight to viper heaven!" *If The Maker created an afterworld for creatures born without legs.*

While we moored *Dixie* to the dock, Merle the Pearl saw us through his screen door. He carried a double-barreled shotgun down the incline, Ace, Spencer, and irritable Jolene hugging his heels. On the landing, he loaded two red shells in the breech and snapped it shut. "Throw the bag over here!"

I clutched the canvas sack packed with Dragon's Breath. "Huh? The remains of our picnic lunch?"

"You heard me, kid." Merle aimed the long gun at my head. Hackles raised a ridge on Jolene's back. The pit bull bared intimidating fangs, champing at the bit to charge. "That duffel was empty when you left. Now, it's filled with whatever you buried in the swamp Friday night. Chuck the bag, and you can be on your way."

I stared down dual muzzles, almost distinguishing the fistful of buck pellets waiting in the chamber to atomize my face. Wondering if I'd feel immediate pain or if, like turning off a TV, everything would fade to black, I missed seeing my mother remove the pearl-handled pocket pistol from her alligator skin handbag.

"Lower the shotgun, Merle." The Colt Model 1908 looked toylike in her hand, the .25-caliber no match for his 12-gauge. The man licked his lips and blinked. This afternoon wasn't going as well as he had planned.

"That your son? Gimme the damn bag, or I'll blow his eyeballs outta the backa his skull."

The "mouse gun" in Jane's grip never wavered. The woman exhibited no timidity as she advanced up the landing. I prayed harder with each step she took closer to Merle. "Pull that trigger, inbred, and I'm gonna put three of these little bad boys in your fat chest, the rest in your fat face. Look at God's green Earth. Do you really want today to be your last?"

Merle the Pearl didn't take a moment to smell the roses. "Lady, you couldn't hit the broad side of a barn with that peashooter."

The sharp crack of the .25 caliber bullet echoed off the rear of the mobile home and into the marsh. Merle dropped the shotgun, his fingers tracing the furrow across his cheekbone and to his hanging earlobe. "Lady, don't hurt my pups!"

Jennifer raced forward to seize the weapon, flinging it into the river. "Hurt your dogs? Who do you think we are? Savages?" She waved us to the car. "Let's get out of this shithole!"

Nobody had to tell me twice.

Chapter Eighteen

Monday Afternoon—August 19, 2019—Day 8

JENNIFER'S EYES ASSESSED THE BUILDING TRAFFIC. "Mom, where did you learn to shoot like Wyatt Earp?"

Underneath her blush, Jane's lips curved upward. "AG & AG."

My wife slanted her ear. "AG and a what?"

"It's a woman's shooting league. A Girl & A Gun. They have local chapters across the US."

From the backseat, I leaned between the two front buckets. "You saved me twice today. Three times if you count the alligator."

"After the event that happened to me as a young girl, I vowed never to be that vulnerable again. I learned to defend myself. Took years of self-defense classes. Boxing and martial arts. I bought my first gun, a Beretta, and signed up for firearms training with an ex-New York City SWAT officer." Jane blew fake gunpowder smoke from her right forefinger, holstering the fake handgun in a fake holster. "Even won a national practical shooting tournament."

Jennifer accelerated the Subaru around a cement truck. "Practical shooting, as in?"

"Event organizers also call it dynamic shooting or action shooting. You're clocked running an obstacle course, firing at various targets. Super-stimulating. Competition really gets your heart pumping."

I understood why my mother schooled herself in the noble art of self-preservation. *Her survival skills should reassure me, but—* "That pocket pistol you carry can't be very accurate. Suppose you missed? How did you know Merle wouldn't shoot me?"

She stared straight ahead, the contours of her face alternating light and dark as trees alongside the road blocked the sun. "I didn't."

My fingernails dug semicircles into my palms. "Still, you wagered and fired anyway? You were confident you'd make the shot?"

"Paul, I couldn't let that thief steal the only thing we had to trade for Sarah and my boys." She pivoted to me. "I'll fess up." The tension in her facial muscles lessened. "I actually aimed for his forehead. My front sight must be misaligned. I should have a gunsmith fix it."

Is she pulling my leg? "You're yanking my chain, right?"

"Ernie and Marvin told me you have a steady arm. You're pretty good to have hit Augustus from a moving boat."

"Lucky shot." I kept at Jane, dissatisfied with her responses. "Please tell me you meant to shoot off that man's earlobe."

"Yes, Paul. I aimed at his ear. You were in absolutely no danger, unless the wind changed direction or he—"

"Okay, okay!" I dropped the subject. "Are you bringing your gun to the meeting tonight?"

"These guys ain't Merle the Pearl. The Silverio drug cartel is known for shooting first and asking questions later."

"So, are you taking it or what?"

My mother snugged her seatbelt. "Haven't made up my mind."

In our haste to drive to the Pearl River Wildlife Management Area and recover the fent, we hadn't spoken more than a few vague words regarding the 10 p.m. rendezvous—*just six hours from now.* I opened *Google Maps* on my phone and retrieved the address in the easternmost downriver portion of New Orleans. When Hurricane Katrina struck land fourteen years ago, storm surges breached the Mississippi River-Gulf Outlet Canal's levees. Streets, vehicles, and buildings in the historic Lower Ninth Ward quickly sank under twenty feet of polluted water. Those fortunate enough to escape the flooding needed to be winched off their roofs by Coast Guard helicopters.

Satellite views of the Saint Claude Avenue and Alabo Street intersection revealed a patchwork of green and brown, with homesteads and empty lots. *Google Street View* dropped me to road level. I scrolled past a derelict motorboat loaded with satellite dishes and through a jungle of weeds.

The deserted turquoise house on Alabo Street (now a pebble path overrun by bunches of greenery) waited for us, where, in short order, we'd be bartering with the Silverio cartel for the lives of Sarah and my two half-brothers. Rescuers had spray-painted a giant red X (faded after a decade and a half in the sun) above the watermark, only inches below the gable vent. The symbol's bottom quadrant contained this morbid notification: 3D. *As in, three deceased, none saved.* Plywood covered the lower windows; however, the front door yawned open as tenebrous as the inside of a killer whale's mouth.

I straddled the floor hump, my elbows on the padded center console. "What's our strategy? We give the cartel the stuff, and then?"

Jane spun in her seat to make eye contact with me. "Before arriving at the meeting place, we'll hide the drugs nearby. Once we see that Sarah and the boys are—"

"That's our course of action?" I thrust my spine against the backseat, smushing my temples between my palms. Unable to restrain my growing sense of foreboding, I shouted, "You're telling me we're just winging it?"

"Paul, do you have a better idea?"

I wanted to scream, *Fucking bitch! You'll do anything—gamble with our lives—to protect Ernie and Marvin, but you left me rotting in a fucking maternity ward!* I exhaled, unclenching my fists. "No."

My mother patted my knee. "It'll be all right. As you said before, Juan Carlos just wants his merchandise."

Although her tender caress helped soothe me, I still felt like a snail stuck in the middle of the road without enough slime in reserve to crawl to either side. *El Gato Montés will eat us alive.* Trained as a quant, I figured our chances were slim to none statistically. I said, "I checked out the address in the Lower Ninth Ward. 235 is an abandoned home at the end of Alabo Street, a stone's throw from the Mississippi River. If you want to live in a ghost town, you can buy a New York City block for the same price as one house in California."

Jennifer spoke to Jane. "Paul and I shall attend the meeting. If you remain out of sight, you can phone the police if everything goes fubar."

"They're my kids." Jane clenched her fist. "I'll be the one walking into that house."

Jennifer waved her hands. "Delgado doesn't know us. We're not in the drug trade, mere civilians—small fry. He won't face getting bad press by hurting a pair of married Americans. We inform him that, *if* he deems making an appearance worth his time, a third party is holding his product, and he's not getting an ounce until he releases the hostages."

I watched my wife's lips move, pondering, *does she believe any of the words coming from her mouth? There's no possibility of us leaving that house on two feet. A vengeful man like the Wildcat does not leave loose ends.*

Jane said little else on the overlong ride to the hotel. I studied her mannerisms—plucking an eyebrow or itching her nose—not knowing my mother well enough to construe her idiosyncrasies. Did Jane agree with Jennifer's suggestion to stay on the sidelines, or is she mentally preparing for her Sarah Connor role in this evening's activities?

I didn't plan to catch forty winks upon entering our room at the Hotel St. Marie, and I don't think Jennifer intended to either, but we were bushed from the day's trials and tribulations. The moment we lay down on the bed, we both conked out.

"Paul, where's your mom?"

When my eyelids opened, the sun no longer streamed through the window as it had when my face hit the pillow at 6 p.m. I had lowered the thermostat before our catnap, so the hotel room was now an icebox. Beyond the panes of glass, Christmas lights twinkled on an adjacent building's balcony. Revelers down on Toulouse Street made merry. "What time is it?"

"Quarter of nine. I just woke up myself." Sleep lines marked Jennifer's pale cheek, and the whites of her honey-brown eyes were bloodshot. "Jane took her handbag and the keys to our rental car, and," she stood upright, "the drugs aren't underneath the bed."

I stared at the digital clock in disbelief. "Huh? Maybe she—"

"You know precisely where your mother went."

I craned my head beneath the mattress. "The fentanyl's gone!"

"You didn't believe me? Put on your pants." My wife grabbed her iPhone while I stretched on a pair of blue jeans. "I'll request a ride."

When my fingers touched the doorknob to leave the room, I whirled. "Jane's gun? Did she bring it with her?"

Clothes flew over Jennifer's shoulders as she rummaged through the dresser drawers. "I don't see it." She dumped the contents of Jane's suitcase across the bed. "Her Colt's not here. Let's move it! The Uber is waiting downstairs."

Our ride-hailing driver, a fit, mid-fifties African-American man clothed in a MARDI GRAS BOURBON STREET T-shirt and tan Bermuda shorts, sized us up as he held the 1960s-era black Lincoln Continental's rear door open. I slid in behind my wife onto a leather backseat as roomy as a football field. "Folks," he said in a mellow Creole accent, "kinda late to be going out to da Lower Ninth Ward. Sure you got da correct address?"

Jennifer bristled at being second-guessed. "Yes, 235 Alabo Street. And, Gervais, we're late for an appointment. There's an extra forty for you if you step on it." She checked her wristwatch and groaned. "Up that to a hundred."

The driver snapped a salute. "Right away, ma'am!" He closed the back door, hurrying around the long vehicle's big front bumper.

Gervais veered past a FedEx truck and into traffic with his right arm resting on the Lincoln's front bench seat. He steered down a maze of dim, cluttered alleys to Decatur.

Out on the Mississippi River, the navigation lights of a gargantuan cargo ship drifted along. The V-8 engine roared mightily as we swooped through Jackson Square and by the Café du Monde, the restaurant my wife asked me to take her for coffee and beignets. *I promise I'll bring her here for breakfast if we live to see the dawn.*

Gervais swung his head rearward. "Where you folks from?"

"California." Pedestrians and stray dogs darted in and out of our headlight beams. I wished our driver would keep his eyes on the road. "North of San Diego."

He nodded. "After Katrina, my cousin relocated to da West Coast. Know where Long Beach is?"

"Near Los Angeles? We used to get tickets for the yearly Bob Marley concerts at the Long Beach Arena until—well," I glanced at Jennifer, "the reggae promoters quit having them."

Gervais sang in a rich voice, "Three little birds pitch by my doorstep singin' sweet songs. . . ." as the Lincoln's rear end skidded sideways making a hard right onto Saint Claude Avenue. "Bob Marley is a legend! Sorry to say, but every musical genre has an expiration date. Da youth always want the latest thing. Dixieland has been New Orleans' traditional style. Nowadays, da majority of kids listen to rap und hip-hop. I tried forever to get my son to learn to play da trumpet or pick up a pair of drumsticks. Knox—dat's my boy—told me, 'Pop, dat music is for de old folks.'" Gervais stamped the brake pedal for an aging woman in a black dress crossing the road, tugging a three-wheeled grocery cart filled with teddy bears. *Where did I see her before?* "Made *me* feel so old!" He sighed. "Und sad we Orleanians are losing our soul, our entire culture."

A railroad track divided the median strip into two sections of dandelion-infested grass. I peered through the windows at the single-level houses and industrial structures, which, judging from their cheerless patinas, must have spent time underwater during Katrina. You had to feel for the people forced to dwell in a flood plain. "How much farther?"

Gervais lowered his brow below the visor to read the street signs. He nodded and flicked the right turn signal. "Just a few more blocks, sir."

If Alabo appeared rough on Google Maps, the road was even worse in reality. Parking lots were heaped with treadless tires, stained mattresses, wooden pallets, and rubbish. A different train track curved out of an overgrown field, splitting the cracked macadam. The Lincoln's leaf springs squeaked over each pothole or bump. We'd see a couple of well-maintained homes or businesses, then come upon rows of uninhabited houses or plots where only the vestiges of cinder block foundations or concrete driveways remained.

Gervais slowed as we passed a wheelless Mitsubishi truck propped up on bricks. "Down here someplace." He gestured at a boarded-up building. "Dere's 229. Hmm. 231. You know which one is 235?"

A beached motorboat overflowing with dish-shaped antennas caught my eye. The narrow lane constricted, the land yacht's chrome prow displacing wave after wave of flourishing vegetation. "235 is at the end of this road. You can pull over by that telephone pole."

"Sir, I'll drop you on da front doorstep. You folks don't wanna be wandering about in da Lower Ninth once Jehovah snuffs out da sun. Ain't safe for you, *oya for me.*"

"Gervais," Jennifer hissed, "stop the car and switch off your lights."

Our Uber driver reluctantly pushed the headlight button and lifted the column gearshift into Park. "Did you drag me all da way downriver to rob me? I don't carry cash."

"You think we're robbers?" She dealt him five twenties and exited the Continental. "Thanks for bringing us. Now go."

I slid outside. "Drive out the way we came." I gently closed the door.

He clanked the transmission into reverse and slowly backed away. We turned toward one another when we couldn't see the Lincoln's windshield glimmering under the moonlight or hear its whitewall tires crunching gravel.

Jennifer's eyes connected with mine. "Ready?"

She looked so beautiful, so full of life, *so equipped for battle.* I drew her face to mine, softly kissing her lips. Overwrought, I implored, "We don't have to do this. Let's just go home."

My wife squeezed my hand. "Come on, Lover Boy. Time's a-wastin'."

We clung to the muddy side of Alabo, careful not to slip into a drainage ditch brimming with raw sewage. I slapped at relentless mosquitoes buzzing by my ear, squashing several that feasted on the veins in my neck.

Jennifer peeped from beneath a scrub pine. "There's the rental car!"

The green Subaru Forester was parked in front of the same tumble-down two-story house I had scrutinized hours ago in *Google Street View*: Number 235. The dim sky's illumination made it difficult to tell whether someone was in the driver's seat. *Is that a head or the headrest?* I moved to the side and squinted. *Headrest.* "Jane must already be inside," I whispered, having no way of knowing my mother's current location. No lights shone inside the domicile's doors or windows, and no other vehicles were parked in the vicinity.

My wife nudged my ribs with her elbow. "Around the rear." She towed me through a dead patch in what used to be a trimmed hedge of Savannah holly.

We stood on a lush lawn of crabgrass. The wreckage of a picket fence fringed the property. A children's swing set and slide rusted in the small yard.

Are those voices? I clutched Jennifer's arm. "Thought I heard—" My straining ears only detected the pounding of my heart and the blood rushing behind my eardrums.

A drum meat smoker sat beside a pair of beach chairs stripped of webbing. I tripped on a plastic Barbie fashion doll embedded in the dirt, my knees and hands almost landing upon a hill of crushed beer bottles.

Jennifer crept to the back door and pressed her cheekbone against the flakes of turquoise pigment. As she mouthed, "Somebody's talking," I saw the whites of her eyes.

Chapter Nineteen

Monday Late Night—August 19, 2019—Day 8

MY HEAD SWIVELED ON A STIFF NECK. A shadowy figure emerged from a box I now registered as a wooden garden shed with a caved-in roof.

"¡Manos arriba!"

After realizing what the man wielded, a shotgun with a large revolving cylinder, I didn't need two years of Spanish lessons to comprehend to put my hands up. He aimed the Armsel Striker at the back door. The street sweeper's ventilated barrel thrust me against Jennifer's back when she turned the doorknob. We both tumbled indoors onto the filthy linoleum floor.

I stood up on shaky legs to protect Jennifer. "We're here to see Juan Carlos Delgado." I felt stupid blurting this next line. "My wife and I have an appointment!"

The man, his pecs swelling the front of a purple NEW ORLEANS JESTERS jersey, pointed at a card table surrounded by four chairs and topped with a lit Coleman propane lantern. *"Siéntate."*

I pulled out one seat for Jennifer, then sat catty-corner to her. The doors on the kitchen cabinets hung open, the crockery and glassware on the bottom shelves coated with layers of dried mud. My eyes tracked the ring of sediment marking the refrigerator, the window and curtains above the sink, the exhaust hood atop the stove, the group family photo on the wall, the doorway to the—

"Who are our new guests?"

A male in a white suit jacket with a matching vest and slacks sauntered into the room. *John Travolta in Saturday Night Fever?* Edith, my adoptive mom, loved reruns of the late '70s TV series *Fantasy Island*. From the black tie hanging from his neck to the black handkerchief neatly tucked into his breast pocket, this man in his early sixties could be Ricardo Montalbán's doppelgänger.

"Where's my mother? Where are Sarah and my brothers?" However much my eyes begged to water, I refused to let them start. "Let me see them!"

The person I now reasoned to be Juan Carlos Delgado nodded at the guy who had captured us. *"Antonio, mira si lo son. . . ."* He tapped his chest.

Antonio laid the 12-gauge on the countertop before roughly patting me down. With surprising delicacy, the thug checked Jennifer for wires and weapons. He confiscated our phones, powered them off, and placed them in a mixing bowl.

"Ricardo" stood close enough for me to see the glint of his golden belt buckle: a snarling lynx. "I am Juan Carlos Delgado." Although Wikipedia listed Delgado's birthplace as Mexico, he sounded American—Northeastern American. Either Juan had spent a lot of time in the United States, or he had strived to conceal all traces of a Spanish accent. *Maybe he graduated with a Ph.D. in drug trafficking at Harvard or Yale?* "You may call me Judge Delgado. You've met Antonio, my first lieutenant." He put out his right hand, the longish fingernails perfectly manicured. "And you are?"

I shook his hand in a daze. "Judge Delgado, I'm Paul Crutcher, and this is Jennifer, my wife. The woman who returned your goods is my mother. Jane."

Delgado crushed my palm, not letting go. "Answer truthfully, Mr. Crutcher. Did you contact the police?"

I stared directly into the Wildcat's eyes, darker *and deeper* than the Mariana Trench. "We just—"

He nodded again to his assistant, this instance extending his right pinkie.

Agile as a whipsnake, Antonio unsheathed a bone-handled knife from a leather case on his belt. Juan swatted my right wrist onto the tabletop and held firm. I curled my fingers beneath my palm until he gnarled, "Open your fist, or we will take hers! I'll begin with the one with the pretty ring."

Jennifer cried out when I splayed my fingers, the fingernails not nearly as well-groomed as his. "I swear to God, we didn't tell anybody we were coming here."

Up to the flash of carbon steel, my pinkie gyrating off the card table and rolling under the refrigerator, I still prayed they were bluffing. I wrenched my arm away, blood spattering a crimson arc across Delgado's pressed white jacket. Horrified, I shrieked—and, as my severed nerves squawked, "Code Red, Code Red—THIS IS NOT A TEST!!!" at my brain's overloaded cortices, I shrieked louder.

Delgado ignored the spreading bloodstains. For some weird reason—*I must be going into shock*—I pictured Juan's significant other scolding him for ruining Ricardo Montalbán's *Fantasy Island* ensemble. "I hate repeating myself, Mr. Crutcher. Did you contact the authorities?"

Woozy, I clutched the bleeding stump against my rib cage. *Don't pass out. Do not pass out. You cannot leave Jennifer alone with this lunatic.* I pinched the sensitive area to remain conscious. "No. I couldn't care less about your drugs." *Don't hurl, don't hurl.* "We only want our family back."

The third time Juan Carlos nodded to Antonio, I anticipated more carnage and reared backward. The chair rocked, dumping me onto the black and white tiles. *"Ayúdalo a levantarse. Consíguele un vendaje."*

Antonio restored the seat to an upright position and guided me to it. He wrapped a semi-sterile hand towel around the amputation. With the fresh wound screened from my sight—except for my whole arm feeling like it was jammed in a supercharged garbage disposal—I almost believed ligaments still attached my pinkie to my hand.

The Wildcat sat across from me. "I'm impressed, Mr. Crutcher. You've got," his cupped palms supported two giant make-believe testicles, "*cojones grandes*. Or," he rapped his temple, "you're *loco*."

"My mother gave you your drugs. Now, let us go."

"And that, Mr. Crutcher, is where our problem lies. Where are they?"

"Look, Juan, I know she's here." *Did I just call the head of the Silverio drug cartel by his first name? Are you trying to get beheaded?* "Her car is parked out front."

Jennifer bowed, clasping her hands in prayer. "Please, Judge Delgado, with due respect, Jane Baker has the Dragon's Breath. This afternoon, we helped her dig the fentanyl out of a hunting shack on the Pearl River. I saw the three plastic containers with my own two eyes. We agreed to come to this meeting together. When we woke up, she and the drugs were gone."

"Rodrigo! Sergio! *¡Tráelos aquí!*"

A door banged against a wall, followed by multiple shuffling feet. Glass crashed to the floor, accompanied by flesh smacking flesh and a muffled grunt. Ernie lurched into the kitchen, blood flowing from a gash bisecting his left eyebrow. Marvin doddered in after his brother. *Is he limping?* Difficult for me to establish with the twin's ankles trussed with rope. *Oh, how can I forget? Augustus shot Marvin in the leg!* Cord secured their arms behind their backs. Jane came next—our maternal bond causing me palpitations—seemingly unscathed. Her hazel eyes surveyed the room, heeding Jennifer, widening as she spotted my bandaged pinkie and the splash of red on Juan's suit. Cloths stuffed into the threesome's mouths prevented speech, but their frightened faces spoke volumes.

The youngest Baker did not proceed through the door as the last in line. Instead, two henchmen stepped into the kitchen, the taller and heavier one wearing a red and yellow XXL CARTA BLANCA T-shirt and the shorter and thinner one dressed for abuse in a medium-sized, white wife beater. My fear merged with my rage. "Where the fuck is Sarah? What have you done with her?"

Delgado swirled his hands, a Las Vegas magician performing his best trick. "The girl isn't in this house, but she's not far. My men are taking excellent care of her. Once I'm holding the goods you swindled, we'll discuss the requirements for her release."

"Ungag my mother."

The Wildcat dropped his chin a millimeter.

Antonio plucked the rag between Jane's lips and tossed it on the kitchen counter. He wiped her saliva on his khakis before unbinding her.

She hawked, spitting on the floor with the vehemence of a cobra. "I'm not giving you anything until my kids are safe."

Antonio, lightning-quick, hooked his arm, punching her in the kidney. My mother grasped for the refrigerator door, her back sliding down the avocado-green surface to land on her butt. Urine stained her tan pants, forming puddles on the white and black tiles. She raised both of her middle digits. "Fuck you, and fuck the ugly bitch that shat you out of her—"

Delgado's first lieutenant twined a fistful of Jane's mane around his one hand, drawing the bone-handled knife from its leather sheath with his free fingers. By Antonio's expression (a man with deep affection for his livelihood), I knew he intended to fillet my mother into strips of meat right in front of my bulging eyes.

Just as I coiled to dive at her aggressor—the two guards restrained Marvin and Ernie—Delgado's fingers sliced his own throat. "Antonio! *¡Deténgase!* We need her alive. Mrs. Baker still must tell us where she hid our product."

My hamstrings slackened when the blade reentered the subordinate's belt as rapidly as it had appeared. As Antonio seized Jane to slam her onto the fourth seat, Delgado's nostrils flared in distaste. He signaled the henchman exhibiting the most gang tattoos. *"Oye, Sergio, limpia a esta mujer."*

Sergio, long-faced with the unpleasant chore of bathing my mother, strong-armed her outside.

Juan put a hand in his jacket pocket and produced a cylindrical object I hoped wasn't a gun silencer. He unscrewed the metal tube's cap and jiggled out a fat cigar. After Juan utilized specialized scissors to snip the tip off, he gradually rotated the tobacco roll, warming the end with a fancy lighter linked to a silver chain. Satisfied with his preparations to inhale nicotine, the drug lord wedged the Havana in his mouth and passed me the sugar skull-embellished S.T. Dupont. "Mr. Crutcher," he requested through clamped lips, "would you be so kind as to light my Montecristo?"

I flicked up the lighter's lid and depressed the button to ignite the spark. The beast of prey's face came too close to mine, blue butane flames reflecting in hellish eyes as he puffed fumes redolent of rain-soaked earth.

We waited for Jane to return, the hissing lantern the only audible noise. Regardless of the Mexican cartel laying its mitts on the fentanyl, I felt certain we'd be leaving this house in body bags or fifty-gallon drums packed with lye. A similar fate for Sarah, wherever she might be. All these introspections saddened me. *Why am I so exhausted?*

A tiny voice spoke to me, Insecurity, the id whose foremost duty is to make me lose my confidence. *Paul, you've had a hard day, and it's way past your bedtime. But you were taking a snooze, weren't you, while your mother snuck out of the hotel to clean up your mess on her own? You're less than useless.* My eyeballs ached as if breaded with grits of sand. *Close your eyes, Paul.* My eyelids drooped farther. *You don't want to see Antonio take out his skinner. Be fast, fast asleep when he slits your cowardly throat. And what degradations will Jennifer endure as you—?*

I heard the back door shut and opened my eyes. Sergio stood Jane in front of his boss, her washed pants clinging to her legs.

"*Gracias, Sergio.* Better now, Mrs. Baker?" She glowered at Delgado. Rodrigo, the beefy guard, set a blue coffee saucer near his boss. Juan tapped cigar ashes into the dish and sighed. "We're all tired. Let's finish this transaction and call it a night. Talk."

"What guarantee do I have that you'll let Sarah and the rest of us go if I tell you where the drugs are?"

"Mrs. Baker, let me assure you, if you don't make full restitution, your whole family shall die—one by one—with you having a front-row seat."

"And if I do?"

Juan sucked on the Montecristo, blowing away a dense fog. He knocked the tobacco roll on the saucer's rim. A chunk of embers broke off and crumbled to gray dust. "Someone still has to pay the price. To be fair—people say I'm a civil man—I'll let you choose."

Jane gazed long and lovingly at each of us, impotent to single out the one to sacrifice. *She'll point at me, the new guy. Or Jennifer.*

"Mrs. Baker, need help?" Delgado touched the top of his head. "Let's put on our thinking caps."

I stared fixedly at the stopped wings on the "Singing Birds" wall clock. *7:45. Was 7:45 a.m. the minute the second levee breached, flooding the Ninth Ward and wiping out hundreds of residents?* I remembered the red X spray-painted on the gable of the house I now sat within. 3D filled the lower quadrant, a symbol you never dreamed of seeing written on your own home. How did the three inhabitants die? Which rooms? Did the family, possibly sleeping at this early hour, drown in their own beds, raveled up in cotton sheets? Were mother, father, and innocent trapped in the attic, clawing at the rafters as the water reached their noses? I peered around the kitchen. Maybe they perished here in this room, as we five no doubt will? The family must be dead, or they'd have returned to get their belongings. I sensed ghosts floating within the space, their restless presences heavy upon my chest. *God, if you help us, I will be your humble servant for the remainder of my life. Please, Lord, let—*

The Wildcat indicated the thrashed twins. "I paid the Baker boys to accomplish nothing more complex than to pick up and deliver my product. Middlemen in a chain of hundreds. Yet, the two ingrates judged my compensation inadequate. Those lazy *pedazos de mierda* cheated me." Juan noticed the blood blotching his white *Fantasy Island* costume and frowned. He spun to Jennifer and me. "Mr. and Mrs. Crutcher, what are your thoughts? Mr. Crutcher, you traveled to Alabama to locate and meet your biological mother. Is that right?" I locked my eyes on his, not yielding a reply. "Your newfound brothers may have roped you into their childlike hustles, but that night, weren't you with them on that boat, the *Chum Runner*? You shot Mr. Dawson, a loyal employee, and then you stole the Dragon's Breath—*my Dragon's Breath.* That sinful act makes you a willing accomplice, even the heist's mastermind."

How does he know all this? I pictured an Amazonian woman standing in the doorway of a Greyhound bus-sized recreational vehicle. *Was it Ruby?*

"And your adoring wife?" Delgado gestured at Jennifer. "Guilt by association. Give your mom a hand. Should we settle the score and let some of us get on with our lives, or do you all wish to be buckets of chum by morning light?"

I didn't know the moisture levels inside Jennifer's mouth, but my tongue became too dry to form words. I could only moan.

Juan pretended to shoot craps on the card table. "How about we roll dice? Or let's have Antonio draw a name out of a hat?" He dipped his fingers in an imaginary top hat. "Sorry, my dear, one of your kiddos must pick the short straw." Juan held up a handful of nonexistent straws, his face elongating into comical shock as he flaunted the shortest. Although the dice, slips of paper, and straws weren't there, I clearly saw these props in his grip, each illusion eroding my stomach lining with surplus bile.

Tears streaked down Jane's cheeks. "Judge, I ask that you just punish me. Don't hurt my kids."

Juan outstretched his palm. "Brave choice—*a mother's choice.* You understand what this means?"

"Yes. I do."

"Your decision will be final. No changing your mind."

She hesitated, then clenched his hand. "I stashed the containers in a motorboat a few lots down the road underneath a pile of DirecTV satellite dishes." The élan vital drained from her lovely eyes, leaving the orbs dull and lifeless.

"Rodrigo, revisa el bote. ¡Apuro!"

The pudgy man readjusted the green, brown, and black camouflaged Glock shoved behind his back before dashing through the back door. Sergio positioned Jane on the floor in front of the refrigerator. He took over Rodrigo's station, arms crossed and teed off. I suspected his acrimony grew from his boss not assigning him the more important task of repossessing the fent.

Delgado smiled. "Now, we wait." He pivoted to me, puffing his Montecristo. "While running background checks on you two, I saw Paul's books on Amazon. The historical novel about the Confederate soldier starting a new life in San Diego sounds intriguing. Alas, my time is too limited for recreational reading. Plus, my eyes get tired, and I always end up dozing off. Are there audio versions I can listen to in the car?"

"No." I questioned his motives, creeped out by the notion that the narcotrafficker had the addresses for our home and the midtown building Jennifer worked in. *The Wildcat probably knows the brand of toothpaste we use and how we buy a slice of pepperoni pizza and a churro at Costco every Tuesday evening.* "I can't afford to pay a professional narrator to record the audiobooks."

Juan waved the cigar. "Newspapers, magazines, paper books—all obsolete media, Paul. 'He who denies change is the architect of decay. The only institution,' Juan scratched his jaw, 'human institution, which rejects progress, is the graveyard.' One of Harold Wilson's finer quotes."

Is Delgado impressing on me that he's college-educated, not just a run-of-the-mill hoodlum?

His brown irises constricted, dilating the pupils to an ominous shade of pitch-black. "Mr. Crutcher, have you considered writing a biography?" His face hovered near enough for me to smell his breath: Cuban tobacco harvested by Cubans in Cuban tobacco fields.

Whatever vile ruminations roamed beneath his clipped scalp, I possessed no desire to let these sadistic cerebrations see the light of day. I shook my head. Seconds later, Curiosity (the malignant spirit daring us to burn our fingertips on every hot stove) forced Impulse (the inciter culpable for getting us all in trouble) to open my mouth. "Why?"

"Are you familiar with *narcocorridoes*?"

I once read an article in *Time* magazine on how some popular Spanish songs glorified the unstoppable smuggling trade and paid godlike tribute to the cruel men reaping the benefits. "Drug ballads?"

"There are a zillion highly viewed music videos praising myself and my colleagues on *YouTube*. Have you read *El Chapo, The Man, the Mind, and the Mystery*?"

I had to mind my p's and q's around this fiend. "No, is it good?"

Juan spread his fingers and wiggled all five. "So-so. I'm dubious that the biographer ever personally interviewed Joaquín. Mr. Crutcher, I am convinced you could do a superior job. Interested in a new project?"

Is he serious? "Judge Delgado, I—"

"I'll pay you well for your labor. Is a million US dollars to start and a healthy bonus upon completion acceptable?"

"The money's not the issue. It's—"

His gaudy gold wedding band (a pouncing lynx with embedded red rubies for eyes and glittering diamonds for fangs) rapped the tabletop twice. "Two mil? Won't go any higher. I can easily find a more enthusiastic author."

To type on a standard keyboard, I'd need to adapt to my present disability by using my ring finger instead of my pinkie to hit the P and the nearest punctuation keys. Quotation marks would be a reach, and an excessive span to spear Enter. I practiced stretching my fourth digit sideways, the raw stub next to it stinging like holy hell. The white bandage turned revolting red as sticky hemoglobin dripped down my wrist. *Will the new skin eventually overgrow the exposed bone? Can a surgeon sew the fingertip back on if I bring my pinkie to a hospital before it rots?* I squinted beneath the refrigerator, unable to see the digit I favored for nose-picking. *My finger is under there somewhere. I'll wash the grime off and put it in a bag of ice.*

Juan brooded, checking his bejeweled wristwatch for the umpteenth time. "Well?"

I angled myself to define Jennifer's demeanor. *Yes? No? Maybe?* Her bloodless skin, jittery eyes, and compressed lips silently screamed, "Paul, the Wildcat will kill us if you don't hurry up and say yes!"

Antonio's street sweeper, a 12-gauge shotgun on steroids, rested on the countertop alongside the sink. *Can I grab the gun before he slices and dices me with his bone-handled pigsticker?* Delgado's first lieutenant held his cell phone to his ear. *Antonio is speaking to Rodrigo. Or it's his wife. "Baby, please don't wait up. I've got gringos to slaughter. Yep, yep, I'll pick up a gallon of milk for Antonio Jr. on the way home. Love you too!" Does Antonio also carry a handgun? No holster, and I don't recall him holding one. He might keep it in the back of his khakis, like Rodrigo. Where is Rodrigo?* Sergio swept sheer curtains from the back door's dirty glass to scan the backyard. He turned to us, shaking his head in exasperation. *The boat is just a hundred yards away. Rodrigo should be back by now. If I'm making a move, now may be the only time.* My quads prepared to spring.

"Antonio, ¿hablaste con Rodrigo?" Juan approached his first lieutenant. *"¿Por qué está tomando tanto tiempo?"*

The back door swung inward, whamming Sergio square in the backbone. He drew his snub-nosed revolver, spinning his body to open the door fully. A male garbed in a MARDI GRAS BOURBON STREET tee and tan Bermuda shorts stumbled through the doorway with his arms upraised. A bald and beady-eyed man prodded the stranger inside the crowded kitchen using the tip of his machine pistol. Come to tell, our new cocaptive wasn't unknown to us after all. *That's our Uber driver, Gervais!*

Juan bellowed, *"Dante, ¿quien es este?"*

Dante raised his shoulders. "I found him in the bushes."

Gervais glanced at me furtively, his lips shaping words I couldn't interpret. I looked away. . .but not fast enough. Delgado had caught me arching my eyebrows.

The Wildcat's fingers dug into my clavicle. "You know him?"

Jennifer spoke out. "Jane took our rental car, so I hailed an Uber. This man picked us up at our hotel and drove us here. We told him to wait for—"

Juan slugged Gervais in the solar plexus. The driver keeled over, uttering an "oof" sound and clutching his middle. The drug baron towered over the crumpled driver in an MMA stance, both fists clenched. "Who are you, and what are you doing here?"

"Like da lady said," Gervais groaned, "I drove dem. Making extra cash to send my son to college."

"If you let me use my phone," my wife held out her hand, "I can show you his profile picture on the Uber app."

Juan gestured at Antonio. Jennifer tapped several icons and handed the device to Juan.

The Wildcat, a Spanish inquisitor jonesing to administer the strappado to an impenitent heretic, ripped into Gervais. "Why were you hiding?"

"No one's hiding." Gervais grunted as Dante poked the machine pistol into his spine. "Drank too much Starbucks. Had to piss." The Uber driver scowled. "Mister, I've driven carloads of tourists down to the Ninth to buy grass, coke, women—you name it, whatever dey want. Don't give two shits about the things other folks do in their spare time. This man can stay in his own lane. Und usually," Gervais winked, "my clients are pleased with my service, und I get a generous tip."

Delgado roared, *"Antonio, ¿qué le pasó a Rodrigo?"*

The first lieutenant selected a contact on his cell phone and activated the speakerphone. We listened to Rodrigo's cheery voicemail greeting. *"Hola, este es Rodrigo. Deje su nombre y número y me pondré en contacto con usted lo antes possible."*

"Dante, go after him." Juan's fingers simulated a cocked gun. *"¡Ten cuidado!"* The bald man rocketed out the back door, raising the machine pistol. Juan flung Gervais onto our card table's fourth chair. He smoothed his suit lapels, then eased into his seat. Now, we had enough players for a fun game of pinochle *or* a not-so-fun game of Russian roulette.

With Rodrigo and Dante gone from the room, that left Sergio, Antonio, and, obviously, the Wildcat himself. Sergio drank water from a bottle while Antonio tried to reach Rodrigo on his phone. Jane remained on the tiled floor with her back against the refrigerator. Ernie and Marvin, muzzled and constrained, stood in the corner as if being punished by a strict schoolmaster for horseplay. The junior twin's posture leaned to the right. *His bum leg must be killing him.*

My eyes passed over the street sweeper—a machine designed to obliterate expeditiously and efficiently in close-quarter situations. *Can I get to the shotgun?* I estimated the steps required to reach the counter without Antonio or Sergio blocking me. *Three, four—five? Can I even operate it? For starters, how to toggle off the safety? Of course you do, Paul. Eddie and Marvin taught you to fire all types of weapons, and you've proven you're a straight shooter.*

Juan lifted his Cuban cigar and examined its smoldering end. The Wildcat resumed our previous conversation as though not a thing was wrong, just another paper-pushin' day at the office. "Mr. Crutcher, have you decided? Will you tell the story of my life?"

I stuck out my palm as if negotiating business deals with pathological drug kingpins was commonplace for me. "Judge

Delgado, I'd be proud to write about you." Jennifer leaned back in her chair, visibly relieved. "If I may, I only request that you allow—" *Is that a siren? Cops?*

"¡Jodeme!" Juan bounded to his feet, flipping the table with both hands. The blue saucer and cigar slid onto my lap as the propane lamp rolled off the edge, struck the floor, and extinguished. The Wildcat, outlined by the heat lightning flashing in the kitchen window, uplifted his snout. "Is that smoke?"

I, too, distinguished the sooty odor of conflagrant wood as the staccato blare of an ambulance, fire truck, or law enforcement vehicle strengthened.

Sergio bent to peek through the back door. *"Probablemente alguien esté quemando basura."*

In a stupor, I gaped at the ceiling. Gray smog flowed from the central hallway, under the doorframe, and across the old-fashioned tin tiles. *The house is on fire.*

Delgado, his head in the clouds, coughed. "*¡Imbécil!* Nobody's burning garbage at this hour." He faced the corridor, cursing under his breath. Red and yellow lights illuminated the spindles and handrail of a staircase leading to the upper level. *"¡El piso de arriba está en llamas! ¡Vamoose!"*

I noticed the sirens had stopped wailing. *The paramedics, firefighters, or police have arrived at their destination—which isn't here.* Somebody thumped thrice on the back door.

Sergio yanked the door open. On the stoop, a bald man with a machine pistol slung over his shoulder gawked downward at something glistening in his hands. As his fingers wrapped around the sheeny object and his biceps flexed—*is he stabbing himself?*—the flat length of steel retracted into his stomach. Dante's bloody lips spluttered, "*Jefe*," before he toppled head-first onto the kitchen floor.

I flew off my seat, arms straining for the shotgun by the sink. Three short blasts, deafening in the small room, whizzed past my ears to drill holes in the refrigerator door inches above Jane's head. The black 12-gauge protruded over the countertop. Not feeling any bullets strike me, my fingers groped for the metal folding stock. The scattergun teetered, fell, ricocheted off my skull, and clattered to the floor as I smashed into the moldy cabinets. I snatched the Armsel Striker and whirled. Flames radiating from the hallway floodlit the erupting mayhem.

Jennifer tugged Gervais out of his chair, towing him by the arm behind the overturned tabletop.

Jane scuttled across the cruddy linoleum to huddle beside me.

Ernie (his wrists and ankles still fettered) hopped as though competing in a sack race to oppose Sergio. Simultaneously, Marvin bounced in Antonio's direction.

Juan had disappeared. *He must have run into the foyer to escape through the front door.*

A man, a hulking goliath, materialized in the back doorway. Long black hair brushed his strapping shoulders. He wore a black pullover and black tactical pants. A short sword—*is that blood on the blade?*—hung from his hand.

I had no time to identify this newcomer or calculate how he fit within this unbalanced equation. Although I had figured out the way to click off the shotgun's safety (a cross-bolt close to the trigger), I couldn't risk taking a shot without accidentally hitting one of my family members.

At the exact instant Sergio aimed his Smith & Wesson at Ernie, my half-brother head-butted him in the breadbasket. Antonio pulled his bone-handled knife on Marvin. Ernie, no longer seeing the snub-nosed revolver in the sinewy guard's fist, flashed shark teeth. Marvin, not so charmed, bobbed and weaved away from Antonio's slashing blade.

My mother unbuckled her belt and slipped the leather strip through the pants loops. She attacked Antonio from behind, standing on her tiptoes to wrap the waistband around the man's windpipe. Marvin used this opportunity to ram his forehead into the first lieutenant's arched groin. The knife fell, the tip impaling the soft linoleum. Antonio elbowed Jane in her side, but she didn't release her garrote until he backed her against a cabinet, the edge jabbing her bruised kidney. When I elevated the gun to let loose a scattering of shot, my wife darted into my line of fire, holding Antonio's blade.

Ernie and Sergio, entwined in struggle, barreled into me, whacking the street sweeper from my grasp. I lost my footing on a slick of Dante's bodily fluids, ass-planting onto the floor. I reached out blindly for the 12-gauge.

A female yelled. *Jennifer? Jane?* In panic, I gazed upward the moment my wife carved a knife across Antonio's midriff horizontally. The skin below his belly button split open like a burlap bag full of angry eels. As the gutted man sank to his knees in dread, ropey intestines spilled through his twitching fingers to splatter the white tiles. I dry-heaved as Antonio stuffed his innards back inside his gaping abdominal cavity.

Gervais unstrapped Marvin's hands and feet. I heard a contrasting high-pitched shout, this one male. *Ernie?*

Sergio had generated the earsplitting squeal. In the heat of engagement, I somehow forgot about the person responsible for skewering Dante. *Is that brute really here to liberate us?* Sergio was lying on top of Ernie (I recognized Delgado's lackey by the white wife beater stretched over his pimply shoulders). *Where is his head?* My eyes watered from the smoke. *Oh, there it is, near the oven.* Sergio rested on his right ear, goggling at me with open-mouthed bewilderment—a man whose daily routine has been ruined by a sequence of unforeseeable and unfortunate events.

Our guardian angel used his boot to roll Sergio's torso off of Ernie's stomach. The tattooed goon flopped onto his back. Blood pumping from his pharynx slowed to a trickle.

I sputtered, "Who *are* you?"

He aimed his short sword at the bright hallway. "Go after the guy in charge. You can't let him get away."

As during the emotional stressfulness of my father's funeral, opaqueness blackened the boundaries of my vision. My alter ego, Powerless Paul, shepherded me to sweet, sweet oblivion. "Wha—did—you—just—?"

The big man slapped my cheek, not unkindly, but with enough potency to reboot my neural network. "He's the only person alive who knows what you all look like."

Outrage spiced with the hottest level of violence coursed throughout my veins. I yearned to watch the Wildcat slow roast on a spit—*to suffer as he had made us suffer.*

Jennifer squeezed Gervais' hand. "I instructed you to leave. Why didn't you?"

"From da funny way you were acting, I knew something bad was fixin' to go down. When I saw," the Uber driver shook his head with disdain at Antonio, "drag you into da house, I phoned 911."

My wife hugged him tightly. "We will always be grateful."

"Save your gratitude." Gervais sulked. "The po-po never showed. Da mayor und his cronies don't give a damn 'bout da poor folks in the Ninth Ward."

I clinched his arm. "Forgive us for putting you through this."

Gervais asked in a low voice, "What about. . .him?"

My eyes traced a wide trail of red slop to the back door. Delgado's first lieutenant had crawled across the kitchen floor—a Herculean effort if I ever saw one. His hand reached for the doorknob. No matter how much I despised him for taking my finger, I experienced a trifling amount of compassion.

Jane gasped. "How is he still alive?"

"Not for long," the nameless man growled, bulldozing past me with the dripping sword gripped in his iron fist. He came close to finishing Antonio off, but Jennifer was nearer and swifter. As the cartel lieutenant twisted his head to plead for his life or perhaps to enchant a dying man's curse, my wife jabbed his own bone-handled knife into his left eyeball, all the way to the hilt. Antonio shuddered once, then slumped against the back door.

For a second, I listened to the upper floor snap, crackle, and pop, trying to blot out the horrors I had just witnessed. Side by side on the couch, Jennifer and I had viewed all nine gory seasons of *The Walking Dead*. How often had we seen Daryl, Carol, Michonne, or Rick stab a walker in the eye socket? *"Get 'em in the brains, Carl!"* Did my better half learn this execution technique by watching a fictional TV series? The former sheriff drawled within my head, *"We don't kill the living."*

"Up and at 'em!" Ernie's defender cut my half-brother's bonds and hauled him erect. "I'll get Jane and your family out of the house before the roof collapses." He pulled the missing street sweeper from the sink and passed me ten pounds of terror. The burly man waved the sword at the front door.

I ran from the relative coolness of the kitchen into the blazing corridor. The super-heated air scorched my lungs. Embers singed the hair off my skin as I bolted through the inferno, speculating, *How did that guy know my mother's name? And that Ernie and Marvin are part of my family?* I slipped on an unseen object, tipping a side table covered with picture frames filled with the sunny smiles of the long-dead. My arms extended, I careened along the entryway, predicting a fall. I bashed into the solid oak front door, clinging to the knob, afraid to discover it locked. The brass lever retracted the latch from the strike plate. *Thank you, God!* I plunged over the doorsill and down the seven brick stairs. In the distance, lightning flashed, and thunder rumbled. The heavens opened, and the downpour began.

Chapter Twenty

Tuesday Early Morning—August 20, 2019—Day 9

I STRUGGLED TO MY FEET, KNEES AND ELBOWS SCRAPED AND BLEEDING, to scan the vicinity for Juan Carlos Delgado. Even though Father Time had rotated Mother Earth well beyond midnight, with the top of the house engulfed in flames, I had no need for a flashlight. The rutted street, uneven sidewalk, rioting camellia, and live oaks draped in Spanish moss were brilliant orange beneath low thunderheads. Our rental car, the green Subaru, sat in the same spot. *How did Delgado get here? Somebody dropped him off? Drug lords don't walk to their drug deals, do they?*

The Wildcat drove away, Dum-Dum. That didn't feel right to me. *We'd have seen his car when we arrived.*

In the lane, my eyes swept past the Forester's wet hood for the only living human capable of sending a hit squad after us. And, of timely importance, the solitary person able to inform me of Sarah's whereabouts.

Not far behind me, the Mississippi River burbled into the Gulf of Mexico. In the direction from which Gervais had driven us, the lights of police cruisers spun blue and red beams onto the trees and houses. *Is that a motorboat? The cops must have discovered the drugs underneath the satellite dishes. That's the reason the sirens quit. But how did the authorities know to stop there? Rodrigo! Juan sent Rodrigo to bring back the stash.* I envisioned our savior standing in the doorway, blood dripping down the short sword swinging in his arm. *Law enforcement found Rodrigo. Rodrigo is dead. The guy with the sword chopped off his head. Time to find Delgado, make him tell me where Sarah is, and put an end to this nightmare.*

And if I catch the Wildcat, will he be armed?

The ravenous fire hadn't finished with the house on Alabo Street. Embers shot out of holes in the roof, and hungry flames licked black soot from cracks in the upper glass. Plywood covered the lower level's front windows. I wondered if this building, soon to be a pile of ash, had a cellar. *Could Sarah be down there? Too hot to go back inside.* I backed away, praying that Jennifer and the rest of my family had exited safely, ill at ease about leaving my loved ones with the strange swordsman. *Why are you worrying about him? That good Samaritan saved us!*

Again, I peered down the road at the police activity. Two officers set up red-and-white barricades and unfurled yellow crime scene tape. *This place should be teeming with firefighters. Where are they?* I remembered Gervais' complaints regarding the city hall. *Maybe the fire chief believes the rain will put out the fires.*

Sarah could be anywhere, the next house or a hundred miles away. Delgado (unless he hitched a ride from a deputy or swam across the Big Muddy) had to be nearby.

In the backyard, at the corner opposite the falling-down shed, a pair of reflective amber disks hovered above a tangle of ivy. A great horned owl screeched, taking wing from the small outbuilding's roof.

Tire tracks filled with rainwater led to a whitewashed garage door. *Locked.* I tracked hurried shoe prints. *Juan's hiding inside.* I elevated the 12-gauge to eye level and kicked the side door. The termite-infested wood gave way, my right heel punching through to the other side. When I withdrew my lower limb from the fragments, someone—*Delgado!*—grabbed my foot. Pain shot up my calf as he twisted my ankle 180 degrees. Crucial internal support mechanisms stretched and snapped. I yelped, my left leg pitching me face-first into the mud.

With dull amazement, I realized I retained the shotgun. I contorted my body to aim the street sweeper's vented barrel at the door. I squeezed the trigger once—the sudden recoil and report bruising my armpit and eardrums—then three additional times in rapid succession. Spherical pellets traced a diagonal line of destruction along the panel, mullion, and bottom rail.

Although the ankle-wrenching ceased after a moan and a thump, the searing ache intensified. And to make matters worse, fresh blood leaking out of the dishrag bandaging my pinkie coated my shooting finger. I extracted my sneaker from the splinters. My shoulder rammed the door. The entrance to the garage was impeded by something heavy.

I hobbled around the building by hanging onto clumps of green ivy. A window on the side of the structure provided a vantage of Delgado's ride, a gleaming Range Rover. The SUV's size prevented me from determining his current location or physical condition. I used the shotgun's metal buttstock to smash the glass, swiping away the jagged edges with the muzzle. I glared at my throbbing ankle—*it feels busted, not sprained*— and my bloodstained fingers. *How am I supposed to get up in there?*

"Need a boost?"

My overtaxed vascular organ practically split a seam as I pirouetted on one pin, almost toppling in astonishment. The swordsman, with stringy hair sticking to the sides of his face, stooped, interlacing his fingers to give me a leg up. I put my foot in the stirrup. "Alley-oop," he whispered, lifting me across the windowsill.

Am I detecting self-gratification in his tone? I nose-dived into WEED & FEED fertilizer bags, solidified by the flood, yet softer than landing on the hard cement. Swordsman—*the man still hasn't shared his name*—passed me the 12-gauge. He stuck up his thumb and grinned—this final bit of encouragement sending chills along my vertebrae.

I ducked under the Land Rover, too dark to discern much beyond the exhaust pipes. The street sweeper's drum magazine rasped the rough floor as I slithered forward. I peeped past the vehicle's fender with my cheek against the chrome grill.

A black, leathery object was lying near a child's blue tricycle. I crawled closer. Bone, fractured and stained red, extended from the inside of a wingtip shoe. Whimpering whirled my head. A few feet from the side door, Delgado wallowed in fluids with viscosities vastly different from Quaker State motor oil. The Wildcat clutched about for his missing paw. His pad, toes, and claws really weren't lost—they were safely tucked within the Louis Vuitton shoe next to me. His other paw, the expensive footwear punctured in a hundred places by birdshot, appeared ready to fall to pieces. The condition of his white *Fantasy Island* suit? An Olympic-sized swimming pool filled with Spray 'n Wash wouldn't clean that bloody mess.

I wondered why the Drug Lord hadn't driven away. Maybe Antonio had the keys to the Land Rover.

Juan's eyelids fluttered. He recognized his visitor—*the Grim Reaper*—his lips parting wide enough to croak, "Let me live—and I'll give you whatever you—money—drugs."

The soles of my Nikes squished in his expanding circle of biofluids. I upraised the wingtip with the inner workings wrapped in the argyle sock. "If you don't tell me where Sarah is right now, I will club you to death with your own shoe." *There's not much time. He's bleeding out.*

A snippet of the vivacity I had seen in Juan's eyes when he clamped my wrist to help Antonio lop off my pinkie resurfaced. *"¡Vete al infierno!"*

My damaged foot stomped on his remaining foot, the brutal force tearing the bands of tissue holding my anklebone together. Surprisingly, I sensed no bodily injury, only wrath. That I had caused this man to howl like a banshee both appalled and intoxicated me. I repeatedly trampled his perforated Louis Vuitton, my mind an awakened hive of killer hornets. At that moment, I didn't care if we ever found Sarah. I just longed to hear Juan scream and scream—each time with more gusto. *All sons become their fathers.*

Incessant pounding on the outbuilding's siding halted my heel in mid-flight. I gimped to the big garage door and turned the lock. The horizontal panels lifted, revealing five sets of legs silhouetted by the burning house. I floundered outside, hoping the rain would cleanse away my mortal sins.

Jennifer rushed to hug me, her eyes welling up. "Sweetie!"

I handed her the shotgun, its lethal weight now a burden. *Jane's here. So are Marvin and Ernie. And there's the swordsman.* "Where's the Uber driver?"

"Gervais took off. Said he had fares to pick up." My wife shrugged. "I got his number, in case we," she caught sight of Delgado, "ever—need—it."

Swordsman's eyes bore into me. "Is he dead?"

Delgado lay in the same position beside the Range Rover. *Is his chest moving?* I replied, "I don't think so."

The not-so-gentle giant stepped forward, brandishing his sword.

Jane deterred him, her gaze swiveling to me. "Did he say where Sarah is?"

I mumbled, "No. I—"

My mother ran inside the building. "Jesus," she muttered, "what happened to him?"

I kneeled alongside her, our pants recoloring maroon.

Jane lightly slapped Juan's face. "Rise and shine, shitbag! Where's my daughter?" He groaned, then fell mute. She cuffed him again, this round hard enough to rock his head. "I know you can hear me! Where's Sarah?"

Is he breathing? I placed my ear an inch above Delgado's nostrils, hearing and feeling nothing. *Call the meat wagon. He's toast.*

The retired caregiver placed her lips over the supine man's open mouth and blew. When his ribs rose, she started compressions. "You ain't dyin' till you tell me where my kid is. Breathe, bottom feeder!"

And after a few more repetitions, Juan began breathing on his own. A miracle, *for us.*

As my mother returned to the business at hand, a task the CIA terms "enhanced interrogation," I snagged her arm. "Hang on." I staggered to a workbench to select a blowtorch with a flint striker from the tools rack. "This should do the job." I cranked the knob on the propane cylinder to release the gas, then pressed the striker's handle. A pinpoint of blue flame grew out of the brass burner tube. "Try this, Mom."

I lowered the garage door, and we got to work.

Chapter Twenty-One

Tuesday Morning—August 20, 2019—Day 9

SUBARU DESIGNED THE FORESTER TO CARRY FIVE PASSENGERS. Somehow, we fit in six adults with Ernie curled up in the cargo area. Although my right hand and ankle hurt like the dickens, I still demanded to drive. My clothing stank of charred flesh, as did my mother's, but I guess the stink was worth the reward. With a little perseverance, she and I forced an address from the Wildcat (his final words). I won't go into the grisly details now—and in good conscience, shouldn't ever. We were on our way to Reynes Street, only a mile and change away.

In the passenger seat, Jennifer peered up from the GPS and unfolded her left arm. "Turn at Forstall Street."

I glanced in the rearview. Jane sat in the backseat, bookended by Marvin and Hank Russman (I pried the name out of the man I had designated Swordsman). My mother appeared tense: her eyelids closed, and her lips clenched. *After what she did, what we did, I don't blame her one bit.* I hunched over the steering wheel, my eyes directed at my own reflection. *Do I look different? No, why would you?* My intestines knotted. *You're a murderer, and you'll always be a murderer—for the rest of your murderous life.*

"Be careful, Paul." My wife, also a new member of the Murderers' Club, caressed my shoulder. "You almost sideswiped that car."

"Sorry." I cranked the windshield wipers to a faster setting.

She pointed. "Pull in here and park."

I locked the Forester, dragging my heels as the others hurried by an unoccupied lot. Russman no longer carried the short sword. *He had the blade when he used the point to puncture the Land Rover's gas tank.* Once Ernie set the gasoline puddle aflame using the sugar skull-embellished cigar lighter, Marvin gave a brief and scathing eulogy. "Juan Carlos Delgado, may you roast in hell for all of eternity."

Holy Cross loomed across a grass field that hadn't been touched by a lawnmower's blade since the day Katrina marched through town. We advanced to the red-brick high school on a dirt footpath partially sheltered from the torrent by a grove of hickory trees. Blue tarp covered expanses of the sparsely shingled roof. Windows not shattered by hooligans hurling stones mirrored the grayness of predawn. On the second-floor balcony, in a section not sprayed with layers of colorful graffiti, a girl's face (portrayed by a talented artist with black and white paint) beamed skyward with a child's eternal hope.

The abandoned schoolhouse looked spooky under the lightning strikes; no radiance from within. *It feels all wrong.*

Marvin had acquired a stout stick to support his injured leg. He leaned on the make-do cane, stretching open a gash in the vine-laced chain-link fence. One after another, we eased past the metal spikes into the asphalt schoolyard. We stood for a moment listening to rainwater run down the building's slanted roofs, flow along lengthy gutters, and finally gush from broken downspouts.

Ernie drew abreast. "This is a big place. Delgado didn't tell you where Sarah is, exactly?"

I squeegeed rain off my cheeks with the crook of my arm. "I don't believe the Wildcat knew what room, just that his men are holding her here. They're probably awaiting his call."

My half-brother patted his waistband for the hardness of Sergio's revolver. "Who is Russman? And why is he still tagging along?"

Out of the corner of my eye, I caught our new acquaintance eavesdropping on our conversation. I bunched my lips in a tight line.

Ernie cupped his hand to my ear. "I don't like that fella. Don't trust him."

A cross, curiously white and immaculate, hung high on the tower. As we approached Holy Cross, beneath the symbol of Jesus' crucifixion, I prayed we weren't in for an equivalent end.

After Russman guided us under a semi-circular arch and through a set of double doors, he upraised his palm. The man thumped his chest, then pointed his index finger sideways. *He's signaling he's going around the back. Former military? Mercenary? It makes sense for us to come at the kidnappers from opposing angles. Right?* When Russman hustled outside, I noticed the butt of a camo-colored Glock tucked in his belt. *Rodrigo's?*

I fingered the crosshatching on the street sweeper's safety. *How many shells remain? Does the magazine hold eight? Ten? Possibly twelve? I used four. That leaves? How do I check?*

Jennifer had scooped up our cell phones as she escaped the burning kitchen. I switched on my iPhone's flashlight. The tiny LED barely illuminated the spacious one-hundred-forty-year-old lobby. Two sets of staircases ascended immediately ahead of us, the ornate stringers flaking, most of the balusters missing. One flight of buckled steps climbed to the left; the other stairs, in worse repair, rose to the right. I swung my head from side to side, only hearing the raging storm. *Which way? Where would the abductors keep Sarah?* I trod upon the white fangs of a roaring orange-and-black-striped tiger medallion that read GO TIGERS! and over a heap of folding tables into the east wing.

Glass shards crunched under my sneakers. Cobwebs clung to my face. Electrical and plumbing fixtures were cluttered everywhere. Cardboard cartons loaded with student directories were stacked adjacent to an administrator's office. A scavenger had ripped a drinking fountain from a wall to cut out the copper pipes.

Rows of corroded lockers lined the water-damaged corridor, their open doors exposing mildewed algebra, biology, geography, and history textbooks. A long-gone teenager had taped a *People* magazine cover image of Lindsay Lohan inside a locker. Green spots grew on the *Mean Girls* star's rosy cheeks like flesh-eating bacteria. On the neighboring vented door, Jamie Foxx, the leading man of the biographical movie *Ray*, sat at a grand piano, a pair of opaque Ray-Bans perched above a veneered grin.

Public address loudspeakers were mounted over bare fire extinguisher cabinets. On Monday, August 29, 2005, these halls had resounded with hurricane warnings—each more urgent than the last. Pure pandemonium must have ensued as the kids evacuated the building, leaving their belongings behind.

We inched past numbered rooms, stopping every few feet to look and listen. Some classrooms prevailed untouched, with wooden desks arranged in orderly rows, children's crayon drawings of people and animals tacked to corkboards, and scientific diagrams or mathematical formulas scribbled on chalkboards as if written hours ago. Other classrooms, seemingly chosen at random by a malevolent entity, were completely trashed, with desks chopped into firewood, tipped metal shelves, floors strewn with books, and blackboards chalked with cartoonish likenesses, violent threats, and graphic pornography.

Smudged windows overlooked a square courtyard. Lightning flashes left afterimages of a two-tier water fountain clogged with muck. Saplings sprouting from cracks in the concrete reached the third floor.

The ceiling had collapsed into the gymnasium, the once-polished basketball court now warped and way beyond buffing. Rain drenched a jumble of debris at half-court. Black and orange Holy Cross Tigers banners, one for each winning year, hung above rows of bleachers, too high for even the tallest gang member to spray-paint gang signs.

Much of the cafeteria remained remarkably intact, despite sagging vinyl ceiling tiles dripping rainwater onto rows of bench tables. Near a pair of looted cash registers, carbohydrate-deprived animals had raided an ice cream cooler containing boxes of Blue Bell Mooo Bars.

Jars of Vlasic dill pickles and cans of B&M baked beans stocked shelves in the industrial kitchen. Atop the gas stove, an open yearbook, filled with the autographed faces of teenage men and women now in their thirties, rested beside a fry pan brimming with rancid cooking oil.

No Sarah.

The west wing contained more defiled classrooms and a row of windows facing another weed-infested courtyard. We entered a stairwell leading upward. Water cascading down the steps washed gum wrappers and cigarette butts past our climbing feet. Forty feet above our heads, a shredded blue tarp flapped against a blustery sky.

On the second floor, recently installed steel crosspieces shored long sections of the bowed ceiling. Repeatedly, we halted to prick up our ears, only catching the sounds of blowing wind and rushing water.

We ducked under scaffolding into the band rehearsal room. An upright piano was lying like a turtle flipped on its back, its black and white keys spread across reams of sheet music. A copper kettledrum converted into a cooking grill collected gray ashes and white bones.

Still no Sarah. Did Delgado lie to us? How could he? My mother held the blowtorch to his balls.

Someone had torn off the door to the girls' bathroom and carried it away. A thief had rifled the Kotex and Playtex dispensers for quarters. Swollen sanitary napkin and tampon packages were scattered on the wet tiles. Boxy monitors blocked the computer lab's doorway. I thrust aside shopping carts jam-packed with printers, keyboards, and mice to peek inside. *Where is Sarah?*

We avoided the library—something reeked among the mounds of moldering fiction and nonfiction. *Dead rats? Bigger? Human?*

After we circled through the rubbish-filled central floor—my right foot miraculously improving—we rallied in front of a different stairway. Each member of our search party understood that if Sarah were in this basementless building, she would have to be on the next level. I clicked off the shotgun's safety, Marvin and Ernie doing likewise with their firearms. Jane, her expression deathly serious, clutched her pearl-handled pocket pistol. *She must have retrieved the gun before escaping the Alabo house.* I wanted to hold Jennifer and tell her I loved her. Instead of expressing my adoration, I speechlessly watched my wife grip Antonio's bowel-stained knife. With our weapons ready, I wondered about our sixth member. *Where's Swordsman? Is Hank Russman upstairs, or did he run back to whatever cave he crawled out of?*

I pushed the panic bar on a fire door, raring to race up the steps and liberate Sarah. *Bam! Bam!* A split second. *Bam, bam,*

bam! Heavy footsteps echoed from the stairwell. A well-built man double-stepped down the stairs. He saw us, quickly aiming an assault rifle with one hand. Marvin minced the gunman's head with a momentary burst from Dante's machine pistol.

We dashed by the guard's body to the third story. Window blinds glowed on the far side of the west courtyard. *Sarah's over there.*

Ernie and I extended our necks around a corner. Light spilled from a room midway along the hallway. My half-brother crept forward, waving at us to stay put. I brushed away his wariness, clinging to his tail tighter than a tick.

Our guns were drawn as we entered the doorway through nose-high acrid smoke. Except for the captive—*Alive!*—and two more captors—*Dead!*—no one else inhabited the room. I gestured for our group to join us.

Jane untied Sarah and pulled the gag out of her mouth. She helped her daughter out of the armchair and took her in her arms. "You all right, sugar? Did these awful men hurt you?"

The girl massaged her stiff arms and legs, her clothes grimy from sitting on the rotting leather. "Thirsty." Her stomach rumbled. "And starving. When these jerks tried to feed me Happy Meals, I spit the McNuggets in their faces. I'm thirteen, for Christ's sake."

The window in the principal's office, located directly below the tower's white cross, had an unrestricted view of the entire grounds. A figure of Hank Russman's size and shape wedged his shoulders past the slot in the chain-link fence and receded into the hickory trees.

Sarah saw the dark craters in the backs of the drug dealers' skulls and the pinkish substance splattering student records. "An old guy walked in and shot them in the head. He said, 'You're welcome,' to me, then ran off." She dabbed her eyes with her wrist and sniffled. "Can we go home now?"

We descended the front stairs to circumvent the faceless corpse in the stairway. The thunderclouds had drifted north, leaving the sky beautifully blue. Gray mist rose from the sodden soil as the tangerine sun soared above luxuriant greenery. I smiled. *Today's weather will be hot and humid, but overall, much better than yesterday's forecast.*

Marvin tugged the slit in the schoolyard fencing open for us. The muddy path under the trees preserved our shoe prints. *Nothing can be done about that now.* The six of us piled into the Subaru (Ernie still scrunched up behind the rear seats). We drove to the Union Passenger Terminal on Loyola Avenue, only making one detour to throw all our weapons into the Mississippi River.

Jennifer embraced Jane. "I won't ask where you're headed."

She cupped my wife's face in her palms. "We'll continue to use *Craigslist* to keep in touch. Check for a free Beautyrest mattress. King-size."

I wrapped my mother in my arms. "Don't cry. It'll just be for a short while. Once everything cools down, Jenn and I will come to you, even if you're on the dark side of the moon."

Ernie hoisted me off my feet. "Love you, big bro!" Not words he'd have spoken to me back in Hurricane, Alabama.

I laughed. "You too. What will you do for money?"

He pretended to dig a hole in the ground and hee-hawed. "Hillbilly bank account. There's enough cash stashed to hold us till we get," he hooked first and middle fingers, "real jobs."

Marvin squeezed me in a grizzly bear hug. "I'm enrolling in school this fall to become a certified public accountant."

I patted his whiskered jowl. "Go for it!" I nodded at Ernie. "Marv, you should take charge of all family matters. It's time to lift the weight off your brother's shoulders."

Sarah stood by herself. I went to her. "I'm sorry this happened to you. Will you be okay?"

"We're not calling the police, are we?"

I whispered, "We mustn't speak of today. Not to anyone."

The edge of her lip curved up. "Well, I'll never look at a candy machine the same way again."

I smiled. "Psychologists say, 'To conquer your fears, you need to face them.' At the next snack machine you see, buy all the candy in it. Eat every bar, or pass them out to your friends. Just save me the Kit Kats."

The girl put her damp cheek on my chest. "*You* are my friend, aren't you, Uncle Paul?"

"Sarah, we will always be family. I'm sad we have to go our separate ways."

"So am I. Can you visit me in college?"

"I'm sure we'll see you before then. Sarah, you're smart. You can be a scientist, doctor, lawyer, whatever your heart desires." I pecked her forehead. "Don't ever doubt how much we love you."

Ernie and Marvin, holding hands with Sarah, strolled to the train station. Jennifer, close behind, wished them well. Jane and I were alone.

"Mom, who was that stranger? Who is Hank Russman?"

My mother tilted her chin up, inhaling and exhaling before her hazel irises lowered to stare into my steel-blue irises. "Paul, he's the man who raped me. Your biological father rescued Sarah." She turned away from me, trotting ahead to be with her kids.

Chapter Twenty-Two

Tuesday Noon—August 20, 2019—Day 9

AFTER WE CROSSED LAKE PONTCHARTRAIN, I BEGAN TO SEE DOUBLE. Jennifer's eyelids had shut several exits back, her mouth ajar to catch flies. I pulled the Forester into a TA truck stop on the border of Louisiana and Mississippi.

Parked under shade trees, I examined the red blotches on the bandage swathing my pinkie. We had stopped at the New Orleans East Hospital's emergency room three hours earlier. After Dr. Patel warned me to be more careful when operating electric hedge clippers, she debrided the dead tissue, using the epidermis harvested from my outer thigh to close the amputation wound. The surgeon informed me that a full recovery might take months or years in the worst cases. Dr. Patel prescribed antibiotics and pain meds. *How much agony will I be in once the anesthetic wears off?*

A line of truckers trudged into Country Pride, later exiting with food containers. Other long-haulers, stubbly and unkempt, carried bags of toiletries and rumpled clothes to the showers, afterward emerging shaved, laundered, and geared up to drive another five hundred miles. A fuchsia-haired woman in high heels and a miniskirt peered into our car, scowled, and kept strutting. I nodded off to the soothing drone of passing semitrailers and the aromatic odor of pumping diesel fuel.

> I was lying on my back in my childhood bedroom. Wild West cowboys-and-Indians wallpaper decorated misshapen walls. A humongous rectangular block floated near the ceiling. *Is that an air mattress? So dark and hard to see.* A corner broke away, the piece drifting out a window. As the voluminous object silently descended, I thought, *Yes, it is a mattress! Same as the king-sized Beautyrests they sell at Mattress Firm.* The bloated padding touched my pajamas, light as a bird's feather. The mass increased uncomfortably against my ribs. *I can still crawl out from under this load if I have to.* The suffocating pressure doubled exponentially. Physically or mentally paralyzed by panic, from a practical point of view, the cause had no significance—I could not move my arms or legs. *Too heavy, can't breathe.* "Jenn! Jenn! Come quick!"
>
> "Son, your wife is downstairs broiling Smokey for supper. Only I can help you now."
>
> I glimpsed black pants and the white stitching of multiple pockets. The blood of ten thousand sacrifices seeped through the bedclothes to stain my bare skin. "Father, I beg of you, lift this burden off of my—"

A hand rocked my shoulder. "Wake up, Paul! You're dreaming."

I gripped the steering wheel to hoist myself upright. "Late, gotta get to work."

"It's okay, sweetie." Jennifer brushed a lock of hair from my brow. "No building castles in the sky for you today. You're here with me."

I wiped a strand of drool off the corner of my mouth. "Had a bad dream. My father—"

"Your father?"

"Uh-huh."

An electrical motor whined as I raised the reclined seat. With my mind's eye, I saw Hunter Rugger's stilt house overlooking the Mallini Bayou, the white Rugger Pest Control van, Blatto the cockroach's petrified eyeballs, and the ground-level storage unit stocked with insecticides and traps.

"Your gurgling scared me. It sounded like you were drowning." My wife's nostrils wrinkled as though she smelled sour milk. "I assume you mean Hunter Rugger, not Hale?"

"Yep."

"What was this dream about?"

The incubus left a foul taste on my palate, but nothing tangible. "Don't recall." I yawned. "Tired."

Jennifer checked her wristwatch. "It's noon." She regarded the Country Pride restaurant with distrust.

I opened the car door. "Let's eat."

We sat at a table with a great perspective of the fueling stations. The stain-proof menu advertised BREAKFAST ALL DAY, EVERY DAY! so my wife asked our waitress, Peggy, for the Farmers Omelet, and I ordered the 2000-calorie Long Haul.

Suddenly famished and parched like a stranded man swimming to shore from a desert island, I drained the orange juice in a single gulp before digging my fork into the buttermilk pancakes. I swabbed the Vermont maple syrup off my lips with a paper napkin. "Wanna talk about last night?"

Jennifer shook her head, her jaws chomping eggs, tomatoes, peppers, onions, mushrooms, and bacon topped with sausage gravy and a pinch of cheddar. She swallowed, drank coffee, then appropriated a triangle of my toast. "Not now. Maybe later.

Maybe never. Did you get a load of how low the prices are for this amount of food? Do we have Country Prides in San Diego?"

Peggy returned and refilled Jennifer's cup. "Everything all right? More OJ, sir?"

"Yes, please." I needed to warn my wife that Hank Russman is, in reality, Hunter Rugger, who, in fact, is my real father—the degenerate guilty of viciously violating my teenage mother. While I contemplated ruining the first proper meal we'd eaten in the last twenty-four hours, Peggy dropped the check on the table with two peppermint candies.

Jennifer pushed her empty dish forward. "Well, not exactly chicory coffee and powder-sugared beignets," she settled back in the booth, "but crikey, not bad for twenty-three bucks." I'd never heard my wife use this British expression of surprise, but after witnessing her disembowel Antonio, I reckoned that I still had much to learn about what made her tick.

I slid the credit card out of my wallet. "Sorry. I promised you breakfast at the Café du Monde."

"It's fine, sweetie. We can fly down for Mardi Gras."

Beaded necklaces and topless women. Even with those sexy images dancing in my head, I had no desire to set foot in New Orleans for the foreseeable future. "Fat Tuesday, all the decorated parade floats?"

My wife grinned. "Might be fun." She balled her napkin. "Let's rent a different car."

"Now? Why?"

"Hunter Rugger will easily spot our Subaru. We need a vehicle that blends in with the environment."

I hadn't the faintest idea how to respond—*no time to gather my thoughts.*

"We'll see what your father is up to, or whatever the man with the sword is naming himself. If he's still assaulting women or anybody else, we go straight to the police."

"You realized Hunter Rugger and Hank Russman are the same person?"

Jennifer nodded.

"When did you know?"

My wife appeared embarrassed. "Could just tell." Her eyes darted from mine.

I touched my hair and pinched the bridge of my nose. "Umm."

"I don't understand how we didn't catch him, but your father tracked our car to New Orleans." She gazed through the restaurant's tinted windows. "He may be out there now."

Dozens of vans crammed the parking spaces, predominantly white—Al's Plumbing, S&G Delivery Service, Mopar Auto Parts. *No Rugger Pest Control, no Blatto.* I checked the seats at the surrounding tables and the stools at the lunch counter. *The men and women are stamped from the same pattern—big, broad, and bulky.* With all the running around in poor lighting, I hadn't seen Swordsman up close in the course of last evening's excitement. I inventoried Hank Russman's features. *Black hair, a longish nose, and blueish eyes—sorta silverish.* I gasped. *My old man looks a lot like me. Bland. Boring. Except for his height, nothing to strike a note, not one thing to speak about later.*

Tuesday Afternoon—August 20, 2019—Day 9

No familiar vehicles popped up in my rearview mirror during the twenty-five-mile journey east into Mississippi. At traffic lights in Pass Christian, I scanned each passing white van. Along Beach Boulevard, I checked out the sandaled beachgoers for someone I couldn't perceive going anywhere near sun, sand, and surf. *Why did my father leave me without saying goodbye?* I felt strangely betrayed by a man I didn't even know.

At Gulfport-Biloxi International Airport, we exchanged the snazzy green Subaru Forester for the most nondescript automobile on the lot, a silver four-door Toyota Corolla. When the clerk at the rental desk questioned our reason for the return, I glanced at Jennifer. She told the gal in the blue Budget Rent a Car polo shirt that we required a vehicle with better gas mileage.

Tuesday night, after my wife and I ate at Claw Daddy's, we checked into a Days Inn on hotel alley, a mile and a quarter from the airport. We rinsed the long, loathsome day down the drain and went to bed early. Although my eyelids were shut, my cerebrum spun like an out-of-control merry-go-round. Jennifer's irregular breathing and continual adjustment of limbs signified she hadn't yet wandered off to Jonathan Swift's Land of Nod. I slung my arm about her waist. "Babe?"

"Hmm?"

"You awake?"

She rolled out from under my forearm to face me. Moonshine sneaking through the gap in the blackout drapes gleamed in her eyes. "I killed a man. Keep seeing all the blood and hearing the dreadful noises he made."

Antonio stuffing his bowels back in his belly wasn't a scene I'd be forgetting any time soon. "I shot Delgado in the legs, then did some things with my mother I'm not proud of."

"Paul, you had no choice. You needed Sarah's location."

"Jenn, I tortured him, and I'm not talkin' waterboarding. I–I used a—"

My wife pressed her forefinger to my lips. "You freed that girl. She's alive. That's what matters."

I nudged her finger away. "Hunter Rugger saved Sarah. I simply drove him to the school. If you hadn't stabbed Antonio, we'd all be dead."

"Your father also helped us flee from the Wildcat."

I propped myself on my elbow. "Are you saying that he's a hero?"

"Hunter Rugger is no white knight in shining armor."

"Should we go home?"

"We can't."

I deflated onto the pillow. "Yeah, I know."

"Hug me?"

"My pleasure, Mrs. Crutcher." I enveloped her warm body in my arms. I cannot say that Jennifer sailed into Jonathan Swift's mythical land of mystical dreams, but I skydived into Adam and Eve's eldest son's land of exile—Cain's East of Eden—without a working parachute.

Out of numerous semi-nightmares broken into pieces by intermissions of getting up to take a leak, I just remembered this doozy before waking up.

> Beneath a new moon, the only illumination reflecting upon the bayou flickered from Hunter Rugger's windows. The flames drew me up the stairs and inside the dwelling like a moth. Wrought-iron sconces held tapers of rendered fat. More yellow tallow drizzled from gently swaying crystal chandeliers. *The storm! There must be a power outage. That's why the light switches don't work!* Somewhere, somebody—*Jennifer?*—cried for aid.
>
> In the kitchen, seawater pooled at my bare feet. "Hello?" My voice—*his voice*—reverberated off shiny industrial freezers. I cupped a hand to my ear. "Where are you?"
>
> A female—*Jennifer?*—called my name. *His name.*
>
> In the living room, a tattered brown recliner faced a television playing the same Technicolor scene again and again: John Wayne scalping an Indian chief. A red chyron moved along the large screen's lower edge at a snail's pace: BREAKING NEWS –

EVERY BOY TURNS INTO HIS FATHER!!! *How is the TV on without electricity?*

Doors, each mid-rail crudely carved with Roman numerals, lined both sides of an endless corridor. A chorus of imprisoned souls chanted my name, *"Hunter, Hunter, Hunter!"* I twisted the skull doorknobs, but all were locked and lacked keyholes. "Hello? Are you still there?" Behind DCLXVI, a stout portal held shut by a robust crossbar, floorboards groaned as something ponderous lumbered back and forth.

At the dreary end of the hallway, cowboys astride frothing white stallions chased Indians astride frothing black stallions across a wallpaper prairie.

"Paul?" The pleading resonated from everywhere and nowhere.

"Is that you, Jenn?" I lay my ear against the peeling paper—talons ceaselessly clawing their way out.

Someplace, a door opened, letting in the tempest. Wick by wick, the candles guttered and blew out. The air stank of soot, sorrow, and now a more potent, unidentifiable funk. *Burnt hair? Burning flesh?* I felt my way in total darkness, my fingertips recoiling when they touched a face. "Jenn?" I stroked elongated antennae, giant compound eyes, and a pair of dripping mandibles below a slick, hard shell. "Blatto? Is that you, my friend?"

A hurricane lantern swung from whence I came. No longer alone, I yelled, "Who's there?"

The hooded man replied, "'Tis me!"

Two ancient swords rested on a two-tiered mount—the top blade long, the bottom blade short. I grabbed the lower weapon and jabbed it into the wall. Jennifer! Are you in there? Powdered gypsum coated my cheeks as I put my shoulders into the laborious task. Chunks of plaster bounced off my toes. Wads of human hair plugged narrow strips of wood. Eyes gaped dumbly through chinks in the horizontal lathing. A woman, her once lovely face now ravaged beyond all recognition, stretched bloody fingers past the bars.

I recoiled. "Babe, is that you?"

A black beak clacked, "You did this, you did this, you did this. . . ."

A hand clenched my throat. I pivoted to see the person I knew would eventually catch up with me: *Me.*

Chapter Twenty-Three

Wednesday Morning—August 21, 2019—Day 10

I AWOKE IN A SWEAT. *5:35 a.m.* I rolled over, comforted to find Jennifer softly snoring alongside me. Outside the window, commercial trucks and early commuters zoomed by on the 49. A normal day, with normal people doing normal things. *I don't feel normal at all.*

Ten days had passed since I landed at Mobile Regional Airport, yet it seemed ten lifetimes ago. I mused over my previous existence: Wake up, breakfast, slog away at my latest novel, lunchtime, read a book or magazine before dozing into an afternoon nap, squeeze out a couple more paragraphs, dinnertime, watch TV, hit the sack—rinse and repeat. Now I was the protagonist in a story that I wasn't authoring. *Are you the hero, Paul, or are you really the villain?* Regrettably, as murderers—regardless of how justified—this account never could be penned on paper. *What if the Mexican cartel hunts us down? And the cops? We left so many fingerprints.*

I checked the Mobile, Alabama *Craigslist.* No ads for free Beautyrest king-sized mattresses. *They're safe—for now.* I closed my eyelids, foreseeing our lives on the run.

"Let's get ready to go."

I hadn't sensed Jennifer coming up behind me. "Rush hour starts early. How did you sleep?"

She kissed the tip of my nose, then flipped on the television. "Looks like I slept better than you, sweetie."

While my wife showered, I listened to weather reports of a tropical storm named Fernand brewing off the North Atlantic coast. I perused pictures on my iPhone, grinning at a cute shot of Smokey lying on his back. I missed listening to the feline's contented purr when I rubbed his furry tummy. Christmastime photos of my smiling parents the year before my dad died misted my eyes. I typed a mental memo to call the Meadows Assisted Living Facility to check on my mother's well-being.

We bought breakfast at Burger King and ate the Croissan'wiches on the drive west to Pass Christian. Sausage grease dribbled down my chin to splotch my white T-shirt. I cast my eyes toward the Gulf of Mexico, disappointed that Cat Island wasn't visible through the fog. Down in the dumps, I clicked on the radio only to hear negative news. ISIS gained strength in Iraq and Syria. Jeffrey Epstein signed a will before he, quote, "killed himself" in his jail cell. *May the Prince of Darkness make you his número uno bitch, Jeff.* I rotated the dial, stopping on a song by Twenty One Pilots, paradoxically "Heathens" from the superhero movie *Suicide Squad.*

Jennifer gestured for me to turn at the UNIVERSITY OF SOUTHERN MISSISSIPPI sign.

I parked near the dorms, lowering the windows to let in the sweltering air. After five minutes of watching my wife stare blankly through the windshield, I took hold of her left hand, the one with the golden ring the Wildcat threatened to cut off. "Jenn, we can leave a tip with the authorities. Let them deal with it."

I had learned that the Gulfport Police Department provided an anonymous online form. Hunter Rugger's present town, Pass Christian, had a drop box for discarding prescription drugs, so it would be easy for us to leave a note for detectives to find in the mountain of pills. Either option ought to start the ball rolling, and if neither of these alternatives produced an expedient outcome, Crime Stoppers claimed to have solved more than a million cases. The national organization paid informants for tips that led to felony arrests. I saw Deputy Dawg counting greenbacks into my outstretched palm. As a senior software engineer, Jennifer earned a decent income. We were getting by financially, but five grand would help with a down payment on a new car or pay off escalating credit card debt. I exhaled. *The problem is, and always will be, he's my—*

"Paul, whatever Rugger's done, he's still your father." Jennifer laid her right hand on top of mine. "Do you really want to see him apprehended and spend the rest of his life in a federal penitentiary?"

I had no inkling of what I wanted anymore. My life felt off-kilter. I had intended for the quest to meet my biological mother and possibly locate my biological father to be a simple meet-and-greet, not the clusterfuck it had become.

A pickup truck parked adjacent to us. Two male undergraduates hopped from the cab, slung book bags onto their backs, and rambled off to classes. With each step they took, a larger, longer laugh came out. God, how I missed the carefree days of my youth.

"Paul?"

I turned my head to look at her. "I've got to question him before we do anything drastic." I inspected my fingernails, not recollecting the last time I clipped them. Whenever it had been, I still had been blessed with ten. "And anyway, we're not completely sure Hunter Rugger *is* my actual father." It hit me. Of late, I'd been letting lots of important details fall through the cracks. *Too much shit rushing down the sluice, all at once.* I pulled my hand from Jennifer's and smacked my temple. "We never contacted the DNA Center for the paternity results."

The slight downturn of my wife's lips made plain nothing so vital would ever slip her mind. "Shall I call them?"

"Be right back," I said, stepping out of the Toyota. The brilliant sun baked my sinuses. Both sides of my head ached—the onset of a migraine. I plodded across the front lawn (more tan sand than green grass), babying my injured anklebone. Students disassociated themselves from the distraught stranger who was tottering aimlessly throughout their seaside campus. *Rugger—my father?* The brightness hurt my sensitive eyes. *Raped my mother.* My heart pounded too fast. *He murders women in that concealed room under his house.* Out of breath, my lungs failed to absorb enough oxygen. *Torments them first—for his own amusement.* I envisioned razor-sharp instruments of pain.

Beside an old Catholic church, I stood beneath a gigantic tree. The magnificent live oak's hanging branches swept the ground. I read the historical plaque, hurried to the car, and opened Jennifer's door. "There's something you must see!"

I led her below the five-century-old hardwood's leafy umbrella. "The sign says, 'Those who enter my shadow are supposed to remain friends through all their lifetime no matter where fate may take them in after years.'" I embraced my life partner underneath the Friendship Oak. "I love you, Jenn. You're all I care about." My wife kissed me and swore she loved me too. We held hands, my headache a memory. "I'm ready. Can you please call the DNA Center?"

The current quandary flopping around on my plate—*what if that maniac, Hunter Rugger, is my real father?*—instantly was resolved during a one-minute phone call to the DNA Center. The technician assisting us asserted that their paternity tests were 100% accurate in determining whether a man is another person's biological parent. Now, in Pass Christian, while we sat in the stuffy Corolla a block from 1086 Pall Mall Road, my overactive brain looped the naked truth: *That maniac is my father. That maniac is my father. That maniac is my father.*

On Poindexter Drive, we had an unobstructed view of the brown cockroach glued to the rear of the white van. At 8:26 a.m., Rugger descended the front steps, grasping a schoolchild's Lone Ranger lunchbox in his left hand, a clipboard clutched under the same arm, and a matching Lone Ranger thermos in his right hand. He unlocked the Chevy, set the vacuum bottle in the console, and laid the other items on the passenger seat. After Rugger opened the back of the van, he went beneath the house to the storage closet and returned with two cartons to stack in the cargo area. He made one additional trip to pick up a long metal pole and a plastic backpack sprayer. Rugger shut the hatches, slid behind the wheel, started the motor, and backed the vehicle out of the driveway. We had parked in the direction we hoped he wouldn't go—a dead end. I sighed in relief as the van headed toward the main thoroughfare. Jennifer cautioned me when I drove too close.

Rugger pulled into a Chevron by the Yacht Club. With a full tank and a clean windshield, he steered the pest control vehicle past Hank's Party Favors to stop in front of a ranch-style home on Russman Avenue. *Did he splice these two places to create the name Hank Russman, or is what I'm seeing here a mere coincidence? And who might Hunter Rugger be an alias for?* Following twenty minutes of Rugger using the pump sprayer to apply pesticide to the building's foundation, he knocked down spiderwebs from the high eaves with the extended duster pole. Finished, he packed the equipment inside the van, hung a bill on the doorknob, and drove to the next residence.

We waited for the pestman to service five more customers—I dozed off occasionally from extreme tiredness or extreme boredom—before tailing him for eight miles to the town of Long

Beach. At 10:50 a.m., he parked at Long Beach High School and unwrapped a peanut butter and jelly sandwich. Ten minutes later, a string of female students in athletic outfits exited the gymnasium to stretch their legs, then jog around the track.

Jennifer, with moisture beading frown lines on her forehead, tied her chestnut hair into a ponytail. "Pretty sick, don't you agree?"

"Sure, but watching kids exercise means nothing. He could only be—"

"Look," my wife sounded as annoyed as she appeared, "I'm hot and dehydrated." She frenziedly scratched a cluster of red bug bites on her elbow. "Your dad ogling sweaty schoolgirls parading about in halter tops and short shorts doesn't seem pervy to you?"

I wordlessly agreed with her. A solitary man parked across from a schoolyard? Creepy, at the very least. Pedophiliac at the very worst. I wondered if campus security ever questioned him or directed him to move along. I studied his right profile from our vantage point behind two rows of cars. No visible scars. *Which side of his face did Jane disfigure with the compasses? He may have had plastic surgery, or the injury naturally faded with age.* I compared our facial characteristics. *Are my eyes, nose, ears, and mouth shaped like his?* I had seen little of myself in Jane, my biological mother. Rugger swiveled his head, his steel-blue irises sweeping over us, not slowing or stopping. I sank into the driver's seat, a jackhammer fracturing my chest. *Those eyes. Bluer and colder than the bottom of Lake Tahoe. Yup, I absolutely take after my father.*

That afternoon, we trailed the white van throughout Harrison County, one trip as far north as Cuevas. Jennifer suggested a break after Rugger exterminated every living creature at five or six different properties. (I lost count long ago—how do legitimate private eyes stay alert?)

"If we leave now," I said, "we won't be able to find him again."

"Paul, you said the night you broke inside Rugger's storage shed and discovered the secret room, that the van's hood was still warm."

"Hot. He just got back from somewhere."

"And this was past midnight?"

"One thirty in the morning."

"After we rest up at the hotel," she yawned as if to emphasize her point, "we can swing by Pass Christian to monitor his late-night activities. And on this stakeout, we bring snacks."

"I'm hungry now. Let's stop at Shaggy's to celebrate."

Jennifer smiled for the first time in recent memory. "Celebrate what?"

Her birthday, the Big Four-O, is in October. I thought harder. *Our anniversary isn't until next July.* I shrugged, then whispered, "Us. You and me being alive."

Wednesday Night—August 21, 2019—Day 10

It took us longer than expected to drag our achy butts out of bed and down to the hotel's parking lot. Three rounds of the hard stuff at Shaggy's left me groggy, but I hardly noticed the pain in my foot or hand with the top of my head hurting. By the time we positioned the Corolla at our secluded place on Poindexter Drive, the sun had dipped below the timberline. Mallini Bayou mirrored a sky russet from uncontained wildfires north of Wolf River.

Jennifer passed me the Deep Woods OFF! as mosquitoes buzzed in the open windows for an all-you-can-eat bloodfest. I squirted the sections of my skin not shielded by cloth with liberal doses of repellent, grateful that Marge at Hurricane Landing had recommended this purchase. The thirsty bloodsuckers hovered above my veins, never touching down.

The essence of DEET (a complex bouquet of cherries and perspiration) led my olfactory nerves, and consequently my brain, to dwell upon the day Jane handed me the fragment of a DDT bag. My mother had bared her soul to me—the savage attack, the rape, and the brave escape. Her parents had sent her out of town to stay with Aunt Vivian before May 15, 1978—my birth date. I checked my wristwatch—*8:29*—approximately the time Hunter Rugger had guided the white van into the alley behind the Ace Hardware store four decades ago.

He deserves to die for the things he did to her.

Would I be able to assassinate my own father? This was a tough question that I had no inclination to answer. The church has a special term for this egregious sin—*patricide.* A persistent mosquito explored an unprotected portion of my neck. I homed in on the swamp angel, squashing it without an ounce of pity. In the dark, I couldn't see the blood staining my fingers, but I damn well knew it was there.

At 9 p.m., a bluish glow emanated from the living room window. I visualized Rugger recumbent in his La-Z-Boy, viewing the evening news. *Or what else does he like? Friends reruns? Dateline?* My gut churned as I imagined what debauchery he'd jerk off to on *Pornhub. No, that's not it. My father is watching*—a hazy image bobbed to the forefront of my mind—*Westerns. Cowboys and Indians. The Lone Ranger.*

At 11 p.m., the television light went out. The front door opened.

Jennifer leaned forward to squint through the bug-splattered windshield. She whispered, "It's showtime."

With no exterior lamps switched on, Rugger legged it down the tall stairway to unlock his van. He unloaded the eradication supplies he had loaded early this morning, stored them below the structure, then drove away quickly.

I pursued the Chevrolet at a sensible distance, not wanting to lose my father among the sea of red taillights.

As the traffic thinned, Jennifer pumped her hand. "Slow, Paul. You're on his bumper!"

The Rugger Pest Control van took a less-direct route inland to Long Beach. He cruised past Valentino's Lawn Mower Sales and Service, Save A Lot, and Massage and Healing by Linda Lee. We rattled across railroad tracks a mile from Long Beach High School. On Ocean Wave Avenue, the vehicle's brake lights lit up. A block farther, they flashed again.

My wife read the sign on the two-story building. "Seaview Apartments. What is he looking for?"

"Maybe—" The Chevy sped off, failing to indicate a hard left. When we reached Finley Street, the man and machine were gone.

"Did," her vocal cords cracked, "your dad see our car?"

My tongue stuck to the roof of my mouth. I figured the sly fox likely caught wind of us.

Jennifer rested her head on the passenger seat. "Pass Christian?"

We circled back to the stilt house on Pall Mall Road, where a white van sat underneath.

Chapter Twenty-Four

Thursday Morning—August 22, 2019—Day 11

THURSDAY MORNING, JENNIFER AND I PICKED UP BREAKFAST SANDWICHES AT THE MCDONALD'S DRIVE-THRU and motored southwest to Pass Christian. Although the brume hanging above the Gulf had dissipated and the rising sun thawed our icy moods, the weather reporter on the radio announced a tropical storm watch. Fernand and his fifty-mile-per-hour winds hadn't turned southward as originally predicted. Without signaling, Fernand swerved north. We parked in our regular spot down the road from Hunter Rugger's house.

I nibbled my McMuffin's toasted edge. *Shoulda got two,* I thought, chomping into the griddle-fried egg. "I slept well for a change." During the past six hours, I dreamed scads of dreams. Now, in the bright of day, I couldn't nail down the gist of any single one—*which is always for the better.*

"Took me a while to drop off," Jennifer mumbled around a mouthful of Canadian bacon, "but once I did," she sipped steaming Americano, "I slept like the dead."

I pictured Rick Grimes, the stalwart Southern sheriff, stabbing his best friend, Shane Walsh, in the chest on a highly controversial episode of *The Walking Dead.* "Did we frighten my father from whatever he was up to last night?"

"Our headlights might have spooked him." My wife shoved the fast-food debris (substantial for such small fare) in the paper bag stamped with golden arches. "Or—who knows?" She finished the espresso, put the empty cup in the holder, and winked at me. "Holding onto this if I gotta pee."

I handed Jennifer the leftover napkins, just in case. "My father may be practicing due diligence, you know, checking properties to decide whether he'll take them on as new clients."

She snorted. "After midnight?"

"Insomnia?"

"Seriously?"

I sighed. "Sorry I dragged you into all this."

My wife's grin melted my growing melancholy. "Sweetie, I was the one banging on *your* hotel room door. Remember? I had a gut feeling you were in way over your head, so I came to help."

I touched my wedding ring to hers. "Till death us do part?"

"Hells yeah, Sugarboo." Her radiant smile dimmed for an instant as if a rain cloud passed behind her eyes. "But I pray the death part comes much, much later."

I spent a long, pensive minute before responding. "Who in the hell is Sugarboo?"

Jennifer playfully poked a finger in my side. "You're Sugarboo, Sugarboo." She sat erect. "8:26 on the dot. It's shooowtiiime!"

We observed Hunter Rugger loading his van with equipment and supplies, then followed him across a bridge to his first job, a hole-in-the-wall Mexican restaurant in the coastal town of Bay Saint Louis. After he sprayed the bejesus out of Loco for Tacos, he serviced several residential homes and a large project that took two hours—the L&N Historic Train Depot. At 10:55, Rugger parked the Chevrolet Express at Saint Stanislaus Catholic to have lunch. *My father really loves peanut butter and jelly sandwiches. Or he prefers to stick to a routine.* Tennis courts and a lap pool equipped the boarding school for boys in grades seven through twelve. At 11:05, whooping youths galloped over the lawn, stripping down to swimsuits before leaping into the pool's chlorinated water.

I expected my wife to make a snide remark like, "Well, your dad is also into murdering young boys," but she only handed me a LÄRABAR and a Diet Mountain Dew. After I read the "REAL" flavors printed on the energy bar's vibrant label, PEANUT BUTTER & JELLY, I lost my appetite.

Jennifer raised her voice above the roar of landscapers wielding leaf blowers, "Do you suppose your dad is eyeballing all the kids or just one specifically?"

I contemplated his motives. With the swimmers jumping in and out of the pool and the range we were at, it was hard to establish whether he indicated an attraction to any individual student. "Not sure," I replied, wishing for a pair of binoculars. "Yesterday, at the school in Long Beach, his head spun whenever a particular runner sprinted by on the closest section of the track."

My wife put her crumpled LÄRABAR wrapper in the McDonald's bag. "Which one? What did she look like?"

Thirty girls had raced around the oval, the majority in packs, pretty much all dressed the same. "Blond hair?" I shut my eyelids, rewinding my mental tapes twenty-four hours. "Her shirt was—dark. I thought she might blow a gasket wearing black on such a muggy day. Something was written on the front."

Jennifer rubbed her first three fingers in unison. "The name of the high school?"

"No, only four letters." I backtracked, stroking my forehead. *Relax, relax, relax.* I envisaged the building, the track, and the young women exercising under the scorching sun. "Oh man, it's on the tip of my tongue." Neurons in my hippocampus sparked the word, as clear as a neon sign. I opened my eyes. "PINK was printed on her shirt. Black letters—capitalized—outlined in white."

"Victoria's Secret sells the PINK product line—not so fashionable with the ladies since the MeToo movement."

"Should we drive to the high school and try to find her? 'Pardon me, miss. See that guy in the cockroach van scoping you out? That's my pops. He wants to chain you up in the dungeon underneath his house. If you're lucky, he'll just rape you and let you go. Still, you have to ask yourself: I saw his face; why would he be stupid enough to let me walk away?'"

"That boy in the blue swim trunks?" She indicated a chubby kid talking to a skinny kid.

I squinted into the glare. "Red hair? On the shortish side?"

"Um-hum. Your dad showed interest in him."

I hate that Jennifer calls my father "dad." Is she attempting to get a rise out of me? If so, it's working. Rugger's head rotated like a radar dish as the boy dashed to the diving board. *Yikes, she's right.* I said, "Yesterday, we left early to eat. Today, we stay. Let's see if he goes straight home after work."

My wife, done using the McDonald's bag for trash, crushed the soda can and chucked it into the back seat. "How many kids *is* your dear ol' dad stalking?"

Thursday Afternoon—August 22, 2019—Day 11

At three o'clock, after two interminable hours of watching "dear ol' Dad" making a living killing, we slowed on County Farm Road when the Rugger Pest Control van's brake lights flashed. I stopped the Toyota in front of Harrison County Fire Service Station No. 2, a cinder-block building with two large garage doors. We were nine miles north of Gulfport Beach in a sparsely populated, forested region. Across a mowed grass field, a huge, white golf ball sat atop a tee—*a water tower.* Banks of spotlights mounted on soaring poles verged fenced-in areas. *A compound of some type.*

I ran the windshield wipers to squeegee away the fossilized bug guts, only to liquefy the disgusting mess. "Is that a jail?" I then saw the fluorescent traffic sign: girl and boy stick figures carrying lunchboxes.

Jennifer checked *Google Maps* on her iPhone. "School felt like a prison to me at that age. That's West Harrison High."

"Don't classes let out around this time?" I gave the engine enough gas to gain on the slowly moving Chevrolet without getting too close to remain inconspicuous.

"Three to three-thirty, from what I—" She pointed.

Students, shouting joyously, capered out of the building's entrance and side exits. Most boys and girls stood in line for yellow school buses. Others waited in the VIP section for parents to chauffeur them home in sedans, SUVs, and pickups. The more energetic unchained their bicycles and pedaled away. Nobody walked; the distance to the nearest housing developments was too far.

Is Rugger concentrating on a single student? "What do we do if he jumps a kid?"

"Alert the police." My wife checked her purse. "We still have one burner phone."

I concocted a cerebral scenario: a fleet of black and whites in hot pursuit, the speeding pest control van running over a spike strip, spinning, flipping, crashing—my deranged father holding his short sword to a terrified schoolgirl's throat as a hail of bullets—

"There she is!"

I scanned right and left. "Who?"

"The kid he's after. See her?"

A female wearing a dayglow-orange backpack peddled an orange Schwinn in the narrow bike lane. The white van cruised past her, then accelerated up the street.

I shouted, "Take a picture when we pass!"

Jennifer aimed her cell phone through the glass and fired off a series of shots. My attention reverted to the road ahead. The Chevy had vanished.

At the next intersection, the cyclist steered onto Landon Road. A half-mile farther, she turned at Hughes Road. We passed a self-storage facility, large ranch houses on enormous parcels of land, and a picturesque lily pond before she coasted into Ridgecrest, a manufactured home community. The girl dismounted the bicycle and wheeled it across the cement driveway to a recently painted double-wide trailer. She chained the frame to the front deck, petted an Alaskan husky lying half inside a doghouse, scampered up the stairs, and unlocked the door. My wife saved the address as we reversed and went south.

We ate at The Rack House. A constant diet of mollusks and crustaceans had started to turn me off, so I ordered a juicy steak, the first red meat since I almost choked to death. Afterward, we purchased a pair of binoculars at Academy Sports. At 8:30 p.m., we parked down the street from Rugger's place for the second evening in a row. The rental car's interior stank of bug spray. *Greedy little devils.* I slathered additional redneck cologne on my neck.

Jennifer lowered the field glasses. "Paul, is your father fucking with us?"

At least she quit calling Hunter Rugger "your dad." Although "your father" still sounds offensive. "What do you mean?"

"He may have detected we're shadowing him."

"We've been careful." *Were we?* I checked the rear and side mirrors, relieved that Leatherface or Jason Voorhees wasn't lurking in the bushes.

Jennifer summarized what we had seen. "At noon yesterday, in Long Beach, Rugger watched the PINK high school girl running at the track. That night, in the same town, he drove along Ocean Wave Avenue, braking at the Seaview Apartments. I don't know why. This morning, in Bay Saint Louis, your father eyed that boy swimming in the Saint Stanislaus pool. Then, this afternoon, he waits for West Harrison to let out, so he can rubberneck a schoolgirl riding her bike. Doesn't tail her the whole way home."

I grunted. This topic of discussion—my father's amoral conduct—made me uneasy.

"He's studying their daily routes and routines." Jennifer held three fingers high. "What do the kids have in common?"

"High schoolers," I replied. "All close to Jane's age when Hunter Rugger attacked her? Two are female, and one's a male." I raised my shoulders. "Why do you say he's screwing with us?"

"It's more of an intuition than anything concrete. In New Orleans, he burst into the Alabo Street house like Deadpool to the rescue. That signifies he's keeping tabs on us." My wife tapped my chest. "You anyhow." She stared into space. "I wonder for how long?"

Since I saw my birth certificate and learned that Edith and Hale were not my real parents, I never considered my biological mother or father "keeping tabs" on me as I matured. Did Hunter Rugger hang around the playground watching me fly to and fro on the swing set or glide down the slide? Did he park beneath my bedroom window, waiting until the ceiling light switched off and the night light switched on? Had the man ached to rob me from my cradle and spirit me away? My basic emotions were at odds with one another: deeply touched to think my blood father might care for me and equally repulsed that he might.

Jennifer spiraled her forefinger downward. "He's leading us on a wild-goose chase."

"Why?"

"To confuse us."

"Too many victims to keep track of?"

She shook her hands by her temples. "Without knowing who your father is picking to kidnap, he understands we'd have to warn *all* the kids. Their parents will engage the authorities—legally bad for us. We left evidence in New Orleans."

"Jenn, we burned it all."

"Not at the high school. Your bandage leaked like a sieve. Your bloody fingerprints are on the rental car's steering wheel. If the police tie your DNA to us, we'll be locked in the interrogation room, not him. What if our Uber driver steps forward?"

"Gervais can keep his mouth shut."

"I agree, but I have no desire to be associated with Juan Carlos Delgado and his goons. We also will put Jane and the rest of your family in more danger if we start blabbing."

I grumbled, "Where does that leave us?"

"For now, let's determine which kids he's observing. If something hairy goes down, we contact the cops." My wife ruptured a TracFone clamshell, pausing to fixate on the umbral shape descending Rugger's front steps. "It's show—"

"Time," I said in harmony with her. The Toyota's four-banger eagerly purred when I pushed the ignition button. Set free, the Corolla sprang. I muttered, "Where is Dad going tonight?"

We followed Rugger's van north across the Popp's Ferry Bridge. The Biloxi Junior High School and the Biloxi High School campuses had extensive sports complexes. On Wells Drive, we drove past a memory care center to a cul-de-sac with an excellent waterfront view of Mullet Lake and Magnolia Bend: Damphman Point.

"What's he doing?" Jennifer inquired as the Chevrolet slowed in the Bay Cove condominiums' parking area.

I swung behind a Winnebago. "We're a five-minute walk from the high school. Maybe a kid he's after lives here?"

We lost sight of the white vehicle while it circled the lengthy building. I hung back, counting the seconds before the headlights reappeared. As we ducked below the dashboard, I swear I heard the Chevy's motor drop a few revolutions as it passed by our Toyota.

Once Hunter Rugger got home, and we returned to the hotel, I slept, but not very well.

My dream. . . .

> Late for class, I sidled into the classroom and sat with two dozen students stationed at long desks. The instructor chalked complicated equations on the blackboard. My fellow pupils took copious notes. I checked my book bag for a notebook, finding nothing but a fanged ball of fur. I looked around the dismal room, which had no windows to let in a ray of light, nor ceiling fans to circulate the stagnant air. On the wall clock, the Lone Ranger's eyes were X-ed black, his gloved hands stuck at 7:45. Anatomical drawings covered the dingy walls. A petite girl—*looks like Sarah, not Sarah*—cranked a pencil sharpener in a corner. Wood shavings snowed onto her bare feet. Alongside a teacher's desk laden with wormy apples, a life-sized human skeleton swung from a rolling stand, its cranium cracked open like a walnut. *If that thing is real, whose bones are they?* A bell rang one, two, three.

My schoolmates stood in unison, lined up, and zombie-shambled into the dark hallway. I rose, anxious to ride my bike home and watch *The Price Is Right* with my mom, only to be reprimanded by a wooden ruler across my knuckles.

A voice boomed, "Sit!" A firm palm pressed me onto the hard chair. "Son, you cannot leave until you complete your exam!" I obediently picked up a No. 2 pencil. "Begin by filling in your name." The lead point formed H-U-N-T-E-R.

"Sir, that's not me."

A yardstick thwacked my spine. "No backtalk! Take the test, boy. I'm late for dinner."

I counted the multiple-choice questions. *Just ten. Okay, I can do this.* I read the first query aloud. "What amount of rat poison is required to kill a one-hundred-and-eighty-pound adult male? A. one ounce, B. one cup, C. one pint, D. one quart, or E. all of the above." *Probably very little. A? Hmm, we're talking about a full-sized man, not a one-pound rodent. B? Or is it C?* I guessed B, hoping the second question would be less baffling. "Which human organs are best eaten raw? A. kidneys, B. spleen, C. lungs, D. heart, or E. all of the above." I examined the attached DISSECTION diagram. *Oh, this one's easy.* In the vivid 8x10-inch illustration, a giant frog lay on its back. The amphibian's pulmonary cavity was sliced open, and the flaps of skin were stretched and pinned to a board. *I've heard about people dining on kidney pie. Healthy for the heart, but aren't the kidneys usually cooked with mushrooms, onions, and a drop or two of*

Worcestershire sauce? Spleen? Lungs? Nah. Aren't those delicacies in certain countries? D, the heart? Don't Native Americans traditionally devour the hearts of freshly killed animals to gain their strength and agility? I X-ed D, but looking again at A, I quickly erased the selection. *Please, God, tell me the correct answer.* The writing implement snapped between my clenched fingers.

A cane smacked my cheek when I twisted my neck to offer an excuse for not cracking the books or burning the midnight oil. "You muttonhead! Didn't Hale teach you anything? The answer is E! The answer is always—"

Chapter Twenty-Five

Friday Morning—August 23, 2019—Day 12

JENNIFER SAT IN AN ARMCHAIR BY THE OPEN WINDOW CURTAINS, HOLDING A CUP. Papers covered the small table. She heard me yawn and turned. "Thought I'd let you sleep in. How do you feel?"

"Fit as a fiddle." I lay sideways on the mattress, kneading my aching anklebone with my sore hand. "What are you going through?"

"The copies you made at the library are a fascinating read. Sweetie, there's a coffee maker if you'd like some. Oh, and can you switch on the TV for the weather?"

"Will do." I tested adding weight to my right foot—*still tender*—hit the power button on the remote, and hobbled to the Keurig. I put down the K-Cup pod, recalling a news item about high levels of black mold growing in hotel-room coffee machines. I passed on the caffeine and opted for an invigorating shower. As I sealed my eyelids to rinse the shampoo from my hair with hot water, fragments of the dream bobbed to the surface. *Something about taking a difficult quiz. The instructor berating me for not applying myself. Poison. Kidney pie. A creepy skeleton.*

I dried behind my ears with a bath towel, leaving wet toeprints on the carpet. While I hopped into boxer shorts and pulled a T-shirt over my ears, Jennifer spread the photocopies of the South Mississippi Sun, The Daily Herald, and The Biloxi Press across the bed chronologically. There were more news articles than I remember printing at the library. She added two sheets to a thickening pile.

I asked, "Why are these separated?" I picked up a feature story. Urban explorers had stumbled upon a middle-aged female's torso at a decommissioned military base. Authorities could not identify the victim due to Jane Doe's skull being "kicked about like a soccer ball."

"They're duplicates," my wife responded, pulling the photocopy out of my hand and putting it with the others on the bureau. She inspected *The Biloxi Press* classified advertisement for Rugger Pest Control. Cartoon Blatto ran for his life, oversized perspiration droplets spritzing from the back of his insectile head. "His eyes! I totally get the reason this pitiful cockroach bugs you."

I attempted to distinguish correlations in Jennifer's arrangement—a strangling at a playground, a knifing in a parking garage, a sexual battery behind a bar, a different sexual battery behind a different bar, a cheerleader not coming home after football practice, a pubescent girl snatched from her bedroom. *So many rapes and homicides. Countless kids were unaccounted for.* Depravity covered every inch of the bedspread. *Fifty? A hundred?* Gulfport and the surrounding areas didn't seem particularly safe, especially for women.

My wife put her hands on her hips. "Still don't see it?"

Once more, I scanned from the left side of the mattress, starting with the August 1977 newspaper articles. My eyes panned to the right, lingering on the date posted below a *South Mississippi Sun's* masthead: WEDNESDAY, AUGUST 24, 1978. *The anniversary of my mother's attack.* My stomach had that free-fall feeling it always gets on roller coasters. The headline exclaimed: COUNTY TEEN WALKING TO SCHOOL GOES MISSING!

As Jennifer jammed the paperwork into her leather satchel, a CNN meteorologist stood beside a swirling green-and-yellow mass labeled FERNAND. He spoke to the camera, "NOAA's National Hurricane Center is broadcasting a tropical storm warning."

My wife turned off the TV. "Paul, get dressed. The Biloxi Public Library opens in an hour."

I parked at the Biloxi Civic Center. As we walked up to the men and women queuing in front of the library, I lobbed the Bagel Bees wrapping tissue in the trash bin. With no wind and the sky so fair, I had trouble imagining Fernand as an enemy. At 9 a.m., the doors swung wide, and we hurried to the Local History and Genealogy Department.

Debbie grinned when she saw me. "Oh, hi! You're the guy who told Professor Evans, 'I'm gonna,'" she dropped her voice, "'rip your balls off and stick them up your scrawny butt.'"

Jennifer appeared flabbergasted, never having witnessed me blow my top.

I waved an admission of bad behavior. "Sorry, I was under pressure to finish an assignment."

The librarian chuckled into her palm. "It's cool. Evans always treats me like his own personal assistant. I'm glad somebody finally put Uncle Sneaky Hands in his place. What will it be this morning?"

"We'd like all your local newspapers—1965 until now."

Debbie handed me a form. "The *South Mississippi Sun* and *The Biloxi Press* ran from the mid-seventies to the mid-eighties. In 1985, *The Daily Herald* was renamed the *Sun Herald*, the only regional paper still hiring journalists."

I swiftly filled out the fields. She went to the file cabinets and returned with three brown envelopes.

I accepted the microfiche, saying, "We appreciate your help. Hope Uncle Sneaky Hands doesn't come in today."

At side-by-side readers, I split the sheet film with Jennifer. I took the largest stack, the long-running *The Daily Herald* and *Sun Herald*, and gave her the shorter-lived *South Mississippi Sun* and *The Biloxi Press*. "We're just checking August the 24th for each year, correct?"

My wife nodded. "Let's begin with that date." She twiddled the machine's knobs. "How do you work this contraption?"

I demonstrated inserting the 4x6-inch film into the glass carrier, focusing on one of the black rectangles, and moving through time. Then, I positioned the first *The Daily Herald* sheet in my microfiche reader: 1965. I scrolled to August 24. That Tuesday, a C-130 Hercules cargo plane crash-landed in Yau Tong Bay immediately after takeoff from Hong Kong. Fifty-eight US military personnel perished. The president of Egypt and the King of Saudi Arabia announced a nine-point agreement: the withdrawal of 30,000 Egyptian troops from Yemen. The KGB imprisoned twenty-six "nationally minded Ukrainian intellectuals" in the Soviet Union. Two well-known authors charged with "anti-Soviet agitation and propaganda" were on the docket to stand trial. A date with a firing squad seemed inevitable. In Gulfport, apart from an armed female wearing an Atom Ant mask robbing a community bank and seven automobiles vandalized outside an Otis Redding concert, no other local crimes were mentioned in print.

I looked at Jennifer. The light emitting from the translucent screen flickered across her cheeks. "Find anything in *The Biloxi Press*?"

"No, Paul. I'd tell you if I did." She scrolled through articles as if *her* life depended on them. "Starting 1978."

Given that tomorrow is August 24, I understood why we were on a tight deadline. *Will one of the kids my father has been so attracted to end up in his mysterious room?* I slid out 1965, slid in 1966, and went directly to the date in question.

In international news, the Russians launched the Luna 11 space probe to photograph the moon's craters. Disastrously, the misaligned camera merely captured the blackness of outer space. In China, a "counterrevolutionary" novelist being "cross-examined" by the Red Guards committed suicide, and a Marxist philosopher succumbed days after the government denied his diabetes medications. Locally, a Biloxi wife shot her husband over the supper table in retaliation for his drinking, gambling, and philandering. Not much else.

1967 was missing. 1968 was not.

Under the August 24 cover story, FRANCE BECOMES THE FIFTH NUCLEAR NATION, and the accompanying black-and-white picture of a mile-high fireball, a smaller headline burned brighter. "Jenn, come over here!"

My wife rolled her chair closer. "The mushroom cloud?" She squinted at my screen, eventually registering the piece that produced my outburst. "Gulfport teen murders his parents." Her voice lowered to read the full text. "Gulfport, Mississippi. A sixteen-year-old male has been accused of slaying his mother and father in their Orange Grove house, Donna Henderson of the Harrison County Sheriff's Office informed reporters. The minor, name withheld, is charged with two counts of murder in the first degree and possession of a weapon during a violent crime. When authorities entered the Savannah Place residence this morning at nine-thirty, they discovered the bodies of Tanya Russell, forty-five, and Wayne Kenneth Russell, forty-seven. Tanya Russell's employer, Drake's Cannery, had requested a welfare check. Tanya did not call in, and her boss could not reach her by phone. 'Coworkers say it was highly unusual for

Mrs. Russell not to clock in early for her Saturday shift,' said Harrison County Sheriff Peter Cook. Asked about the state of the crime scene, Cook replied, 'In my thirty years in law enforcement, I've never seen this level of brutality. All the gratuitous violence on the idiot box is driving our youth off the path of righteousness. Bring your kids to the house of God to partake in the Eucharist, not to the movie house to gobble Raisinets while watching *In Cold Blood.*'"

At the jump line, Jennifer turned to page seven. "As stated in the arrest warrant, the son, who lived with his parents, initially told deputies his mom and dad were vacationing for a week in New Orleans. Deputy Harris and Deputy Porter spotted bloodstains on the boy's dungarees. They searched the premises, finding the husband and wife's corpses in the master bedroom beneath a bed. According to Harrison County Coroner Mark Fuller, the couple had numerous injuries to their upper torsos and lower extremities. 'Detectives found a knife and an antique tomahawk buried in the backyard garden. We have confidence these sharp-edged implements are the murder weapons.' Donna Henderson said the suspect is being held at the Harrison County Juvenile Detention Center. Autopsies for Tanya and Wayne Russell are scheduled at the Mississippi Forensics Laboratory in Pearl." Jennifer exhaled.

I recalled Jane telling me her attacker said the name Tanya or Tabitha. I said, "Hunter Rugger was sixteen when this was written. Same age as this kid!" I browsed Sunday, Monday, and Tuesday, pausing at this Wednesday feature.

GULFPORT TEEN KILLS MOTHER AND FATHER IN THEIR SLEEP

GULFPORT, MISSISSIPPI – Tuesday's autopsy divulged new details about the deaths of an Orange Grove couple. Tanya Russell, age 45, and Wayne

Kenneth Russell, age 47, died Saturday, the twenty-fourth, at the hands of their son.

The autopsy results are significant, as they disclose that the parents were slain as they slept.

A representative at the Harrison County Sheriff's Office says the two first-degree murder charges were filed in adult court on the grounds of the seriousness of these offenses. The defendant's name, Henry Trenton Russell, age 16, has been made public now that County District Attorney Zachariah Alden has charged him as an adult. "That this young man butchered his own folks while they dreamed of a better life for him categorizes this felony as willful and premeditated."

The Tuesday document describes the fatal injuries.

Harrison County's Coroner, Mark Fuller, alleges Henry Russell lacerated his sleeping mother's throat with a serrated bread knife before slashing his father, who slept in a separate room. Both bodies were posthumously mutilated with a tomahawk (a cutting tool akin to a hatchet). Only prescriptive medications and slight traces of alcohol were detected in either of the adults' bloodstreams. The son tested negative for tetrahydrocannabinol (the psychoactive compound found in marijuana).

Late Tuesday, Russell's lawyer, Hiram Baskin, formally petitioned media organizations not to publish the parents' autopsy. "If these photographs are splashed across *The Daily Herald's* front page, my client won't have a chance in [expletive] of being assigned an unprejudiced jury." Editors at *The Daily Herald* ran Baskin's appeal up the flagpole. The in-house legal staff advised limiting specific aspects of the autopsy to government records, which, under Mississippi state law, are accessible to the public.

Harrison County's Sheriff, Peter Cook, said two full jerrycans of gasoline were hidden behind Christmas decorations in the attached garage. "We believe Henry Russell was preparing to burn down the house to conceal evidence when Deputy Porter and Deputy Harris arrived to check on Tanya Russell. [Her manager phoned the authorities after she didn't report to work.] The offender had a book of matches in his pocket."

The Russell family has been active in various charity groups. Tanya Russell, a factory worker, regularly volunteered at a soup kitchen. Wayne Russell, a shipyard electrician, coached the Blue Jays, the local Little League Baseball team. Wayne's brother, Emmett, affirmed that Henry Russell served several years at Saint John as an altar boy and competed for a single season on the Gulfport High School fencing team. "To be frank," he said, "I always thought my nephew was a bit off."

Neighbors often saw the teenager shooting hoops in his driveway or riding his bicycle late into the evening.

"Henry was polite to me," Gretchen Allen declared from her front porch on Savannah Place. "Kind of quiet. A loner, but no matter the weather, the lad waved hello to me on his way to school. A few

> months ago, he fetched my Sunday newspaper out of the ditch after Bryce, he's the paperboy, didn't have the muscles to pitch it over the fence." Mrs. Allen went inside her home and returned with a discolored photograph of a small boy in a Lone Ranger outfit. She flipped the print to read the date. "1960. I took this picture on Halloween. Henry looked cute in his black mask and cowboy duds. When he got older, he came wrapped in Japanese robes, swinging one of those long swords. Samurai? Not so adorable. Don't suppose I kept snapshots from that year."
>
> Harvey Cohle, a civil servant living across the road from the Russell family, said Henry once helped him search for his lost puppy. "The kid brought me Daisy's collar—nothing else."
>
> Donna Henderson, a spokeswoman for the Sheriff's Office, stated deputies were transporting Henry Russell from the Harrison County Juvenile Detention Center to the Harrison County Correctional Facility, where he will be incarcerated until a judge sets bail.

Jennifer finished reading the text. "The name Henry Russell sounds a lot like Hunter Rugger."

"Yeah, it does. And what about the Lone Ranger stuff?" I scrolled through the rest of the week, hoping to find a photo of Henry Russell or a trial date, but only saw a brief funeral notice for Tanya and Wayne.

"I'll rake the papers for other weird occurrences on August 24th." She rolled her chair back to her machine.

I stood to stretch. *Is Henry Russell Hunter Rugger? If so, my father murdered his parents.* I felt the walls closing in on me.

Hacked them to death as they were lying in their beds. At the reference desk, Debbie smiled cheerfully. I willed my lips to upturn, the magnitude of this demonic act smacking me hard. *He killed my grandparents—grandparents I'll never have the opportunity to meet.*

In the preceding decade, Hale's parents, Grandpa John and Grandma Lillian, breathed their last from radon poisoning—radioactive gas seeping over time through fissures in their basement foundation. They lived in South Dakota, so I just saw them during the holidays. Edith's mom and dad sold their house in Oradell, New Jersey, to spend their retirement tooling around the country in a recreational vehicle. Grandpa Charles and Grandma Katherine's golden years sadly ended a fortnight short of their 50th wedding anniversary. They had been overnighting at a Glacier National Park campground when both were asphyxiated by carbon monoxide poisoning. Investigators faulted a disconnected generator exhaust pipe for their premature deaths. My mom broke down at the double funeral, almost toppling Grandma Kate's casket.

"Paul."

"Hmm." I pivoted to Jennifer.

"Please go to the printer for me?"

I scooped up the two Henry Russell printouts and a new one from the *South Mississippi Sun*, dated Sunday, August 24, 1980.

GIRL FOUND IN TRASH AT CHINESE RESTAURANT

> GULFPORT - A man scavenging for scraps at daybreak behind a popular restaurant on 25th Avenue uncovered a human arm. The vagrant notified the Red Lotus' owner, Feigang Fei, then left the premises without leaving his name. Fei, a US citizen, called the Sheriff's Office. Detectives

> discovered parts of a young female in three separate garbage cans.
>
> At noon, Harrison County Sheriff Preston Perkins announced, "Although we haven't located her clothing, it's too soon in the investigation to verify if our Jane Doe had been sexually abused. The coroner has confirmed the victim is of Asian descent, and, from the condition of her dismembered body, she expired today shortly after midnight. Our department artist will complete a visual likeness and release the sketch to the public. Hopefully, someone shall provide a name."
>
> Sheriff Perkins said Feigang Fei is not a suspect, but had no comment when queried if a serial murderer ran loose in Gulfport.
>
> Due to the tremendous backlog of cases at the Mississippi Forensics Laboratory, autopsy results may not be available until the end of this week.

As I reclaimed my seat, picturing flies buzzing over swill bins full of human remains, Jennifer sent me back to the laser printer. "I came across another match in the *South Mississippi Sun.*" She depressed a key. "Printing now."

This August 24, 1982, article made me ill.

HUNTERS FIND A WOMAN'S LEG INSIDE AN ALLIGATOR

> PASS CHRISTIAN – This morning, three men not carrying hunting permits shot an alligator in the Wolf River Marsh Coastal Preserve. While brothers Earle and Boone Abernathy and Army veteran pal, Vernon Fortner, skinned, cleaned, and deboned the thirteen-footer in the bed of Fortner's pickup truck,

the poachers were shocked to find an unexpected meal in the beast's stomach: a female's mangled thigh, calf, and foot.

Once Fortner got to town, he used a pay phone at Harpy's Saloon on Menge Avenue to call the Mississippi Department of Wildlife, Fisheries, & Parks. "Even knowing the staties would fine the boys and me $750 for gatoring out of season, my gut told me, 'Vern, get some of them government suits down here to get a look-see at what we reeled in.' That girl's ma and pa must be worried to death." Fortner wiped his eyes. "Such a [expletive] shame."

MDWFP interfaced with the Pass Christian Police Department. Sergeant Rhett thanked the men for performing their civic duty, but wondered why the hunters had broken the law. "Alligator season always opens the last Friday of August. That's only three days away. In the future, get your $25 hunting permit, grab a rifle, and go have a blast!"

This reporter further questioned Sergeant Rhett about the leg recovered from the dead alligator's belly. "Jane Doe had a tattoo of a seahorse blowing bubbles on her left ankle and five stitches on her knee. There has been a slew of runaways this summer. Our office is checking the churches and shelters. We need the public's support to give this poor girl a name. Not a great deal to work with."

Harrison County Coroner Deacon Holt revealed preliminary examinations of the female's limb could exhibit foul play. "The shape of the marks on Jane Doe's upper thigh indicates that a sharpened instrument similar to a knife or machete may have

> been used to cleave the appendage from the hip cleanly. A full-grown alligator has eighty conical teeth." Holt clamped his hands to simulate a snapping jaw. "No mistaking the damage those choppers can do to human flesh."
>
> Sergeant Rhett requested that parents missing a 14-17-year-old daughter contact the Pass Christian Police Department.

Friday Afternoon—August 23, 2019—Day 12

I needed a breather after reading that ghastly article. The library's printer spat out page upon page as I plodded past the reference desk to the exit. *Jennifer is unearthing more stuff. Terrible stuff.* Debbie heard the deepness of my sigh and looked away from her computer. "Finding what you wanted, Mr. Crutcher?"

"Sure. Thanks for the assistance."

"No problem. Be safe!"

I halted in my tracks and twirled. *Did the librarian see the material we were researching?* "'Be safe'?"

"The storm. The forecasters calculate Fernand will slam the Gulf Coast as soon as tonight. People are boarding up their houses and businesses or even evacuating." She crooked a finger upward. "When I get off work, I'm driving to Saucier to stay with my parents."

I told her, "My dad always used to say, 'Better safe than dead.'"

Outdoors, I circumnavigated the Biloxi Civic Center under a dark sky markedly darker to the south. A stiff breeze blew the Padres baseball cap off my head and into the parking lot, making me have to stomp on the brim to prevent the souvenir from being sucked down a storm drain. I perched on a concrete bench beneath a newly planted tree, nature's fury denuding the spindly branches of leaves. Across the street, an elderly man struggled to nail plywood over a picture window at a run-down house. I deliberated whether I should go over and lend a hand, now too physically and mentally beat to lift a finger.

I visualized Tanya and Wayne Russell being slaughtered by their own child in their own beds. Henry Russell? Hunter Rugger? Pillows smothering gasping mouths. Bedsheets soaked in ancestral blood. *Henry and Hunter are one and the same!* I felt pain for the girls I believed he had abducted. Overwhelmingly, I bemoaned my own existential crisis. The man responsible for sexually assaulting my mother is a monster in the ilk of John Wayne Gacy, Ted Bundy the Killer Clown, Son of Sam, Charles Manson with his flock of homicidal women, and that sick fuck Jeffrey Dahmer. And let's not forget the list of psychopaths never apprehended: the Alphabet Killer, Jack the Ripper, the Boston Strangler, and someone biologically close to me—*my father.*

Jennifer emerged from the library's front entrance, gazing from side to side before spying me. She walked through the wind, clutching a bundle of photocopies, and sat beside me. "Hanging in there?"

Her closeness made my reply, "I'm fine, babe," a wee bit easier.

My wife flattened the newspaper clippings on her thigh. "Want to see more?"

"I've seen enough." My eyes strayed to the top page of *The Biloxi Press*. I couldn't help myself from reading the SUNDAY, AUGUST 24, 1986, headline: BELOVED TRACK STAR RAPED AND MURDERED.

"Today's been a strain, but I have an item of interest to show you." Jennifer sorted the articles. "Check out this *Zillow* listing! Hunter Rugger purchased his residence in Pass Christian for one hundred and fifty-six thousand in 1996." She held up four news pieces from *The Biloxi Press* and five from the *South Mississippi Sun*. "In the years since your father bought the house, the only crimes on August 24th were for missing women. No women wound up in dumpsters or inside alligators."

I frowned. "That's when Rugger built the damn room." I envisioned a young girl shrieking her lungs out, no one hearing her pleas through the soundproof walls. *Dexter Morgan's saltwater boat—the SLICE of LIFE.* "My guess is, he uses *THE TERMINATOR* to discard the bodies in the Gulf after he—you know—is finished with them."

She checked the time on her phone. "Now what? It's three o'clock."

I spread my hands. "Why didn't the police ever figure this out? Aren't detectives trained to recognize patterns?"

Jennifer shrugged. "Deputies arrested the Golden State Killer last year. He began his raping and killing crime spree in the seventies. And the Zodiac Killer might be a friend, coworker, or neighbor. Hell, Zodiac could have been the handyman on *Captain Kangaroo*."

I scowled. "Say it isn't so!"

She patted my arm. "Paul, I know you loved Mr. Green Jeans. The Golden State Killer's mug shots were posted all over the media. Joseph James DeAngelo, an ex-cop."

I snapped my fingers. "Didn't a cold-case investigator upload his DNA into a genealogy database, then link him to other family members?"

Jennifer nodded. "DeAngelo's DNA was on file in a rape kit. They dug a fresh snot rag out of his trash. Bingo—perfect match. DeAngelo kept saying, 'Don't blame me. Jerry made me do it.'"

I perceived my father's pernicious chromosomes flowing throughout my veins and felt an ice cube skate down my neck and along my spinal column. "Let's spin by Rugger's to see if he's home."

I glanced at the fast-encroaching cumulonimbus clouds as we plowed through powerful gusts to get to the rental car. The rain hadn't begun to come down yet, but the streetlights turned on four hours ahead of schedule.

My wife got in the Corolla. "What about the storm? The librarian told you she's evacuating?"

"To her family." A thirtyish man carried water jugs and sacks of groceries into the house across the lane. *The old fella's hanging tough.* "If it gets too nasty, we'll go north." The car door handle nearly flew from my fingers as I shut out the gale.

We swung past the towering home on Pall Mall Road in Pass Christian. No pest control van. I stifled the impulse to run under the structure, bang on the storage room's walls, and yell, "Is anyone in there?"

Jennifer extracted newspaper photocopies from her brown satchel. "We have enough circumstantial evidence to hand over to the authorities. The Sheriff's Office will haul your father in for interrogation."

I evaluated her proposition. "Jenn, the deputies are busy with Fernand just miles from making landfall. They'll be on the streets directing traffic out of town and pulling people from submerged cars."

She shook the fistful of papers. "They can't just ignore us!"

"It's all inconclusive. No hard evidence."

"There's the space behind his exterminating gear! Investigators shall find his little shop of horrors and scour the place. A judge will lock up Hunter Rugger for a thousand years."

The DNA Center has my father's and my DNA samples. I knew I'd receive a backblast, yet self-preservation talked me into:

"Babe, you ended a man's life. Law enforcement can't become involved."

My wife's cheeks flushed with anger. "Delgado's first lieutenant intended to eliminate us! After the cartel got their claws on the drugs *your brothers* stole, they'd make your whole family cease to exist!" Her lower lip quivered. "I stabbed Antonio in self-defense."

The look on her face as she—

"Paul!"

"Jenn, I know that and you know that, but the cops don't—"

"What did *you and Jane* do in that garage? The Wildcat had no legs!"

"Like I said. When I booted in the side door, Delgado twisted my foot. I shot him in his calves to free myself."

She clenched my hand. "After you let us back inside the garage, I saw what was left of the man. Skin, black and blistered. Not a hair on his head. And, oh, what happened to Delgado's chest?"

I killed the Wildcat. My mother breathed the Wildcat back to life. Then I killed the Wildcat again, this time permanently. I said softly, "Once Juan told us where to find Sarah, I put the scumbag out of his misery."

"How?"

"I burned a hole through his rib cage to get to his heart."

Jennifer's complexion waned to the shade of bleached bone, and I worried she might throw up. By sheer willpower, my wife held down the toasted sesame seed bagel with a schmear of jalapeño cream cheese. "So," she consumed half of a water bottle, "if we don't go to the police?"

"We kill my father," I answered, "and toss his body in the swamp."

The corners of Jennifer's lips curled. *Is that a grin? Does she think I'm joking?* "Sounds like a plan, kemosabe."

It started to drizzle at 4 p.m. I set the windshield wipers to intermittent. Whitecaps formed as we crossed the Bay Saint Louis Bridge to Saint Stanislaus Catholic Boarding School. There were no cars in the parking spaces, no teachers in the faculty lounge grading exams, and no students partaking in extracurricular activities. *Classes let out early because of the storm.* We roved the area seeking high and low for a short, chubby, red-haired boy. Those scarce kids splashing through puddles were indistinguishable from each other in their hooded raincoats.

We drove back across the bridge to Gulfport, the wipers on medium, the water in Bay Saint Louis foaming white. Headlights on, we circled Long Beach High School, scouting for a blond girl in a black PINK shirt dedicated enough to run laps in a rainstorm. Minutes later, I stopped the Toyota at the Seaview Apartments on Ocean Avenue. A FOR RENT sign blew over and pinwheeled down the deserted street.

We proceeded east to the Bay Cove condominiums on Damphman Point. Nobody stood outside braving the weather to admire the waterfront view of Magnolia Bend and Mullet Lake. At 8 p.m., even if we knew what Rugger's subject of intent looked like, it was now too dark to identify anybody. *A colossal waste of time.*

Northbound, en route to West Harrison High, Jennifer turned on her phone to study the photo of the cyclist shouldering a dayglow backpack. In Ridgecrest, I rolled the Corolla past the schoolgirl's double-wide. The orange Schwinn was chained to the wooden front deck. *No room within that shoebox to keep the bike dry.* An unoccupied doghouse. *At least the husky is indoors.*

My wife glared through the water streaming down the passenger window. "This girl is the only potential target we're able to speak to. She's in that trailer with her family right now."

I ticked off the kids my father had watched and the places he had driven by—the blond female runner in PINK exercise apparel, a resident at or near the Seaview Apartments, the red-headed boy at the school pool, the Damphman Point condominiums, and this teen now only yards away.

Jennifer chewed on a fingernail, a nervous habit she had quit long ago. "What are our options?"

I shrugged. "This is the only address we have. You suspect Hunter Rugger is toying with us. Is he clever enough to know we'd tail this one here?"

"Conceivably." She spat a sliver of white keratin at the floor mat. "The first two, the sprinter and the swimmer? At midday, they were in school, three hours till the bell rang. We trailed your father without determining where each of the students lived." My wife stared at the beam of light shining from the mobile home's window. "I'm afraid this bicyclist isn't a lot to go on, but she's all we have."

I wondered how many other kids my father had pursued before we pursued him. Strategic decisions filled my belfry to the rafters. I wanted to recline the seat, close my eyes, and fantasize about lying on a Caribbean beach sipping cocktails with Lilliputian rainbow umbrellas stuck between floating cubes of ice. Rather than resolve any issue, I switched the windshield wipers up a notch and shoved our rental car into drive.

We reached Pass Christian—twenty miles of pouring rain, three downed trees, and a detour around a flooded major avenue. The Mallini Bayou seemed inclined to overtop its banks as we turned onto Pall Mall Road. No van at Rugger's unlit house.

Jennifer's eyelids narrowed at the dashboard clock. "Where is he?"

The scattering of hail striking the Toyota's metal roof sounded as though we were trapped inside a steel drum.

We returned to the Days Inn, hung our sodden clothes over the shower rod, and crawled into bed. I can't vouch for Jennifer, but I dreamed.

> I sat in a room with three other children. The Lone Ranger wall clock chimed nine times. A severe matron garbed in Victorian black bustled into the space, calling, "Madeline McFarland!" An athletic young blond woman in a shirt printed with the word PINK raised her arm not holding a Chihuahua. "Here, Mrs. Moriarty!" Madeline lowered the dog to the floor, then scurried to the corridor. The whining animal trotted in circles chasing its tail. Ten chimes. "Thomas Pullman!" Mrs. Moriarty shrilled with heightened ferocity, "Thomas Pullman!" Four chairs down from me, a carrot-topped boy in a blue swimsuit sprang to his feet. "Please don't hit me, Mrs. Moriarty. I was daydreaming. Won't do it again." Thomas scampered out the door, leaving a puddle of water on his seat. Eleven chimes. A dark-haired female remained with me, a luminous orange pack on her back. Mrs. Moriarty peered at me, then pointed at her, who put on a helmet, mounted an orange bicycle, and pedaled into the hallway. Isolated, I listened to the ticking of the clock's internal mechanism. When the black-masked Lone Ranger's black gloves touched XII, bells chimed. Bong, bong, bong, bong. . . . The undertaker's wife clapped her hands in rhythm. *"Paul! Paul! Paul!"*

Chapter Twenty-Six

Saturday Morning—August 24, 2019—Day 13

"PAUL!"

"Huh?"

"You're having a bad dream."

I sat upright, checking the clock on the nightstand. *9:07 a.m.* "I was in this room filled with—"

"Wow, look at that!" Jennifer had the television tuned to the Gulfport news. Scenes of gigantic sea surf pounding the coast, capsized fishing boats, roofs blowing off of industrial buildings and residential houses, and flooded streets flashed across the screen in an endless loop.

"Walter Coleman is out in the field," a female voice announced. "Walt, what are you seeing at the beach?"

A hooded man gripping a WXXV microphone angled 45 degrees into the windstorm. His yellow slicker flapped as a cloudburst doused his face. "Rachel, I'm standing in front of the old Biloxi sea wall. Constructed in 1927, engineers designed this stepped structure to withstand the force of a Cat 5 hurricane. Over the decades, sand built up on the seaward side, leaving only a few of the original steps exposed." Walt extended a portable device with a tiny propeller embedded in the top. "As you can see on this anemometer's display, we're getting steady squalls of sixty miles per hour. The National Hurricane Center still classifies Fernand as a tropical storm. If these winds increase to seventy-four miles per hour, the NHC may upgrade Fernand to a hurricane. Hey Joe! Get over here and give the viewers a closer shot of the size of the waves coming in." The picture tilted, moving jerkily toward the cement wall. "If a storm surge coincides with high tide, there's speculation this aged coastal defense will breach." When Joe inclined past the edge, the crest of a giant breaker knocked the camera from his hands. White static filled the screen as the distorted audio cut out.

Rachel Martin, a statuesque gal in a clingy green dress, stood at a mammoth monitor illustrating a mostly yellow and red Doppler image of the Gulf coast. "Walter?" She tapped her ear. "We're trying to get Walt back online. In the meantime, stay tuned to WXXV for the latest on Fernand."

My wife lowered the volume and went to the window. "It's raining cats and dogs out there."

I settled beside her as a convoy of law enforcement vehicles, sirens howling, raced east. "Just like us, Hunter Rugger can't drive anyplace. Anybody he has in mind will remain indoors until the storm passes. Those kids will be free from harm."

She yawned and rubbed her arms. "Unless he already took them. He wasn't home all yesterday or last night—till midnight, anyway."

I stood up. "We'll go downstairs, eat breakfast, and plan our next steps."

Jennifer frowned at the words on the scrolling ticker: BREAKING NEWS – NHC UPGRADES FERNAND TO HURRICANE. "Look! The map shows all the flooded areas." She retrieved a paper pad from her purse and typed into her phone. "I have the address for that girl in Ridgecrest. The *Whitepages* claims Alexander, Isabella, and Lorena Gonzalez have occupied that mobile house since 2014."

I rubbed my eyes. "How does that knowledge benefit us?"

"Lorena Gonzalez recently won a debating competition at West Harrison High. That's gotta be her. Oh, here's a photo." My wife rotated the screen. An attractive adolescent woman in a black jacket stood at a podium, one hand upraised, her expression earnest. "She's definitely the person riding the orange bike."

I asked, "Is a telephone number listed?"

Jennifer did more *Googling*. "Hmmm. I'm not seeing any."

I overfilled a bowl with Tony the Tiger and 2% milk in an alcove off the hotel's lobby. My wife ladled whitish goop into a waffle maker. After the cooker's timer dinged, she joined me at the table. Sweet syrup drowned the pockets in her batter cakes.

I spoke with my mouth crammed with soggy Frosted Flakes. "I want to go to Pass Christian."

"Will we make it?" Jennifer spread a pat of butter onto the goo. "The meteorologists are designating Fernand as a hurricane. I looked up that word in the dictionary. The definition of 'hurricane' is 'a big-ass storm that kills a shitload of people.'" She added two squares of fatty goodness. "Paul, you really want to do this? It's insane."

"Babe, you can stay here at the hotel."

"Ha!"

"I mean it. It's safer for both of us. If something happens to me, dial 911."

"And say what exactly? 'Hello? My husband vanished out hunting for his serial-killer dad. Paul was driving around all by himself in the *hurricane*. Yes, Officer Fife, I know what a *hurricane* is. Sure, Barney, I'll listen to hold music while you noodle for catfish at the fishin' hole with Ron "Opie" Howard and Andy fucking Griffith.'" My wife threw down her napkin. "Do you recall how you screwed up by not bringing me with you in the first place? I go where you go, and you go where I go. Us alpha wolves hunt in a pack." She kicked back her chair. "Got it, my little buckaroo?"

Saturday Afternoon—August 24, 2019—Day 13

Thunder rolled in from the south as we entered the seashore town of Pass Christian. Aside from expanses awash with tides (which we niftily circumvented using the *Waze* app), the journey west was easier than I anticipated. We made good time on the empty streets. The shallow root balls of the palm trees bordering Pall Mall Road were being put to the test as a windbreak. With no white van in sight, I swung the Toyota into Hunter Rugger's driveway.

Jennifer clinched my arm. "What are you doing?"

"Wait here." I jumped out of the Corolla and shut the door. Below the stilt house, I joggled the padlock securing the storage room. *Locked.* I groped the top of the doorframe and under the doormat for a key. *Too easy to happen a second time.* I circled the structure, hammering the walls. "Anybody in there? Hello? Hello?" I squeezed my ear flap to the plywood, only hearing the wind wailing. Inside the car, I rested my damp forehead on the hard steering wheel. "If somebody *is* in that box, they're tied up and gagged, or—" Tired from running on fumes, tired from trying to stop "dear ol' Dad" from grabbing some kid, I sobbed.

My wife swabbed my face with her shirt sleeve. "Sweetie, you're a courageous man doing your best. That's all anyone can ask."

"My father is a serial murderer."

"Well, my dad left me the day I was born. Not sure which is worse. Jesus preached to his twelve disciples, 'You *can't* pick your family, but you *can* pick your friends.'" She smooched me on the cheek. "Rev up the Batmobile, Robin. We'll check the same places as yesterday."

We bypassed the schools—closed on a stormy Saturday—motoring up the water-washed coast to the Seaview Apartments on Ocean Wave Avenue. Outside of a guy dashing to get a suitcase from a station wagon, no one else was nearby.

High beams flashed in the rearview mirror as we progressed north to the condominiums on Damphman Point. I groaned. "Oh, no!"

Jennifer sighed. "What now?"

I steered onto the muddy shoulder, opening my window to the driving rain and screeching wind as the City of Gulfport Police vehicle pulled alongside.

The policewoman lowered her passenger window to shout, "Where are you folks headed?"

My wife, reacting to my speechlessness, leaned across the console. "We're delivering medications to my grandmother at the Bay Cove Assisted Living and Memory facility at Damphman Point."

A garbled voice squawked a command. The officer spoke into a two-way radio microphone. "10-4. Unit responding." She returned her attention to us. "Fernand is approaching at hurricane strength. You should keep off the streets." The blue-and-white SUV, lights flashing, sped to the next emergency.

I raised the glass and guided the tires onto the roadway. *Fortunately for us, the cop was summoned away.* We traversed the Popp's Ferry Bridge to Deep Point, a marshy crescent of flatland surrounded by Big Lake, Little Big Lake, and Mullet Lake. In plainer words, too much lake and too little terra firma.

"What *is* that?" Jennifer mopped condensation from the interior glass with a napkin. "Stop! Stop!"

A swell drenched the hood as I smushed the brakes, the Toyota fishtailing into inches of floodwater.

My wife spun to the rear window. "Back up and turn around. Find a different way."

Pigheaded, I eased the wheels in ten more feet. "Not that deep. I see a high point beyond those trees. We will get through if we go slow."

"Paul, we'll get stuck."

I waved away her protestations, inch by inch, rolling the automobile into a pond that had not existed moments earlier. The whirling radiator fan splashed, the dashboard lights flickered, the automatic transmission shuddered, and the engine's four cylinders filled with a liquid lacking the explosive properties of gasoline. Steam emerged from cracks in the hood.

"Paul, the water's rising. We need to get out."

I cranked the starter motor. "The battery's dead." I dialed the Budget Rent a Car office to hear, "Due to a high call volume, you may experience a longer hold time than normal. We apologize for any inconvenience this might cause."

"Paul, it's up to the guardrails."

I phoned Triple A, only to be notified, "Sorry, Mr. Crutcher. Thanks to Fernand, no tow trucks are on hand."

Jennifer opened the car door. Turbid water poured into the footwells. "Hurry!"

We waded through water up to our knees to reach dry ground. Despite packing our rain jackets, we hadn't prepared for anything comparable to Fernand. Both of us were sopping wet. "This span is the only way to cross."

"Forget Damphman Point. We can—" She stood still. "Will our insurance cover that?" The silver Toyota Corolla slowly floated off toward Mullet Lake. "Crap, I forgot to charge my battery." My wife waved impatiently. "Give me your cell phone. I'll try Lyft or Uber."

"Good idea, but I doubt drivers will work in this weather." I probed my pockets. "Christ, I left mine in the car. Do we still have the burner phone?"

She scowled as the rental car's roof sank below the roiling surface. "Now we have to walk."

While we descended from the top of the drawbridge, a Mississippi Power bucket truck advanced in the opposite lane. I vaulted the concrete barrier, jogging into the street with my arms upraised. Once I explained our predicament to the driver, he reversed the cherry picker and carried us as far as Cowan Road. We thumbed another ride (a waterlogged jounce in the rear of a pickup overloaded with crated chickens) to the Days Inn.

Out of the elements, Jennifer plugged her cell phone into the charger, stripped off her saturated clothes, and showered. I blew our garments with the hairdryer before my turn beneath the massaging head. My wife was asleep under a quilt when I limped from the bathroom. Wide awake in bed, I watched the clock's digits increment upward. As the five o'clock hour transitioned to the six o'clock hour, I drifted into. . . .

> My father—*my dead-on-Christmas-morn father*—greeted me in a room crowded with kinfolk. *Grandma Lillian? Grandma Katherine? Is this a birthday? Or a funeral?* Hale appeared tall, bright-eyed, bushy-tailed, and very much alive. "Son, you have no choice. You must do it."
>
> "Do what, Dad?" He about-faced, striding past Grandpa John and Grandpa Charles and out the back door. I rushed after him. "What does that mean, 'I have no choice'?" The faster I ran, the farther he got—my father evanescing down a forest trail. In a clearing, a crow on a stone altar pecked the entrails from a snake's belly. The black bird spread vulture's wings to caw, *"Kill him, kill him, kill him—"*

I roused to urgent squawking. Jennifer's glowing iPhone lured me across the darkened hotel room to read an emergency notification.

> Amber Alert Aug 24, 2019, 10:02 PM
>
> Gulfport, MS Amber Alert: LIC/NA white late-model Chevrolet Express van. License plate unavailable.

The hyperlink led me to *missingkids.org*.

> Name: Lorena Gonzalez
>
> Issued for: Mississippi
>
> Date: Since Aug 24, 2019, 6:00 PM
>
> Location: From Gulfport, MS
>
> Age: 17
>
> Sex: Female
>
> Race: White
>
> Hair: Brown
>
> Eyes: Brown
>
> Height: 5'4"
>
> Weight: 115 lbs.
>
> Description: An Amber Alert has been released for Lorena Gonzalez. Lorena is a 17-year-old white female, 5'4" tall, 115 lbs., with brown hair and brown eyes. Lorena was wearing gray sweatpants, black boots, and a camouflage raincoat. A white late-model Chevrolet Express van had been seen in the area. If you have information regarding Lorena's whereabouts, contact the Gulfport Police at 423-555-0111. Check local media for more info.

The attached photograph of the smiling youth left no ambiguity in my mind. The West Harrison high school girl pedaling a bike to her Ridgecrest house trailer, the girl on the same school's winning debate team, and the girl in this Amber Alert were all Lorena Gonzalez. *The person Hunter Rugger followed.*

"Jennifer! Wake up!"

My wife groaned, then resumed snoring.

"Wake up!"

She sat against the headboard, rubbing her eyes. "What's the matter?"

"My father kidnapped Lorena Gonzalez!"

I clicked on the TV, flipping past movie channels until I landed on WXXV. Lorena Gonzalez's face (the picture in the Amber Alert) hovered over the anchorwoman's left shoulder. I increased the volume and moved closer.

"We couldn't drive a satellite truck up to Ridgecrest; however, we've got Lorena's mother on the line. Mrs. Gonzalez, what can you tell us about your daughter's disappearance?"

A woman's voice vibrated with tension. "After the rain let up, Lorena took Balto for a walk. We just bought our daughter a raincoat at Walmart, but one of her classmates swiped it. Alex, that's my husband, gave Lorena his waterproof hunting jacket. The roof leaked something awful, so while Alex emptied the pots in the bathroom, I was in the kitchen roasting a rack of—"

Rachel Martin cut her off. "Mrs. Gonzalez, when did you realize your daughter was missing?"

"Oh, I removed the lamb from the oven and hollered, 'Lorena, dinner!' She took too long to answer, so I asked Alex to check on her. My husband looked out the windows, only seeing the dog. I heard him hollering, 'Lorena, Lorena!' He ran inside, yelling about a white van driving off. Whoever has my daughter, please don't hurt her. We'll do whatever you want to get her back!"

The over-the-shoulder graphics box changed from Lorena's photo to the Gulfport Police phone number.

"Chief Calvin Riley of the Gulfport Police requests you to call 423-555-0111 if you've seen Lorena or have additional information. Now to Walter Coleman at the weather desk. Walt, Fernand gives all indications of intensifying. What is the forecast for the next five days?"

"Rachel, Doppler radar shows—"

I muted the volume. "We've got to get to Pass Christian, but we're dead in the water without a car."

Jennifer opened the Lyft and Uber apps on her iPhone. "Only ducks dare to be outdoors in this rain."

I inwardly paged through a list of alternatives. *Take a bus? Another jaunt in the back of another pickup truck? Hike twenty miles in a hurricane? Talk to law enforcement? We can't contact the cops anonymously now that the burner phone is at the bottom of Mullet Lake.* Flustered, I paced the mauve carpet. *Excluding my family, wherever they might roost, there's only one person within a hundred miles I trust.*

"Babe, you told me Gervais gave you his phone number?"

"Before he left. Why?"

I pointed at her cell phone. "Can you call him?"

"Gervais Romero is in New Orleans. Too far to Uber us anywhere."

"He may know someone in Gulfport. A friend or relative? Otherwise. . . ."

She selected the ride-hailing driver and the speakerphone icon.

"Hello?"

"Gervais?"

"Who is dis?"

"Jennifer Crutcher."

"You got da wrong number."

"Wait! Don't hang up! You don't know our names. Um, you drove us to the place on Alabo?"

"Alabo Street? Are you okay?"

"Paul and I are, but a child is in jeopardy. You remember the man with the sword?"

"I'll never forget da eyes of dat scary motherfucker."

"We just found out that 'scary motherfucker' is my husband's biological father. He goes by Hunter Rugger, but we've learned his true identity is Henry Russell. A few hours ago, he abducted a high school student while walking her dog. The Gulfport Police Department issued an Amber Alert. It's all over the news. He has assaulted many women, including the lady held hostage at the vacant house. Jane is Paul's birth mother. Russell raped her as a teenager. Gervais, we don't have time to go into it all."

"What can I do to help?"

"Our rental car was washed away in the storm. Gervais, we need a lift from Gulfport to Pass Christian. We think—we're certain Henry Russell has Lorena Gonzalez locked in a room underneath his home. Is there anyone in Gulfport who will take us to Pass Christian?"

"Where you at now?"

"The Days Inn on Poole Street. Off the 49?"

"Be dere in ten."

"Ten minutes?"

"After surviving dat crazy bitch Katrina, I'm riding out Fernand with my sister. Delphine lives near da Gulfport Dragway. Meet me in da lobby."

Gervais hung up. We got ready.

Gervais Romero zoomed up to the Days Inn in Delphine's new red four-wheel-drive Jeep Wrangler instead of his classic black Lincoln Continental. He avoided as much destruction as possible by navigating roads on elevated terrain, the high-clearance vehicle capable of fording sections inundated with water.

Jennifer, seated in the front bucket, swiveled to regard Gervais. “Why are you once again risking your life for us?”

“You yanked me behind dat table when da shit hit the fan.” He shook his head. “You saved my bacon, ma’am. I owe you.”

“Gervais, quit with the ‘ma’am’. Call me Jennifer or just plain Jenn. You watched over us and contacted the police. If you hadn’t waited to see if we were all right, that nutcase—”

“Five-O never showed their snouts.” He sucked air through his teeth. “The pigs only come to the Lower Ninth Ward to shoot innocent folk.”

“Not entirely the cops’ fault that night.” She directed the Jeep onto Pall Mall Road. “Running a squad car over Rodrigo’s severed head probably distracted them. Stop here.”

Gervais killed the engine and opened the door.

I clasped his arm. “Stay. If we’re not walking out of that house in an hour, call for help.”

Gervais reached within his poncho. “Here, Paul.” He put a well-worn revolver in my palm. “You might need dis. I filed off da serial number. Untraceable.” The Uber driver threw up both hands. “Keep da gun. That thing’s got a wicked history. Don’t want it back.”

Chapter Twenty-Seven

Sunday Early Morning—August 25, 2019—Day 14

AT MIDNIGHT, WE CLIMBED THE TWENTY-ONE SLIPPERY STEPS TO THE WRAPAROUND DECK, the handgun in my jacket pocket thumping against my hip. Instead of pressing the doorbell, I banged three times on the front door.

Fifteen heartbeats later, the exterior lights switched on, and Henry Russell (aka Hunter Rugger or Hank Russman) opened the yellow door without showing a hint of surprise. He peered past my shoulder at the glimmering red Jeep. "Who's your friend?"

I shouted above the howling wind, "Nobody. Where is she?"

"Come on in. I've been waiting for you." He swung the door, giving Jennifer the once-over as if grading cuts of meat at the neighborhood Winn-Dixie. We stepped across the threshold into the dark foyer, the blowing precipitation beading on the waxed hardwood flooring.

My father—at this point in our limited relationship, I could not refer to him as Hunter Rugger, and the name Henry Russell bothered me even more—led us by the living room/TV room and the corridor to the bedrooms and bathrooms. With cowboy boots on, the man had to be six inches taller than me, his broad shoulders grazing the kitchen entryway. I was powerless to resist the familial pride puffing out my chest. *That's my dad.*

"Will you lend me a hand, Paul?" He went to a table leaning against the wall. Dutifully (as though I had done a thousand household chores for him during my childhood), I helped my father move the brown table to the midpoint of the space and unfold the legs. He carried over a chair and set it down. "The laundry room has extra seats." My father didn't gesture at the bi-fold door, so I figured he knew my familiarity with where he washed his clothes. Jennifer, preferring not to be alone with him, accompanied me across the sandstone tiles. Three brown folding chairs hung on a rack above a blue basket filled with beige RUGGER PEST CONTROL coveralls. I unhooked two dusty seats from the wall, and we transferred them to the kitchen.

We sat under a candlestick chandelier, me facing my father and my wife at a diagonal to my right. The light shining directly on his face gave me my first real opportunity to scrutinize the man who begat me. He appeared younger than his sixty-seven years, only a patch of scalp peeking through hair darker than mine. The facial hair (somewhere between stubble and a full beard) softened the harsh contours of a face that needed to interface with customers. The white bristles sprouting from the bottom of his rectangular chin, extending up his jawbone to his sideburns, concealed a jagged scar. I saw my teenage mother ripping the compasses across his cheek to extricate herself—racing home as fast as her cross-country legs would propel her. *Hope it hurts every time you open your goddamn mouth.* Self-conscious, I rubbed my nose, the prominent bridge feeling much as his looked. My eyes, ostensibly drawn upward by powerful mental magnets, gaped into his steel-blue irises.

"Like looking in a mirror, isn't it, Paul?" My father bent forward with unabashed zeal. "I've taken hundreds of pictures of you, but they come nowhere close to seeing you in the flesh."

"Pictures of me? When?"

He stood, then paused. "Don't you dare run off."

Jennifer whispered, "Where's *he* going?"

I shrugged.

My father seemed grateful we were still here as he reentered the kitchen carrying four large red scrapbooks. He laid the cloth-bound album hand-labeled PAUL RUSSELL 1978-1991 before me, opening the front cover to the first page. A photograph showed a toddler, *me*, crawling on uncut grass. In the background, laughing children holding long ribbons danced around a Maypole adorned with flowers. This sharply focused image had been shot with a telephoto lens, as indicated by the photographer's distant angle of view. Next came a snap of my adoptive mother, Edith, and me playing with a black-pawed dog. *Bootsie!* A picture of my adoptive father followed—Hale pushing me down a street on a tricycle. Birthday parties, band practices, soccer games—sheet by laminated sheet, I observed myself evolve into the proud fourteen-year-old waving an eighth-grade diploma. I visualized the photographic darkroom in the master bedroom's walk-in closet—the orange lights, the enlarger, and the three chemical trays. *My father developed these black-and-white prints himself, so he didn't have to use a commercial lab.*

After I reached the final page, Jennifer took the scrapbook from me, haltingly leafing through the highlights of my youth. She fondly patted my baby photos, her eyes crinkling at my winsome smile. My wife oohed and aahed at a color Polaroid of me cradling Bootsie and once giggled at the "Toothless Wonder" holding a shiny quarter. *Has she forgotten the purpose of us being here, or is she trying to build some kind of rapport?* Jennifer turned to my father. "Mr. Rugger, Paul grew up in New Jersey. Living so far away in Mississippi, how did you arrange to take these pictures?"

He smiled. "Operating your own pest eradication business has its advantages. I can travel wherever and whenever I want.

Mr. and Mrs. Cockaroach patiently wait for my return, thirsty for a squirt of Permethrin or, if they've been extra good little buggies, a dose from my stockpile of DDT." He groaned, tapping his temple. "Forgive me for being such a poor host. I rarely entertain. Would either of you care for a drink?"

With gallons of poisonous chemicals within his grasp, I shook my head. "We're fine. Why all these photos of me?"

His bushy eyebrows raised in dismay. "It's not obvious to you?"

"Not yet."

"Paul, you're my son. *I love you.*" My father clasped his hands in astonishment. "I don't believe I've ever said that word to anyone." His Adam's apple bobbed as if he had just swallowed a horse pill. "Love."

I waited for him to lift his bewildered eyes and for my heart to stop fibrillating. *Is he acting? Don't psychopaths learn how to mimic basic emotions?* "My parents would've seen you and contacted the police."

He touched his chin. "My face is easy for people to dismiss. And walking a miniature poodle gives you a valid justification to be outside day and night."

"You own a dog?" I pictured the big man with an animal off the "Ten Meanest Breeds" list, not an ankle-biter with a pompom on the end of its tail.

"No." He chuckled. "Not me."

I paged through PAUL RUSSELL 1992-1995, viewing high school teachers and schoolmates long since relegated to my brain's DELETE folder. *Mr. D'Ambra, British Literature. Had fun times hanging out with Richard Fand. There's Lisa Wright. I never learned why she dumped me the day before the prom. Oh yeah, she went with my back-stabbing buddy, Billy Ranzetta. Wonder how Lisa looks now? Bet she's three hundred pounds with a trailerful of rug rats.* I questioned his story. "After four decades skulking in the shadows, somebody must have become suspicious."

"As far as I can tell," my father twisted his palms outward, "no one did." He beamed. "Until you tracked me down."

It's a bald-faced lie if I ever heard one, yet he doesn't care if I know it. I skipped PAUL RUSSELL 1996-2000, my time at the University of San Diego, to pick up the last album. The front panel of this red book had no label. These color photographs likely were shot with a digital camera and printed on an inkjet printer. I skimmed past images of my career choices following graduation—San Diego Credit Union, Palms NC Capital Group (*God, how I hated my boss*), and the government job for the State of California that I quit to start writing. Interspersed with these candid shots of me trudging to and from work and eating lunch with associates on park benches were pictures of Jennifer and me shopping at Costco, hiking the local hills, riding our bikes, or lying on towels at the beach.

Recent photographs filled the final sheets. These glossy prints exposed almost everything I had done in the days since I arrived in the Southern states—Jane and me talking at the family barbecue, gun and drug runs with Ernie and Marvin, the shootout with Augustus and Jasper, grainy surveillance images of me searching this home, lunch with Jennifer at Shaggy's the day she flew into town, the ill-fated meeting with Drug Lord Juan Carlos Delgado in the Lower Ninth Ward, and Sarah's rescue at the Katrina-devastated high school. Thankfully, the indistinct shot of my mother and me in the garage with the Wildcat brought no infliction of exquisite pain to daylight, only a glowing flame.

"Still don't get why you have these photographs." I slid the latest scrapbook across the tabletop.

My father opened the earliest album, casually flipping the pages. He held up a square photo. "My favorite. You must have been five years old when I took this at the Bergen County Zoo. You had a ball watching the zookeepers feed the mountain lions." He closed the cover. "I can't explain why. If I couldn't be with you, I'd at least record your life. Buying a decent SLR to take the pictures and setting up a darkroom to develop the film made me feel—"

"Fatherly?" My voice dripped with sarcasm.

"Paul, what is *your* definition of fatherly?"

"You're smart. *You* know what paternal protection is."

"No, actually, I don't. A loving father raised you. Hale. I didn't have anybody to—"

"You had Wayne, and you had Tanya. You went nuts and cut them to pieces."

"Paul, you don't—"

"Try me. Did they molest you?"

"No. When I look back, I realize Tanya and Wayne were always—"

I raised my hands. "Then why do it?"

"Tanya, she. . . ." He frowned. "I had to."

"Because?"

An object crashed outdoors with enough mass to shake the dishes. My father crossed to the window. "A tree fell on the Calloways' house. Right through the roof." He snickered. "Must have hit a gas line. The upper story is on fire." My father sat down, his bemused expression morphing to frustration. "What shall I say? 'Oh, I went berserk when they forced me to clean my room'? Or 'Voices in my head ordered me to do it'? I'm not David Berkowitz or Herbert Mullin."

Prepared to comment about the lack of mirrors in his house, I noticed his vintage wristwatch: the Lone Ranger astride a rearing horse, whooping, "HI-YO SILVER!" I nodded at the matching wall clock. "You've collected plenty of cowboy stuff."

He smiled. "You mean the Lone Ranger?"

"Him and Silver are everywhere. Even on your lunchbox."

My father scratched his jowl. "That's a long story. Not sure you need to hear it."

Jennifer spoke cautiously. "That's why we came to visit you, Mr. Rugger." She clenched my hand. "Paul wants to learn as much about you as he can."

"Paul, we have more in common than genetics." My father reached out his fingers, presumably to grip my arm, then withdrew. "I, too, was put up for adoption." He breathed in heavily. "One frosty morning in February 1952, the sisters at Saint Therese of Lisieux nearly tripped over a box on the front stoop. They opened the case of Ballantine Ale, stunned to find a newborn bundled in a blanket. The nuns brought me to the hospital. I checked out okay, aside from having a pinch of hypothermia and a dash of anemia. Of course, the police sought the person accountable for delivering the foundling. A neighbor who let his dogs out that day reported seeing a young woman in front of the church. He assumed she dropped off food or a clothing donation. The cops never learned her identity. How do I know all this? Like you, I've spent a lot of time in newspaper archives. I stayed in foster care for two years until Wayne and Tanya Russell adopted me.

"They named me Henry, and everything went smoothly till I hit my teens. I became angry—big mood swings. Felt like nobody wanted me. I started cutting myself." He pulled up his sleeve to reveal multiple rows of fifty-year-old scars. "The only possession I owned binding me to my biological mother, was the cloth she swaddled me in when she left me at Saint Therese, a Lone Ranger blanket. At bedtime, I'd fall asleep fantasizing that I smelled my real mom's scent. I came home one afternoon from school and went up to my room. My cherished Lone Ranger blanket wasn't on the bed. Looked everyplace. I asked my adoptive mother where she put it. 'Haven't seen your blankie,' she said. I checked the trash cans in the backyard. Ran indoors, waving the only surviving piece of my blanket—a burned corner. 'Oh, Henry, you're too old for such baby things.' Liar! Jealous thief! Tanya torched the last keepsake I had of my birth mom. Wayne pulled into the driveway as we were fighting. He called me a weakling and a sissy boy. Wayne told me he had been against adopting me. 'Go ahead, leave, but don't expect us to take you back. You'll die on your own.'" My father's lips shut, his eyes glazing over.

Jennifer glanced at me with concern. "Tanya shouldn't have destroyed your property, and Wayne had no right to say those things." When my father remained unresponsive, she asked, "Mr. Rugger, are you ill?"

He elevated from whatever level of Hades he smoldered on. "I'm aware you went to the library and read the news reports. There's no cause to dredge up days gone by."

I envisioned Tanya and Wayne lying in their beds, gore spattering the walls, furniture, and floors. "They tried you as an adult. Did you go to prison? For how long?"

"Nine years. I started the pest management company after my release."

"Why choose my mother? What made Jane Gibbs so special to you? And how many other women did you abuse before her?"

My father scraped his chin whiskers. "You found nothing before 1977?"

"Just articles on your arrest for killing your parents."

"Jane Gibbs was my first. If you do the math," he splayed five fingers on one hand plus four on the other, "from sixty-eight to seventy-seven, I earned thirty-five cents an hour stamping license plates in Harrison County Correctional Facility."

"That's all for a double murder?"

"The judge saw a tearful kid full of remorse. She let me off with a minimum sentence of nine years to life. The liberal parole board gave the perfect inmate a hundred bucks and a one-way bus ticket."

"So, you get out of the slammer horny as hell and go on a raping spree?" Inflamed, I spread my hands. "Is that what happened?"

He sighed in exasperation. "It's not about sex."

I pounded the table. "Tell me! You raped my mother on the anniversary of the date you slaughtered Tanya and Wayne."

"I confess I had pent-up urges, one of them being sexual, but I—"

"You planned to kill her." I dragged a fingernail along the side of my face. "Lucky for me, Jane got away." My father absently stroked the white scar tissue rippling down his left cheekbone. "My mother said you knew her dad's name. Michael, right? Were the Gibbses your customers?"

He nodded. "Regulars."

"You had other clientele with juvenile daughters. Why stalk her?"

"With a new business, I had few jobs. Jane Gibbs was—available—and she was—"

I shouted, "Young? Sexy? Did it turn you on, fucking her, then choking her to death? Sadomasochism?"

"It's ironic, isn't it, Paul? You wouldn't be here questioning me if I hadn't picked her."

I thought about what would have happened to us if he hadn't been in New Orleans to save us from the Wildcat. An advanced college class in chaos theory helped me wrap my mind around the butterfly effect: *a butterfly flapping its wings can eventually cause a tornado somewhere else.* "Why didn't you take care of Jane afterward? You know, 'Dead men tell no tales'?"

"I considered making her—" He snapped his fingers. "For months, I watched Jane Gibbs walking to school and spending time with her friends. She never went to the authorities. If the girl had informed her parents, they would have decided to spare her the public embarrassment. Not long after, her belly pumped up like a beach ball. Her folks drove her to Wiggins to room with a relative. When she returned empty-handed, I learned Edith and Hale had adopted you. I couldn't harm the woman who bore you."

Jennifer put her palms together. "Mr. Rugger, you must allow Lorena Gonzalez to go home to her family."

Henry Russell's head pivoted on a neck roped with muscles. His steel-blue eyes looked through my wife as though she didn't exist in his universe. "Can't do that, hon." A vein pulsating in his forehead belied his composed demeanor. "That girl is mine to do with what I wish."

At that instant, I comprehended my latest dream, what Hale tried to communicate from beyond the veil. *I have to kill him.* My right hand dropped below the tabletop.

Tears filled Jennifer's eyes. "Why hurt her? She's just a child."

My fingers slipped into my rain jacket pocket, rotating the gun until the grip fit my palm.

Finished with my wife, my father swiveled his spotlight to me. "Paul, although I wasn't there to nurture you, you're still my son—*my only son.* Joined forever by blood. I truly care for you and think you feel the same way about me. You are the sole person with enough intelligence to understand my motivations." His feral grin made my skin crawl. "And the reasons I will never let her go."

Lightning flashed. Thunder boomed. *Fernand is at the door and wants to be invited inside.* The chandelier's bulbs flickered twice, then extinguished. In pitch darkness, I extracted the revolver from my jacket, drawing the hammer back with my thumb. I chanted to myself: *Shoot the man, free the girl, shoot the man, free the girl.* More dazzling flashes. More rumblings. *Shoot him, shoot him, shoot him.* I flicked off the handgun's safety, aiming at the spot I had last seen Henry Russell's head—*my father's head.* I put my finger on the trigger as light filled the silhouette, forming a face. My hand trembled. *Fire, fire, fire.* The short barrel's sight wavered from his nose to his brow to his jaw to the Lone Ranger clock on the wall behind him. I lowered the weapon, whimpering, "Please, Dad, free Lorena."

Lightning blazed across Russell's bestial features, and milliseconds later, a volley of thunderclaps. And when the heavens cut loose again, no eyes stared back at me.

The kitchen lights suddenly came back on. My father was lying face up on the sandstone tiles, a small hole in the center of his forehead. Blood splattered the Lone Ranger clock.

I bounded to my feet, tipping the chair. "I didn't pull the trigger!"

A hint of white smoke rose from the muzzle of a pearl-handled pocket pistol. Jennifer released Jane's Colt Model 1908 and crashed to her knees. I embraced my wife, unable to hold back my tears. She wiped her cheeks. "Paul, we must be certain he's dead." Jennifer squeezed my father's wrist for a pulse, exhaled, then turned out his pockets. "Here are the keys."

As a consequence of the combination of storm surge and high tide, the banks of the Mallini Bayou overflowed. Six inches of brackish water lapped at the storage area's plywood door. In the room secluded behind the shelves of extermination equipment, we found Lorena Gonzalez gagged and strapped to a vertical padded bench, her arms extended horizontally as on a lethal injection table. Blood slowly dripped into a five-gallon Home Depot bucket from transfusion tubing dangling from a needle inserted in the crease of her elbow. Jennifer unclasped Lorena, covered her with a towel, withdrew the catheter, and bandaged the punctured skin with a Band-Aid she took from a first aid kit. My wife methodically checked the girl, not discovering visible external injuries.

Amazingly coherent after the terrors Henry Russell had put her through, Lorena asked us who we were and, of prime concern, "Where is the Lone Ranger?"

Jennifer assured Lorena that the man in the cowboy costume was no longer a threat. She made known our legal conundrum. The two spun a plausible, repeatable yarn to tell her parents and law enforcement. In a nutshell, while Lorena's captor was elsewhere, she chewed through her bonds, ran away, and hitched a ride home. We escorted Lorena outside to freedom and into the front seat of the borrowed four-wheeler. Gervais consoled the high school student in his pleasant Creole drawl as my wife and I hurried through the floodwater to tidy up the house.

When we ransacked the main bedroom, Jennifer unzipped a bag on the bed filled with fake IDs and fat wads of cash. I yanked the cedar box from under the mattress and pried the lock open. My wife took in an eyeful of the knives, swords, and tomahawks, and made a suggestion. "Let's chop Henry Russell into a thousand bite-sized chunks with his own tools."

I could not relate to this bogeyman as my father, so I agreed.

Disposing of a human being isn't especially backbreaking if you have easy access to alligator-infested waters. We used Russell's boat, *THE TERMINATOR*, to throw pails of his body parts into the Mallini Bayou. Odious work at the tail end of a hurricane—a heck of a lot easier if you have someone you love to do it with. Logically speaking, feeding the gators might be the most honorable thing Henry Russell ever did.

We lit the white Rugger Pest Control van on fire, but not before I peeled Blatto, the scared-as-shit cockroach, off the rear doors to bring him with us. The Chevy's tankful of gasoline flared nicely, but the stilt house with the torture chamber hidden underneath burned spectacularly. With Fernand wreaking havoc across the land, it is improbable that nearby residents caught Jennifer or me carrying out any of these actions. And if a neighbor saw the flames, he or she may have reckoned God, in His infinite wisdom, flung down a lightning bolt.

Gervais let Lorena off a block from her home in Ridgecrest. We watched her rush through the tempest, waiting until she stepped safely indoors. I imagined how relieved her parents were to see her. Gervais and Jennifer likewise displayed delighted grins.

Beneath the Days Inn's green canopy, Gervais urged my wife and me to stay with him the next time we were in town. He promised to give us "a VIP tour of da authentic New Orleans." We hugged our friend and told him we looked forward to seeing him again.

Will we return to the Deep South? Too many memories were born in Alabama, Mississippi, and Louisiana—the majority of them horrible. But the most important thing I've learned since Hale, my only true father, died is that you never know what Destiny has in store for you.

Now

Monday Night—August 24, 2020

I TURN THE FINAL PAGE OF HENRY RUSSELL'S FINAL UNLABELED SCRAPBOOK FOR THE FINAL TIME. Jennifer saved the four photo albums by stowing them in the rear of the Romeros' Jeep before we set Hunter Rugger's white pest control van and his blue house afire. I have spent innumerable self-indulgent hours staring at these faded pictures of myself growing up. With each review, I become increasingly despondent.

Tonight, on this yearly occurrence of the twenty-fourth day of August—*my 9/11*—I shall rid my life of my father's strange mementos. I'm at a stone firepit on a deserted beach in Carlsbad, California. Although fall is weeks away, as the orange globe sinks below the yellow horizon, chills wash over me in clammy waves. I light a match and throw the spark upon the pile of red books soaked in clear lighter fluid. The cloth covers, cardstock, laminated sheets, and paper photographs flare up, warming my outstretched hands. White-hot embers spiral toward the sky to join the multitudes of stars. Gray ashes whirl—handwritten labels marking my advancement from infant to adult—and blow out to a reflective sea. Soon, nothing will survive but a spot of soot.

Do I feel any better? When will I know?

I tuck a black-and-white photo of my youngest self into my back pocket: a happy boy watching zookeepers feed the mountain lions.

A year has passed since the afternoon we flew out of Mississippi and returned to San Diego. It took me these many "blursdays" to write this journal detailing the events transpiring throughout the two weeks I searched for and found my biological mother and father.

Since March, Jennifer and I have been in pandemic lockdown, so I've had lots of time to think, chiefly about my mortality. The United States is nearing two hundred thousand COVID-19 deaths. Alarmingly, medical experts predict this number will double by the end of 2020. We wear N95 masks whenever we go outdoors for a taste of fresh air, which isn't often. With the bulk of our necessities delivered to our doorstep, we feel imprisoned in our own home.

It has been rough not being able to interact physically with my mom at the Meadows Assisted Living Facility. Alongside other visitors, we blow kisses through the windows and raise handwritten signs. I question whether she comprehends what is happening. Mom needs to know how much I appreciate her and Dad raising me.

Smokey loves having us both around 24/7. The needy cat gets oodles of attention and has put on weight.

Positive news is on the horizon. Pfizer, Johnson & Johnson, and a few other pharmaceutical companies are undergoing clinical trials and plan to distribute emergency vaccines by December. Here and now, we Purell our hands a jillion times a day, Clorox the dirty doorknobs, and stay six feet away from anything breathing.

When we first got home, I resented what Jennifer did to my father, but I knew she had no choice. Still, I needed to ask him about dozens of topics. The essential one—*why do you kill?*—was not answered to my satisfaction. I also puzzled over why he didn't remove the magnetic RUGGER PEST CONTROL signs from his van when cruising neighborhoods for potential victims. Did my father want to get caught?

Amid these bleak hours, I lie awake wondering how alike I am to the predator who procreated me in an act of sexual violence. After I tortured Juan Carlos Delgado, I've become convinced that a shard of Henry Russell bides within me. Jennifer frequently moans in her sleep, and not from pleasure. Once, she sat up in bed screaming, "Antonio, I'm sorry I stabbed you!" Another time, she murmured, "Let her go, Mr. Rugger. Please let Lorena go." I hold my wife close on these cold nights, waiting for Sol, the sun goddess, to show her warm smile.

If Jennifer—acting on my hesitation—hadn't squeezed the trigger of Jane's pocket pistol, Lorena Gonzalez wouldn't have graduated valedictorian from West Harrison High. Alone in the room beneath Henry Russell's stilt house, she'd have bled her last drop into that five-gallon bucket. We haven't followed up with Lorena to learn how she's recovering from her ordeal. Communicating with each other wasn't part of the bargain we struck on the stormy day we rescued her. I'm not overtly religious, but during the quarantine, I began talking to the Man Upstairs regularly, and Lorena ranks high on my prayer list.

I miss my clan. Hopefully, Sarah will fulfill her college goals and graduate as someone who cares for Mother Earth as much as Greta Thunberg. Morning, noon, and night, I monitor the Mobile, Alabama *Craigslist.* I cannot say whether not seeing ads for a free BEAUTYREST KING-SIZED MATTRESS is good or bad. My mother, Jane; my half-siblings, Ernie and Marvin; and my niece, Sarah, are safe and sound in some foreign land, or else the

Silverio drug cartel caught up with them. In either case, I will continue to check *Craigslist* until the moment I stop breathing. Together with Jennifer, Edith, and Smokey, those four family members top my invocations.

In these dark times, when the light at the end of the very long tunnel is the size of a pinhole, the Deity Hotline's switchboard must be overloaded with urgent calls.

I'm still afraid sicarios will turn up on our doorstep to give us the Mexican equivalent of a Colombian necktie. Sometimes, without warning, I have panic attacks. My chest constricts, or my stomach cramps, and I need to check the windows and doors. I'm sure Jennifer worries about retribution as well, but we don't regularly discuss the possibility. It could be that, naïvely or not, we have faith we can defend ourselves come what may. I bought ourselves protection from a sketchy guy down by the Mexican border: familiar items—a Desert Eagle handgun and a Remington shotgun. We practice shooting at the nearby range, take self-defense classes at the local dojo, and pray that everybody tied to the Wildcat died in the house on Alabo Street or at Holy Cross School. These haunted places fill my dreams.

Blatto keeps me company. His bulging bug eyes watch my nine fingers type away from sunup to sundown on my new laptop. It might be just me, but the vinyl cockroach seems happier now, and less scared shitless.

Naturally, Jennifer is itching to get her hands on what I've drafted. Each time she inquires, "How's it going?" I tell her, "When I've proofread the complete document, you'll be the first to read it." My wife doesn't push me, so maybe she's not as eager as she appears to relive her days on the Mississippi and Louisiana coasts. The past has been hard for me, too. In the future, I may be mentally prepared to hand this text over, and she'll be ready to read all the way to the "happy" ending.

Meanwhile, I start over at the beginning, modify a word here, delete a word there, and shed a tear everywhere. An acclaimed wordsmith once declared that editing written material is very therapeutic for the soul. Self-cleansing my system from "mommy and daddy issues" is probably far cheaper than paying a psychiatrist to inform me, "Paul, your hour is up. See you the same time next week?"

Even if these pages are the best literary work I've authored, I suspect *Kin and Clan* will be the last thing I'll ever write. The truth is, my heart no longer beats to be Stephen King's successor. What's discouraging for me? I can't publish this manuscript as a hardcover or an ebook on Amazon or on the dozens of other online bookstores. *Kin and Clan* shall never sit on a library shelf wedged between other inkslingers whose surnames begin with the letter C. To insulate ourselves, I suppose I could alter the identities of everyone involved and add this notice to the copyright page: "Any similarity to actual individuals, living or dead, is purely coincidental." What's the point of putting on that charade? Life happens. Every contented moment. Every moment of sheer terror.

I toss a stack of *The Daily Herald*, *The Biloxi Press*, and *South Mississippi Sun* photocopies onto the fire. As the papers blaze, I see faces in the dancing flames—Jane, Sarah, Lorena—as well as boys and girls I don't recognize. Kids snatched while they walk home from a friend's house, walk to a candy machine, or walk their dogs. I want to exterminate the evil men who prey on the innocent.

To calm my nerves, I close my eyes and inhale deeply. I dwell on the days, months, and years to come, not knowing what I'll do to keep busy—*to keep sane.* Henry Russell's bug-out bag contained more money than we first realized, along with four one-kilo gold bars. I regard those rolls of hundred-dollar bills and the Suisse fine gold as my rightful inheritance.

I compulsively study my hands, my father's hands. He stares back at me from every mirror. Perhaps I'll employ my quantitative analysis skills to hunt down these predators. Jennifer will help—possibly enjoying the task too much. My wife is as ruthless as they are.

Finding my real family changed me. Killing Juan Carlos Delgado changed me. Killing Antonio and Henry Russell changed Jennifer. Alabama, Mississippi, and Louisiana transformed our lives forever. And forever, when you stare Chronos in his hoary face, is a mighty long time.

One last thing:

If you are reading this and not Jennifer, it's doubtful you will give credence to my written word. I'm with you. The narrative sounds far-fetched, a work of fiction, and not even a great one. But if you believe I'm delusional, once COVID-19 is stamped out once and for all, hop on a plane to Gulfport. Drive to the Biloxi Public Library and look up every August 24 news article, the same way Jennifer and I did twelve months ago. Perform the research. We made bringing the darkness to light as easy as searching for a date.

Once you connect all the dots—murders and missing persons—you'll hit the print button and hand the evidence over to the police.

Or will you?

www.ingramcontent.com/pod-product-compliance
Lightning Source LLC
Chambersburg PA
CBHW020559310726
48979CB00008B/1275/J

* 9 7 8 0 9 9 8 5 4 4 7 5 5 *